T MacBri
cBride, Laura,
ound midnight /
30.99   ocn984898968

Sm   OCT 1 2 2017

'ROUND MIDNIGHT

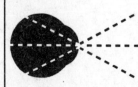

This Large Print Book carries the
Seal of Approval of N.A.V.H.

'ROUND MIDNIGHT

LAURA McBRIDE

THORNDIKE PRESS

A part of Gale, a Cengage Company

Farmington Hills, Mich • San Francisco • New York • Waterville, Maine
Meriden, Conn • Mason, Ohio • Chicago

Copyright © 2017 by Laura McBride
Thorndike Press, a part of Gale, Cengage Learning.

ALL RIGHTS RESERVED
This book is a work of fiction. Any references to historical events, real people, or real places are used fictitiously. Other names, characters, places, and events are products of the author's imagination, and any resemblance to actual events or locales or persons, living or dead, is entirely coincidental.

Thorndike Press® Large Print Basic.
The text of this Large Print edition is unabridged.
Other aspects of the book may vary from the original edition.
Set in 16 pt. Plantin.

LIBRARY OF CONGRESS CATALOGING-IN-PUBLICATION DATA

Names: McBride, Laura, author.
Title: 'Round midnight / by Laura McBride.
Other titles: Around midnight
Description: Large print edition. | Waterville, Maine : Thorndike Press, a part of Gale, Cengage Learning, 2017. | Series: Thorndike Press large print basic
Identifiers: LCCN 2017019033| ISBN 9781432841720 (hardcover) | ISBN 1432841726 (hardcover)
Subjects: LCSH: Casinos—Nevada—Las Vegas—Fiction. | Interpersonal relations—Fiction. | Life change events—Fiction. | Las Vegas (Nev.)—Fiction. | Large type books.
Classification: LCC PS3613.C284 R68 2017 | DDC 813/.6—dc23
LC record available at https://lccn.loc.gov/2017019033

Published in 2017 by arrangement with Touchstone an imprint of Simon & Schuster, Inc.

Printed in the United States of America
1 2 3 4 5 6 7 21 20 19 18 17

For my mom

■ ■ ■ ■

June:
The One Who
Fell in Love

■ ■ ■ ■

March 11, 1960
In the Midnight Room

Coming in the casino's main entry, the Midnight Room was on the right. A scantily clad ingénue waving a golden star in front of her torso — its two jeweled points artfully covering the money bits — adorned the neon marquee above the door. Below, a man in black tie greeted those lucky enough to have a ticket, and escorted the ones who slipped him enough cash to the better seats in the room.

It was a straightforward showroom: a hundred-foot stage, with a narrow apron, about four feet above the main floor. There were twenty or so small round tables, and chairs with red velvet seats. Along the back wall were a row of booths, higher even than the stage, and the velvet there was closer to maroon, and the stained glass lamps cast a warm but not revealing glow on the table where the drinks would sit. The sound system was excellent, and the lighting was standard, and there was room for a pretty good-sized band on the stage if someone wanted it.

That night, there was a man playing the piano, another playing the sax, and a third on the drums. When the curtain parted in the back, a top light rotated to catch the singer's face. He'd been doing this awhile; he swung to the light intuitively and let it accent the plane of his cheekbone, the hollow of his eye, the curve of his lip.

He was thinking he might never play there again.

He knew what was coming later.

And when he saw her, sitting at the back, at the booth she always sat in — still he was startled, it had been a long time, she had not said she was coming — he signaled to the band to quit playing. He thought he might say something, just say it, put it out there, but in that split second in which he would have had to decide what to say, in which he would have had to find the courage to say it, he suddenly remembered the first time he'd seen her.

He'd had no idea who she was. He was new in town, didn't know anyone at all. And of course, she was the only white woman. She'd looked up — damn, she was good-looking — and the horn player had sounded a note, and he'd swung his hip, just a little, instinctively, and her breath had caught — he'd actually seen that; he'd never forgotten it — and right that minute, maybe he'd fallen in love.

So tonight, four years later, when it was probably the last time he would ever sing for her, he lifted his finger to Jamie, who played the sax, and when the note sounded, he closed his eyes and remembered the rotten little bar, the white woman's face, the flick of his hip, and he let his body take over, repeated the one instant of that fateful night, and as he did so, he remembered, he thought of her face, the intake of her breath. He remembered, even though, of course she would not.

1

To celebrate victory in Europe, June Stein dove headfirst off the Haverstraw Bridge.

A few months earlier, she had bought an eighteen-inch silver cigarette holder on a day trip to the city — snuck into the shop while her mother was choosing a hat next door — and spent the spring flicking ashes on the track as she smoked behind the stairs of the boy's gym. In April she wore stockings to school, and bent over the water fountain to highlight the brown seams running along the backs of her legs. Leon Kronenberg said he had touched her breast. When Mr. Sawyer came back from the summer holidays with a goatee, June Stein breathed in, licked her lips, and shuddered.

She was bad for the neighborhood.

Things happened to other girls because of June Stein.

When she married Walter Kohn at nineteen, most people figured she was pregnant.

June Stein would get her due. She'd be stuck in Clinton Hill for life; Walter Kohn was going to be bald in three years, like his father and his uncle Mort.

But at twenty, June Stein disappeared.

She was gone for six months.

When she came back, Walter Kohn had become something of a catch. People thought it was wrong that his wife had left him. They said she'd gone to Reno, gotten a divorce, that she'd never been pregnant, she had just wanted to have sex, and now that she'd had it, now that she'd used Walter Kohn — who did have beautiful blond hair and the bluest eyes — she'd gone and left him, and who knows what man she might try to take up with next.

June Stein returned a pariah.

It was a role she had cherished, but at twenty-one, she found it less amusing.

She had not gone to Reno.

She had gone to Las Vegas, and the lights and the shows and the desert air, the dust and the heat and the way one felt alone in the universe, were more appealing in memory than they had been when she lived them. There had been only a handful of Jews in town, and none she found interesting, so while she was waiting for the divorce, she hung around a different crowd: locals

14

mostly, born and raised Nevadans, and some that had come in for the gambling boon. And they rose in stature after she moved back to her parents' house, after even her friends expressed sympathy for Walter Kohn — who had taken the newspaper into the bathroom with him each morning — and there was the way her mother looked at her in the evenings, and the way her father kept asking if she would like to take a stenography course. One day June Stein packed a suitcase, including the eighteen-inch silver cigarette holder, called a taxi, and flew all night from Newark to Las Vegas.

She didn't even leave a note.

But that was June Stein.

Prettiest girl in Clinton Hill.

And the only one who ever dove headfirst off the Haverstraw Bridge.

2

"June, you shouldn't be on that ladder. You look like you're going to fall right off."

"Don't you think I would bounce if I did?" Del laughed.

"I mean it. Get down. What are you doing up there anyway?"

"There's one of those atomic bomb favors in this chandelier. You can see it from that side of the room. It's been bothering me for a week."

"Well, tell Mack to take it down. Why would you climb on a ladder when you're eight months pregnant?"

"I did ask Mack. Three days ago. He really doesn't have time. And I'm bored to death. Even the baby's bored. He's been kicking me like a trucker."

"A trucker? I don't think our daughter's going to be a trucker."

"Well, then, our daughter's going to be dancing with the Follies down the road."

June jumped backward to the ground from the second rung of the ladder. She had meant it as a graceful note, but her weight was unwieldy, she landed on the side of her foot, and caught herself awkwardly before she could fall.

Del darted forward, and June grinned.

"I'm fine. Maybe it'll get labor started."

"Okay, just try to be reasonable this week? I need help. The hotel's booked solid for the holidays, and Ronni wants to visit her dad, who's sick. We're short everywhere. If you feel like going through the applications in the office, maybe we could get some folks started this week."

"Hmmm. All right. If you're sure I can't help Mack hammer at things. Baby and I love hammering."

June reached up to give Del a kiss, her belly snug into his, and he distractedly returned it. He didn't notice her puzzled gaze, or the way she walked with a slightly duller step toward the office.

Cora was already there. She was sitting at the table where June usually did the books, with one cigarette between her lips and another smoldering in an ashtray, her long legs stretched out in front of her — an old lady who looked as if she had once been a showgirl.

"You looking for people to hire too?" June asked.

"Odell's single-minded. How ya feeling?"

"Fat. Bored. See if I let your grandson knock me up again."

Cora smiled at June. Her language, her sultry ways, did not bother her. These were the qualities that had left June needing Odell. And without June, Odell's life would be different in ways that Cora did not want it to be. Cora had given up a lot for her grandson. She didn't regret it. When her son and his no-account woman had dropped Odell off the last time — his bottom covered with neglect sores, and the marks of someone's fingers on his thin arm — Cora didn't waste any time making her choice. She and Nathan had picked up what they had, locked the door on the little Texas house the Dibb family had lived in for ninety years, and headed to Vegas. There was a railroad job there for Nathan, and a new world for Odell. She and Nathan had done some things well and some things poorly, but in the end, the only thing worth taking out of Texas was a two-year-old child.

June was even prettier pregnant. Everything about that girl was pretty. Her hands, her feet, her skin, her hair. When she spoke, her voice trilled as if she were about to laugh. You listened to her in the same way you couldn't stop looking at her. Cora figured that if everything went to pieces, June might stand in as the club's entertainer. If she could sing a note, she'd make it.

Entertainment was why the El Capitan was a success. That was why she and June were going to spend the afternoon reading through letters — pages and pages of them, some handwritten, some done up on an Underwood (with all the *n*'s and *l*'s faded to a slightly lighter gray), some folded around photos. All these people, young and old, wanting to start a new life in Vegas. Yep, the El Capitan was a hit. And it was the showroom that brought people in — or more to the point, Eddie Knox. Eddie Knox and those atomic bombs.

There had been a bomb detonation every five days all summer and fall. Operation Plumbbob. June called it Operation Plumb*rich.* Tourists flocked from all over the country, from Canada, from Mexico. People who wouldn't have come to Las Vegas otherwise. But everyone wanted to see an explosion. Ever since *National Geographic* had described a bright pink mushroom cloud turning purple and then orange, spraying ice crystals like an ocean surf in the sky, people had been coming. They drove up the dusty road to Charleston Peak and leaned against their cars to watch the white dawn burst against the night, or they crowded into tiny Beatty and asked the locals if the air was safe.

Afterward, they returned to Vegas, to the air-conditioned hotels and crystal-clear pools, and giddy with the awesomeness of the power they had witnessed, with the strange menace of invisible rays, they gambled more than they might have, ordered another round of drinks, splurged on a second show. When the showgirls came out wearing mushroom-cloud swimsuits and headdresses that looked like explosions, they hooted with glee, and cheered when Eddie ended his set, dead silent, and then one word: Boom.

It was fun and dare and newness. If danger lurked, the Russians, a nuclear bomb, polio, distant nations and foreign religions and dark skin, then there was also the thrill of a mushroom cloud, the sound of doo-wop, Lucille Ball, the clickety-tick of dice rolling on a craps table, feather and sequin and mirror, red lips, breasts, Mae West onstage with muscled men in loincloths, anything goes, anything went, a small town in the middle of nowhere, and already, eight million people a year coming to see what was happening.

Cora herself had little to do with the El Capitan's success. Odell and June were doing it on their own. She would help them out by going through a few applications this week, but for the most part, she stayed away from their business and their marriage. She liked her little apartment downtown, liked her habits there, and if she had learned one thing from her own son, it was that it would be better for her to leave June and Odell alone. There would be no option to rely on Cora Dibb when things got tougher.

They would get tougher.

Cora could see this already.

June didn't seem to see it. How could someone so quick not see what was coming?

Well, life was hard. For pretty much everyone. June Stein had made her bed long before she married Odell Dibb. And in the long run, marrying her grandson was going to be the best decision June ever made. Though it might be awhile before she understood that.

"I'm going to find Del. I need a backrub."

Cora thought it unlikely that her grandson would stop what he was doing to rub June's back, but he might. She hoped he would.

June left the office and headed upstairs to the casino floor. Del might be there, but she wasn't really looking for him anyway. She liked to spend time in the casino, watching the players, listening to the dealers calling for chips in, tracing the pattern of lights that swirled against the hard surfaces as the machine wheels spun dizzily. She could wander around there for hours, her stomach wobbling in front of her — a little startling to the patrons that did not know who she was — and it was good for business, her wandering. She noticed which dealers got the best action, or when a customer headed off to the bathroom at an odd moment, and whether or not the girls were getting drinks to the right gamblers.

From time to time, surrounded by the swirl and stir and smoke of this new life, June's former life would come back to her: the look of low-slung clouds as she walked down the block to school; her mother singing the blessing on Friday night, her father's hands over her head; later, the way her body had melted into Walter's, and how for a while they would couple over and over, and she would wonder if everyone could see this, in her gingerly walk if nothing else.

When she moved to Las Vegas, she was free of her marriage, free of certain expectations (not just those of others, but also her own) — free of a past she had never fully shouldered. And it was Vegas in the fifties, when it was a small town and a big town, when no one she had ever known would be likely to visit, when a young woman who enjoyed men and adventure and the casual breaking of conventions was something of a community treasure. For a while, this life had been entertaining — entertainment was high on June's list of values — and when it had become less so, when June started to notice the long, slow slide that some of the older women had embarked on, Del was there waiting. Persistent, loyal, unlikely Del, someone you wouldn't notice on your first pass through a room, but who lingered in the mind later — who showed up at unlikely moments, and always with the right drink, the right idea, the right equipment for the task — his charms grew on her.

Also, Del had a plan. He was hell-bent on running his own casino, and he knew how to make it happen, and for some reason, June was part of his vision. They would revamp one of the old casinos, right at the center of the Strip. They wouldn't try to compete with the new places, but their games would be fast; he had a way to run some tables without limits. Certain gamblers looked for these joints. He would talk to June about it, a bit flushed, excited, exposed in a way she never saw him exposed to anyone else. It caught her attention.

Little by little, Del's dreams became her own. Perhaps Del was right that they could make one of these joints go, perhaps she would be good at it. She knew what people liked, she knew the atmosphere they wanted, she knew what they were trying to escape and what they wanted Vegas to be. This desert, this odd town; maybe they were June's future too. It wasn't what she had imagined for herself, but then, what had she imagined? Did lives look sensible if you were outside them, and startling if you were in? Or was it that some people stayed in the groove in which they were born, while others skittered and skipped and slid unexpectedly into a new groove? She, June, was one of those.

June and Del gave the El Capitan everything they had, and by the second year, it was growing faster than their wildest early hopes. Not every tourist was hot on the new carpet joints: the Dunes and the Flamingo and the Sands. Some liked the old-time feel

24

of the El Capitan, especially now that she and Del were cleaning it up, now that Eddie Knox was as good as it got when it came to nightclub entertainment. Yes, Eddie. Eddie had made the difference.

She and Del had known what good entertainment would mean — how a really great act could draw people in, create the right buzz — so they had gone to Jackson Street to see who was singing in the clubs. At the Town Tavern, a pretty good singer named Earl Thurman had invited his friend Eddie, just in from Alabama, to join him onstage. And Eddie had come up, soft-shoeing across the floor, and before he had opened his mouth, before a single note came out, he had swung his hip, a small move, in perfect erotic time to the horn behind him, and June's private parts had clenched, and she had known. Known that Eddie Knox would make them all rich. She grabbed Del's hand and squeezed. This was it.

And then, the voice.

People started whooping, calling out, a woman stood and lifted her arms above her head; he wasn't even through the first verse.

After he finished singing, June and Del waited while he was introduced around. June saw the women watching Eddie, noticed that he had his arm around one and was keeping her with him even before he had stopped meeting folks, even while Earl the pretty good singer was back at another tune, and nobody was listening to him, because all the energy in the room — all the hope and buzz and sex — was already around Eddie Knox. That's the kind of impact he had.

But June and Del were there first. The only white folks in the place. The first in town to hear him. Del said he would like to talk to Eddie. They had a nightclub at El Capitan, they were looking for a regular act; could he stop by the next day? And Eddie said, "Sure, that sounds good," but June knew he might not come, because he was brand-new to town, he didn't know the lay of the land, and how could someone like Eddie Knox not know that plenty of offers would come his way, of one sort or another?

So she named a figure. An amount per week. Plus a percentage. She could feel Del about to protest, so she pulled his elbow tight into her rib, and they were friends enough, real partners, that he trusted her even though her number had surprised him. She added: "The offer lasts twenty-four hours. Come tomorrow if you want it."

June Stein. Barely twenty-seven years old. Too pretty and too featherbrained to have managed such a thing. In a crowded room, on the wrong side of town, with nothing but chutzpah to make her think she could do it. But then, she had also dived headfirst off the Haverstraw Bridge.

And Eddie was there the next day.

They pulled Mack off the kitchen, which badly needed renovating, and they put nearly the whole budget into the nightclub, into the lights and the sound and the velvet-backed booths around mahogany tables. June handpicked the girls who would serve the drinks, served some herself the first months, wearing a ten-inch silver skirt and a studded headband and a sort of bra made of a thousand tiny mirrors.

The first time Del saw her in the outfit, he drew in his breath, and the sound of that breath played in her mind for months, even years after, because she could hear the desire in it, and because it told her that Del could feel that for her, that he could be knocked off his reasonableness, his deliberations, his kindness; if she had not been in the middle of the casino, with employees around, she could have had him on the floor, right there, her way.

And they had all made money.

The figure she named for Eddie was

doubled in six months. Plus, he had a take. Which was easy because they liked each other. Sometimes it even seemed like Eddie was in it with them, that he was just as much a part of the place as she and Del were. They spent so much time together, into the dawn hours after his show closed, and at dinner, which was more like breakfast for Eddie, before the act started up again.

Eddie liked to gamble, mostly on the Westside but sometimes at the El Capitan, at the back when the tables were slow. Negroes weren't allowed to gamble on the Strip or downtown, they weren't allowed in the shows, no matter who was playing. Once in a while, someone came in and said he was a friend of Eddie's, and then Del told Leo just to seat him in booth nine, where he and June sat. Del got away with these things. They were done quietly, and he had grown up here, so he had a little room in which to work.

And, of course, women liked Eddie. Sometimes he liked one of them long enough to bring her to dinner or for a drink after the show. They would sit in a private room at the back of the bar, June and Del and Eddie and whoever-she-was: a Jewish woman, a white man, a Negro singer, a colored woman. They would sit there, laughing and trading stories and sipping one another's drinks, and maybe that's why June didn't understand how things really were in Vegas; what it really meant to be Eddie or the girlfriend or any of the people working in the back of the El Capitan.

June overheard the doorman say that Vegas was the Mississippi of the West; she listened when the California tourist told his friend that even Pearl Bailey and Sammy stayed in a boarding house off the Strip, but she didn't pay them much attention. Del had grown up here, and his closest friend was colored; he and Ray Jackson had lived on the same block on North Third Street, had gone to the same elementary school, had worked the same job hauling wooden crates at the back of a downtown casino when they were about twelve. When she and Del married, at the county office in the middle of the night, laughing and excited and with a little whiskey to make them do it, Del had stopped to make one phone call. June figured he was calling Cora, but he had called Ray, and Ray made it there while they were still filling out the papers, with a ring of his wife's that he said June could borrow as long as she liked. So what the tourist said, what the doorman thought, it wasn't the whole story. She knew for herself that Vegas was not as simple as that.

Usually June's new home made the rest of the country seem slow. Hung up. Here there was money and music and gambling and sex and drinking late into the night. And all of that was the center of town, was the domain of the prosperous, was what the town celebrated; it was out in the desert sunshine, not in the backroom alleys and dark bars of New York or Chicago or LA. To June, this world felt free and fast and stripped clean of the conventions that had closed in on her in New Jersey. Hollywood stars came to Vegas to play. The richest and the newest and the most beautiful, and they were there every night; they flocked to the big casinos, and they came to the El Capitan pretty often too.

Las Vegas was the future. She saw this in the entertainment, in the way people lived, in the way the town kept growing; the future was there in the atom bombs and the magnesium plant and in the dam south of town. To see that dam, one drove a winding road up the side of a steep treeless mountain, and when June looked out the car window, down a thousand feet to an angry Colorado River, she imagined the people who had come to this desert before her: the ones who had taken the measure of Black

Canyon, narrow and deep and forbidding, scorching hot, and decided that they could stop that river, they could turn it aside, they could conquer these sheer rock faces, pour three million cubic yards of cement in a raging river's path. It was extraordinary, it was inspiring — surely humans could do anything. That was the lesson June learned from her new home.

But then what about the Negroes? Cora said the bad times for colored people started when that dam got built, during the Depression. Workers poured in, from all over the country, but especially from the South: sharecroppers and farm laborers, some Negro and some white, and all dirt poor. Southern white folks brought their ideas about colored folk with them. A quarter century later, if you were Negro, you shopped and ate on the Westside, your kids went to schools without windows or floors or chalkboards, and you worked in the back of a casino as a driver or a maid or a janitor. Or your band played in a casino, for huge money, but you couldn't spend it in Vegas, because there was nothing you were allowed to buy, no place you were allowed to go. It was 1957, and some people thought things were changing in the country, but in Vegas it had gone the other direction.

Anyone could make it in Las Vegas, anyone could be a winner, just by being smart and playing the game the Vegas way. And most of the time, the Vegas way left tired old ideas in the dust, but not when it came to Negroes. When it came to Negroes, Vegas was worse than New Jersey, and June did not understand how that could be.

But even so, she and Del and Eddie did pretty much what they wanted in their own casino.

3

Three months after Marshall was born, June and Del flew to Cuba. They brought along Cora, and she watched Marshall as June learned the mambo from some dancers she met at the Tropicana, and Del talked business. By day, they sat next to the pool at the Sans Souci, or on striped loungers dug into the white sand of the beach. The air was moist and salty, and the baby was happy in his little cave created of an umbrella and a towel. People called Havana the Latin Las Vegas, and Del was thinking about the growth of the El Capitan; to June, the whole world seemed open and lovely and possible.

When they returned, Marshall got sick, and June stayed home with him and did not go to the casino at all for a week.

Del walked in mad on Thursday.

"Eddie didn't get the house."

"What? I thought it was already done."

"Owner backed out. Said his kids had

gone to school with the neighbors' kids, and he just couldn't do it. Couldn't sell the house to him."

"Can he do that?"

Del didn't answer. Eddie wanted his own house. He was sick of paying rent for a shack made from wood stolen from Nellis Air Base; for the same money, he could own a new house almost anywhere in town. But every time Eddie tried to buy a house in another part of the valley, it went off the market. All his money couldn't buy Eddie a house with hot water, or an indoor toilet, on a street that didn't turn into a muddy creek in the August rains. "Negroes like to live together" is how June heard it said. Del said, "Negroes'd like to have hot water and a decent school." But that's all he said.

It had looked like Eddie was finally going to get a house. He'd told the owner he wasn't the fathering kind, wouldn't be having any kids to send to the schools, and maybe that's why the guy had considered it long enough to tell Eddie he'd sell it to him, long enough for Del and Eddie to get the cash together. Cash deal. High dollar. But it still hadn't worked.

In the meantime, Eddie had taken to staying in the apartment at the back of the El Capitan. Del had offered it to him for nights

34

when he didn't want to drive home, but bit by bit, Eddie had started staying there most of the time, at least the weeks when he was playing. When he wasn't playing, he was mostly out of Vegas. He flew to New York, he drove to LA, he liked to show up at a club in Baltimore, where friends from Alabama had a combo.

And he talked about Cuba. He wanted to know everything about June and Del's visit there, what they thought of the Sans Souci, who was playing at the Montmartre, what the people acted like, on the street, in the cafes, on the beach. Eddie liked to say that Cuba would be his bit of heaven.

June figured that Eddie stayed in the apartment because he'd had too many girlfriends, and the 'Side was a small community. She'd heard some of the blackjack dealers grumbling about him being at the El Capitan; how a Negro shouldn't sleep anywhere in a Strip hotel. But she didn't say anything about this to Del, and the employees got quiet when they realized she was around, and soon she never heard anything said at all. It wasn't worth telling Del and making trouble.

Also, June liked having Eddie nearby, especially now that she had Marshall. She brought the baby to the casino every day. Del had suggested that maybe she would want to stay home, join a mothers' group, meet some of the ladies in the houses nearby. And June had laughed. Having Marshall hadn't turned her into someone else, hadn't turned them into some other couple; she loved the El Capitan. So she and Del had switched offices, and she had set up a playpen and a basket and a little set of drawers in the larger one, and Marshall was growing up there with them. Several afternoons a week, when the sun shone straight in from the west and Marshall started to get fussy, she would head upstairs to Eddie's apartment at the back. Usually he was just getting up.

Eddie might not want kids, but he was a natural with a baby.

"Eddie, you're so good with him."

"Honey, I'm good with everybody. Babies, women, children." He rubbed his nose on Marshall's chin, and the baby laughed.

"It's a black thing? Black men are good with babies?"

"Black men? We're good with everybody." June laughed.

"Actually, I got four little brothers. And an older sister. You didn't know that, did ya?" Marshall reached up and pulled at

36

Eddie's lip and ear. "Bertie helped Ma with the cooking and the washing, and I took care of the babies. We had some adventures, my brothers and me, because I didn't have no sense with the first ones."

"You have four brothers? Are they all in Alabama?"

"Most of 'em. We lost Jacob. He died just before I came out here."

June waited, wondering if Eddie would tell her, but not wanting to ask. Not sure she could ask.

He lifted Marshall into the air.

"How you doing, little guy? You gonna grow up in a casino, with your pretty momma and your rich daddy? You gonna run this place someday, Marshall Moses Dibb? You gonna be the rich daddy?"

Eddie was talking to Marshall in a low rumble that was almost a croon, but he didn't look at June. He didn't offer any more information about his brothers, about Jacob.

June sometimes thought that Eddie was probably just about as far from home as she was. Del belonged here. He grew up here, watching the casinos grow, seeing people move to southern Nevada from all over the country. So he was rooted in, part of the landscape, but she and Eddie, they had left different lives behind — so different that they were hard to imagine from here.

"Vegas is really different, isn't it? I mean, it's not like home."

"I don't know about that. Vegas is a hell of a lot like Alabama some days. A hell of a different, and a hell of the same. That's what I think."

June was quiet. Vegas wasn't like her hometown. She shook off the thought, and danced a few steps toward Eddie. "Want me to show you the mambo?"

"You going to show me the mambo?"

"Yeah. I got pretty good in Havana. At least, that's what people said."

She smiled her devastating June smile, and Eddie laughed. He whistled a little mambo rhythm, and she took Marshall from him. The baby laughed and waved his arms wildly, trying to clap, or catch his fetching mom's cheek. She rubbed her nose on his face, and he opened his mouth and slobbered on her chin.

"Marshall, that move is not going to take you very far."

She held the baby in front of her and swung his feet from side to side as she stepped and turned. Eddie sang a few lines. June was happy.

After awhile, she stopped dancing and set

Marshall on her hip.

"Let's go home, baby man. Let's go home and make some dinner for Daddy."

Eddie looked at June straight, held her eyes a minute, but she simply shifted Marshall's weight, winked, and left.

She and Del were working late when the call came in. The count was down at the poker tables, and Del was worried that someone was running a game while he was busy at meetings in Carson City; it would be bad if one of their own dealers was in on it. All this left Del quieter and cooler than normal. He wasn't one to get worked up, but June knew he was bothered; that his mind was spinning. She had returned to the El Capitan after dinner to keep him company, and even though Marshall would have been asleep for hours by now, she was anxious to get home. When the phone on Del's desk rang suddenly, she felt slightly irritated, not alarmed. Then she heard him telling the operator that yes, June was here, go ahead and put someone through.

Del's voice dropped lower. He was asking questions. He shot a look at her across the hall, and her heart dropped. Something was wrong.

It was her father. Dead beside her mother

in bed. Maybe a heart attack. Or a stroke. No sound at all. Her mom had just tried to give him a push, move him from where he had rolled in the center of their bed, and he was gone. Her mom was confused on the phone; she'd called the police, she was about to call June's aunt. She said she could hear the siren coming down the street, and hung up before June could take the receiver from Del.

June's body turned to stone. Tears trickled down her cheeks as Del repeated what her mother had said. She concentrated on the possibility that this was not true. Her mother panicked easily — how many times had she panicked at something June had done? — so perhaps her father was not dead. When the ambulance driver examined him, perhaps he would be revived. They would laugh together at the fright her mom had given her.

Del reached out to hold her, but June stood stiffly. To fold into Del would be to believe it was true, and she did not believe it. Her mom was in shock, it was the middle of the night for her, she had called before the ambulance even arrived. Del stroked her head. "June, I'm sorry," he said, and then, "June, it's true," because of course he already knew what she was thinking.

She stepped back then, and Del said he needed ten minutes before they could go home. He had to take something to the safe. He would make the flight arrangements from the house. June thought she could not bear to be alone, even a moment, but she nodded yes, and then she walked upstairs, to the back of the casino, and knocked on Eddie's apartment door.

He was getting ready for his late show, and a woman was with him. When June told him, he wrapped her in a big bear hug, and rocked back and forth. June shuddered there. She saw the surprise in the woman's eyes.

"You're going home, June. You're going home, but you'll be back. You'll be okay."

"He never saw Marshall."

She could hardly get the words out.

Eddie held her. And he hummed as he did it. Just a soft hum, and a rock.

"I didn't take him home, Eddie. We went to Cuba. But I didn't take him home."

Eddie didn't reply. Just the hum, the rock. They stood that way for long minutes, June collapsed into Eddie's rocking, and eventually the woman looked away from them, and then she left the room. When June stepped away from Eddie, they were alone. She looked at him — the tears had swollen her

41

eyes nearly shut — and Eddie looked back, his eyes moist, and June thought that if not for Eddie, maybe she wouldn't have stayed in Las Vegas after all. Maybe she didn't like running a casino that much, and what did it mean that Eddie Knox was the person who held her while she cried on the night her father died?

4

June and Marshall were in New Jersey for two months. Marshall learned to crawl there, and June tried to share this with Del.

"How's our little man?"

"He wants to crawl. I'm trying to keep him from doing it. But if I set him on the ground, he rolls on his tummy, sticks up his bottom, and starts waving his arms and legs to get going. When I'm holding him, he flips down and reaches out to the floor. He's just set on it."

"Why would you stop him?"

"I want you to see it. I don't want you to miss this."

"It's okay, June. It's good for your mom to see. And I've got a lot going on here."

Sometimes June wasn't sure quite what Del meant. She tried to shake off the way her husband's voice on the phone made her uneasy. Del loved her, he loved Marshall, they talked every night. But there was

43

something in his voice; some distraction even when he was saying he loved her. What did Del feel?

Marshall crawled across her mother's kitchen, started to pull himself up on the chairs, grew out of the overalls June had brought with her. And still they stayed in New Jersey. Still Del did not insist they come home. Lying awake at night, with her son asleep beside her, June thought often of her father. She remembered how it had felt to hold his dry, bony hand, and how his brow would wrinkle when he asked her about what the teacher had said, about what the neighbor had reported, about what her best friend's mother had suggested.

"June," he used to ask, "what are you thinking?"

And sometimes June would feel bad, and she wished she knew what she had been thinking, or why she had done what she did. But other times, she would flash her blinding smile, laugh, say, "Poppa, it was fun."

June's father was an amateur photographer. He had built a darkroom in the basement and spent his evenings there. When she was very small, she hadn't even known he was home. She thought he went to work after dinner the way he did after lunch.

Later, when she knew he was in the basement, she'd been afraid to follow him down into it. An eerie red light glowed when he opened the darkroom door, and often it smelled as if he were striking matches, so in June's mind, the darkroom was associated with fire. In second grade, a new girl in school told June about hell, and when she described the fires where sinners would burn, howling and howling without ever being incinerated, June thought of the basement, and pictured her father, with his sore red hands, as the flaming miscreant. It made her cry. Hazel, the new girl, took this as the sign of a guilty conscience, and for the next four months, until she left the school as abruptly as she had arrived, she called June "sinner" under her breath.

Hazel frightened her, because by eight, June already had the sense that she wasn't quite good. Why couldn't she wear a dress that her mother had carefully sewn and pleated without tearing the skirt or getting ink on the pale cotton? How did she lose her book on the way to school, and why did pencils break and cups drop and pages get ripped whenever she came near? June was easily distracted by the sense of things: the rub of a neatly stitched hem on her thigh, the round, hard smoothness of that pencil, the sound of paper fibers splitting one from the other, the intoxicating scent of a pink flower shooting out of a crack in the sidewalk. The idea that her parents had somehow ended up with the wrong little girl — one who was hapless and pell-mell when they were deliberative and precise — had already formed vaguely in her mind.

The great work of her father's photography was June's own childhood: hundreds of two-inch black-and-white squares, carefully documenting a little girl with perfectly combed hair sitting at a piano, a baby lifting her dark head to stare at the white muzzle of a whiskery dog, three children dressed as Indians with feathers stuck in their headbands, a toddler resting a fat finger on the base of a flickering menorah. Her father's photos were perfect. In seventy years, they would still be detailed representations of a time hardly anyone remembered, but to June, even as a child, they spoke to her mostly as depictions of how she was meant to be: clean and silent and still, instead of rumpled and impetuous and inclined to pull at any stray thread.

And yet she had been loved. Her quiet, careful parents, not given to demonstrative acts, had somehow made this clear. She was loved.

So how could she have gone so long between visits? How could she have left them at all? She didn't know. If there was any answer, it was that she hadn't done any of it — as she hadn't knocked over the cup, as she hadn't lost her sweater — she had merely lived, from this moment to the next, in this day or that, and there had been so much to attract her gossamer attention. June didn't think forward and back in quite the way that her parents did, but when this caught up with her, when she had made some error she would never have chosen to make, if she had thought it possible for her father to die without seeing Marshall — for her father to die at all — then she grieved her lack of foresight. And again she felt like the little girl who broke the pencils and snorted at the teacher and said the wrong thing when the rabbi asked what it was that a child should do.

"June, what are you thinking?"

"Poppa, it isn't thinking at all."

So she stumbled through this time, with Marshall doing something new every week, and her mother thrilled with every sound and gesture. Now and then, her mom would pull out a jacket and say, "Would you like to take this to Del?" or "I'm going to give these shoes to the auxiliary; is that fine?"

Their days filled up with visits. Nearly everyone she'd ever known was still in Clinton Hill, but they didn't ask about her life in Nevada. Perhaps Vegas was a taboo, embarrassing to ask about, like whether or not she was a virgin when she and Walter got married (of course not) or whether Leon Kronenberg had really felt her breast (he had, more than once).

It rankled her that people found it awkward to talk about Vegas. She imagined that they looked at her and thought instead of the showgirls in Minsky's Follies. They disapproved, when topless dancers were not that big a deal, though it was amazing when they all walked out in a line, their backs to the audience, and then spun around in unison, pasties whirling. All those beautiful girls, tall, with long legs and false eyelashes — the effect was dramatic. It did surprise one.

Of course, people here would not approve of the way she and Del lived, the things they did: Marshall in his playpen in a casino, the late nights in a club, the drinks and the cash and the energy of it all. June wanted not to care about this — nobody would ever expect she did care — but it lingered in her mind.

Finally, she bought her own ticket back

and didn't tell Del or her mother until after it was done. Once she had made the decision, she could feel sad about leaving Clinton Hill. Something in her responded to this place: to its gray sky, its squawk of seagulls over the bay, its light, its air, the way people talked, even the smell of the tanneries in summer. These all moved her, they were so familiar, and yet it was impossible. Vegas was her home now.

Del picked her up at the airport.

June was anxious, so her hands shook. She walked down the stairs from the plane with Marshall in her arms. He looked suddenly like a little boy, wearing red pants and a blue jacket. He had on shiny cordovan shoes, with laces, which June had bought him in New York. She was wearing a brown-and-white dress, with a wide patent belt, and a small hat pinned on the side of her head. She had given a lot of thought to their appearance. She was rarely nervous, but here she was, about to see her husband, to show him his adored son, and she felt light-headed and wondered if they were wanted.

Del was standing in the sun about twenty feet back from the bottom of the jet stairs, just behind a woman and her two children who were waiting for someone else. He looked uneasy too. He had his hat in his hands, and when he saw them, he raised it high, as if to wave them in. June relaxed and held up her hand, and Marshall dug his face into her shoulder and kicked his new shoes into her stomach. Then Del was holding them both, and he was kissing her head and kissing Marshall, and Marshall was not sure whether to laugh or cry, and June couldn't remember why she had been afraid; why she had imagined that Del had not missed her.

"Well, my grown-up man. What tricks have you got to show your dad?"

Del had Marshall in his arms, he was grinning, and Marshall seemed to remember him; he dropped his face toward Del, and their heads cracked together, like a shot. Marshall started to cry, and June made a sound, and Del rubbed his head ruefully. Then June reached up and kissed Del, and he kissed her back, and she felt the warmth of it right through her middle, and knew she was right. This was where she belonged. Where Marshall belonged. She was so glad to be home.

5

On the day Ray Jackson was killed, June was at the house with Marshall. When the door opened, she expected Del to be bringing ice cream, but instead, her husband stumbled in, looking raw and panicked in a way she had never seen. He wrapped his arms around her and cried. When he finally spoke, his words were almost unintelligible. Just for an instant, June wondered how Del would react if something ever happened to her.

He choked out that Ray had been shot — by some lousy drunk, a drifter — and June thought that Ray must have had the night's take with him. When he was in town, he took the money to the bank for Del. *It could have been Del.* It could have been Del who was shot. Later, June questioned this thought. Cora slipped that Ray had been on his way home from the bank when it happened, and Leo told the pit bosses not to bring their kids in to swim for a while.

That didn't sound like a drifter.

But that first day, when she barely recognized her husband for the enormity of his grief, June kept silent about the relief that flooded her, imagining that it had been a drifter after the take, and that somehow, incredibly, it had not been Del with the cash that morning.

Del's friendship with Ray was part of the life he had lived before her. She knew how much he meant to her husband, but she didn't really know him. He was on the payroll. Security. He went back and forth between LA and Las Vegas. Whatever Ray did for Del rarely put him at the El Capitan, and when he was there, he was formal with June. He called her ma'am, in a way that made her feel silly. She didn't want him to treat her this way, and yet she hadn't known how to make him stop. The few times she had tried, smiling or laughing or offering an inside joke about Del, he had been quiet, and she had felt embarrassed.

Ray had the capacity to be still. Twice, June hadn't even realized he was in a room with her. He was large and very dark, and June had seen him dance, sinuous and graceful. He spoke softly, even when everyone around him was excited, or in the middle of a casino floor, with the racket of dealers calling bets and coins dropping into bins. There had been only one time when Ray had treated June with any familiarity. She was pregnant with Marshall, and unexpectedly, he had placed a thick finger on her stomach and then leaned in to whisper how glad he was that she and Del would have a child. This gesture had moved June; somehow he cared for her baby.

Of course, Ray had children of his own — two or three; she wasn't sure. In all these years, she and Del had never had him and his wife to dinner, the two had never joined them at their booth in the Midnight Room. This seemed strange now, that June would not know someone Del loved so deeply, that she would have met Ray's wife only once, that she would not know his children's names or exactly how old they were. When she returned his wife's ring a few months after they were married, June suggested to Del that they all go out to dinner, but Del looked at her oddly — where would they have gone? — and said that he would send the ring over with one of the casino hosts. June should pick out some flowers, and perhaps a hat. Ray's wife liked hats.

So June had ordered an extravagantly expensive hat from New York, and she thought Del might comment on the price, but instead he simply thanked her for choosing it.

In the weeks that followed, June worried about Ray's wife and his children. She asked Del if they could do something for them, and he answered sharply that of course he already had.

"How's Augusta?" June asked, the name unfamiliar on her lips.

"Not very well," he said, in a clipped way that hurt June. After that first day, when Del had sobbed against her, he had not shared his feelings about Ray. It was as if he were angry at her for not caring in the way he cared, though she had done everything she could: sent flowers, attended the funeral, dressed Marshall in a navy-blue suit though the church was small and hot, and he had struggled fiercely to get out of her arms.

Ray's oldest child, a girl, had jumped into Del's embrace after the funeral. This startled June, and Marshall had burst into tears, so June had walked away to console him without learning the little girl's name, without getting a chance to talk to Ray's wife. She wondered if this is what had made Del angry.

■ ■ ■

If it wasn't a drifter, who was it?

Who would kill Ray Jackson? Who would kill anyone associated with Hugh?

Hugh had put up the money for the El Capitan. He lived in LA and didn't come to Las Vegas because there had been some problem in the past; some reason he couldn't return to Nevada. Ray handled things with Hugh.

June didn't like Hugh, and she had been grateful that it was Ray who took care of what the man needed, and she wondered whether Del would now be the one to go back and forth to LA to see him.

She wanted to ask her husband about this — to ask Del what Hugh knew of Ray's death, to ask him what Hugh might do in response — but Del was closed and angry these days, and she didn't dare. He had asked her to stay home with Marshall for a few weeks until things quieted down — whatever that meant — and working at home, doing the books while the new maid, Binnie, made Marshall's lunch or set him down for a nap, June wondered about Hugh.

Eddie had once asked Del about him. They'd all been drinking — even Del was a little in his cups — and Eddie asked how Del and Ray had ended up working with Hugh. June was surprised when Del answered. He never talked about Hugh, and sometimes he didn't even acknowledge that he knew him when his name came up in conversation.

Del told Eddie that it started when he and Ray were just kids, maybe twelve. Hugh had come to the casino where they worked. He was in his midtwenties, and he'd been on his own awhile. He already had a reputation.

"How much this place pay you?" Hugh said to Ray.

"Thirty cents an hour."

"And him?"

"Forty."

Hugh looked from Ray to Del and back to Ray again.

"You're bigger than your friend. How come you making thirty cents?"

Ray didn't say anything. Kept his head down.

"Shut up, Hugh," said Del.

"Shut up? You telling me to shut up?"

"Yeah. Shut up."

"Those are dangerous words, *Skinny.*" Hugh moved closer to Del, near enough to speak in his ear. "You think you're safe

56

'cause of your friend? Your friend who isn't making as much money as you are?"

"Ray and I split our pay."

Hugh whistled. "Is that so?"

Neither Del nor Ray said a word.

"That true, Ray? He give you a nickel for every hour he works?"

"Yup."

Del stepped away from Hugh, then leaned down to pick up another crate and go back to work.

"Well, that's another thing altogether."

Ray joined Del. Hugh didn't move, just watched the two boys.

"How'd you guys like to make a dollar an hour? Each?"

"Yeah, right. You gonna pay us a dollar an hour, Hugh?" Del was mad. He didn't want any trouble with Hugh, and his grandmother would take a belt to his backside just for talking to him.

"I might. If you're up to it."

"What we got to do?" said Ray.

"Collect some tickets. That's all. Just the tickets. No money."

And June gathered that that was how it all started. Del and Ray collected the slips of paper on which people wrote down their bets, and dropped them off with Hugh at night. Somebody else collected the money.

It wasn't until Del got a lot older that he ever collected any money.

By the time Vegas got too risky for Hugh — by the time he was well known for a short and dangerous fuse — he and Ray and Del had been working together for more than fifteen years. Hugh was making a lot of money, running a lot of games. But the county and the state were cracking down. They wanted to keep the feds out of Nevada, and guys like Hugh made that tougher. It was Hugh who figured out that the real money was going to be in the legal casinos; that Del should get one of the new gaming licenses, that he was the only one of the three who could.

So Del had applied for the license, and eventually Hugh put up the money for the El Capitan. Mostly he stayed in California, where he was safe from the Nevada authorities, and it was Ray who attended to whatever Hugh wanted done. For years, June had seen Hugh only in the middle of the night, in their living room, and always with a couple of men standing bodyguard.

Very early on, though, she'd met Hugh in more ordinary circumstances. He'd come to a show when she and Del were dating, and after they said their good-byes, just as he started down the street, Hugh turned and called, "You bet, Del. She's perfect. She's gonna be just perfect!"

It irritated her to remember this. The way he'd spoken as if she weren't there. Who was Hugh to say something about who Del was dating? And why had Del let him?

"I don't like Hugh," she had told Del that night. "I don't like him at all."

"Well, that's good. He's not someone you should like. But don't worry about it. You're not gonna have to worry about Hugh, darlin'."

She had liked the way Del said "darlin'."

6

At lunch, Shirley said that it was nice how colored people could sing and all, but that didn't make it right that white and colored should mix in a restaurant. Nancy said that nobody did anything when Harry Belafonte swam in the Thunderbird pool, but that the Flamingo had burned Lena Horne's sheets after letting her stay in a room. Shirley said it all came back to money: that the casinos made so much money on the colored performers, they would let them do anything. Sleep in the hotels, play at the tables; Lena Horne's kids swam in the pool all day long. Colored entertainers used to always stay in one of the rooming houses on the Westside, and then some of them had refused. They brought in so much money, what could the casino hosts do?

And there was going to be trouble, Nancy said, now there was that colored dentist saying he was the head of the N-A-A-C-P in

Las Vegas. She drew out the offending letters slowly, enunciating each one, and hitting the final two sounds slightly harder.

June was silent. She was silent more and more now. Now that Del had made it clear he wasn't going to hire any Negroes for the front of the house. Del said he couldn't. It was wrong, but he couldn't fight every battle. He had to keep the El Capitan going. A lot of people's jobs were at stake. And what about all of the people that worked in the back of the house? June wouldn't be doing much for them if people stopped coming to the El Capitan.

Eddie was out of town more than he was in. Hadn't even showed up for one of his weeks in the showroom last month, and didn't even bother to explain when he came back. He looked bad. June didn't want to know what he was doing, or what he might be on.

But when he was at the El Capitan, the days Eddie stayed in the apartment, she went and found him there. Sometimes, she brought Marshall, who was two now and called Eddie "Master Knox." June didn't like this, but Eddie thought it was funny. June had wanted Marshall to call him Uncle, but Eddie had looked at her as if she

61

were daft, so she had told Marshall to say Mister, which he had turned into Master. Now he climbed on his knee, put his fat white hands on Eddie's cheeks, and told Master Knox about the rabbits in the park.

Eddie was good with Marshall even when his eyes were shot through with red, and his clothes smelled and his hair, and even when he couldn't keep down anything June fixed.

And Eddie was good with June, too.

They didn't talk about their troubles. June didn't tell him that things were different with Del; that she was alone most of the time. Eddie never told her what was bothering him — what the women troubles were, or the money problems, or how damn sick he was of living in a town like Vegas.

June could guess. Eddie probably guessed. But what they did was race trucks with Marshall on the floor, smoke, play some fierce games of canasta, and listen to Cubop or mambo. Celia Cruz, Dizzy Gillespie, Compay Segundo. Eddie would listen to the same six measures a dozen times in a row, and then Marshall would hum the notes as he packed his toys into a basket or sat and splashed in his bath at night.

Sometimes, listening to a singer like Olga Guillot, June would lean her head onto Eddie's chest, and he would step back and say, "No, June, you're a death sentence for me. For you, it's fun. For me, it's the end."

And she would knock it off, because of course she desired him — she liked men in general, and all women liked Eddie. Also he was her best friend, and he loved Marshall, so of course she sometimes wanted him, and even thought about tempting him, because she was sure she could. But something held her back, had held her back for four years. Maybe it was Shirley and Nancy at lunch.

Del came home for dinner that night.

He didn't always. He said he had to go back to the El Capitan later, that maybe she would want to go too, catch Eddie's show. He didn't know how much longer Eddie was going to hang around; didn't know how much longer the El Capitan could keep him.

That was Del's way of telling her, she supposed.

She knew that Eddie would go — he would have to go — and she would be left here in Vegas; the place she had chosen, her place. She had cut every tie, but the bloom was off the rose, as they said. She was lonely. She was lonely and she felt stranded, and somehow it all had to do with Del, even though there was nothing she could put her finger on exactly.

"I want a baby."

"What?"

"I want another baby. I'm ready. And it will be good for Marshall."

Del was quiet.

June didn't care. She felt a little wild all of a sudden. Maybe because of what Del had just said, or maybe the way Eddie had looked that afternoon, or maybe just that she couldn't think of anything else to say. Something big enough to balance what was happening to them.

In fact, the thought of having another child hadn't crossed her mind.

It would be pretty hard to do, given that Del hadn't touched her in weeks.

He wasn't mad. They didn't fight. The other night, she had slipped into bed naked, and when he came in late, smelling of smoke and casino — the way he always did, even though he never smoked — she laid her narrow warm body close against his, lifted her leg over his hip, reached her hand around to his middle. And he stood up. Apologized. Said it had been a long day.

Well, Marshall was already in bed. Binnie never came out of her room once he was asleep.

June didn't have anything to lose.

And she didn't really want to have a conversation with Del; she just wanted him to touch her.

June smiled slyly at her husband.

"Only you . . ." she sang, with a slight tease.

It was the smile that worked. It always worked.

And probably Del didn't want to talk about things either.

June unzipped her dress, slid it partway up her leg, kept her eyes on Del.

She could feel his ambivalence, that resistance that was always there — that was Del, but no other man she'd ever known — but he also felt a pull. She knew that too. He smiled at her.

June ran her hands through his hair, then her finger in her own private area.

She licked.

And the deed was done. Del took her there, on the dining room rug, which felt great, which felt mad, which didn't last long, but at least they had coupled. At least she could still move Del. Later, June said she would go back to the El Capitan with him. She hadn't been in the nightclub, hadn't heard Eddie sing, in a long time. And Del thought that would be terrific, though he wouldn't be able to join her for the show. Should he send someone to their booth to sit with her? She said no, it didn't matter one way or the other. She was fine on her own.

Leo saw her before she entered the room.

"Mrs. Dibb," he said. "The boss told me you were coming. Let me take your coat. Here's your seat. Will Mr. Dibb be joining you?"

"Maybe."

"Gimlet?"

"Yes. Please. And a second."

"Of course, Mrs. Dibb. Eddie was in good form last night."

"That's nice to hear."

Eddie wasn't out yet. The band was playing low, and June watched as Leo seated the guests; the women wore long gowns and the men wore jackets and ties, handing their hats to the coat check girl as they walked in. Leo was a master at filling a room. There was an art to it: to knowing who would want a quiet booth, who would laugh and play along with the band from a front row table, how much cash someone might be willing to slip a maitre d' for special consideration. Leo's bald head shone with the effort and the heat from the stage lights, but his face was relaxed; his compact body moved easily through the crowded room.

June wondered if Eddie had a warm-up act tonight. He liked to mix it up; didn't like to be held to a plan. She and Del figured out early on that they might suddenly have to pay a singer they hadn't known they'd hired, or a bill for a set of instruments they'd never ordered. It had worked out. Their partnership with Eddie had lasted longer than most shows on the Strip, and when you figured what Eddie might have made somewhere else — how big some of those rooms were in the newer casinos — really, she and Del owed Eddie a lot. Maybe even all of it. Because Eddie Knox and the El Capitan were just a *thing:* something everyone who came to Vegas knew about, something a lot of people wanted to try. And the three of them had done it together, keeping it kind of easy, just making one another happy most of the time and not planning too far ahead.

Eddie came out alone.

The music stopped. The crowd quieted.

He looked right at June, lifted a finger to the horn player, and swiveled his hip in time to the one long horn note — the exact note, the exact swivel, of the first instant that she had seen Eddie Knox four years earlier.

Her whole body leaped.

And then he stood, silent, the horn silent,

the room silent, still looking at June.

And she knew. She knew right that minute.

She loved Eddie Knox. She was in love with him, had been in love with him, would always be in love with him. She was doomed. Eddie Knox was not the man to love.

But it was total, and it was absolute, and the only thing that was notable was that she had kept it from herself for so long.

He was singing now.

A little bebop song, lips into the mike, flirting with a row of women in the right front.

He didn't look at her again.

She barely heard the show.

He was great. She could hear that. He was Eddie at his best. Not Eddie of the bloodshot eyes, not Eddie rail thin, not Eddie puking into a toilet. But Eddie as he had been, and Eddie as he was, with everything he'd learned in four years of carrying a nightclub, carrying a casino, carrying a whole certain kind of dream, night after night after night.

He was better than they'd even known.

And he sang and sang. He brought up some women to dance with him. He let an old man croon three verses into the mike.

For a while, he sang from a booth on the other side of the room. And the audience knew it was a special night. They were all with him, pulling with him, hanging on his every note; they would talk about this night for years.

When it was over, nobody in the room got up to leave. They just sat there, waiting, watching. June could feel the longing. She caught Leo's eye, and he walked her out the door at the back. Her body was trembling, and she did not dare see Eddie.

Leo had a security guard drive her home; said he knew Del was working late and that she would not want to wait for him. June let him tell her what to do. She couldn't think about her husband; she didn't want to see him. Had they actually been on the dining room floor that night? Had Marshall been sitting on Eddie's lap that day? Her world spun and spun, and all these ordinary parts of it, these things that had made perfect sense, did not make sense at all. What was she doing? And what would she do now?

She didn't get the news until late afternoon the next day.

Del told her. Came home from work early again. Came in and put his arms around her and told her that Eddie had been beaten the night before; that it was bad, that it had happened behind the El Capitan. He was in the hospital, and he would probably make it, but he looked real bad.

7

They'd taken Eddie to Las Vegas Hospital on Eighth. He was at the back, in a room with six beds, and the nurse who showed June where to go mentioned that there wouldn't be much privacy. It was hard to tell what she was thinking. Perhaps she disapproved, perhaps she wanted June to say who she was, perhaps she was just a fan of Eddie Knox.

June said nothing. She wore heels and a narrow skirt and a jacket with wide lapels that she had ordered from the Bloomingdale's catalog. Eddie's bed was in the corner, and it was the only one partially obscured by curtains.

"Hey, Eddie."

He looked at her, one eye fully shut, the other open just enough for her to see his pupil rotate toward her. He looked worse than she had thought he would. As bad as she had imagined, it was worse. There was no way to tell he was Eddie, his face was so swollen, and his mouth caved in a bit where his teeth were gone. She had meant to be cheerful, but it was all she could do to hold back the shock, to keep the tears in. She sat on the small green chair next to the bed, placed her fingers oh so gently on his arm, leaned her head near his face, but did not touch. He did not move or make a sound, and it was a few minutes before she could speak.

"I'm sorry. I'm so sorry."

He mumbled then, and she strained to hear him. "Go away. Stay away from me."

"I'm not going away. I'd never go away."

"This is my doing, June. Please. You can't help me."

"I can help you. I can. Del can."

Eddie made a sound then, when she said Del's name, but she didn't know what it meant. She couldn't tell if he agreed that Del could help or not.

"Have they given you enough pain medicine? Can you eat?"

Eddie didn't answer.

June didn't try to keep talking. She laid her head on the pillow near him, her body bent awkwardly from the chair, and she stayed there, quiet, inhaling Eddie's hospital smells: antiseptic and gauze and sweat and something it took a minute to recognize as blood. Eddie didn't move to push her away, he didn't protest. They lay there, head near head, silently, a long time.

June heard someone, a nurse, an orderly, pass nearby. There was the sound of breathing, a sharper step, a slowing step. She didn't care. She didn't care what they thought, didn't care what they said, didn't care what happened next. She had been naïve about all of it, about what Eddie was up against. She hadn't spoken out when she should have, and it wouldn't have made a difference, and still, she had sat silently at lunch with her friends, she had picked this town, she had seen the Westside, she had gone to all the big shows, many times. She knew as much as anybody could know. And she had known nothing.

She had been too stupid even to know what she felt.

But this was the man she loved, and if he were lying here, in pain, in this bed, in this place where not even Del could get him a room on the second floor, then she would lie here too, and they could all say anything they wanted. She didn't care.

The nurse's voice was brusque.

"He needs rest. And he doesn't need someone laying on his pillow."

June sat up. The nurse glared. June had given birth to Marshall in this hospital. She had a private room with a window that looked out over downtown and toward the mountains. The nurses brought her apple juice with ice chips every time she asked, and they brought the baby in too. He slept in the nursery, and every three hours or so, he came in to nurse, and afterward, Del would sit in the chair and hold his boy. The sun would stream in, and the white of the bed covers and the white of the baby clothes and the blue of the sky out that window fused in her mind, and felt like happiness manifest. Until today, June had loved this little hospital with its adobe walls and its red stucco roof, and she had loved that her son was born here, in Nevada, in the West.

"He's had enough visitors for today. You're not the only one."

June sat up, pushed the green chair back from the bed, and went to stand in the corner. The nurse placed a glass thermometer in the side of Eddie's mouth, laid the palm of her hand expertly on his forehead, lifted his wrist and watched the second hand on her watch to count his pulse, then wrapped a tan rubber cord around his arm. She inserted the needle with practiced efficiency, drew two vials of blood, carefully marked each with his name, and placed the purpling beakers in a basket marked "Lab — Colored."

"He needs to rest, so you're not helping him just standing around here all day. That's what I told the other woman too."

At this, June almost laughed, and she saw Eddie's lip curl upward. He wanted to laugh too, knew what she was thinking, and so June smiled brightly at the nurse, who was, after all, good at her job, and the woman just shook her head and walked out.

June angled back to Eddie's bed, tilted her head near his battered face, and said again, "I'm so sorry."

"It's time to go."

"I want to stay. I don't care what they think."

"Please go. Please."

"Eddie, I . . . I didn't . . . I want . . ." Tears welled in her eyes, obscuring Eddie's face. She didn't know what she wanted to say. Just didn't want to leave.

He turned away. Shook his head slightly when she said his name again. And June left.

In the lobby, she picked up a newspaper and sat down to collect herself. There was another article about the NAACP. They wanted the casinos desegregated. Negroes would be able to gamble, eat, stay in the rooms. There were rumors of a march. Inside, a small notice: "El Capitan Headliner Eddie Knox Beaten, Recovering in Hospital." There was no indication of what had happened, just that the performer had been found hours after his show by a security guard from the El Capitan, who had rushed him to the hospital.

June folded up the paper and set it on the chair beside her. She didn't want to think about who had found him, how long he might have lain there. She considered the front page story instead. The casino owners would hate a march. Would hate the publicity. Del said that there were some who would die before they would serve a black man. Others remembered watching their biggest headliners take off for the Moulin Rouge at midnight, had seen people flock to the Westside casino for the six months that it was open in 1955 — paying customers who walked right out of their fancy carpet joints to see a third round of late-night shows, and to play and gamble and drink in an integrated hotel. Those owners wanted the business.

"I visited Eddie today."

"I heard."

"He's bad, Del. It was bad."

"I know."

"Who did it? What happened?"

"It's complicated. I don't know, exactly."

"Exactly?" She wanted to shake him, he was so calm.

"Hey, I'm not the enemy. Eddie's been taking a lot of risks; he's been out of control for a long time. Something was going to happen."

"Out of control? Whose control?"

"June, I can't talk to you if you're going to be this way."

"What does that mean? What am I not getting? Eddie Knox was beaten to a pulp outside our hotel. *Eddie.* He could've died."

"Yeah, he could've died."

"Please. Tell me what's going on."

"It's better if you don't know."

"Can't you protect him?"

"He's gotta get out of town. He's gotta stay away."

"Because you can't protect him?"

"Obviously I can't."

"What about Hugh? Have you talked with Hugh?"

She and Del never talked about Hugh. For a split second, he looked startled that she had said his name. Then he shook his head.

Looked straight at her and said slowly, "Hugh isn't going to protect Eddie Knox. That's the last person to protect him."

June did not want to dwell on Hugh. But Del had to understand.

"We have to do something. We owe Eddie. After all the money he made for us. And . . . he's Eddie."

Del didn't answer right away. June knew she was pushing too far; that he was composing himself because he was angry.

"I don't owe Eddie Knox. We had a business deal, and we both made money. He made his own choices after that."

"I don't even know who you are. A business deal? That's what you call it?"

"That's what it was."

"I know you care about Eddie. I know he's not just a business deal to you."

Del said nothing. Got up and walked out of the room. June heard him talking to Marshall, offering to go outside and toss him a ball.

Leo told her what he had heard about the NAACP threatening sit-down demonstrations, but he said nothing about Eddie. Nobody said anything. Not if it was drugs. Not if it was gambling debts. Not if it was a woman. Not even if it was Vegas. Eddie was

78

always going somewhere on the weeks he was off. And June didn't care, really. It didn't matter what it was.

Every day, she visited him at the hospital.

Some days he was glad to see her, and other days he asked her to leave. Told her that she was making it worse. That he had earned what he got, and she had to stay away.

After two weeks, they were ready to let him out. Eddie didn't want to tell June what his plans were, just that he was going away, would lay low awhile. Del had already negotiated a new headliner act, a band that had appeared at the El Capitan before. But Eddie was really banged up, both his arms were broken, the vision in one eye wasn't back yet. He couldn't take care of himself; he couldn't move somewhere on his own.

June approached Del after dinner, when he was reading the paper and sipping a whiskey sour.

"I've told Eddie to come back to the apartment for a few days. He can't leave yet."

"That's a bad idea."

"What do you suggest?"

"He's got family in Alabama. He can go there."

"I've already told him that we agree. That he can come to the apartment."

"And he believed you?"

"He said he would come. He said he'd be out of there fast, that he had to be."

"Okay, June. You're on your own here. He stays there. He doesn't come out. He doesn't come out of that apartment until he's headed out of town."

"I'll tell him."

"And Marshall doesn't visit him."

"Marshall loves Eddie."

"Marshall's never going to see Eddie again. That's a deal breaker. Marshall does not go to that apartment."

She had gotten as much as she could. And she hadn't really thought about Marshall and Eddie anyway. She didn't want him to see Eddie the way he was now. But what Del said: that their son was never going to see Eddie again. Never. She couldn't think that far ahead; couldn't think about next month. June needed to take care of Eddie right now. She couldn't bear that he would leave, and she would never have any chance to show that she understood — that she finally understood — what he meant when he said she was a death sentence; what it meant that Nancy and Shirley didn't want to sleep in a hotel room that someone colored had slept in. She had known all of this, she had known all of it, but she had not understood what it meant.

And that's where it happened. Maybe that was predictable. But it wasn't what June was expecting, it wasn't what she had planned, it wasn't why she brought Eddie to the apartment for those days.

He needed a lot of help. He couldn't get dressed on his own. Couldn't wash himself. Del didn't say anything when June had one of the maids take a night shift in Eddie's apartment. He didn't say anything when she left Marshall with Cora all day, and when she disappeared most of those days into that apartment.

In Del's mind, this was a problem that would go away on its own, that would disappear when Eddie did, and one of the reasons he was so good at running a casino was that Del didn't take on problems that would solve themselves. He kept the focus on what he needed to do. If Del wondered what June was doing, he didn't say it.

At first, June felt uneasy in the apartment with Eddie.

She had spent so much time there; she and Marshall had spent hundreds of hours there.

But now it was different.

Different because Eddie was vulnerable, different because he needed physical help, different because he had been beaten, and he was afraid, and he did not sparkle with energy and optimism and confidence — everything that had made him Eddie Knox, and everything that was probably the reason he was sitting there, broken, defeated, unsure.

But different as well because June had never been this close to Eddie when she was in love with him, or when she had known she was in love with him.

Had she ever been in love with anyone? She loved Del. She loved him even now. But had she ever been in love with him? Had she ever trembled with the possibility that he did not love her? Had she ever felt the terror of being in love with someone, knowing what one would risk for that feeling — for an instant of that feeling?

Until now, she had thought that love felt like power.

They were talking about Marshall. June told Eddie that her son had decided to become a robber. He said he liked robbers better than soldiers, better than pilots, better than cowboys. He said he would grow up and be a robber and steal all the money, and he would be rich, and he would give some to June and to Del and to his grandma. Also, robbers used swords. So everything in the house had become a sword. A towel could be a sword. He would plant his feet wide apart and challenge his dad to fight with *"sowds."*

Eddie laughed.

"Jacob liked to fight with swords too. Almost took my eye out once, when he was about five."

June felt the tears in her eyes. She didn't know why. Eddie hadn't mentioned Jacob with any sense of pain, he hadn't ever told her anything more about his brother. But everything felt fragile right then, everything important teetered, a rounding drop about to fall, glistening with light, an instant before dissolution.

Eddie reached over, caught one tear with a finger that emerged from a graying cast, and June leaned in, and finally, after four years, they kissed. It was as sweet and demanding a sensation as June had ever experienced. And if their lovemaking looked awkward from a distance, with Eddie's casts, and his bruises, and the difficulty in finding just how to move, just where to embrace, it didn't feel awkward. It felt tender and absolute, exhilarating and un-yielding, inevitable, glorious, terrifying, gentle. And when it was over, they lay tangled on Eddie's bed, and they kissed more, and they tried to say words, but then they kissed, and they made love again, and this is what they did, pretty much all they did, in those hours — for those days — in which June was in that apartment, and Marshall was at his great-grandmother's, and Del ran the casino.

June knew that it would end, though she told herself that something would happen. There would be a way; she would take Marshall and go with Eddie. Something. It was not possible that she would never see him again, and they did not speak of it. Then on Friday, Del asked her if she would like to have coffee with him before she went to see Eddie, and Mack asked if she had seen the plans for the new card room. By the time she got to the apartment, Eddie was not there. Some of his clothes were gone, and his wallet; and he was gone too. No note.

8

She was five months pregnant.

It might be Del's.

She and Eddie had been careful. She and Del had been on the dining room floor. The doctor's due date split the difference between these events — a perfect split, though she had given him no dates.

It had to be Del's.

They planned as if it were Del's.

Del never asked her anything about Eddie.

Of course, she had asked Del. She had gone straight to Del when she found Eddie gone, demanding to know where he was, whether Del had shipped him off, why he had asked her for coffee that morning.

Del had been patient, and then been annoyed, but all he'd said was that they both knew Eddie had to leave — there was never any doubt about it — and didn't she realize he could have ended up dead?

"Is he alive? Do you know he's alive?"

"He's alive."

"Where?"

"I don't know where. But he'll start singing somewhere. We'll know."

"Will you tell me?"

"Yes."

And six weeks later, Del had told her. Eddie was in Cuba. Things were a little different there than they had been, but Havana was still a great place for him. He could work. He'd do well. He'd been smart to get out of the country.

And that's all Del would ever say. He made it clear he would not speak of Eddie again.

And maybe June could have chipped away at that resolve, but by then, she knew she was pregnant and she was calculating the odds, and wondering whether Del would ask, and wondering what she wanted — what she really wanted — except she knew. She knew the baby had to be Del's.

She wrote Eddie a letter. Mailed it to a casino in Havana after she overheard a guest saying he was appearing there. She didn't say much in the letter. Just wanted to know that he would get it, that they would be able to stay in touch.

She thought about the letter every day. Where it might be, what day it would arrive in Cuba, how long it might take to wind from the casino's mailroom to Eddie. Did he have a regular gig? Had he appeared only once? Would they know how to forward it to him?

But one day, Del dropped the letter on the desk in the study.

"You can't write him."

"How did you get this?"

"No letters."

She stared at the envelope. It hadn't been opened. She'd put it in the mail slot to be delivered; how had Del gotten it? But, of course, he could get to any mail in the casino. If he were watching it, if someone at the hotel were watching it. Her face flushed hot.

"I'm not messing around," Del said. "Eddie Knox is out of our lives. No letters, no phone calls. Don't cross me on this."

Don't cross him? Del had never spoken to her in this way. It was a tone of voice she had heard him use only in rooms with men talking about cardsharps. He had no right to speak to her like that. Hot fury coursed through her.

"You're going to have a baby." Del's voice was strained, in a way June almost never heard it. "We have Marshall."

Was it a threat? Did he also wonder about this baby inside her? Even as they repainted the nursery, even as they told Cora that a little girl would be named for her, even as he ordered bottles of champagne?

She had betrayed Del.

She had betrayed him, and he might know it, and he had allowed it, and maybe even he had understood. And that was worth something. But still, he didn't have the right to stop her letters. He didn't have the right to speak to her in this way.

She took the car and drove.

It often relaxed her to drive without knowing where she was going: to get in the Chrysler and drive west, toward the mountains (she might not stop until the sea); or north, toward the proving ground (she might watch a nuclear bomb explode); or east, toward the rest of the country (she might go home to her mother). Today June drove up Charleston until the road turned to dirt, and then aimlessly back on Sahara. She crossed over the Strip, and turned on Maryland Parkway before remembering that a school was right there and the children would be leaving now. Sure enough, a nun in full habit stood in the street holding a stop sign. June turned at the corner before the walkway, thinking she could avoid stopping, but it was not a street, just a drive into a small parking lot. She turned off the car. A giant oleander bush, with its hot-pink flowers finally fading and wilting and starting to drop, blocked her view of the building. She breathed in and thought.

It was possible that Del knew about her and Eddie. How could he not, when she had been so wild last spring, when she cared not a whit what anyone thought; when the sight of Eddie lying unrecognizable in the hospital bed had driven her mad? Del was not someone who needed to share what he was thinking. Of course he knew. He must have known then. He had said nothing.

What sort of husband would say nothing?

It was unbearable to think of never seeing Eddie again. But what other choice was there? She and Del owned the El Capitan. They had Marshall. She was pregnant. There had to be another choice.

There wasn't another choice.

The fury with which she had taken the car and started to drive had already begun to ebb. Now, in this strange little parking lot, with pink flowers draped lasciviously across her window, June felt a thick heaviness descend. For an instant, she wanted to close her eyes and stop. Stop everything. Sit in this car until something forced her to go. Anything not to move.

There was only one way to play this hand, and Del had already figured that out. She had trouble gripping the steering wheel. Del had known before she did. But he was right. She would have to accept this.

June started the car and nearly backed into a man walking behind her. She heard his startled "Whoa!" and saw him in the rearview mirror.

"Oh, I'm so sorry. I didn't look."

"No harm done. I hopped."

He was young and very good-looking. He wore a priest's collar, and June realized that the parking lot probably belonged to the church or the school next door.

"Thank you. I was thinking about something. I'm really sorry."

"Do you need anything? Were you here to see someone?"

"No. I . . . I pulled in because the children were crossing the street. And I got distracted."

"It's not a problem, but if you wanted to talk with someone, I'm here. Father Burns, at your service."

His blue eyes twinkled.

June couldn't think of anything to say.

"Or you could talk to Father Fahey?" He

seemed embarrassed that he might have been forward.

"Oh, no. I'm Jewish. I didn't even know I'd pulled into a church."

"Well, we're happy to talk with anyone. Even Jews." He smiled when he said this.

Why would someone who looked like him be a priest? She hesitated a moment, because suddenly she *did* want to talk with someone. Someone who would hear the whole story; someone who might understand. Weren't priests sworn to secrecy?

He waited.

He was so young. No. She didn't need to talk to a priest. She was June Stein. She knew what she had to do.

"No, I just made a wrong turn. Thank you, though. Sorry." She was starting to babble.

"Sure," he said easily. His eyes flitted to her rounded belly, and June thought, maybe he could bless the baby. Which was a strange thought, and unsettling. She drove away quickly.

If she hadn't had those days with Eddie, then she might never have noticed certain things that Del did. The way he answered the phone in the study, even if the hall phone was closer. The way that Leo or

Mack sometimes told her where Del was before she had asked. Even the smell of sweat, of salt, on his skin: some nights she noticed it, some nights it caught her attention, but she couldn't put her finger on why.

And one day, when Mack offered to drive her home because Del would be late, June asked.

"Is he in a meeting? Do you know where he is?"

Mack wasn't expecting this, and there was a split second between her question and his answer, a second imprinted on his face; a moment where he recalibrated what she had just asked and how he would reply.

"He had a meeting with some guys from the golf course. It's a charity event for that new school on Sahara."

June didn't answer. She didn't look at Mack. He was loyal to Del, and she didn't want him to know what she had seen in his face. When he drove up to the house, she said lightly, "Marshall's going to be so excited. Del told me your car was a rocket, and Marshall thinks it *is* a rocket."

"Should I give him a ride?"

"He'd love it. Let me go and get him."

She tried to decide if it mattered to her. What she felt. She wondered how long it had been going on. She'd noticed things only in the last month or so, but the truth was, she hadn't been looking for anything. Before having her own secret, June hadn't considered what a secret looked like.

But who?

Del didn't seem to pay particular attention to anyone at the hotel. In fact, she couldn't remember any time when she had noticed Del notice someone. She had noticed Eddie notice, from the first night she met him. It was an instinctive part of being around him, the way women looked at him, the subtle ways he indicated interest back. She'd practically done a study of it, long before she had admitted she cared. She and Del had sometimes mentioned it; heck, she and Eddie had laughed about it. So June tried. She tried to remember a time when Del had suddenly noticed a woman, and she could not.

Nor did she see it now. Now that she was watching for it.

He was a cool cat, Del. He played a long game, following beginnings out to their possible endings, and adjusting course before his competition knew the race was on. June knew this about him. Perhaps she hadn't fully considered what it might mean for her.

Well, he wasn't tougher than she was. She

could play a long game too.

And did it matter if Del was seeing some-one? Maybe it mattered if he were in love. But if he were, he'd missed his opportunity to move June out. And it wasn't like Del to miss an opportunity he wanted.

So who was she?

June smelled something, a different salty, sweaty something, on his skin.

9

June's pregnancy stretched into the long, slow months, and she experienced the world as simultaneously leaden and diaphanous. There was the not knowing whose baby she carried, there was the knowledge that her husband was capable of hiding things from her that she would not have been able to hide from him, there was the small boy who chattered at her side, there was the extraordinary sensation of a new person shifting within her. And then there was Eddie: the way his face had been swollen, how his skin had tasted, the words he had said, what she had felt in that room with him. All of this echoed in her mind, night and day.

In November, Cora stopped by the El Capitan to have lunch with June. They sat outside because the weather was warm, and June arched her neck to feel the sun on her face. Del's grandmother wore an olive green hat and carefully positioned herself in the shade, though her deeply lined skin revealed decades lived in the desert.

"Del's pleased about the baby. He thinks it's a girl." Cora slipped a cigarette between her lips, offered another to June, then placed the pack on the table where she could easily reach for it.

"Yeah, he's sure it's a girl. He says I look different than I did with Marshall."

"I don't see that, really."

"I feel different. I feel bigger. Like a car."

"You carry your babies right up front. From the back, you don't even look pregnant."

"Well, from the side . . ."

"From the side, you look pregnant."

"I look like a car."

"Or a train."

June snorted. Cora could make her laugh. She was huge. Twice, she'd hit her stomach on the side table. She grew so fast, she couldn't figure out where her body started and stopped. Marshall could crouch directly under her belly, and she couldn't even see him. She'd told him this, and after first saying "I don't like it, Mommy, I don't like to be inbisible," he decided it was funny. He would slip underneath her and yell, "Daddy, look! Mommy can't see me here."

And then he would peek out, give her a

long sideways glance — his lashes so lush they looked fake — and say, "Hi, Mommy. It's your Marshall."

In the evenings, June sometimes lay next to Marshall in his bed. Stroking her belly with his fat, soft fingers, he placed his ear on her stomach and said, "Can you hear me, baby? Can you hear me, my brother?" One time Del was there and whispered, "What if it's a sister?" And Marshall said, "It's not."

Which was why June tended to think it was a boy too.

She did feel different this time. Not just wider. But different. She was queasy every day.

Still, it seemed as if Marshall might know. Her son was so aware of the baby. He would talk to him while he played with his cars, or ask if the baby liked what June was eating. Maybe almost-three-year-olds had some special knowledge. From the day he was born, June could sometimes look in his eyes and think that he saw things, that he knew things, she didn't see or know.

"Daddy, is Chuck coming?"

"Chuck?" June asked.

"A runner at the Sands," Del told her. "He brought some papers here last week. You were home."

"Oh, yeah. I didn't see him."

"Chuck has red candy, Mommy."

Del winked at June.

"That's right. He had candy. He gave Marshall a piece. I might have told him not to tell you."

June smiled. She had thought there might never be a time like this again. And yet here it was. Even after Eddie. Even after Ray. An easy moment, just the three of them. It was Marshall who made this possible. And maybe there would be more moments like this. Maybe they would come more often. She placed her hand on her stomach and found the lump of her baby's foot. *Please,* she whispered to herself, *please.*

Marshall stood up on the bed and jumped.

"Hey, little man," Del said. "Let's read a book."

"*I Know a Lot of Things!* Let's read *I Know a Lot of Things.*"

"That's just the one I was going to get. Up you go."

And Del carted Marshall off to the big chair where they liked to read, and June got up and poured herself a glass of wine. Then she straightened up the kitchen, and thought about two little boys, riding their bikes, and kicking a ball, and going off to school hand in hand.

■ ■ ■ ■

Her pains came early.

The baby was Del's.

That was her first thought.

She waited with them through the day, and when they seemed to ebb at dinner-time, she didn't mention them to her husband. She'd had contractions for a month with Marshall, and it was early. Del put Marshall to bed, June ran a bath. Getting into the tub was a bit of comedy; things like this made her laugh. She concentrated on her balance as she stepped in, but from the corner of her eye, she could see the absurd watermelon of her stomach, and the dark line that divided it vertically. It was funny being human.

It happened all at once. The baby kicked, her belly contracted sharply, her foot slid on the damp tile floor. Painfully, bent forward, June started to fall, grabbed wildly at the air, caught her legs on either side of the bathtub rim, and slipped sideways into the tub. A surge of water landed on the floor. She could not catch her breath. Her stomach hurt, her private parts hurt, she had twisted her back, she was panting heav-ily, afraid. She gripped the edge of the bathtub and pulled herself upright, willing herself to relax. Breathe. Relax.

A contraction came again, so sharp she let out a sort of whistle. This didn't feel the same as Marshall. She'd had an easy birth. He'd come quickly. Dr. Bruno had said she was made for giving birth; that not many women had such a simple time with a first child.

Again, a contraction.

"Del!"

"Del!"

Where was he? He couldn't have left. Had he fallen asleep next to Marshall? Suddenly Marshall's new room all the way down the hall seemed like a terrible choice. They couldn't leave Marshall on the other end of the house. What if he cried, and they didn't hear him? Another contraction. June gritted her teeth and watched it grip its way across her belly. It was something separate from her, this force that kneaded her from within, that was making it so hard to breathe.

She couldn't stay in the tub. Were babies born in tubs? Hadn't she read that? Well, she couldn't stay in. She'd drown if she slipped underneath; if she loosened her grip on the rim. June was beginning to panic, the panic was rising in her, she couldn't stop it. She could drown, the baby could die, was the baby coming, why was this so different from Marshall, where was Del, couldn't he hear her, if she tried to get up, she might fall, she would fall, she could hit her head, what would happen to the baby? And another contraction. And another. What was this? Her body was bucking in the tub, and she was screaming, and holding onto the side, and suddenly, finally, there was Del.

"June! What's happening? Is it the baby?"

"The baby's coming! I feel his head. He's coming right now."

"He can't be coming. You haven't even been in labor. Just breathe. Take a breath. I'll get you out of the tub."

June screamed.

Del lifted her, wet and slippery and awkward, her belly bucking again, again, from the tub. He wrapped his arms around her shoulders, held her upright, half carried her, half walked her toward their bed, murmuring, "It's okay. It's okay, June. We did this before. I'll call the doctor. I'm going to set you on the bed, and I'll call Dr. Bruno, and you're okay, we did this before."

The bathtub was pink and red with blood, her legs ran with blood, there was blood on the floor, there was blood on Del's light-brown pants. June closed her eyes. It was too early. It was too fast. Something was wrong. She had never felt this kind of terror.

Del laid her on the bed and piled the pillows behind her. When the contraction came again, he held her shoulders with his hands and stared right into her eyes. He said, "You can do this June. It's okay. We're having a baby. It's going to be okay." And she was hoping he was right: they were having a baby, this was somehow normal, but she was also afraid, and she had lost control of her body, and this baby wanted out, and Del needed to call the doctor, and she needed to get to the hospital, and how would she possibly get to the hospital? Would they take her in an ambulance? Oh, the pain. Would the baby be born in the ambulance? Was the baby okay? This was not what she had planned. Why was this happening so fast?

"I'm scared."

"I know you are. But you're okay. I'm going to call the doctor. I'm just going to the hall. I'm calling the doctor."

Another contraction came, and this time June felt the head. She remembered Marshall's head, and there was no doubt: she could feel the baby's head.

"He's coming! He's coming now."

"June, I'm just going to call the doctor."

"Now!"

And she arched her back, and gave one great long push, and the baby's head was out; she could see the wet black crown between her legs, but not his face, and she was crying, and Del was saying, "Oh! Oh!" and he was holding the baby's head, and now he was afraid — more afraid than she was — and she pushed again, and the baby turned slightly in Del's hands, and then his shoulders slipped out, and then one last push, and he was free: a glistening, perfect Negro girl.

The next seconds were all feeling — exhilaration (a baby), shock (this was not Del's baby), chaos (June's body was still heaving, she was pushing, there was everything else to be born) — and Del was gripping the wet, slippery baby, and he was crying, and he was holding the cord and watching as everything else came out. He looked at June, and there was so much there, in that look, in that instant; June would never forget it. And then the baby hiccupped, and Marshall opened the door, said: "Mommy, I'm scared."

Somehow, Del put the baby in her arms, and he hoisted a fascinated Marshall on his hip, and went to the hall to call Dr. Bruno, but he didn't call an ambulance. And Dr. Bruno, who had known Del since he was a child — since Del's grandfather Nathan had helped him lay pavers in his carport — came by himself. He cut the baby's cord, and he washed her gently, and squeezed something into her eyes, and estimated that she was small, perhaps six pounds, but healthy. He left the baby at June's breast, with Marshall asleep on the pillow beside her, and he and Del went in the living room. June could hear the low rumble of their voices, and the doctor giving Del instructions, and Del saying something else. The conversation lasted awhile.

For three days, June and the baby stayed in the bedroom. Del did not go to work. He took care of Marshall, and of June, and of the baby. They didn't say anything about a name. He didn't call his grandmother. Nobody from El Capitan phoned, at least that June heard. She wouldn't have thought it possible that the three — no, four — of them could live entirely in a bubble alone, even for three days, but they did. Dr. Bruno came each afternoon. He was cheerful. He said nothing about the baby's skin, her hair, her face. He didn't ask her name. He came to see June, and he checked her carefully, and he was kind to all of them, but he didn't say anything.

Marshall stayed in the room with them for hours. He brought in all his cars, and his stuffed animals, and his favorite books. He chatted to his "brother sister" as he always had, telling her which car was fastest, which one she could drive, how many races he had won. He liked to watch the baby while she nursed. He would stroke her head, and say, "Did I do that, Mommy? Did I eat you too?" And June would pull his blond curls away from his forehead, and nod, and say yes, Marshall had done everything just like baby.

Marshall seemed to think her name was Baby, and did not ask for any other.

Del was the most surprising. He held the baby tenderly. He sat and rocked with her in the chair in the nursery, and June could hear him humming, and she could hear him talk to the baby while he changed her diaper, while he carefully washed the skin around her cord, while he jiggled out a burp.

He did these things with love.

This was what June remembered.

This was what she would cling to for all the years after. How Del had loved the baby. How Del had been tender.

And for three days, they lived in this way, and Del did not say anything about how the baby looked or about Eddie, and June began to believe that it was going to be okay — that as impossible as it seemed, this too was going to be part of the deal between her and Del.

Perhaps they were never going to speak of it. Perhaps it would just be this little girl, a little bit different, who was their daughter, who was Marshall's sister. Would they name her Cora? Did Cora know yet?

On Sunday June dared to hum to the baby. Until now, she had cared for her almost in silence, talking with Marshall as he played, answering Del's questions about what she needed, but caring for the baby, holding her, nursing her, dressing her, washing her, in silence. It was as if her voice could break the spell, and she couldn't risk it. But by Sunday, she'd begun to relax. She loved Del more than she had ever imagined she could love him. And even the love for Eddie seemed small, seemed tawdry, next to this: next to a husband, a proud man, who was singing to their baby girl — their Negro baby girl — in her nursery.

But that night, Del came into the bedroom with a basket. She had never seen it before. A baby basket, with a beautiful pink blanket. And her heart stopped.

"No."

106

"There's no other way, June."

"No! Never. This isn't the Middle Ages. You can't take my baby."

"I can take Marshall."

June was standing, her body swaying, unsteady beneath her.

"Del, you can't possibly mean this. You wouldn't do this."

"What do you think we should do, June?"

"Keep her. What do we care what people think? What do you care?"

"What about Marshall?"

"What about him? I don't want him to be like these people anyway. You don't want him to be that way."

"That's not the point. What about Eddie?"

"He's in Cuba. He doesn't even have to know."

Del shook his head then. He looked away from her as she said, "It's better if he doesn't know. It's safer for him."

"Nothing's safe for him now. Not now. Not with her." He motioned to the baby. "This he would not survive."

"But why? If you accept it?"

"It's not what I accept. It's the way it is."

"No. No, Del. I will *not* give her up."

"You will, June. You will. We will."

"No!"

She was crying, she was shrieking, she was

holding on to him, with the basket in his hands, with the baby now in it. Marshall wasn't home. He had taken Marshall somewhere. He had known how this would go.

But Del didn't take the basket out the door while she was crying, while she was screaming.

Like a man shot, he folded. His back to her, he was standing, holding the basket, and then suddenly, he set the baby on the ground, and folded to the floor. She could hear him start to cry, and then to sob. His sobs came in convulsive bursts, and June crumpled to the floor next to him, and they sobbed until they were spent, until the baby woke up. Until one of them — it was Del — lifted her from the basket, and she nursed, and they cried together watching her.

And then Del took the baby from June, and he bundled her softly in the basket, and June watched, depleted and desperate and silent, and then Del kissed June's head, and her tears came faster, faster, and he stood, and he took the basket out the door.

Dr. Bruno came the next morning and showed her how to bind her breasts. He had kept Marshall for the night; he had known what Del was going to do.

The day after, the doorbell rang and the first of the bouquets arrived. "In Sympathy." "For the Loss of Your Baby." "In These Sad Times."

Cora came over, but June drew the line. She told Del that she didn't care what he said, what lies he told, but Cora could not come in. Nobody could come into the house; she would see nobody. She let Cora take Marshall for a few hours every day.

June understood that she owed it to Marshall to stay alive; the thought of him without a mother was unbearable. But for now, that was all she could do. She was not capable of anything else. She didn't want Del to tell her what he told people about her, she didn't want him to tell her how Marshall had reacted, she couldn't bear to think of the questions or the answers.

One day, she was able to ask Del where their baby was.

He said it would be better if she did not know.

She said that she could kill him as easily as look at him.

He didn't flinch. But he told her. The baby was in Alabama. With one of Eddie's brothers. He was a nice man. It was a nice family. They hadn't asked many questions. Del had given them money. A lot of money. He would give them more.

"Then Eddie knows."

"I don't know. They haven't talked to Eddie in years. But they know she's Eddie's daughter. And they're nice people. Two little boys."

And June thought about the two little boys she had imagined. Riding bikes. Playing ball. Heading off to school hand in hand.

10

"Baboooppboop booopp booopp."

That was good. That felt good.

He could hear it. And the little heat in his veins, that was good too.

The room tilted oddly, faded and blurred, moving. That was okay too. That was like being in the bath. Warm and woozy.

And someone was yelling.

"Eddie!"

"Eddie!"

"Eddie, shit."

Stop yelling at me.

"Eddie, damn it."

"Eddie, again?"

"Goldarn it, Eddie."

Someone was always yelling. Women were always yelling.

Mama. The teacher. Wanda and Bertie and Patricia, and on and on and on. Some woman. Mad at him.

He didn't want to hear those voices.

He took another drink. Another.

The room tipped the other direction.

His blood still ran warm. It was good.

He could feel his pants, wet where he had probably pissed himself, and his shoulder against something that protruded hard from the wall, but these didn't matter. He felt these things, but they didn't bother him. Like the voices: he heard them, but they didn't hurt.

"Eddie, your daddy gonna get hanged. That's what my daddy says. Your daddy gonna hang."

Not that voice.

"Eddie, Daddy's gone away. Daddy had to go away."

Not that one.

"You nigga shit. You think you something? You think you can sing?"

Not that voice.

"Get your hands off her. Get your hands off before I count one, or you're a dead man."

"Eddie, don't go."

"Eddie, don't leave me."

"Eddie, I'm pregnant."

"Eddie, he'll beat me."

"Eddie, stay."

"Eddie stay, Eddie stay, Eddie stay."

"God gave you that voice, child. God gave

you that voice."

"Whew. That cat can sing. That is some singing."

"Eddie, can I sing with you?"

"Eddie, sing in church."

"Eddie, that is the Lord's voice."

"Eddie, what you singing with that voice the Lord gave you?"

"Eddie, where'd you get that? Where'd you get that money, where'd you get that bottle, where'd you get that girl, where'd you get that dope, where'd you get that voice, where'd you get that face, where'd you get that song? Eddie, where'd you get that?"

"Eddie, where you been?"

"Where were you all night?"

"Don't come around here, you gonna be singing that stuff."

"God gave you that voice, and you give it to the devil?"

"Eddie, can you sing for me?"

"Eddie, will you sing?"

"Eddie, make it better."

"Eddie, I got something for you."

"Eddie I got money I got pussy I got champagne I got money I got dope. Eddie, Eddie, Eddie, will you sing?"

11

Marshall refused to go to school. He locked his feet against the floor of the car, wrapped his hands around the loop over the door, and elevated his six-year-old body like a two-by-four above the seat. Everyone in the drop-off zone heard him screaming. "No, no, no! I won't go! I'm not going to school, Daddy!" Plenty of them heard Del begging Marshall to calm down, offering him a new GI Joe tank, threatening to spank him. There he was, Del Dibb, in a white Cadillac, arguing with his six-year-old son in front of John S. Park Elementary School, and wondering if he could wrench him out of the car without hurting him. And then what?

Marshall had picked a really tough day. Binnie had gone to help her sister recover from a surgery. Cora was in Texas, visiting a cousin Del didn't remember having. He had meetings scheduled all morning, and he had to be at the county commission hearing that afternoon, and he was already late, since he wasn't expecting to have to fix Marshall his breakfast and take him to school.

Of course, June was home. She was swimming. Had wandered downstairs while Marshall was eating a bowl of Cocoa Puffs. "Good morning, Mommy!" Marshall had said, but June looked at him as if she had never seen a child before, and then said, wearily, to no one in particular, "I'm late to start my mile, and I wonder if there will be any fish in the water."

Del had not thought to look at Marshall's face.

What Del had noticed was that June was calm. It was a relief that she was calm.

So he had raced, trying to get Marshall ready, on the phone with Leo about how to handle his first appointment, feeling a little sorry about the Cocoa Puffs, though Marshall was pleased. He had said, "Thanks, Daddy!" in his sweet, high voice, and then a rich brown stream had slipped out of his mouth and onto his pale-blue shirt.

But now Marshall was lodged in the front seat of the car like a stick in a cog, and Del was out of options. He couldn't leave his son home alone with June.

"Okay, Marshall. You'll have to come to work with me. But I have meetings, so you'll have to stay with someone else."

"No, Daddy, no! I'm not going to work! I'm not going!"

"Marshall, what are you doing? What do you want?"

"I don't want to go to school! I don't want to go to work! I won't, I won't, I won't!"

"I have to go to work today. Grandma's in Texas. Binnie's sister is sick. So you have to go to school, or you have to go to work with me. Now which is it?"

"I want to go home!"

"You can't go home!"

Marshall screamed. He screamed so long that he started to choke, and then he threw up, brown Cocoa Puffs all over the clean shirt and his pants and the front seat of the car.

Del gave up.

"Okay, Marshall. We're going home. It's okay, buddy. It's okay. We're going home."

Marshall pulled his knees to his chest, and rode home with his cheek resting on his knees, looking at his dad.

"Buddy, I know it's tough. But you got to pull it together. A man has to do the right thing. He has to go to school, he has to go to work."

Marshall just stared at Del, expressionless, his eyes rimmed in red. He didn't look away.

When they got home, Del called Leo and told him he wouldn't be in. Send Mack to the commission meeting. Tell him to handle things the best he could. Things at home had come to a head, so he didn't know when he'd be in. Screw it. He'd make this up to him. Then Del sent Marshall in to find clean clothes, and walked outside looking for June. She was there, stretched out on the lounger, her body still wet from her swim.

"June."

She didn't answer, didn't open her eyes.

"Marshall wouldn't go to school today. He's upset. You didn't say anything to him this morning."

June didn't open her eyes. He couldn't tell if she was listening.

"Did you notice him? Did you see him sitting there?"

She opened her eyes, staring at him blankly.

"What are you on? What'd you take?"

His wife rolled to her side, facing the wall.

"Miltown?"

She said nothing.

"Where'd you get it? One of your friends?"

She moaned, rolled back over, and looked at him.

"Well, I'm not waiting for it. I'm not sitting here, with Marshall, waiting to find you dead. My son is not living his whole life with what you are doing to him right now. You were better — I thought you were better — but today . . . today it ends."

She sat up.

"There's a place in LA."

She shook her head slowly.

"I've called them, and as soon as someone's here to watch Marshall, we're going. You don't need to pack. You won't need anything."

"I don't want to go."

"It doesn't matter. You're going."

"You can't make me go. You can't make me do anything. You can't just do anything you want."

Her voice was rising, reaching a squeak. It was an old argument. They had both heard it, over and over.

"I can make you."

"No!"

"I'm going to take you to this place, and if you refuse to go in, I'm going to leave you there at the door. I've already drawn up all the paperwork. We'll be divorced in six weeks. And you won't see Marshall. There isn't a judge in this town that will let you near him."

"There's other towns."

"Try it."

She puckered her lip and spit at him, but she was so wrecked that the saliva simply dribbled down her chin. Del felt sick.

But that afternoon, June went with him. He was afraid he would have to restrain her in the car, but she sat without moving, staring blankly out the window for most of the five-hour ride. As they drove onto the clinic grounds, down a long drive with walls fringed in bougainvillea, she finally spoke.

"When it's over, let me come back."

"I'll let you come back."

June hadn't recovered from the loss of the baby.

That's how the world understood it. That her baby had died, and she had never been the same. Del supposed that Cora guessed there was more, but she didn't ask him. His grandmother had never asked him about any of it. About Hugh. About Ray's death. Any of it.

Of course Dr. Bruno knew about the baby. He was the one who had given June the pills first.

"These will help her through, Del. She

needs some relief."

Damn.

And, really, losing a baby was what *had* happened. June had lost a baby, and afterward she had fallen down some hole, gone down so deep that some days he couldn't even remember who she had been. And then, when he had more or less given up — was actually wondering if committing her was the one option left — she had crawled back up. He and Marshall had lain down at the lip of that hole, with their arms outstretched, reaching for her, for June, for Mommy, for the woman who had once been so joyful, and almost, almost, they had pulled her up. They'd had her fingers in their hands; they had all been smiling.

They'd had eight months of the old June. Looking back, it was moving that had made her better. Selling the house and buying another one on the other side of the Strip. A house where no baby had been born and lost. A house without neighbors who had noticed June, too drunk by ten in the morning to get to the mailbox without tripping, or who had heard her boozy "Haaaaayyyyr-rooo!" to the newspaper boy and then watched her fall down laughing at how funny the word came out. A couple of those neighbors had even seen June climbing the ash tree, sawing off the branches as she went up, dressed in a pink silk robe and singing "Yankee Doodle Dandy." Binnie was there that day. It was the maid who had noticed that Marshall was alone out back; that his mommy had climbed up a tree. After phoning Del, she bundled the boy off to his bedroom and read him stories while the drama at the front of the house played out.

So they moved. Del hadn't known what else to do. The psychologist didn't help. The pills Dr. Bruno prescribed: they definitely didn't help. (It took him awhile to persuade Dr. Bruno to stop giving them to her, but then it was so easy for her to get more. He couldn't plug every damn hole.) Del had moved without any hope that it would actually make a difference. But it had. June had seen her chance. She had made Marshall her captain, and they had planned and painted and purchased: the new house a project that worked when doctors, when pleading, when medicines did not. For eight months, he had his little family back.

And then, just like that, for no reason that he could figure, she had disappeared back down the hole. One evening he came home from work — it was Binnie's day off, but June was fine being left alone with Marshall then, they were all so happy — and as soon as he opened the door, Del heard the dog barking, smelled something burned in the kitchen, knew something bad had happened.

He found June passed out drunk by the pool. And where was Marshall? Where was Marshall? The pool? Thank God, no. He started yelling "Marshall! Marshall!" and he shook June. "Where is he? Where's Marshall?" and the dog barked faster, and Del was frantic, racing through the house: not in the kitchen, not in his bedroom, not in the bathroom. He dashed to the front door, ran halfway into the street, grabbed Mrs. Walkenshaw: "Have you seen Marshall? Did you see Marshall outside?" She looked alarmed and then said, "I'll help you look," but already Del was running back to the house. Where was he?

A neighbor called the fire department, and it took an hour, but someone finally found Marshall huddled in a cabinet in June's dressing room. He had closed the door on himself, and Del hoped he had fallen asleep curled up in the dark, but he thought probably his son had just sat there, having seen or heard whatever he had seen or heard to send him there, and unable to answer all the people, even his dad, calling his name.

And that had been the beginning of it all

over again. Only this time, Del didn't believe she would get better. And Marshall was different too. The little boy who'd weathered all that had come before, who had seemed cheerful and loving and marvelously obtuse about his mother's behavior, disappeared. In his place was a nervous six-year-old who would throw fits in public places, and who had night terrors, and who crawled into their bed and slept curled against Del night after night, sucking his thumb and shuddering in his sleep.

Del never knew what made June fall back down. He would lie in bed, listening to Marshall's light snoring and to June's footsteps as she restlessly roamed the floor below, and he would remember. He remembered holding June's hand — so tiny, such thin fingers — in that bar on the Westside. He had been able to feel the excitement coursing through her. It hadn't bothered her to be the only white woman there; she was not uncomfortable. She liked the pulse of the place, everyone a regular, the bartender sliding drinks over without needing to be asked, three couples dancing, their feet whirling. That was the night they met Eddie Knox.

And he remembered June laughing, spilling the night's take on the table as he and

Eddie and some woman — who was she? — drank champagne and sang "Bye Bye Love." They had sounded pretty good, drunk as they were, with June and Eddie taking harmony, he and what's-her-name taking the melody. There was a moment — there was often a moment on those nights — when Del felt perfectly happy, perfectly at ease, when the four of them singing and drinking and celebrating felt like everything that could be right in the world.

One night, he had taken Eddie to the vault to get him some cash. They were sloshed, of course, and June had gone to bed. After Del handed him the money, Eddie got sentimental. He told Del he'd never had a friend like him before, pulled him into a hug, and Del's body, flat against Eddie's, reacted instantly. Del should have been horrified, but he was on fire, he couldn't bear to move away from him. And Eddie waited, still, just a second, and then said, "Sorry, man. Man, I'm really sorry." Eddie stepped back. Del looked away. They left the vault, quiet.

And from then on, Eddie knew it all, knew what Del kept secret. He knew it all, but he didn't do anything with it — at least not then, at least not for a long time. If only Eddie could have left it that way. If only Eddie hadn't threatened Hugh. If only Del hadn't been the one with the gaming license, the one who couldn't be guilty of a crime. Eddie was smart, but not smart enough to figure out how dangerous a thing he knew.

Del remembered other moments.

Laying his palm on June's belly and waiting for the flutter-kick move that was the first sign of Marshall. Then later, June's belly would roil so fiercely, and he could make out the shape of Marshall's foot rolling from one side to the other. They hadn't known it would be Marshall. It might have been Marilyn.

And the girl. The real baby girl.

Del had known the baby would be Eddie's.

He'd pretended that it could be otherwise, but he'd been planning, thinking, calculating all along. He had thought he would have to pay off the nurses at the hospital, so he'd kept a roll of cash in his coat pocket that whole last month. Weeks earlier, Dr. Bruno had helped him with the arrangements. There was a place in California, near Anaheim. It mostly took in unwed teens, but it also placed babies.

Of course, nothing happened the way he had planned.

Because Del hadn't known he would fall in love. He hadn't known that the color of her skin, the awareness of who she was, wouldn't make any difference. He would fall in love with her, just as he had with Marshall. She would be born, and there would be the instant of shock, of sadness, and then, without warning, there would be that same mad total falling in love that he had felt when Marshall was born. And maybe knowing who she was, seeing this tiniest, newest human being, knowing how things were going to go for her, made the experience more intense. Del couldn't bear to take her from her mother. He couldn't bear not to set her on June's breast. Poor thing. She needed her mother.

No, Del had not imagined he would feel this.

From there, the plan just kept unraveling. Because he didn't feel the way he thought he would. Because he loved her mother and maybe he had loved her father, and mostly, he loved the baby. He had thought there was nothing he could not do, if it needed to be done. But that turned out not to be true.

And this is why he put up with June. This is why he continued. Because what had happened to June shouldn't happen to anyone, and not just Eddie, not just the baby, but him, Del. *He* shouldn't have happened to June. Marrying June had made everything possible for him, but she was a calculated choice, and she had not known, and Del was not such an operator that he did not appreciate the magnitude of that betrayal. It was not June who had betrayed Del.

What she wanted, what she begged for, what he would not give her, was to know where.

Where was she?

Wherewasshe, wherewasshe, wherewasshe.

How could he tell her?

He would never be able to tell her. That was the mistake he had made, when he was driving around with a baby in a basket, when he drove past the spot where he had agreed to bring her — drove past it one time, two times, three, thinking all the while, What could he do? What were the other options? None of them was possible, all of them were worse, because what if Hugh found out? Hugh would not tolerate this risk. And then the baby had started to make her little mews, her little scratchy yowl, her hands and feet pushing the blanket into a storm of pink silk and cotton beside him, and he was out of time, she was hungry, she had to eat.

He had wished he could talk to Ray. He had wished Ray were next to him, in that car, with that baby. Ray would have known what to do. Or Ray would have told him to stick to the plan. And Del would have listened. He would have listened to that deep, soft voice, to the one person who knew everything there was to know about Odell Dibb and who loved him anyway. He could have taken care of things if he'd had Ray next to him.

So that's how it happened. How Del made the choice he did. How he went to the one place he should not have gone. How he put them all at risk, when risk was what he had been trying to avoid.

This was what he couldn't tell June. He couldn't tell her where the baby was, because it would be piling error on top of error, because he wouldn't ruin another mother's life, because Hugh was a dangerous man. There was no way to predict how Hugh might react, and Del couldn't risk finding out. June had the right to know where her husband had taken her baby, but Del would never be able to tell her.

He had tried to help, but he'd made the worst choice of all.

■ ■ ■ ■

HONORATA:
THE ONE WHO GOT
LUCKY
AND
CORAL:
THE ONE WHO
ALWAYS WONDERED

■ ■ ■ ■

OCTOBER 19, 1992
IN THE MIDNIGHT ROOM

The priest noticed the woman, but she did not notice him.

She was small and dark. Asian, maybe Filipino. She had on evening clothes, a silk dress beaded at the front and gold sandals with heels that seemed too high for her tiny feet. She was carrying a plastic bucket of coins, and it was heavy; her shoulder drooped slightly with the weight.

He had noticed her the night before, dressed in a similar way, carrying the same heavy bucket, wandering disinterestedly from one area of the casino to another. He often noticed the people in the casinos where he played. The regulars. The tourists. It was an occupational hazard to wonder who they were, what brought them there, whether they were having a good time, whether they believed this place would change their lives. He could think like this — he could think about other people gambling and how foolish they might be, how vulnerable — but he couldn't stop himself from playing, couldn't stop thinking about the whir of the reels spinning, the lights, the feel of the heavy metal ball in his hand as he pulled on the machine's arm. No, he couldn't stop thinking of these things, even as he sat and listened to a confession or helped an altar boy lift the heavy book to a stand.

He was sorry for his weakness. Sorry and embarrassed and discouraged. He tried to make up for it in other ways.

The small woman stopped to read the playbill outside the Midnight Room. Father Burns had seen the show: it was a "Psyche-delic Sixties Revue" whose pulsing lights and electronic sounds had only made him want to play more, so here he was hours later, in this dark corner of the casino, sitting at a machine that had not hit in a long time. An employee slowly moved a carpet sweeper back and forth, an older woman with a cigarette turned mostly to ash stared blankly at the reels of her own machine. The Filipino woman studied the poster of the 1960s revue, opened the door that led to the nightclub, and looked inside for a moment. Then she turned and walked unsteadily toward the oversized Mega-bucks machine just a few feet away.

Megabucks was even more of a sucker's game than the slot machines to which he and ash-lady were tethered. He watched her climb onto the slightly too high seat; he saw her look for a place to set down the bucket, and then decide to balance it between her knees, with the silk dress stretched along her thighs. She played slowly and without enthusiasm, mechanically dropping in three one-dollar coins, lifting them from the bucket one by one, letting each one drop and settle before adding the next. Then she leaned forward, reached out her hand as far as it would go, and pulled down the oversized arm. She did it again and again. The priest could have set his watch to her methodical motions, and somehow it transfixed him: the tiny woman, the huge machine, the drop-drop-drop of coins, the body stretching to catch the great arm and pull it down.

When the machine hit, when the lights and the bells and the horn sounded, the woman reared back as if there had been an explosion. The still-heavy bucket slipped and fell to the floor. Coins rolled. The woman with the cigarette yelled. The employee dropped the handle of the vacuum. Father Burns jumped to his feet. And the woman looked stunned, afraid, confused.

People started running toward her, toward

the machine. Before the crowd descended, the priest saw the words and the numbers running across the top of it.

"Jackpot! $1,414,153.00! Winner!"

12

Of course, they had sex first. They went directly from the airport to a room at a nearby hotel. He had paid someone to take her things: the gray plaid suitcase her mother had given her and the small leather-like one that had belonged to her uncle. And when the sex was over — when he had showered and then offered his cock for a blow job after (it surprised her that he could do this, as fat as he was, as pale and large and soft as her uncle's old couch) — after that, he called someone on the hotel phone. A few minutes later, a man in a round hat, such as a young boy might find in the boxes left by missionaries, brought the bags to her room. Jimbo said she could take a shower, that she could change her clothes, but not to unpack anything; the car would be coming to take them home in an hour.

So it was done. She was going to his house. According to her uncle's agreement,

he would marry her now. Just as he came
— the first time, his heavy body pressing
the design of the bed's brocade cover onto
her skin — he had cried out that they would
be getting married in Las Vegas, that he had
already made the arrangements, that his
friends at the El Capitan would show her a
wedding she could write home about.

He also mentioned the ring, as if he might
give it to her then. He had showed it to her
at O'Hare. Not two minutes after she had
emerged from customs, hungry and disoriented, still in shock that this thing had happened to her, that the whole string of
impossible, unlikely, unbelievable events
had occurred one after another (as if some
diabolical cherub had been given control of
her fate and was wildly stacking the least
likely scenarios on top of one another,
laughing as the madcap pile teetered and
grew), right then, with her fellow passengers
still bunched around her, looking for whoever had come to meet them, he had caught
her eye, called out her name, and held open
the small black box with the ring in it. When
she walked up to him, he closed the lid of
the box and handed her only the receipt,
which showed exactly what he had paid to a
jeweler on East Walton Street.

The ring was her trump card. At least her

uncle thought it was. He thought it was why she had agreed.

"You'll be wearing a five-thousand-dollar ring," her uncle said. "You can walk away anytime. It's yours, and it's on your finger. You'll both know what that means."

Honorata tried to imagine five thousand dollars. One hundred thirty thousand pesos. In Manila, she had laughed when Kidlat told her about the businessmen who paid fifteen hundred pesos for dinner in Makati. At the *tinapayan,* she made three thousand pesos a month, and gave a third to her mother in Buninan. It had been her mother's whole income.

"I don't want a ring."

"Silly little fool. Do you think it was easy to talk him into that ring? Do you think it was easy to persuade him to give you something you could walk away with? You're pretty, Honorata, but you're spoiled meat. You think you'll get another deal this good?"

She'd never known it was possible for her uncle to talk like this. She'd never known any man to talk like this, and certainly not her uncle, who walked with her mother up the hill to where the priest said Mass on Sunday mornings, and who had come to Manila after Kidlat disappeared, telling her that even after all this time, after everything that had happened, her family still wanted her; she should come home to her village.

She showered quickly, her body like a thing tethered to her. She wished it were something she could unhook and release, something that would slide off her and down the drain, something to be dispersed into the sewers beneath the airport. She didn't bother to change her dress when she finished. It was wrinkled and limp, but even the tiny act of choosing another one seemed too much in that moment.

In the car — a big black sedan, with a driver wearing another one of those stupid hats — Jimbo brought up her name.

"You can't be Honorata here. We'll call you Rita."

For an instant, something rose in her. The deal did not allow him to choose her name. Then, what did it matter? It wasn't her body that had slipped down the hotel room drain, but her name.

He had not given her the ring.

She wondered when he would give it to her. If she would have to wait for Las Vegas. The car moved slowly in traffic. Outside the air was cold, there were heavy clouds, white and black and gray. She could only occasionally glimpse the lake, but it looked metallic and angry. She could not see more than a few hundred yards in any direction.

Next to her, Jimbo busied himself with papers in his briefcase. There was a phone in the car — her left knee kept bumping the plastic cradle that held it to the floor — but Jimbo had his own phone, with an antenna that extended rigidly from the top, the sight of which made her slightly sick.

She was starting to feel as if she might not be able to ride calmly after all. Her head ached. She had not eaten in at least twenty-four hours. All that had happened to her in the last two days was brewing in her now: kneeling on the dirt floor with her mother before the statue of the Sacred Heart; kissing her mother's frail, sad face good-bye; her uncle's clipped instructions, vaguely threatening; the long flight, and the smell of the man sitting next to her, who eyed her from the side, pressing his knee into her leg; the speed with which her uncle's deal had been consummated. It was all brewing and stewing and fermenting in her to the rhythm of the phone's wagging antenna as Jimbo talked and leaned forward and dug in his case for something the lawyer, the accountant, whoever it was on the other end, wanted.

What kind of name was Jimbo?

■ ■ ■ ■

The black car pulled into a curved driveway and stopped. Jimbo kept talking on the phone. When the driver opened the door, she stepped out.

"Be careful, ma'am. The stones are wet."

The stones were wet. Wet and slick and uneven. Not far from her was a mound of what she realized must be snow — so dirty, not pretty, not what she had imagined. She tottered unsteadily in the narrow strapped sandals that had seemed right back home. The driver offered his arm.

"I'll do that," said Jimbo. And there he was, at her side. The mass of him was alarming. She thought of the neighbor boy, the one with the Nike shirt, who brought his basketball to the park near where she and Kidlat had lived. "Kidlat, you are *matangkad at mataba,*" he would say. Jimbo was *matangkad at mataba.* Thinking of his size made her dizzy. She wobbled in her ridiculous shoes, and Jimbo steadied her.

"It's okay, Rita. I've got you."

He said it softly, kindly. Rita. That's not my name, she wanted to say.

"Martin. Miss Navarro is hungry. Please ask Gina to prepare her something."

Honorata steeled herself. The slight note of kindness in Jimbo's voice was worse than what had come before. She was very close to losing control, to beginning to cry; she imagined herself dropping to the cold wet flagstones, begging for mercy. The driver, Martin, was still there. She could feel him looking at her, and this kept her upright. Already, so many men had stared at her today. It was as if she were wearing a sign — who she was, what she had done — and that imaginary sign was blood in the water. The man next to her on the plane had smelled it. Jimbo smelled it. The driver, the bellhop at the hotel, they all smelled it.

Jimbo held her arm as she climbed up the two steps, and then just as she was about to enter through the door, he squeezed her waist.

"This is your home now. I hope you'll be happy here."

His arm held her body. She did not look at his face.

There was a huge vase of flowers in the entryway: orchids and sampaguita, gumamela. Flowers from home. The container looked like the one her mother used to catch rainwater. Honorata felt dizzy. Was she being welcomed?

"You're tired. Let me take you to your room."

It was too much to imagine she would have her own room, but she did. It was larger than the apartment she had shared with Kidlat.

"I bought the bedding to match the dress you wore in the photo you sent."

Honorata could not speak.

"This door leads to my room."

She looked at the heavy door on the far side of the sitting area.

"I'm very tired," she finally said. "I'm so tired."

It was not the right thing to say, but it was all she could manage. Jimbo looked at her, his thoughts hidden, and helped her sit on the bed.

"Gina will bring you a tray. You can sleep. I'm going to go out, and I'll see you when I return."

"Thank you," she said. She didn't want to thank him, but it was bred in her: to thank someone who had been kind.

That night, the woman named Gina woke her for dinner. She said that Mr. Wohlmann would like her to dress for their first evening together, so Honorata wore the green sheath her uncle had given her.

■ ■ ■ ■

Later, Jimbo knocked on the door between their two rooms and then entered immediately. He was carrying the small black box.

"This is yours," he said without ceremony. When she looked in his eyes, he opened the box, and reached for her hand. Slowly, he slipped the ring, studded with diamonds, onto her left hand. She had narrow fingers, but it fit perfectly. She wondered how her uncle had managed to find her ring size; whether he might have measured her finger one night when she was sleeping. Anything was possible; nothing made sense. She was caught in some other life: one that disconnected her from everything she had known; a world in which her once-pious uncle might indeed be an incubus.

"You're older than your uncle said."

Honorata trembled. She had no idea what her uncle had said.

"But you're more beautiful in person. Even more beautiful than your photo."

He undressed her then, and they had sex. Honorata fell asleep after, but when she woke up, he was lying next to her, awake. Without speaking, he rolled her over and entered her from behind. Only then did he get up and go through the door to the room Honorata had not yet seen. Lying alone, she stroked the ring on her finger. A bitter taste rose in her throat, but she did not cry.

Their days settled into a rhythm.

Jimbo woke her every morning before it was light. He left when the first timid rays of dawn peeked through the curtains. They had dinner together, sometimes at the house, prepared by Gina, and sometimes in a restaurant downtown. Afterward, they came back to her room. They watched television, sitcoms like *Cheers,* or Jimbo read to her from the book he was reading: a crime story about a woman who had been raped and murdered, which Jimbo read as if it would mean nothing to her. Some nights, he would ask her if she wanted a bath, and her trembling excited him. He liked to wash her back, rub soap over her small body, and then lift her up and take her to bed still wet and slippery.

He was not, however, a cruel lover. He liked to talk. He could talk without stopping, about his work, about Las Vegas, about mystery novels, about his time as a young man. The army had sent him to Japan, and he had gone to college late, when he was twenty-five. He despised rich college students. Often, his talk washed over her. She would lie in bed after he left, back through the door to his own room, and be unable to remember anything he had said.

On the weekends, they sometimes played cards. Jimbo liked blackjack and poker and pinochle; Honorata found a cribbage board in a drawer, and they played this instead. She liked the language of cribbage: 15-2, 15-4, 15-6 and nobs is seven, your cut, in the stink hole, his nibs. She would call out "Muggins, I'll take two!" in the tickatick rhythm with which she spoke, and Jimbo would play game after game with her, though at first he had said that cribbage was dull. Sometimes when they were playing, sitting in the room that Gina called the study, with the game laid out on a heavy oak table and the light coming from the stained glass sconces and a ray of sunshine striking the leaded bottles of scotch and whiskey that Jimbo kept on the sideboard, sometimes, Honorata was at peace.

There were no locks on the doors. Jimbo was away at work all day, and on Tuesdays and Thursdays, Gina did not come, and so she had the house to herself. Martin came each morning and drove Jimbo to work. She wondered if her fiancé — if that was the word for him — knew how to drive.

In any case, Honorata didn't know how to drive and didn't have a car. She was free to go where she wanted, and she often took long walks in the neighborhood, lacing up the heavy boots that Gina had bought her. She had found a grocery store — a big American one — with pale leaves of lettuce and tall stacks of canned food, which seemed as if they might collapse on top of her when she hurried down the aisle, but she didn't have any money. She fingered the ring, realizing it was not quite the same as money.

Jimbo had never invited her into his room on the other side of the door, but she had gone in there once. She was surprised to find that his room was smaller than hers. There was no sitting area, and the bathroom was in the hall. Honorata liked the room better than her brightly colored one. The walls were a deep gray, and the mix of gray and tan and chocolate colors calmed her. Honorata looked at everything in the room carefully — she stared at Jimbo's things — but she didn't touch anything, didn't open a drawer, or move anything sitting on his dresser.

After awhile, the days became more difficult than the nights. There was nothing for her to do. She didn't know anyone and didn't have anywhere to go. Gina took care of the house and the food. Trembling, she asked Jimbo if she could buy some groceries and cook dinner. At first, he said that she did not need to cook, but the next day, he left a hundred dollars in an envelope and told her to take a cab home from the store.

Honorata carefully smoothed out each bill and studied it. She thought about the pesos she had sent to her mother and wondered if her uncle was giving her mother money now. She had let her uncle tell her mother that she had fallen in love with an American, that she was leaving with him, and she had not written her mother since. There was no phone in Buninan, and she could not have risked hearing her mother's voice anyway. She knew she should write, but Honorata could not find the courage to tell her mother that she was fine, that she was happy, that she was rich. This is what she would have to write, and even thinking about it made her cry. No, she could not write her mother.

Instead, she went to the American store and tried to find what she needed to make a meal. The rice was dry and fell off her fork when she tried to eat it, but a customer pointed her to tamarind one day when a clerk said that they did not carry sampalok, and another time, a man gave her directions to an Asian market not too far away. The market was mostly Chinese, but she found good rice there.

That night, Jimbo asked her if she liked the ring.

"It's pretty," she said.

She didn't know how to answer his question.

"Do you know why I gave it to you?"

Honorata thought of her uncle. She thought of Jimbo's house, of Gina, of Martin taking him to work each morning. It didn't seem likely that he had given her the ring because her uncle had bargained for it.

"I gave it to you because your uncle asked for it. Because I wanted you to be happy."

She trembled involuntarily.

"I didn't trust your uncle. But here you are."

Honorata began to shake, and tried to hide it by wrapping her arms tightly across her chest.

"I wasn't sure you would walk off the plane."

Tears filled her eyes, so she lowered her face. She could feel him waiting, waiting to hear what she would say, but she could not speak. The silence stretched out, and Honorata knew that she had to look up, she had to speak, but before she could, she heard him turn and leave the room.

"Good night, Rita."

Jimbo didn't come to her room that night. He didn't give her a bath, he didn't have sex with her. Honorata was relieved. She crawled into bed and pulled the covers completely over her head. In the blackness, hot and without enough air, she slept deeply.

A few mornings later, after Jimbo had finished with her, he brought up the ring again.

"It's an engagement ring. I have the band that goes with it. Would you like to go to Vegas?"

How strange that he would ask her this. What did he imagine?

"I've never been there."

"Of course you haven't."

They sat quietly.

"Are you wondering why I want to marry you?"

She looked up at him. She didn't want to say anything, but she stared straight in his eyes. She didn't often look at him this way, though she already knew it moved him.

"I want a wife. I know my money . . . I

know that you are here because . . . because your country is poor. I understand that. But I want a wife. I don't want a whore."

Honorata noticed that his foot was shaking as he spoke, though his voice was measured, matter of fact.

"I want a family."

She looked in his eyes still, not answering.

"You'll have to sign papers. I'm not giving away my money. But I'm a generous man. When you're my wife, those papers won't matter."

Honorata looked down then. Her heart fluttered with the faint memory of the woman she had been, the girl. She saw Kidlat's face, the smile she had known her whole life, the narrow plane of his back, and the knees that rounded out too large for his calves. She thought of her father, before he died, and the lime green of the rice fields, and how her stomach had lurched when she had taken the jeepney up the Mountain Trail with him. For a moment, she remembered the soft island air on her skin, the slap of wet fronds against her thighs, the slosh of water running through the fields, the trill and mutter of birds, and the squawk of the rooster being beaten for *pinikpikan.*

She should never have gone to Manila.

But she had loved Kidlat. And how would her mother have lived if she had not gone to the city?

Jimbo was waiting. Honorata said nothing but pulled him back toward her pillow, buried her head in the thin strands of hair on his wide chest, and flicked her tongue against his nipple. He moaned. This was the only way she knew to avoid answering.

13

"I had a rooster, and the rooster pleased me," sang Coral, after stepping through the arch of paper flowers that festooned the door of the kindergarten classroom.

"Cock-a-doodle-doo!" yelled Faraz, which Coral ignored. Sara dropped her box of crayons, and Coral ignored that too. The rest of the children hurried to put away their things — the construction paper to the middle of the table, the crayons and scissors into the slots of their desks — and two boys raced to be first to sit on the color block mat.

"I fed my rooster on a green berry tree."

The children on the mat joined in.

"The liiiiittttle rooster went cock-a-doodle-doo, dee doodly doodly doodly doo."

"The duck!" called Aaron from his desk near the bookshelf. Coral ignored him.

"I had a cat and the cat pleased me."

More children were on the mat, singing

now. They wiggled a little, scrambling for place, and Coral slowed the tempo of the song, without quite looking at any wiggler.

"I fed my cat on a green berry tree."

No more wigglers, and even Aaron was putting his art project in the correct spot on the bookshelf.

"The liiiitttttlle cat goes meeeeow, meeeeow, the little rooster goes cock-a-doodle-doo dee doodly doodly doodly doo."

By the time they got to the duck, all the children were assembled, each on his or her own color square, and Coral had motioned for Aaron to sit cross-legged next to her. They finished the song with the lion, roaring with wide-open mouths, and just after the last doodly doo, Coral paused, raised her hands high, and then all together, in perfect time, every child clapped once.

"Hoorah! Mrs. Barrosa's class, you are on top of the world today."

"Hi, Miss Jackson." "Hello, Miss Jackson." "Miss Jackson, are we doing the love song today?" "Yes, the love song!" "Can we do the love song?"

Their voices came in an excited rush, but nobody jumped up or shouted. They sat eagerly waiting.

"We can do the love song today. But first, can anybody tell me what we are learning about music this month?"

"About music writing!"

"Yes. About music writing."

Coral held up a card with a treble clef.

"And what's this?"

"It's an *S*!" "It's a cliff." "It's the high voice sign."

"Good. It's a treble clef." Coral sounded out the two words carefully. "Let's say it together."

"Treble clef."

"And again?"

"Treble clef!"

"Three times, like bells ringing."

"Treble clef, treble clef, treble clef!" the children sang out, pitching their voices even higher than they were naturally.

"Perfect. Does anyone remember the name of the other clef?"

"Basic clef!" yelled Faraz. "It's the basic clef."

"Good! *Bass* clef. Let's try that one together."

"Bass clef."

"Three times, like a choo-choo train."

"Bass clef, bass clef, bass clef!" the children chanted, puffing out their chests in the effort to deepen their voices.

On Tuesdays, Mrs. Barrosa's kindergarten had music right before their day ended at

11:40, so Coral would stop five minutes early to line them up; she was the one to give each child a high-five good-bye and to watch until everybody had left the playground with an adult. The children who spoke Spanish had someone waiting to walk them home, but most of the rest walked or skipped to a designated pick-up area, where a driver with a van marked Happy Daze Care or Kids Korner waited. Last week, one child had been left after all the others were gone. Coral wasn't sure why, but she had already decided whose turn it would be for the love song today.

"We have five minutes left," she said to the class.

"The love song!" "It's love song time!"

"Yes, it is. And today the love song is for Melody. Do you all know that *melody* is a music word too? It means a series of tones that we like. Melody, did you know that?"

Melody shook her head shyly.

"Do you want to have the love song today?"

The little girl nodded.

"Do you want to tell us someone who loves you?"

She shook her head.

"Well, then, we'll start with me." Coral sang, *"You're the one that I love, I love, I love,* you're the one that I love, sweetest one of all."

The children joined in. *"You're the one that we love, we love, we love. You're the one that we love, sweetest one of all."*

Melody was wearing a faded purple T-shirt, with a peeling green Baby Bop on the front. *"You're the one that Baby Bop loves, Baby Bop loves, Baby Bop loves, you're the one that Baby Bop loves, sweetest one of all."*

Melody smiled and touched the hem of her shirt.

"Butterflies," she said so quietly that Coral almost didn't hear her. *"You're the one the butterflies love, butterflies love, butterflies love, you're the one the butterflies love, sweetest one of all."*

The children sang brightly, beaming at Melody as they picked up their cues from Coral, and when she motioned for them to stand, they kept singing, more quietly, as they found their backpacks and unhooked their sweaters, and the ones who were going to day care retrieved their lunches from the shelf near the door. Melody stood on the mat the longest, listening to them sing about her, and saying softly to Coral, "Minnie Mouse." "Puppies. "Mrs. Barrosa."

■ ■ ■ ■

Coral watched the children line up and thought about how her life might be if she had not come home last year; if Augusta hadn't casually mentioned how many teachers the district was hiring; if the thought, initially so ridiculous, hadn't grown on her — after an argument with Gerald, after she had washed her favorite sweater three times and it still smelled like smoke from the club, after her check for the PG&E bill bounced, after Tonya mentioned that she had seen Gerald at a bar in Bernal Heights, on a night that Coral thought he had driven home to help his aunt replace her water heater.

Little by little, the option her mother was suggesting took hold. Coral had her teaching certificate, she'd never intended to become a singer. Singing had started as a dare. They were all at a club in San Francisco for someone's twenty-first birthday, and there was an open mike call. Some of the guys started chanting "Sing! Sing! Sing!" until, laughing, she and Tonya went onstage. After that, it happened fast: someone in the club offered them a gig, for tips, and soon after that, there was another offer.

Tonya dropped out to manage their book-ings — that surprised Coral — but Coral kept going to school, showing up first to class and then to her student teaching bleary-eyed and hoarse. Whether she had done so because she wanted to finish col-lege or because she would never have dared tell Augusta that she'd quit, she wasn't sure.

And was that whole life a detour? For most of the six years that Coral had sung with Tonya and then with the band, she felt like she was doing exactly what she should be doing — that the music, her voice, the way people responded, the songs she wrote in her head, over and over, all the time, this was who she was and who she was born to be. And what did it mean that she could simply drop out of who she was born to be? That one day she would wake up and re-alize she was so tired; so tired that not be-ing tired didn't even seem like a real state. That she would wake up and know she had fallen in love with the wrong man, and that she wasn't strong enough to fix this. She would wake up longing for a morning, miss-ing daytime; she was so damn sick of living at night, of a pink-fingered dawn meaning it was time to go to bed. If she didn't get out of there, if she didn't get away, she'd go under. Music or no.

She wasn't Tonya. She wasn't Gerald. She was weaker than they were. And she needed her mother. She needed to go home. Coral laughed when she told her friends that she was back home living with her mother — she was careful to make it sound like a drag — but, really, she had been so grateful for the sound of her mama in the next room, for the blue sofa with the lumpy pillows, for the wooden swordfish Ray Junior had made in shop class hanging on the wall, for the mesquite tree dropping spinners on her window sill, for the suffocating, sweltering, clean, dry heat of a July noon. It was all beautiful, it was all home, it was all the way the world felt right.

So when the principal at Lewis E. Rowe offered her a job teaching music, she didn't hesitate, she didn't waste any time worrying about what anyone else might think of her decision. She said yes. And from the first week — when she couldn't find the fourth-grade classroom, when the air-conditioning hadn't worked, when the fire alarm had gone off just after she'd sent one small child to the bathroom — from the very beginning, it seemed to Coral it was a pretty good choice.

Still, not everything about coming home to

Vegas was easy. Just this morning, she had woken to that old sense of something not right. Coral kept her eyes closed, but the pressure was there: an emptiness so vast it had presence, pushing against her like a force, daring her to wobble, lean, tumble in, tumble back. If she didn't open her eyes, she might fall back asleep, the pressure might go away: it might not be there waiting when she woke again.

This was a Vegas feeling, as old as she was, a feeling that stretched as far back as her own memory. How many mornings had she felt it? This dread or sadness or longing or fear — she was never sure quite what. When she was small, perhaps five or six, she had asked her mama:

"Who is it that sits on my bed in the morning?"

"Who sits on your bed?"

"On my chest. When I wake up, and I can't breathe."

"You can't breathe?"

"I can't breathe. And then I try really hard, I think about how I want to get up, and she goes away."

"She?"

"The person, sitting on my chest."

"Do you know what she looks like?"

"No."

"I sometimes come in the morning and look at you. I might even give you a kiss. Do you think that's what happens?"

"No. It's not you, Mama. I would know if it was you."

"Hmmm. Well, I think it's a dream, Coral. I think you're not quite awake. It might be a nightmare that you have."

"It feels like I'm awake."

"Yes. I'm sorry. It must be scary."

"It hurts."

"It hurts?"

"Yes."

Years of practice had taught her to get up as quickly as possible. The impulse to lie still, to fall back asleep, could ruin a morning. She sat up and swung her legs over the side of the bed. The sun slanted through the slats in the windows, striping the pale carpet with bands of light and shadow. Long ago, she had shared this bedroom with Ada, and they had made up a rhythm to step on these stripes of light. Coral placed her feet carefully along them now and stepped the rhythm again, remembering her sister's raspy voice and the way she would suddenly pinch Coral at the waist to try to make her lose her footing.

Their twin beds were still covered with the same blue-and-yellow blankets. Some of

Ada's dolls were lined up on top of the chest of drawers, and the teddy bear that their older sister Althea had won at the Clark County Fair still sat, slumped and dusty, in the corner. When Coral reached the door, she leaned down and touched the bear's nose. Then she turned to look back at the room. It was almost time to leave her childhood home. She'd never live here again — and that was good — but still, it ached a bit.

That was another thing about living in Vegas. Houses were cheap. She'd already saved up enough for a down payment. She never could have bought a house in California, but here, even with 10 percent interest, it didn't make sense to rent. The Realtor suggested she wait to buy until the first houses were built in the northwest, next year, but Coral didn't think she would like a master-planned community or a neighborhood filled with the thousands suddenly arriving each month from Ohio and New York and places farther away. Vegas had always been a boomtown, but things were changing much faster now. At her interview, the principal had said that Steve Wynn's new casino would need to make a million dollars a day just to stay open; that a hundred thousand people would live in Summerlin alone; that eighty-nine new schools were going to be built.

When she drove across town, Coral could see that the vast vistas of her childhood — rock and hill and sky — were already disappearing, replaced with rows and rows of red stucco roofs, the sky above blue and streaked with the puffy white plumes of commercial jets or the slowly twining ribbons left by F-15s flying in formation. When she was growing up, the streets had simply ended in desert. And there was a certain odor — dusty; maybe it was creosote or another plant — but Coral almost never smelled that now. Sometimes, if she were way out by the dam, there would be a whiff. When she was a child, the neighborhood would flood — though there might not have been any rain in the valley, just in the mountains — and everyone would put on swimsuits, moms and teens and toddlers, and race outside to splash in water that seemed bewildering, almost mystical, though it was crowded with bits of trash left in the desert and the dead bodies of pocket mice and shrews. Once, there had even been a gray rabbit, soaked to half its size, with its ears absurdly long by comparison.

Memories like these could make her feel unsteady again.

What would Augusta say if she knew what Coral was thinking, here in her childhood room? If she knew what really brought Coral stumbling downstairs for a coffee, for a sniff of the way her mother smelled, for the sound of the voice that made the world shrink back to its proper size and made Coral feel safe just by saying hello? Did Augusta know that her daughter still woke up with a heartsick feeling, that her thoughts turned so often to what her mama had told her a dozen years earlier? Did Augusta guess that her youngest child didn't feel quite solid at the center?

The other day, a first grader raised his hand and asked not if he could go to the bathroom or if they were going to sing about alligators, but what color was she: black or white? Coral started to laugh, and to tell him that she was the color of a milkshake, or a malt ball, but just in time, she caught the expression on the face of a little girl at the back, her hair in tightly-braided rows, and so Coral answered directly, "I'm black."

And the little girl smiled, carefully looking down at her desk as she did so. This feeling, too, Coral remembered.

14

It was summer in Chicago before Jimbo asked about the letters.

"Rita, did you write these?"

"What?"

He stood there in a striped silk bathrobe; a giant with a packet of letters in his hand. She could see bits of pink stationery, words in blue ink handwriting, a couple of airmail envelopes. She had never seen any letters. She went blank, and then, in a flash, realized what they must be. Her face must have shown her shock.

"You didn't sign them, either?"

The magnitude of her uncle's betrayal loomed. That's how it was done. That's how it was usually done. Manila pen pals. Poor women who wrote letters to rich men, in the States, in Russia, other places. They wrote letters back and forth, and the women always knew what was coming; they wanted out, the letters were their chance.

But Honorata had never written a letter.

Honorata had never been one of those women.

Is this what her uncle did? Was this the job that made him travel to Manila? Did he find the women, find the men for them to write to, negotiate the deals?

He had planned it all. He had written letters for her.

Except her uncle didn't even know how to write. He would have had to pay someone to write those letters. Did the same woman write all the letters, for all the girls?

How long had he been planning for her trip to Chicago?

Honorata knew enough about Jimbo to know that her uncle would not have let him slip through his fingers. Big fish. Her uncle liked big fish.

The scope of his betrayal, of his scheme, made her dizzy. He had come into the bakery one afternoon as if he were just dropping by. Then he whispered that he knew about the movie she had made, about *Filipina Fillies.* He said he had come to help her; to take her back to the village for a while.

"Is anything in them true? Did you write any of those things?" Jimbo demanded.

Honorata couldn't speak. She looked

down. For the first time, he became angry.

"I'm asking you a question. Answer me."

His enormous white hand gripped the edge of her chair. He leaned toward her, but he didn't touch her.

"No." ·

"You refuse to answer?"

"No, I didn't write the letters. I don't know about any letters."

There had been no time for letters. Her uncle had come to the bakery on Sunday, and by the next Sunday, she was boarding the plane to Chicago. It had taken twelve hours to go from Manila to her mother's home in Buninan, and eleven hours to return. The days in between had been desperate: her mother thin and sad; her uncle's story about Kidlat, about the people who'd come looking for him; and then the VHS tapes, everywhere in Manila, even in Bayombong and Solano — where the bus had broken down — and even in her uncle's home, though he had no television. She hadn't known these tapes were possible; these tapes from what was until then the worst time in her life: a time that changed everything, a time that ruined her relationship with Kidlat, which was why, she supposed, he had disappeared. She had made the movie to help Kidlat, because he had said a man would kill him if she didn't, that everything was special effects anyway, and the movie would be shown only in Canada.

She had gone to Manila with Kidlat eight years before. She had chosen him over her family because Kidlat did not want to live in a village — not his, not hers — and her mother would never have given her permission to go with him unless they were married. But Kidlat would not get married. Kidlat said that in America, people had stopped getting married. And if leaving the village was a choice Honorata had made, it hadn't felt like one; there had been no thinking at all, just feeling: longing and sorrow and then sudden joy (this, then, was what it was all about). After that, there had been nothing left to do but go with Kidlat, whom she loved, and who knew what he wanted, and what he was willing to do or not do, better than she did.

Always she sent money home. Sometimes her uncle came to get the money from her, sometimes someone from the village came, and sometimes she mailed it with the letters she sent every week. By the time she returned home, by the time she finally saw the thatched roof and wood posts of her family home in Buninan, by the time she saw her mother again; running away with

Kidlat meant nothing. The movie — the movie she'd never seen and never would see — meant everything.

It had not all been special effects. Did Kidlat know that?

"So what did you know?" Jimbo asked. "If you didn't know about the letters, what did you know?"

Honorata said nothing. There was no way to explain. She didn't know what had happened, but now she knew it had started a long time before her uncle came to get her at the bakery in Manila.

Jimbo grabbed her then. His fingers dug into her arm. They were fleshy and strong. She stared at those fingers, at her own arm, without being able to look away. He saw her staring at the arm, and silently, without looking at her, he twisted her elbow back.

Honorata gasped in pain. But she didn't look at him.

He released her.

"Whore," he snarled, and stood up abruptly.

Honorata sat without moving, afraid to be heard. If she could stop her own breath, if she could will herself to stop breathing, she would.

He'd shocked himself. Grabbing her arm.

Bending it backward. He'd almost kept going.

The rage and repulsion and roar he felt was a physical thing: a wave. Jimbo's body dripped sweat, his jaws gripped painfully, the room pulsed with the realization of how Rita's uncle had played him.

Ramon Navarro was a nasty man: insipid, pandering, unrelenting. He operated independently, no agency, and his clients had to be referred to him by someone he knew. A salesman in Miami had made the connection for Jimbo. From the first approach, Jimbo had had no intention of working with Rita's uncle. He'd told him to stop calling, to stop sending letters, but when the man asked him to read just this one letter, this one very special letter, Jimbo had done it.

"I go to the bakery at four in the morning, before it is light. The streets are not quiet even then, and they smell of all the people who live here, and sometimes I feel so sad for someone sleeping on the ground, right in my path, that I am tempted to wake him up, to take him with me to the bakery, to give him one of the rolls left from the night before, but I know this would be dangerous, and so I step around him, careful not to wake him up."

He was a fool. A sucker. And her uncle had played him.

He had worked with Honorata's uncle only because her letters had been so different, and because Ramon had told him that this was his niece; that she did not correspond with anyone but him, that she was not one of the women who had come to Ramon for help.

What a fool.

A pathetic, fat, sweaty fool.

And from eight thousand miles away, Ramon had known.

For months, there had been no photo. Usually the photo was the first thing to come: a half dozen photos, each with a name and a short introduction. But everything about corresponding with Honorata had been different. The letters were sent directly to him, and he wrote directly back to her. Jimbo used his post office box, of course, but the letters did not go through Ramon.

He bit his tongue remembering this, realizing.

So there had been no photo, and after awhile, Jimbo wasn't sure he wanted one. The niece was likely misshapen, there was something wrong about her — he imagined acne scars, dwarfism, obesity, a birthmark, what could it be? — but as they became friends, as he found that he was able to tell her the most intimate details of his life, the slights he kept hidden, the embarrassment he felt, he realized he didn't care what she looked like. It was absurd, that this mail-order bride idea might actually work, that he might actually have met someone he could love and who would love him. He hadn't really believed it was possible.

And he would help her family. They could visit whenever she wanted. She wouldn't have to leave them all behind. Maybe he would buy a vacation home in the Philippines, something on the beach; it would be a place to go in the winters.

When the photo finally came, in a brown envelope with Ramon Navarro's name scrawled across the back, Jimbo was dumbfounded. How could Honorata be this beautiful? Why would such a woman write to him? For a while, he had once again doubted the uncle. So Ramon Navarro had explained. About *Filipina Fillies.* About the way his niece was taken and forced to make a movie that ruined any chance of a normal life for her. How this experience had nearly destroyed her. How it had been months before she would leave the one-room house of her mother. How afraid she was that Jimbo would find out.

His niece had been naïve, and Ramon was

sorry that she was not a virgin, but could Jimbo understand his predicament: a beautiful niece, his sister's only daughter, no one had known what to do. He hadn't meant to introduce her to men, but when he had learned about Jimbo, he had thought maybe this would be an answer; maybe his sister would trust his judgment and agree. He should have explained it all to Jimbo from the start, but he hoped Jimbo would understand why he could not. In the interest of honesty, he felt he should give Mr. Wohlmann the name of the movie, *Filipina Fillies.*

He was stupid, ugly, useless slime. And her uncle had known it.

He'd watched the movie.

Not right away. He'd waited awhile. Spent days thinking about it, knowing he shouldn't watch — that Honorata deserved better from him — but, of course, he had watched it. He had seen horror in the way her body shuddered, fear in the way her lip trembled, sorrow in those wet brown eyes. It was terrible what had been done to her. And he could not get any of these images out of his mind. He read the letters, and he watched the movie, more than once, and after he made himself return the movie to the porn store, he imagined her in it over and over.

That had almost been the end. He stopped

173

writing to her, ignored the two letters that arrived, did not return the calls that came to his office in the city. He had sickened himself, and he felt overwrought, and he wished it would all go away.

Then a telegram arrived from Ramon Navarro.

Honorata was ready to leave the country. She could come very soon. It was important for her to get away quickly. And insanely, Jimbo had said yes.

When he thought of the day she arrived, of how it had felt to wait for her, of how he had made Gina work to get ready for her, of the way Gina had looked at him, surprised, and then — most powerful of all — when Rita had stepped out of customs, and he had seen the wolf look of the man walking behind her, the rush of tenderness and desire, of caring and lust, that he had felt in that moment.

That first time in the hotel room, it was . . . it meant . . . it was sacred to him. That's how it felt in his mind: sacred.

But she had known nothing about him, had taken him with the expertise of any paid hooker.

It was not to be accepted. He wouldn't accept it. He wanted to hurt her. Of course he had twisted her arm back. Of course he was enraged.

The only thing to do now was leave the room.

Jimbo didn't return in the morning. She didn't see him for two days, and she didn't know whether he went to work or not; she stayed mostly in her bed, slipping out to eat some chicken left in the fridge and pretending not to hear Gina when she asked if she had any laundry to do.

On Tuesday, a bouquet of flowers arrived for her. She ignored the card, left it unopened on the table, and Jimbo continued to stay in his room.

The next day, more flowers arrived. No card.

The evening after that, Jimbo knocked on the door between their rooms. For the first time, he waited for her to say he could come in. Then he stood in the doorway, looking smaller.

"May I come in?"

She shrugged.

"I'm sorry. I won't hurt you."

She looked down.

"I thought you'd written the letters. I thought you'd agreed to come here."

"I did agree."

He said nothing.

Honorata thought about her uncle. Her uncle saying that the tape was killing her mother — that running away for love had been one thing, a devastating thing, but this, this tape, it would kill her mother.

How could her mother have seen a tape? Where would her uncle have taken her to find a television? A VHS player?

Honorata still felt the hands of the man on her, her eyes still blinked at the white light of the camera; over and over, she heard the noises of the men who had watched.

"I'm not that kind of man," Jimbo said at last.

She looked at him then.

"At the airport. I thought you'd written those letters. I thought you knew me. I thought you'd chosen me."

For the first time, Honorata's eyes teared. She looked down quickly. She wanted him to leave her room.

"I wasn't looking for a prostitute. I made arrangements for a wife. Your uncle assured me, he . . . the letters . . . what you said . . ."

Honorata focused on breathing. One breath in, then one out. Her stomach knotted, turned.

She didn't look up. She stared at the floor in front of his feet, and imagined his hand coming down hard on her back, knocking her forward. But he didn't hit her. There was silence in the room, and then she heard him move, heard the door open. He was gone.

All night, Honorata lay in bed with bile in her throat. "At the airport . . . I thought you knew me . . ." The room dipped, turned, she would be sick. She thought of herself as a little girl: the yellow dress she'd worn for her first communion, the red frogs the children caught in pails, her mother's voice, singing *bahay kubo, kahit munti.* Her grandmother had called her lucky. In the Spanish that no one else spoke aloud, Lola had said, *"tienes suerte"* — "You are lucky" — over and over. So often that when Honorata was four, she told her new teacher that her name was Hono*suerte.*

Honorata didn't remember confusing her own name, but the story was family lore. And she did remember a teacher's strangely angry face, and a child's giggle, and she remembered hitching up her skirt so that she could rub a finger across the stretched elastic of her faded blue panties in a way that soothed her — in a way she would repeat right now, if it could still soothe her, if she could still feel that sudden enveloping calm that would come over her the instant that her sensitive first finger slipped across the softened elastic edge. Honorata also remembered the teacher leaning in to her ear and whispering that she would not be so lucky if she lifted her skirt in school like that again, and that the word was not *suerte,* but *lucky.* In the Republic of the Philippines, one said lucky.

For a week, Jimbo avoided her. And Honorata avoided him back. But then one night he slipped into bed beside her, and gradually they returned to something like their former routine. They didn't discuss the letters; Honorata never saw them again. Jimbo still spoke to her with tenderness, but the sex was rougher. Once, he left town for five days without telling her he would be going. And after that, he was gone more and more: a night here, three days there. Honorata eavesdropped on Gina talking on the phone and learned that he was going to Las Vegas.

Jimbo didn't say anything to her about these trips. He didn't speak about Las Vegas anymore, he never mentioned gambling. He also said nothing about a wedding. One night when they were naked, he slapped her bottom hard, and another night, her cheek. Now and then, he told her a dirty story.

Honorata spent hours roaming the streets surrounding Jimbo's home, her eyes averted, imagining that Jimbo had someone watching her. She walked dully, her knees aching with the miles traversed, timing the speed of cars passing on the busy road. Timing them, estimating when they would pass her, thinking about what would be possible. The awareness of what she was doing would rend her nauseous, weak limbed. She would think carefully, *It's not true that I've missed my last chance.* Her father used to say that tomorrow might always be better than today. He had said she was a strong girl, that God did not forget his children. And what would *Tatay* think of his daughter now?

Tatay had told her lots of stories about his parents, who had died in a bus accident when she was only five. They had gone to Manila and ridden on the top of a double-decker bus all the way down Roxas Boulevard. But there was an accident — her father never learned exactly what happened — and the bus flipped on its side right near the church. Many fell out of the top, but only Lola and Lolo were killed. Every year, Tatay went to Manila in June and prayed for his parents. When he came back, he would tell Honorata again the stories he knew of them and of how they had grown up. How Lola had been an orphan and lived on the streets. How Lolo had met her when he was in the army. How they had come back to his village, and, at first, the family had not accepted Lola, who was not from the mountains, but when she died, the whole village had mourned her.

In this story was something about Lola's past. Even as a child, Honorata had known it. But she didn't know what Lola had done or why the villagers mistrusted her initially. Tatay had wanted her to know about his mother. Maybe not everything, but the important thing: that once she had been shunned and then she had been loved.

Honorata thought about this story, and about Tatay telling her this story, nearly every day.

In October Jimbo came to her room excited.

"We're going to Vegas tomorrow. Martin will be here to take us to the airport at seven. Bring that green dress."

She looked at him, surprised.

He didn't say anything more, and she didn't ask any questions. He took her from behind on the bed, her face pressed into the flowered satin, and then he left.

"Be ready at six thirty."

That night, Honorata packed the small bag her uncle had given her. Jimbo hadn't

180

said how long they'd be gone. She packed four dresses and several pairs of sandals. She packed a swimsuit. Was it always hot in Las Vegas? She added a white sweater. She didn't have any identification. Jimbo had taken her passport when she arrived, nearly a year ago now. The passport her uncle had ready and waiting.

15

Years ago, when Coral was a junior in high school, her mother had kept her home — on a day she had a world history test — to go to the funeral of Odell Dibb, who owned the El Capitan on the Strip. It was a crowded service, but they had arrived an hour early and had seats even though many others stood or waited outside. Coral had never been in the First Congregational Church, and the only thing she knew about Odell Dibb was that her mother thought he was a good man. She didn't know why her mama had made her attend the funeral; she didn't like to miss school, and Ray Junior could have gone instead.

They weren't the only black people, though. There were quite a few, and the Reverend Sherrell, from Antioch Baptist, was one of the men who spoke. He said that Mr. Del Dibb had been good to the African American community, had been part of the desegregation of the Strip in 1960, one of the negotiators of the Moulin Rouge pact, and even before that, he had been a champion and a fair man to whom plenty of local people owed a debt. There were other speakers too, and Coral shifted around in the hard pew, thinking about whether she could make up her world history test at lunch the next day and whether or not the teacher would be annoyed at her.

There was a large photograph of Odell next to the casket at the front. He was a white man, tall, with fine blond hair; the only interesting thing was his tie, which was fuchsia with narrow silver stripes instead of plain navy or red. Coral gave him credit for the tie. She glanced at her mother, who would not appreciate knowing her daughter's not-very-solemn thoughts. Sometimes, her mama could tell what she was thinking, but Augusta just sat there, large and calm and elegant, with a black hat and the small white Bible she always held in church.

There weren't many young people there. Why had Mama brought her? Mr. Dibb's son, who looked about her age, sat with his mother at the front. They faced out, toward the congregation, which struck Coral as cruel. She gathered that Mr. Dibb had died suddenly, maybe a heart attack or a stroke.

People kept saying he was only fifty-four, which didn't seem that young. Anyway, his son was trying hard not to cry, and his face had a strained, purply look to it. He had wire-rimmed glasses and the same blond hair as his father, and Coral felt sorry for him. She'd never had a dad, but it would be terrible to lose one, and maybe Odell Dibb was a pretty nice guy, because his son was so upset. Mr. Dibb's wife wore a hat with a low brim, and sunglasses, even in church, so Coral couldn't tell what she might be like. She was small, and even though she had to be old too, she was wearing high black heels. She did not move the feet in those heels, even once, even a twitch, in all the time that Coral watched her.

When the service was over, Augusta nodded her head to one or two people but hustled Coral out quickly. They did not walk over to the reception hall afterward and they obviously weren't going to the burial.

"I'll drop you off at school. Then you'll only miss half a day."

"I don't want to go to school in this dress."

Her mama just looked at her, with one eyebrow raised.

"I already missed my world history test. I really don't have anything I have to do there now."

"Well, I'll let you figure that out, Miss Coral, whether you have anything to do with your afternoon in school."

Mama was mad. That sort of thing made her mad. Fine. She'd go to school, in a dress, but she was taking off these nylons as soon as she got there. Mama would never know about that.

It wasn't until a day later, after she'd told her friend Monica that her mama had made her go to a funeral even though she had a test, and Monica had asked, "Well, who's Odell Dibb to you?" that Coral had wondered. Monica hadn't said anything more, but Coral had the feeling that she was going to and then thought better of it, and that had made her suspicious more than anything.

She'd known for a long time that she probably didn't have the same dad as Althea and Ray Junior and Ada. There were photos of Ray Senior all over the house, and her mom talked plenty about him, always telling them how hard he worked, what good care he took of his family, how he'd grown up in Vegas — one of the only African American men in town back then. She'd met him after she'd come from Tennessee, and they'd fallen in love at a dance at

Carver Park when Augusta was only four-teen. Coral knew all that, and everyone could see that Ray Junior looked like him, and Althea too, but what nobody said, not even Ada, who loved to tease, was that Ray Senior was just as dark as Augusta, and just as dark as all the kids, except her. This wasn't talked about in her family. How Coral was born after he died, how Augusta must have known another man, how it would have been when Ada was a baby; how else could Coral exist?

She couldn't really remember the first time someone had said to her that she was a halfie, a zebra, salt and pepper, or that her skin was cafe au lait, caramel, high yellow. By first grade at least. And not long after that, the faster kids, the rougher ones, they made it more explicit. "Your mama's black, so who's your daddy, Coral?" "Who gave you that white girl name, Coral?" And of course, she'd come home crying, and Augusta had told her to stop crying, to be proud of who she was, and to ignore an ignorant child who didn't know what he was saying. Ada had punched a boy in her class — she could punch hard — and Ray Junior had told every kid in the lunchroom that Coral Jackson was his full 100 percent sister, and anyone who didn't believe it could talk to him about it after school. She was a full 100 percent Jackson, and her skin, well, her skin just didn't make any sense, and nobody ever explained anything about it.

One thing Coral never told anyone was that she had overheard a conversation between Althea and Mama when she was only seven. She hadn't really understood what Althea was asking, but it had worried her, and for a long time, she had jumped out of bed and checked the locks on the doors before she fell asleep.

"Mama," Althea had said, "Ray Junior and Ada are too young, but I was seven years old. I knew where babies came from."

"Well, maybe, you don't know everything about where babies come from." Mama's voice held a warning note. "But you'd better stop talking like this. You want to lose Coral? You want someone to take Coral from us? If I ever hear you talk about this — if I ever hear you say one word about it, to your friends, to your brother — I will take a switch to you. Do you understand me?"

"Yes, Mama. I'm sorry."

"Oh baby, I'm sorry too."

Augusta had wrapped Althea, so thin and awkward then, in her arms. "Honey, this is a harsh world. And there's plenty of mysteries in it. But Coral is our baby girl. And it's just gotta be something we don't talk about. I ain't never talked about it, not to anyone, not to Reverend Cole, not to anyone. It's better this way, Althea. People accept something if you just don't give them anything else to think."

But what had her mother meant? That they could lose Coral? That someone could take her away?

A few weeks after Odell Dibb's funeral, Coral finally asked her mama about him. They were alone at home. Ada was in Reno, visiting the university. Althea was already married. Ray Junior had decided to enlist, and he was at the gym, getting ready for boot camp.

"Did you love Odell Dibb?"

Her voice cracked like thunder out of her mouth, even though she'd meant to say it quietly, and after, the room was still and silent, like a stone.

"What?"

Coral could not repeat the question. She had meant to ask if Odell Dibb was her father, but in the seconds when she was trying to say it, trying to spit out the words, so many possibilities flashed through her mind

— that Augusta had been forced, that Augusta had loved him, that Augusta had cheated on Ray Senior — and somehow, this other question had just come out of her mouth.

Mama moved about the kitchen, sliding the broiler pan into the drawer under the oven, and setting some glasses to dry on a towel.

"Child, that is quite a question."

Coral did not look at her.

"I had to take you to that funeral. God knows I would rather not have done it. But there's things that are right to do. They just are."

She was going to tell her. Augusta was going to tell her.

"Come on in to the living room. Let's sit here together, and talk about some things."

So they sat down on the sofa, and Coral put her head on her mother's shoulder, and Augusta stroked the side of her head for a bit.

"I didn't love Del Dibb." Her mother's hand rested on the side of her head. "I loved Ray Senior, and I never loved anyone else."

Then it was going to be bad, what came next. Coral wished she hadn't asked, didn't know why she had.

"Coral, you're my child, you're my daugh-

189

ter, I love you exactly the same as Ada and Althea and Ray, do you understand?"

It was going to be really bad. Because why would Augusta need to say that? The air left her chest like someone had pounced on it. She couldn't breathe.

"I don't want to hear anymore," she choked out. "I don't want to know."

Augusta spoke anyway.

"Coral, I didn't birth you. I'm not your mother that way."

What?

This couldn't be. Of course she was Augusta's daughter. Of course Augusta had given birth to her. What did she mean? Nobody had ever said she wasn't Augusta's daughter.

Coral bucked her head, jamming it sharply into her mother's chin, and for a second, they looked at each other stunned. Coral's hand flew to touch Augusta's face, and then she drew back, looked down. Tears were spurting now.

Her mother wrapped her arms around Coral and settled her back onto her body. Coral kept her eyes down. She would ever after remember the heave of Augusta's chest and a small yellow button that jiggled there, when she thought of this conversation. Mama spoke softly.

"Del Dibb and Ray Senior were good friends. Real good friends. From childhood. And after Ray Senior died, it was a terrible time. I was distraught. I didn't know how I could live with what had happened."

Augusta paused.

"Mr. Dibb helped me out. He gave me money. Ada was just a baby. He put down the payment on this house."

Coral wanted to move. She wanted Mama to stop talking. She wanted to be somewhere else. But her body was solid, like a plank, and she sat perfectly still.

"He came over and visited us too. He showed Ray Junior how to ride a bike. He bought a dress in Los Angeles for Althea to wear to her first day of school. He told the principal that Althea was like a daughter to him. That all the Jackson kids meant the world to him, that he would be watching out for them."

Augusta wanted Coral to understand. She wanted her to believe something.

"This meant a lot to me, Coral. It meant a lot to this family."

Coral watched the yellow button and did not move. Her breath stuttered in and out, and her heart pounded in a lopsided rhythm; she was still afraid of what was coming. If she wasn't Augusta's daughter,

191

who was she? This was worse than she had ever imagined. Why had Monica asked her about Odell Dibb? She hated people. Mama had always taught her to ignore what people said.

"One night, it was a Sunday. It was December, and Althea had a holiday program at school the next day. She was so excited, I had a hard time getting any of the kids to bed. And I was just sitting in that chair, missing Ray and feeling sorry for myself. Those were dark times. I heard a knock on the door. I almost didn't answer it. But when I did, it was Mr. Dibb. He was standing there, crying. He didn't say anything. I asked him to come in, but he shook his head."

Coral was afraid of what was coming. But she couldn't stop listening.

"Mr. Dibb said, 'Augusta, I need your help.'

" 'Sure, Mr. Dibb. I would do anything for you. You know that.'

" 'This is a little bit more.'

" 'Please come in.'

"He shook his head. Then he turned and went back to his car. I thought he was going to leave, but he opened the door, and lifted out a baby basket.

"And that baby was you."

Coral started to cry then. She cried so hard, she got the hiccups, and then her head hurt, so Augusta did not say any more. She slept in Augusta's bed that night, for the first time since she could remember, and in the morning, at breakfast, her mama told her what else she knew.

Del hadn't said whose baby it was. He told Augusta that he would never be able to tell her anything about the child. That was not negotiable. But he had money. He had money to raise her, and to send her to college, and he would take care of everything legally too.

"I don't know where else to go," he had told her. "I know I can't ask you this, but I don't have anyone else."

"Why did you say yes, Mama?" Coral asked. "You had three babies."

"Well, I thought about saying no. I had said I would do anything for him, but I don't think that did include taking on a child."

Coral closed her eyes. What if Mama had said no? Where would she be? What would have happened to her?

"Mr. Dibb was awfully broken up. And you started to fuss. So I picked you up, because he was too upset. You were a pretty little baby, and you had on a pink silk nightie. I still have it, upstairs in the closet. You were real small; smaller than my babies. But it was the way you looked at me, straight into my eyes. I'll never forget it.

"I fell in love with you. Right there. My mind had been racing, thinking how I was going to tell him it wasn't possible, that I couldn't take another child. How could I explain another child? How could he ask me for this, with all I'd been through?

"And I knew he meant it, that he wasn't going to tell me who you were. And who was your mama? Where was she?

"But I also knew that he wouldn't have brought you to me if there was anyone else to take you. And I could see you were mixed. I knew what that meant.

"So I just looked at you, this tiny little girl in a pink silk nightie, and I knew you were meant to be mine. Whatever happened, you were my fourth baby. God works in strange ways, and you came to me after Ray Senior died, but you were our baby, sure as Ada and Ray Junior and Althea.

"So I said yes."

That was all Augusta said that morning, but the next day, Coral asked her, "Odell Dibb never came to see me?"

"No." Augusta's eyes filled. "He never

194

came to see you."

"Do you know who my mother is?"

"No. I tried to figure it out. Las Vegas wasn't very big in 1960. Our community was tight. I couldn't think of any woman who was pregnant, who had lost her baby. We were living all the way over here then, but I asked around in the 'Side, people at work. I had to be careful."

"What did people say to you about me?"

"They didn't say nothing. I introduced the kids to you the next morning. Althea was all broke up, because she had to leave for school, but I told her she had to go and the baby would be there when she got home. I just kept everything real normal. Just didn't let anyone ask me anything.

"I brought you to church. Folks said, 'Who's that baby you got?' And I said, 'This is my daughter Coral.' And nothing else. And I don't know what they thought. Maybe they just thought I was a big woman and they'd missed something. Maybe they figured it wasn't their business.

"But that's one thing I learned from Ray Senior. You don't owe an explanation to anybody but the Lord, and most people will stop asking if you act like you won't be telling."

"Do you think she's alive?"

Coral couldn't bring herself to say "my mother," but Augusta knew what she meant.

"I don't know. I have wondered and wondered. I think he must have known her somewhere else. Mr. Dibb traveled a lot. You could have been born anywhere."

"You mean, you think he just put me in the car and took me away? When I was born?"

"I don't know, baby girl."

Augusta hesitated. Coral waited.

"You weren't brand new."

"What?"

"You were new, you still had some cord, but it was all shriveled up. Getting ready to fall off."

"How old was I?"

"Well, I figured you were about a week old. But when your birth certificate came, it listed the Thursday before. So maybe you were just three, four days old."

"Where was I before?"

"I don't know."

"Did he take care of me?"

Her mom looked down. "I think your mama did."

It might have been the way Augusta's voice dropped, but Coral suddenly felt as if she might cry.

"You wouldn't take a bottle. You cried so much."

"So?"

"So I think you were nursed. I think your mama nursed you those days."

Augusta was silent then, and Coral was too. She didn't want to imagine her mother, herself: newborn. She didn't know how to imagine them. Couldn't get any picture in her mind at all.

Suddenly Coral stood up.

"My birth certificate. What does it say?"

Augusta pursed her lips.

"It says I'm your mother. It says you were born at this house."

"But Mama, that's my birth certificate. It has to say who I am."

"Yes."

"That's wrong, Mama. I'm a person. Someone just can't make up my birth certificate."

"I know, baby girl. I know."

To this day, that's what Coral knew about it. That was everything she knew. Who her mother was, what the story was, Augusta never learned. Augusta saw Odell Dibb only a few times in all the years after, and always by accident. He didn't come around and play with the kids anymore. He wasn't there for Ray Junior's first day of school. But there was always money; things always worked out in town for the Jacksons. Even after Mr. Dibb died. Ray Junior had gotten that good job, Ada was chosen for a scholarship, things like that.

And though Coral and Augusta had talked it over many times, although her mother had repeated the details she knew as often as Coral needed them repeated, in the end, they hadn't talked about it with Althea or Ada or Ray Junior. When she first learned the truth, Coral had wanted to tell her sisters right away. And Augusta had said that it was her story — she could tell anyone she wanted. But she had also said that she had kept it quiet, that she had never told the truth to a soul, so that Coral would be free to keep it a secret too. She always had the option to tell someone, but she would never have the option to keep it a secret again.

Coral had said, "Althea and Ada won't tell. They'll keep the secret."

"They love you, and they'll keep your secret. But life is long. There's a lot of ways for a secret to come out. If you tell someone, it might not be your secret anymore."

"But why should I keep it a secret? Are you ashamed?"

"Oh baby girl, I'm not ashamed. I kept it a secret at first because I was afraid of what would happen if I didn't. Mr. Dibb made that clear. That something bad could happen if anyone knew who you were."

"Could something bad still happen?" Coral felt a jolt of fear.

"Oh, I don't think so. This isn't 1960. I think he was afraid of something that would never happen now. There's no reason for you to be afraid."

"Well, what would have happened?"

"I don't know. Those were strange times. Maybe he was just worried about his son, his wife. Maybe he was worried about your mother. I don't know. But he wouldn't have told me that just to protect himself. He had a reason. I just doubt that it makes any difference now."

This had frightened Coral enough not to say anything to her sisters, and even now, she wasn't sure what Althea or Ada or Ray Junior might know. She supposed they believed what she had once believed: that she was a half sister, that she had a different father, that he must have been white, or nearly white, that he certainly wasn't Ray Senior. They all knew that Augusta had a secret, but which one of them would dare ask her to reveal it? Or did Althea know

something none of the rest of them did?
How strange that Coral didn't know.
As strange as the real story.

16

Marshall was in love. June could see it on his face, flushed. Some of that was wine, but not all of it. Not that giddy smile, that funny laugh. It surprised her. She hadn't noticed anything special about this girl, who worked in reservations and looked like all of Marshall's girlfriends: doe-eyed, dark, thin.

She had never seen Marshall in love. At least, not since he was a sophomore in high school and lost his heart to a senior girl who had simply wanted a good-looking date, some easy fun. It hadn't gone well. Marshall was besotted, but she dropped him three weeks before the spring dance to date someone in her class.

Del had been alive then.

He had tried to talk with Marshall, and June had tried, but their son had sat stony-faced and red. Stayed in his room, playing Lynyrd Skynyrd and eating Butterfinger bars. The candy stuck in her mind; at sixteen, Marshall already looked like a man, but was still a boy.

After that, Marshall figured things out. Waited awhile to date, but had a steady girl all through college and ever since. At first, June had sized up each one, observed their relationship, wondered if this one would be part of their little family. She had liked one in particular: her name was Kari, and she'd been around awhile; stayed at the house for a few school breaks. Now, a decade later, June had stopped paying much attention to who was dating Marshall, to what woman he brought to what opening, or to whether or not she was the same one who had come before.

This could annoy Marshall.

"Mom, you've met Sheila before."

"Oh yes, hi, Sheila. You're a lawyer, right?"

But no, Sheila wasn't a lawyer. Marshall would tighten his lips, June would give him a smile. Really, Marshall could play all the games he wanted, and June did not mind, but she wasn't going to play them with him.

Del had never gotten to see this grown-up, confident Marshall.

He had waved good-bye to his son, driving off in a car packed with skis and a sleeping bag and a bike strapped on top, the extra things that Marshall had decided would fit in his dorm room after all. And they had waved until the car turned the corner, standing in the street, knowing they looked foolish. And June had been just about to say something funny, something about how sentimental they had become, when she saw the tears in Del's eyes; when she saw how very close he was to losing control.

Had he known?

Had he sensed that he would never see Marshall again? That six weeks later, someone from housekeeping would find him slumped at his desk?

What would they have done differently if they had known?

What would she have done differently, had she known?

There were two ways to look at this question: you could size up your life and yourself, and think that you would not change a thing. After all, the tough spots and the mistakes were as much a part of who you were as anything else. June didn't disagree. But to say that it all led to where one was struck June as a bit smug, a bit of a punt. What about that second option? To spot the change that would have made the difference. To know the choice that set the rest in motion.

She could have stay married to Walter Kohn. Or she could have divorced him but returned to Clinton Hill and led an entirely different life. She could have moved back to Vegas but resisted Del's intentions, met someone Jewish, walked a more predictable path. Could she have admitted that she loved Eddie earlier, and gone away with him — before Marshall was born? They could have gone to Cuba.

No Marshall?

And what about Eddie's women?

Or Cuba?

Should she have grabbed her daughter and run out in the night and returned to New Jersey with a second, more surprising child? This is the fantasy that had played in June's mind, over and over, until she imagined that it occupied an entire territory of her brain: all the images and dreams and stories she had told herself about her daughter — a daughter who learned to laugh and crawl and talk, who took up dancing and read *A Tree Grows in Brooklyn* and won the seventh-grade spelling bee.

But then always, what about Marshall?

Could she have found a lawyer? Could she have persuaded him to take her case? Could she have fought Del for their son? Eventually she would have won. The world came her way. How many years would it have taken?

Del was not the one who had made the mistake. It was not Del who had risked Marshall's world. And how far is one obliged to carry the weight of a single mistake?

Because she had been wrong. She had risked Marshall's world for the love of a man who would not have loved her for life (as Del, in his way, had) but it was the world's cruelty, its inanity, that had amplified that mistake. It was the world that had put June and Del and Marshall and a little girl in Alabama in a hold they could not break. Or was this the real issue at the heart of everything else in her life? That she could always blame something other than herself?

Once she had been the girl smoking on the high school track; once she had let Leon Kronenberg touch her breast; once she had run away to Vegas; once she had opened a casino; once she had believed that the world could become new again, that the right people in the right place could make up any rules they wanted. And none of that was true. They had all paid the price. And, really, where was the moment that should have happened differently? Which was the choice that had set all the others in motion?

And would a different choice have been the right one?

June and Del had been good partners at the El Capitan. She and Marshall were good partners there now. They made a lot of money; Del had been right about the opportunities he saw. But how long would it last? For all the millions they had spent, for all that it seemed there had always been something under construction, something being added, some area being renovated, the El Capitan was tired and small and old now. The Strip was moving south, the El Capitan was at the edge of being in the wrong part of town, closer to Circus Circus and the Stratosphere than to the empty land that would surely be the grand casinos — the carpet joints — of the next century. If there had been a niche to carve out for the El Capitan three decades ago, it was not clear that there would still be one for three more.

Already, she was fighting to hold on to their cash cow: to the entertainment that drew everyone in. She had stuck with the formula that she and Del had initiated. Four months after he died, she had signed a brother-and-sister magician act from Belarus, paying them twice what anyone else would have offered. And once again, her instinct for talent had been true. The act grew into that salary and past it, and the pair lured the gamblers, the drinkers, the players, the shoppers, the eaters, the lookers. Casinos were all about people and how many hours you could keep them in your joint. What they did there really didn't matter, because sooner or later you always made money from them. All you had to do was get them in the door and keep them too distracted to walk back out.

And she owed her life to this challenge, she supposed. To this simple trick that was not simple at all: how to keep people coming in, how to make them stay, how to keep up in a town that raced and bucked and reared and roared, ever forward, ever faster. You had better be ready for the ride, because Vegas wasn't for the weak and it wasn't for the cowardly; if you really wanted to win, you had better take off your hat, wave it to the crowd, and smile like an idiot. You had to make it look fun. Would any other life have sucked her up, taken her in, kept her going, held her fast? Would an easier life have kept June Stein Dibb alive?

Could she have climbed up on any other steed and survived the moment when Del walked out with a basket trailing a soft pink blanket and weighted with six pounds of her soul?

It had not been easy. She had fallen off again and again.

For weeks after Del had taken the baby, June had refused to see anyone. For years, she had stumbled through her days, death-eyed with pills, with gin, with crazed antics that had finally forced Del to sell the house and buy on the other side of the Strip. There was the time the man next door called Del to say his wife was naked on the street; the time she had terrified the newspaper boy with a pair of kitchen shears; the time when Cora, in her eighties by then and already sick with cancer, had run from house to house, from the park to the school to the wash, trying to find Marshall, who had wandered out on his own, looking for help with his mom, who was passed out on the stairs.

She didn't remember Marshall's first day of school. She might not have been there. She didn't remember him learning to ride a bike, or catching his first baseball, or sounding out words in a book. Those years were gone for June. Del had done it all: run the El Capitan; taken care of Marshall; hired the sitters; managed his grandmother; held a sobbing, vomiting June; and found the center that she had finally agreed to try — where she had gone for the spring that Marshall was in the first grade, and where she had finally, finally, come back to herself.

She had come out of rehab just in time for summer.

Every day, she and Marshall would swim in the early morning and in the evening. He wouldn't leave her those first months; didn't want to play with friends, didn't want friends coming over. So they canceled day camp, and they ignored the phone, and they spent those months — that hot, blistering summer — together. Seven years old, and he drank his mother's nearness like a wilted plant sucks water. Del came home often, running in for an hour in the middle of the day, and leaving work early most nights. He made Marshall laugh by jumping in the pool in his dress pants and tie, by wearing his shoes with his swimming trunks, by banging off the low diving board and cannonballing in to swamp June when she was trying to keep her hair dry.

If there had been three years of misery, there were then three months of joy. And after, it was true, there were years and years of a good life. They had been to hell, but they had come back. You could say what you wanted about what they each did, about the choices they made — she and Del and Eddie — but in the end, her little family had been happy.

Still, when Del died, the first thing June did after calling Marshall and arranging a way for him to come home, was to go to her husband's office and dig through the one cabinet that he kept locked from her. She didn't want Mack or Leo or his attorney to get there first. But there was nothing about the baby. There were some papers about Hugh, which she knew would be there. There were receipts; she didn't look at the ones for hotels in other places. There were cards, and quite a few letters from someone named Charles; she looked at one of those because she saw Eddie's name on it, but it didn't say anything more than that they had met, not long before Eddie left. There were records having to do with Augusta Jackson and her children. Del had stayed true to his word and taken care of Ray's family. But there was nothing from Alabama, no record of those receipts, nothing from Eddie, no birth certificate, nothing about a school, nothing about expenses, nothing personal, nothing official.

How could that be?

There had been times, in those first terrible years, when June had doubled over with the fear that her daughter was not alive. In the middle of the night, strung out, it was possible to imagine that Del had done something insane. And June could not stop the thought from slipping in then, as she stood in Del's office hours after he had died, the long-watched key in her hand, and all those files, all that paper, with nothing, nothing. But it was unimaginable. This Del could not have done. He was capable of dismaying acts; his life was not simple, and she knew it. But she had heard him singing to that baby; she had known who he was with Marshall. He had promised that her baby was alive and that she was safe. He had promised over and over. But never, in the great cruelness that was somehow also possible for Del, had he told her where she was.

Of course, she had written to Eddie despite Del's ultimatum.

She had mailed the letter at the post office herself.

He had not replied.

She had written again, several times, in the years when it was still possible to send mail to Cuba. She had asked about his brother in Alabama, she had begged him to send her word. And Eddie had never replied.

He was gone now too.

Died in a fight or in an alley — the stories were not clear. One newspaper had said it was a love affair gone bad. Another mentioned a husband. A third said gambling debts. She had showed the articles to Del, and he had said he knew about it. He also said that Eddie never could get past his own history; never could take the success the world wanted so much to give him.

"I'm sorry, June."

"I'm sorry."

And they had held each other then, and she had cried, and he had cried, and later they had even played some of Eddie's records: the song he had made famous at the El Capitan, and the album that must have made him very rich after. Eddie's music played all the time in Vegas, and mostly it had lost its power to bring June and Del back to any other moment. But that night, curled up on the sofa, listening to his debut album — with its scratch on the third track that made the word *cheer* repeat, repeat, repeat — his voice took them back to how it had been when they were newly married, when they first heard him sing at the Town Tavern, when they used to eat dinner and share drinks in the private lounge behind the Midnight Room.

Months after Del died, after she'd signed the magicians from Minsk and after Marshall returned to college, June had traveled to Alabama on her own. She had not told anyone where she was going or why. She flew to Mobile, and rented a car, and drove to the tiny town where Eddie Knox, the singer, had been born. There was a hardware store, two bars, a record store, kept in business, she supposed, by tourists; there were three intersections but no stop signs.

She asked at the hardware store first, but the greasy-haired kid sorting nails said he didn't know anything about Eddie Knox's family, and she stepped away from the record store when she heard one of Eddie's songs on the loudspeaker. That left the bars, so she chose the closest one: a dilapidated shed that looked like it might have been standing there a long time.

"I'm looking for information about Eddie Knox."

"Yeah? You buying a drink?" The bartender wasn't much past fifty, but he looked older, lined and sallow with ropey veins on the backs of his hands.

"I'll buy that bottle. The scotch."

"A whole bottle? You got a lot of questions?"

"A few. But I don't drink. You can share it with the house."

He nodded. Looked around the almost empty room, at the one customer seated in the corner, apparently asleep. Then he set the bottle aside and leaned on the counter, looking at her.

"I'm looking for his family," June said.

"Yeah. Not much left. Around here anyway."

"Who is here?"

"Well, his brother. Jacob."

"Jacob?"

"Yeah, that's Eddie's brother. I think he had a sister too, but she's long gone."

"I thought he had four brothers?"

"Eddie? Yeah. He told that story sometimes. But Jacob's his only brother. I lived here my whole life. I knew the Knox family. The sister was a lot older. But Eddie and Jacob, they were pretty close in age. About the same as me."

"Did you go to school with them?"

He looked at her without speaking.

Of course: he was white. They would not have gone to school together.

"So where's Jacob? Do you know his kids?"

"Jacob's kids? Jacob hasn't got any kids. Not that he knows of anyway."

"He doesn't have kids?"

"No. He's a drunk. Always has been. He lives in a shack pretty close to the old property. Course they lost it. They say Eddie tried to give him money, tried to buy him a house, but Jacob can't hang on to money."

June felt dizzy. She was going to be sick. She bolted up suddenly, left a fifty on the counter for the bottle — three times what it was worth — and got outside before she started to heave.

She made it back to the rental car, sat there stunned and dismayed and thinking about a drink for a few hours at least. But she did not take a drink. She did not go back to the bar. When it started to get dark, she turned the key in the ignition and drove all the way back to Mobile.

There wasn't anyone she could tell about what she had learned. There wasn't anyone to ask. Del was dead. Eddie was dead. Marshall had never known. Whomever Del had told, whoever had helped Del, was probably alive. But who was it? Leo? Mack? If they knew, and as much as they loved her, they wouldn't let on. Not if Del had told them no. Not even now. How would she

215

ever know? She had never felt more alone.

June flew to Vegas that night. Went straight to the El Capitan from the airport. She had always thought she would know someday. But Del had taken care of that. Why? Would he ever have told her?

Somewhere a sixteen-year-old girl did not know how long her mother had been looking for her, how much she wanted to find her, how hard she had tried. Somewhere, a sixteen-year-old girl could not know that her mother's heart was still broken.

That trip to Alabama was a long time ago now — a dozen years at least — and mostly June did not let herself think about it. She had learned how to let go, she had learned what she could not control. It had been that or die, and in the end, she had loved Marshall enough to live.

17

It was the second house on the cul-de-sac. Coral chose it because it was on the east side of town, not far from Augusta and near Rowe Elementary. Out back was a pool, which she hadn't wanted, but Althea brought her kids over to swim the first day.

"Auntie Coral, I'm going to the basketball game!"

"You are?"

"Yeah. Rob got me a ticket. It's been sold out since last summer, but I get to go."

"That's so cool." Coral high-fived her nephew, who then raced to join his sister at the pool. She looked at Althea. "Rob?"

"Don't say anything. He's just a friend from work."

"Who gave your ten-year-old son the hottest ticket in town?"

"Malcolm was in the office with me. And he was going on and on about how the Rebels are the best college team in the

217

country. How they're going to win the whole tournament. So Rob just invited him. They're going together. It's an exhibition game, Friday night."

"Wow."

"Yeah, Keisha's whining, of course."

"Is there anything interesting about Rob?"

"You mean other than he's the accountant?"

Coral laughed.

"How about you? Mama said you went on a date with Paul Ormsby. Didn't he take you to prom?"

"No, he didn't. We went out Saturday, but it wasn't a date. He teaches at the high school, and, you know, we just had a drink."

"Okay. Well, Mama's very interested in your dates. You better be careful."

"Should I tell her you're dating Rob?"

"I'm not dating Rob. This fine woman's done with men, whether Mama believes me or not."

"She doesn't believe you."

"Well, I'm counting on you to distract her. I need some relief."

Augusta walked in from the backyard. "That child is mad for those Rebels!" She reached for the beach towel Keisha had left on the counter. "You'd think a college basketball team made the world the way he talks about them. Larry Johnson. Stacey Augmon."

"Yeah, isn't that ridiculous, Mom? Almost like someone who had to be taken to the ER after a certain team lost to Indiana?"

"That was a different group, Althea. My Freddie scored thirty-eight points that game."

"Remember the Oklahoma game? Mama called me and would not stop talking about that two-point shot."

"His foot was behind the line. It was a three."

Coral and Althea laughed at the same instant.

"Well, I'm not doing that anymore. The Rebels are a great team, but I'm not having a heart attack for them. They're so good this year, they oughta win. That's not the same."

"Right, Mama. We don't care if this team wins or not."

"Well, we care. We can care."

Coral wrapped her arm around her mother, and the three of them went out back to watch the kids swim. She was glad she'd picked the house with a pool. Glad to live in Vegas with Mama and Althea and her kids.

Coral didn't want her mother or her sister

to know some things about the life she'd lived in California. About Gerald, for example. The sort of boyfriend he'd been.

Gerald was the one person Coral had told about her birth. The only time she had ever choked the words out of her mouth, the only time she'd ever repeated the story her mama had told her, was to Gerald one night, very late. And, of course, he'd made it worse. He had focused on Augusta. Why had she kept it a secret? How much money had Odell Dibb given her? (That was a big one. He brought that one up a lot.) Was any of it even true? Perhaps Coral *was* Augusta's child — and the story a way of keeping secret whatever had happened that had made her pregnant. After all, that's what Coral's birth certificate said.

Coral had started to cry as Gerald was spinning these scenarios, one after another, as if it were a movie plot and not her life — not her own most personal truth, something she had shared only with him. Finally, she had reached a kind of wail, screaming "Stop it, stop it, stop it!" But he didn't stop, so she kicked at him in her rage, and he just laughed to see her so out of control. Yet even then, even after that, she continued to live with Gerald.

This was a private shame, one of many

things Althea and Augusta didn't know.

At twenty-nine, the story of her birth didn't loom quite as large for Coral as it had at sixteen. It was true that her heart could still skitter unevenly if she thought of the instant before Augusta said yes to keeping her. It was true that it still nipped at her not to know how she had come to be, how her hair and face and feet had formed. And sometimes, the thought that this was a mystery to her but not to someone else galled her; didn't she have the most at stake in knowing this particular truth? But the empty space at the core, the blankness she had spent years not thinking about — even the way she had felt when she first moved back home with Mama last year — it surprised her that these feelings were starting to fade. Or fading wasn't the right word. She felt them still. They just didn't hurt as deeply as they once had.

Maybe it was getting older. Maybe it was teaching: seeing a lot of children in ruinous situations. Maybe it was having nieces and nephews, watching her brother and sisters raise their kids, seeing all the different ways a childhood might play out. She had been lucky to be a Jackson.

Still, she wondered about the woman who bore her. She felt loyal to that unknown person — who might have been afraid, who might have been treated badly, for whom her birth might have been tragic.

Who was her mother?

Had Odell Dibb loved her? Had she loved him? Had he forced her to give up their child? Could he have raped her? Where was she now?

Augusta thought Coral should let go of these questions. There wasn't any way to find her mother, there wasn't anyone alive who knew anything, and why did she have to imagine such terrible things? Why would Mr. Dibb have asked Augusta to take the baby if he hadn't cared about her mother? Why would she have been dressed in a pink silk gown? Why would he have been so upset? That was Augusta's hole card: the way Odell Dibb had cried the night he brought Coral to her. "A man doesn't fall apart if he doesn't care; if you aren't a love child. He doesn't ask someone to take a baby, to keep a secret, if you aren't important, Coral. A man like Mr. Dibb doesn't risk me knowing this about him, me having this over his head, unless you are someone very special. That's what you should think about your birth."

Coral saw the sense in Augusta's words, but she felt things too. Felt her mother deep down, in her skin, in her bones. These were things she couldn't explain to anyone else, but it was as if she owed her birth mother something, or her birth mother exacted something from her; she really didn't know which.

And what about Odell Dibb?

A long time ago, Coral had done what research she could. She'd sat in the Clark County Library on Flamingo, squinting at microfiche that listed where he had given his money, how much he had paid in personal taxes, who was listed on his private trust. Once she had seen a photo of him standing outside a bar called Le Bistro. He wasn't identified, but Coral recognized him from all the other pictures she'd seen.

And it caught her eye, that photo, because of the way her father was standing. He was smiling, maybe just about to laugh, and held a cigarette a few inches from his mouth — about to take a puff or just having taken one, there was no way to tell — and his long frame was relaxed; his arm rested slightly on a smaller man to his left. That photo stayed in Coral's mind. You wanted to look at Odell Dibb in that photo: something about his stance, that hint of a smile, even his fingers in the air. It was arresting.

There were lots of records to find, articles

about El Capitan, donations to various charities, things he had said in response to one local issue or another. People thought highly of Del Dibb. He had been influential. He had treated his employees well. And yet Coral never felt much in these records; never got a sense of him from all the photos wearing black tie at galas, nothing like the way he leaped out of the photo in which he was not even identified.

Now that she was older, now that she'd had her own experiences of love and sex and the wrong choices one could make, Coral sometimes imagined Odell Dibb differently than Augusta had described him. What sort of man had he been? Why did his face leap out from that one photo? How had he ended up with a baby in a pink silk gown?

Still, the questions about her father didn't burn in her as the questions about her mother did. She knew who he was, and years ago, she'd figured out that what really mattered to her about him was that he'd given her to Augusta Jackson. To Mama, who had allowed the rest of the world to believe whatever it would about her: to believe she had given birth to a mixed race child while married to a dark black man; to believe she had a secret life, a lover; to believe she was raped; to believe she had sold her body; to believe anything it wanted — any possibility at all — for how Coral had come to exist.

Augusta was proud. And she was a religious woman, a churchgoer; she stood for something. And still, to protect Coral, from the first instant — even without knowing anything about her, where she came from, who might have a claim to her — she had sacrificed that. She had given up being known for who she was. She had carried the secret by herself, she had done this for Coral.

That's what Coral knew of her own origins. She knew what her existence must have cost Augusta, and she knew what Augusta's choice had meant to her.

So if she got frustrated teaching at the school sometimes, if there were parents who thought music class was a waste, if there were children who showed up with bruises, if there was a little boy who kept stealing food from other kids' lunches, if the local paper ran an editorial railing against the benefits given to teachers, if the principal could not find money for supplies, if some days being the only music teacher in a school with 654 children seemed Sisyphean, then Coral always had her own mother to inspirit her: she could live how she wanted, she could take the actions she believed in. It didn't matter whether anyone else understood, it didn't matter that others did not see the value in the choices she made. She was Augusta's daughter, and this was Augusta's legacy to her.

For Christmas, they all came to Coral's. It took Ray Junior and Lynda fourteen hours to make the ten-hour trip from Fremont because Lynda's morning sickness was so bad they had to stop every hour, and because four-year-old Trey had an ear infection that made him cry whenever the Tylenol started to wear off.

"Never again," said Ray Junior.

"Do you promise, Daddy?" said Trey.

Althea wrapped her brother in a hug, while Coral took Lynda to the spare bedroom so she could change. Coral nearly twirled down the hallway; she was so excited to be hosting Christmas this year. They had always gone to Augusta's, but her mama had asked if they could move it to Coral's. Augusta said that four adult children, five grandchildren, but just one in-law (this with one eyebrow raised) was getting to be too much. Coral knew this wasn't true. Moving Christmas to her house was Augusta's way of anointing Coral's home.

Coral had been buying and making gifts for weeks, and she and Althea had picked out one of the biggest trees on the lot. Malcolm insisted on colored bulbs, and Keisha had persuaded her aunt to buy a string of plastic lights in the shape of candles. It had taken seven strings of lights, and dozens of ornaments: all of the ones Coral remembered hanging on her child-hood tree — including the green star with her second-grade face on it and the angel Ray Junior had carved one year when he went to Camp Lee Canyon — and some that the younger kids had made. When he was seven, Malcolm had carefully written "Mery Christmes Momy" and "Hapy New Yere Grandnan" on two cards that now hung at eye level.

In the middle of one night, Coral heard a loud bang and came downstairs to find the whole tree lying on the soaked carpet. She didn't leave it for morning; she found a screwdriver, a hook, and some wire, and hung the whole thing from a beam in the ceiling. It was the first thing Ray Junior mentioned when he looked around her new house.

"Nice job with the tree, Coco."

Coral laughed. "It fell over. In the middle of the night."

"I could have guessed that."

"Well, it won't fall over now."

"Nope."

"Come on! You never had any trouble getting a tree to stand up?"

"Oh no, I always have trouble. I've tied trees to the wall, piled sandbags on the base; the year Trey was a baby, the tree fell over twice. I threw it away and bought a smaller one."

Lynda grinned. "Yeah, and what was Trey's first word that Christmas, Ray?"

"*Darn.* It was *darn,* right?"

Everybody laughed.

On Christmas night, with Teenage Mutant Ninja Turtles strewn the length of the house, and Keisha's talking bear Teddy Ruxpin put safely to bed — "If that thing tells me his name again, he and I are going to have some words," said Ada — Coral and her siblings sat around drinking rum brandy punch. Lynda had fallen asleep with Trey, and Augusta had taken the three older kids to see *Home Alone.*

"What was it that Ray used to say when he got dressed up?"

"Ain't I trassy!"

"Yeah, ain't you trassy, Ray?"

"I have always been a classy guy."

"You is trassy, brother. You is definitely a trassy guy." Ada and Ray clinked glasses.

"Remember when Althea said a boy was going to come over to study with her?"

"And Ray went in her room and pulled all the underwear out of her drawers, and hung her bras from the bedposts?"

Their brother snorted. "Mama took a belt to me for that. I got one belt for going in her room, one belt for embarrassing her, and one belt because I better not be looking at any girl's underwear."

They all laughed.

"Hell, I lived with three sisters. How was I supposed to not see any girl's underwear?"

Ada stood up. "Remember when Ray murdered my doll for his Halloween house?"

"Oh yeah, I remember."

"I walked in the garage, and LilyBelle was covered in ketchup with a knife stuck in her chest. I had nightmares about that for years. I might still have nightmares about that."

"I was nine years old. I didn't know you'd be so upset."

"Yeah, and I never told Mama. Which was lucky for you."

"I kept so many secrets for *you,*" Ray retorted. "If I hadn't messed up that doll, you'd probably have a whole different life.

Mama would have figured you out and set you straight when you were young."

"Nobody was ever going to set Ada straight."

"That was Coral's job," Ada explained. "She was good enough for two of us. Right, Coral?"

"I spent my whole life hoping you guys weren't going to get in trouble."

"Oh yeah, remember how Coral would cry when any of us got a beating? She'd cry so hard, Mama would stop hitting us."

"Can I get a thank-you for that?"

"Remember when Coral came to breakfast, all upset because she was going to be late for school?"

"Yeah, and she told Mama, 'How can I be on time for school if Althea is occuuupeeing the bathroom?' " Ray winked at his youngest sister as he mimicked her eight-year-old voice.

"The best was when Althea decided to teach Coral to drive —"

"And the cop pulled them over —"

"And asked Coral if she would drive off a cliff if Althea told her to do it —"

"And Coral said yes!"

"You bet she said yes!" Althea poured another shot of brandy. "When I told Coral to do something, I meant it. And I didn't tell her to turn down the street the wrong way. I told her to turn left into the inside lane, and bam, she just drives straight into traffic."

"I slammed on the brake when I saw the headlights, and then it was a police car." Coral took the glass Althea offered. "The officer flipped his siren on. I about passed out."

"I was grabbing the wheel and telling you, 'Move over! *Move over!*"

"But I turned the car off!"

They laughed again. Lynda walked in, her rounded stomach showing through the buttons of some red flannel pajamas, and curled up next to Althea on the couch.

"What's so funny?"

"Oh, we were just remembering old times. Kid stuff."

"The talent show!"

"Coral's talent show!"

"Coral had a talent show?" Lynda looked at her sister-in-law.

"No, it was Althea's game. We used to play it quite a lot. We'd set up a stage in the dining room, or outdoors, and then everyone just performed whatever talent they could think of."

"Remember when Greg next door popped his shoulder out of the socket?"

"Yeah, that was his talent! He could do 'weird shoulder.' "

"Weird shoulder! That was a great one."

Lynda shifted position, trying to get comfortable on the couch. "So why was it Coral's talent show?"

"Well, Coral was little. Maybe three?"

"Yeah, I think she was three."

"And her talents were always pretty odd."

"Oh yeah. Remember her feet talent?"

" 'My feet have names!' " the siblings said in unison. " 'This one is Petey, and this one is Noodle-ah.' " Ada hooted.

"I don't get it."

Althea saw Lynda's skeptical look and explained, "That was her talent. Her feet had names."

"But I was really little then."

"Oh, yeah, you were small."

"And that was Coral's talent show?"

"Oh no. That was later. She was three, and she said she wanted to sing something, so she stood on the dining table, and she belted out . . ."

All four siblings started to sing: *"So won't you plee-eze . . . Be my, be my, be my little baby? Say you'll be my darling. Be my baby now-ow-ow. A-whoa oh oh oh!"*

They could sing. Lynda tapped her foot to the beat.

"I mean, she belted it. We'd never heard her sound like that."

"She could have been a Ronette. Remember the way she was swishing her hips?"

They all started singing again. Ray stood up and camped his way toward his wife, and Ada took Althea's hand and pulled her from the sofa to dance a few steps. When they stopped, Ada spoke.

"Yeah, I think that's the first time I figured out Coral was different from the rest of us."

Coral shrugged her shoulders. "Come on, stop it. I hate that."

"I know, but I mean, Coral, your voice was unbelievable."

Althea wrapped her arms around her sister. "It's okay, Coral. Ada has wanted to be the baby of the family her whole life."

"It's true. I did want to be the baby of the family."

Coral blurted it out: "Someone gave me to Mama. When I was four days old."

There was silence. Althea squeezed Coral a little tighter, but nobody said anything, not even Lynda.

She realized they already knew. It had been so hard not to tell them, not to talk about it, all these years. And they knew.

"Mama told you? She told me she didn't."

Nobody said anything for a minute.

"Mama never told us anything. She didn't have to."

"But . . ."

"Mama wasn't pregnant." Ada's voice went up a notch. "Althea was seven. She would've known if Mama was pregnant."

Coral was crying now. Althea was wiping away the tears with her hand, and Ray had let go of Lynda to sit down by Coral's feet.

"You're a one-hundred-percent Jackson," he said. "That's what we always knew."

"But when did you know? Did you all talk about me?"

Her voice cracked. Of course they had talked about her. She talked about them. Still, she couldn't stand it. Althea was crying now too, Ray looked sick, and even Ada was bouncing on her toes and shaking her fingers the way she did when she was upset. Only Lynda sat quietly, watching.

"Coco, we didn't talk about you. It wasn't like that."

"I mean, we all knew that there was something. We always knew."

"Always?"

"Well, for a long time. And we didn't talk about it. Ever. You know how Mama is. She told Althea not to talk about it, and Althea told us, and that was it."

"And then Ray was here a few years ago,

and he was telling us what you were like singing in that club, and we were all so proud of you."

"And Ada just brought it up."

"Hey, I'm not the bad guy here!"

Coral looked at Ada, who had tears in her eyes now.

"Coral, it wasn't like that. It just came out. I just asked Althea if she knew about you, where you came from."

Tears spurted from Coral's eyes at these last words.

"Honey." Ada was piled up on the other side of her now. "Honey, that doesn't sound right. I just thought Althea would know."

"Did you?"

"No. I asked Mama when I was younger."

"I heard you."

"You heard us?"

"Yeah. For years, I thought someone was going to kidnap me — take me back."

Ray laid his head on Coral's knees. It was all she could do to ask, "Did you talk to Mama?"

"We wanted to talk to her, we always say we're going to ask her, but —"

"We don't." Ray Junior and Althea spoke in unison.

This made everyone laugh, as they sat huddled around their youngest sister.

Coral spoke: "My father brought me to her in a basket. He was Daddy's friend. But he wouldn't tell her anything about my mother."

She could feel the question in the air, feel how they wanted to ask about her father, but she didn't want to say his name. She had carried the secret so long. It was too much. They all sat there, wrapped up together like one unit: Althea petting her cheek, and Ada holding her hand, and Ray's head on her knee. Nobody asked Coral for anything more, not tonight, and Coral didn't say anything more. And then Trey called out in his sleep, and Lynda leaned over to kiss Coral's head before checking on him, and Ray said again, "You're a one-hundred-percent Jackson, Coco," and they sat like this, quiet and entwined, for a long time.

18

A man wearing a jacket that said "El Capitan" met them at the Las Vegas airport. They rode in a limo that was as long as a tourist bus; it reminded Honorata of a black cat. In Manila, she had often fed a cat with a particularly long body. At the El Capitan, the man who greeted them said, "Welcome Mr. Wohlmann, Mrs. Wohlmann. Let me take you to your suite."

The suite, on the seventeenth floor, had a living room, a den, a bar, a bedroom, and floor-to-ceiling windows overlooking the Las Vegas Strip. There were fresh flowers, champagne in a bucket, a plate of cheese and grapes. Everything in the room was gold or black or mirrored.

Jimbo was effusive. He called the man Denny, clapped him on the back, handed him a small roll of bills. Honorata assumed they would have sex. Instead, Jimbo told her to put on the green dress and the gold sandals; he had some things to show her. When she was ready, he pulled out a long white box in which a necklace with a large emerald nestled.

"The hotel gave this to you to use for the weekend."

She put it on.

Jimbo leaned forward and kissed the stone of the necklace.

They left the room and took the elevator to the casino. Honorata had never experienced anything like it. Lights twinkled, glowed, flashed, there were machine sounds of dings and whistles and whirrs, coins clanking in trays, voices calling numbers, people talking, the whish of air moving: cacophonous, psychedelic, disorienting, galvanizing. Beside her, Jimbo seemed to expand; she could feel the transformation as he lifted on the balls of his feet, his chest swelling, eyes lifting. He took her to the back of the room and walked casually through an entryway where a woman stood at elegant guard; they nodded to each other slightly. This room was quieter, there was more space between the tables, and the people playing sat in concentrated silence. Jimbo introduced her to someone named Richard, who smiled. Then he pointed to the people playing and said the game was baccarat. There was poker too, behind the curtain. A woman brought him a glass of scotch, which he drained quickly. He told Richard that his wife would have a gin and tonic; the woman brought it immediately along with another scotch for Jimbo.

Honorata did not react to the word *wife,* as she had not reacted to *Mrs. Wohlmann.* Jimbo had said nothing about marriage. It was conceivable that he would surprise her with the once-promised wedding, but she doubted it. The conversation about the letters, the act of having gone directly to the airport hotel when she arrived from Manila, told Jimbo that the wedding itself was no longer necessary. He could call her his wife when he liked, he could present himself as a married man when he wanted, but the marriage itself would not happen.

This made as much sense to her as it did to him.

Jimbo had said he would show her around, teach her how to play some games, but he couldn't resist stepping up to a table when someone left. He told Richard to give Honorata some tokens, so Richard handed her a bucket filled with a hundred or more heavy gold coins marked with the El Capitan logo. It made her almost dizzy. She hadn't held money since arriving in America.

"Do you know how to play?" Richard asked.

He had a lovely voice, slightly accented.

"No."

"I can have someone show you. Perhaps roulette?"

"No."

"As you wish."

"Can I walk around? Can I go out there?" Honorata gestured to the casino floor.

Richard looked at her. Honorata saw something flash in his eyes. Then he smiled and said, of course, she could do anything she liked. Mr. and Mrs. Wohlmann were guests of the hotel, and she could go anywhere, she could order anything she liked, she need only say her name.

My name is Honorata Navarro, she thought.

"Thank you. I think I'll just walk around."

Honorata kept the bucket of coins with her for three days. She put a few coins in some slot machines, pulling the long handle and staring as the spinning figures spun into lines of color and then slowed . . . and stopped — never giving back even a single coin. She liked the feel of the bucket in her hand, the shake of the coins, so she stopped throwing them away like this. She supposed someone would give her more coins if she ran out; at least they kept giving her other things: drinks, round glasses filled with shrimp, a private table at the buffet. She never had to say who she was. They all seemed to know her, and many of the workers were kind.

She saw Jimbo only when someone from the casino came to get her, politely indicating that Mr. Wohlmann was looking, and would she mind returning to her room? When she did, he undressed her or bathed her or offered up various parts of his body to her. His moods varied. One time he talked rapidly, the next time he was distracted — sullen, even. Honorata lost her sense of time quickly. She came back to the room thinking that it was time to go to bed, and was startled to see from the windows that the sun was just setting. Jimbo seemed hardly to sleep at all. From time to time, she wandered by the exclusive area of the casino where he played. She would see him sitting there, oblivious to anything but the cards, or once, laughing with a woman bringing him chips. The woman wore a skirt of gold metal that barely skimmed her bottom, and she had the largest breasts Honorata had ever seen.

During the fourth night, Honorata could

not sleep. Her body had begun to rebel, and she turned restlessly in the king-sized bed. She thought that Jimbo would come in; she hadn't seen him in hours, and when she had, he'd said they might be going back to Chicago in the morning; she should be ready to go if he decided to leave.

Honorata didn't want to be alone in the suite. If she opened the blinds, then the lights of the Strip made the room bright as day, but sitting with them shut made her feel claustrophobic. She had not been outside once. She thought about going down to the casino. At night, the play was more serious. People stayed longer at the same machines, they were less likely to look up when a leggy woman brought them another drink. There was almost always a group of loud young men.

She turned from one side to the other, bunching up a pillow against her stomach, and then throwing the pillows aside, lying spread eagle without a sheet over her. Honorata checked the clock beside her bed: 2:18. She got up, drank some water, picked up one of the chocolate coins left every night on their bed, set it down again. She tried sitting on the chaise near the window. She had already examined everything in the room. Finally, as if it were a talisman, she picked up the bucket of El Capitan coins and shook them slightly. They weren't money; they'd be useless in Chicago. She might as well play them now.

Downstairs, she turned away from the side of the casino where she thought Jimbo was. She walked toward an older area of the floor, marked by a lower roof and a general sense of abandonment. The space was nearly empty, and Honorata wondered why the El Capitan had not updated it; why it didn't look like the rest of the gleaming, throbbing casino. Maybe some people liked this sort of thing, but Honorata could almost smell the sadness in the place. In the corner, a man wearing a black shirt played a poker machine. Nearby, an older woman played another; she was smoking a cigarette and a half empty pack of Camels teetered at the edge of her seat.

There was a showroom over here, which Honorata had not noticed before. A sign read "Psychedelic Sixties Revue, Playing Nightly in the Midnight Room." She wandered over, and pulled on the door to see if it was open. It was, but when she peeked inside, the room was dark, and the air smelled of dust and smoke. Behind her, the luminous face of a Megabucks, one of the giant slot machines that was almost always in use, stared blankly. Honorata had watched hordes of people play these, feeding their coins in quickly or slowly, kissing their fingers or their wives, rubbing a button, a penny, a rosary before pulling the handle.

She knew Megabucks was for fools. But Honorata didn't much care. She would play out the coins. It would take awhile, and perhaps she would get tired. She was far from Jimbo. It was quiet, and she didn't feel like talking to anyone. No one had even come to bring the smoker a drink.

She hit on the fourteenth pull.

Forty-two tokens in.

The machine exploded. A round light on the top spun like a police car flasher. There were bells, horns, dings, the whooping sound of a siren. Honorata cracked her knee as she jumped up; her first impulse was to flee.

Within seconds, people started running toward her: a cocktail waitress, a valet attendant, the woman with the cigarette, two young men — the collars of their pastel shirts turned up, one with a cigar, the other with flushed cheeks — all running at her. She heard excited yells and then someone clapping. She looked at the machine: "Jackpot! $1,414,153.00! Winner!" flashed across the top. She heard someone say "Get Mr. Wohlmann, in the VIP room," and time stopped, sound stopped, the room went pale.

There was a huge bouquet of flowers, champagne, the hotel photographer. The owner of the hotel hurried in, his hair sticking up and his tie slightly crooked, as if he had not stopped to shower when he got the call. He was young. He knew Jimbo. He kept saying things like "No problem, man. We'll have this worked out." And then he would look at her, give her another hug, ask her how she was feeling, again, again, again.

The shock of the initial excitement was wearing off.

She had been dizzy with the chaos of it. With the intensity of everyone's interest: the people who worked at the casino, the ones who were gambling, the boss who had clearly been home asleep. Jimbo had gotten to her side within minutes. And right away, she realized that something had changed. He hesitated before he gave her a hug. He seemed uncomfortable.

Everyone was calling her Mrs. Wohlmann. She heard a casino employee spelling out her name for a reporter: "R-i-t-a W-o-h-l-m-a-n-n." Honorata said nothing. The casino owner called her "Mrs. Wohlmann" too. He said that Mr. Wohlmann had been a special guest for twenty years, that it was exciting that the El Capitan's first Megabucks hit had been for a patron they valued so highly. His mother would want to say hello too.

Honorata stayed quiet, but she let them drape a mink coat over her shoulders. "For the photo," someone said. Honorata was not sure what was going to happen, but she could feel Jimbo's fear. Like a tide pulling at their feet. The casino's print department made a large check, five feet long, which said that one million, four hundred and fourteen thousand, one hundred and fifty-three dollars would be paid to Rita Wohlmann. Rita and Jimbo posed with the owner, and the photographer took that shot, and then another just of her.

At six in the morning, a small woman, only slightly larger than Honorata, entered. She was elegantly dressed, in a pale-pink nubbly suit, with an ivory silk blouse and tall ivory shoes that showed off her narrow heel and the bone at the top of her foot. Her hair was a neat, dark bob, and she did not look like she had just gotten out of bed. Her makeup was perfect; she smelled lightly of perfume.

"Marshall, did you get up out of bed to come here?"

"It was three o'clock. Yes, I got out of bed."

The elegant woman lifted her face to her son's, and he kissed her cheek lightly.

"Thank you, honey. I really appreciated that sleep." She turned to a man wearing the casino's black-and-gold uniform.

"Carmine, get us some breakfast. We can eat at the back of the club. I want to congratulate our winners."

She stepped forward then.

"James. It's always lovely to see you. And this is your wife? Is this your first time in Vegas? Did you have beginner's luck?"

Honorata nodded her head, but she felt suddenly overwhelmed. They all knew Jimbo.

"Please, will you join me for breakfast? You must be very tired, but you can sleep all day." She turned to Jimbo. "Are you still planning to fly out today?"

"I don't know. We're a little discombobulated, June."

"Then stay for breakfast. That will give Marshall time to do all the paperwork. Winning Megabucks does not protect you from Uncle Sam, you know."

Honorata felt the fear rise in Jimbo. With

247

every minute, she felt stronger, cleaner. Something had changed. More than the money.

Marshall was talking to Jimbo.

"Sir, thank you for the identification cards. The feds are really strict with us. Since your wife is a native of the Philippines, and her name is different on her passport, I will need to see your wedding license. That's the only way that I can deposit the money."

Jimbo explained that they were engaged, but not yet married. "Is that a problem?" he asked.

"Of course not. Technically, the money is hers. If she wants to take it and go, we can't stop her. We'll just need her account information, and she can sign the paperwork."

"She doesn't have a bank account. We'll set one up now. We can go to a bank here and do it."

"Okay. Well, sure. We'll deposit the money as soon as we have an account with her name on it."

Honorata was too far away to hear what the young owner was saying to Jimbo. After breakfast, he had collected their passports from the front desk and given them to the owner. She had not known that her passport was in Las Vegas — had not seen it since that first day in the Chicago airport.

Jimbo came over.

"We'll have to go to a bank, Rita. You'll need to set up an account. We can open a joint account, which they will do for me very quickly."

Honorata said nothing. Her heart beat faster.

Just then, the other owner, the woman called June, walked up.

"Rita, may I speak with you a moment?"

Honorata stepped forward, and Jimbo started to catch on to her arm, but dropped it when June looked at him. The two women walked to a door nearly disguised by the swirling wallpaper that covered it; behind the door was a set of offices. June chatted idly about the weather, about Chicago, about the good time Marshall had had there last summer. The largest office was hers.

"Please sit down."

Honorata sat.

"Is your name Honorata?"

"Yes."

"Honorata Navarro?"

"Yes."

"And you're a citizen of the Philippines?"

"Yes."

June said nothing. She looked down at her

desk for a moment.

"Does that mean I can't win? Because I'm not American?"

"Oh no. You've won, Honorata. You pulled the handle, and according to the Supreme Court of the United States, the person who pulled the handle has won the jackpot."

Honorata tried to calm herself.

"The thing is . . . Are you married to Mr. Wohlmann, Honorata?"

Honorata stared at the floor. Jimbo was an important person in this hotel. She'd had most of a week to see how important. She thought about how nice everyone had been, how they had all known her name, how they had known what she was doing at all times.

She was alone now. She didn't know how to get back to the casino. Who would help her anyway? She felt dizzy, unmoored.

"Ms. Navarro, are you okay? Please don't be afraid."

Everything swam in front of Honorata. She was going to be sick.

June stood up and asked someone to bring some water. She placed her arm on Honorata's back, making her flinch. A woman brought in the water, and June closed the door firmly behind her.

"Honorata. I can see that you're upset. I think that you're probably afraid. But there

250

is no need to be. I'm not going to let anything happen to you. If you're not married to Mr. Wohlmann, the money's not his. It's yours. It's yours alone. And nobody can do anything about that."

Honorata started to cry. She gulped in air and sobbed.

Later, June and Marshall met to decide what to do.

"Mom, Jimbo Wohlmann has been coming to the El Capitan since I was fourteen years old. I can't simply send him home without her."

"You can. And you will. And if James never returns to the El Capitan, then good riddance."

"It's not like when you and Dad managed this place." Marshall ran his fingers through his hair, a gesture that always reminded June of Del. "Our investors are different. They look at our take every month. Jimbo has dropped millions here. We could practically make him a line item in our budget."

"The El Capitan may not be the same as it was. But it's still my casino. So I say, and the law says, that Honorata Navarro has won over a million dollars. She's a single woman, and she's the sole owner of that money."

"Jimbo isn't after her money. He doesn't need another million dollars."

"He doesn't want Ms. Navarro to have it. And we both know why. Now, I don't know what you're thinking, Marshall, but we're not going to be part of keeping that money from her. Whether it is the law or not."

"You've known Jimbo for decades. He's not a beast. She's not a slave. Why can't we extend the courtesy of a few days to him? He says that's all he needs."

"Because we are not going to extend the courtesy of a few days to him. He's going to leave our hotel, and if he wants to go down the street and stay in another one, he most certainly can. But Ms. Navarro is staying here." June rapped the table with her pen. "She's staying here until she has her money, and her passport, and then we'll take her to the airport, and she'll go wherever she wants."

"You act like I'm the one getting in the middle of this. *You're* the one getting involved. You're the one orchestrating this."

"I'm not discussing this for another minute. I'll talk to James myself. Do you think your father would have given him a couple of days to persuade that woman that she isn't free to leave? James had his chance with her, and if she doesn't go back to

Chicago, I'm sure he'll know why."

"Mom, that's not fair. Don't throw Dad at me that way. I'm not evil here. I'm trying to keep the El Capitan going. Which I remember as being pretty important to Dad too."

"Honey, we'll keep the El Capitan going. We should have a line of people waiting to play Megabucks tomorrow." June smiled.

"Like that'll help."

"You're going to get your chance to make all the decisions. And you'll be great. But this is my call."

The woman had offered Honorata a new room in the hotel. The minute she was alone, Honorata lifted her dress over her head, and crawled beneath the sheets. When she woke up, she was disoriented. The sky above the Strip was dark; she had slept all day. She didn't remember getting into bed; she barely remembered coming into the room. Little by little, though, everything returned to her. Tossing about in the bed alone. Going down to the casino. Climbing onto the high seat of the Megabucks machine. It couldn't be true.

She sat up. Where was Jimbo? Did he know where she was? Honorata struggled to get out of the tightly wound sheets. What would she do with the money? Could her uncle get it? Would Jimbo call him? She stepped onto the thick carpet. Was someone watching her? Could she leave? She didn't have any money. She didn't even have her passport. Her heart rattled in her chest. Honorata was alone, and maybe she was worth a lot of money. And Jimbo, who mattered to these hotel people, was going to be angry.

She had only dresses to wear. Sandals with heels. She had a lipstick in her clutch, and a tissue. Nothing else. She looked around the room, frantic for something more useful. A basket of fruit and cheese was on the table. Next to it was a note, two hundred-dollar bills, and her passport. "Honorata — I didn't know if you had any cash. Call and ask for me when you wake up, and we can make arrangements to have your winnings placed in an account. You're welcome to stay here as long as you like — June."

She leaned against the table and let herself cry.

The next morning, someone at the hotel took her to the First Interstate Bank and waited while she set up an account. Later, she walked in her sandals to the Fashion Show Mall, which appeared much closer than it was. At Bullock's, Honorata stood and looked at the mannequins wearing low-cut metallic dresses and long blond wigs, then bought two pairs of pants, three blouses, and flat leather shoes. She found a travel agent in the mall, and booked a ticket. The agent had to call the bank, because she had only temporary checks.

Jimbo phoned on Thursday. The hotel operator asked her permission to put the call through. She trembled but said yes. She would not have been able to say no. Also, Jimbo knew her uncle. Her uncle was with her mother.

"Rita. Thank you for answering."

"My name's Honorata."

"Honorata. I'm sorry. I thought you'd like Rita."

She was silent.

"I'd like to see you. I don't want it to be like this. Could we have dinner?"

She didn't want to have dinner. She wanted him to go away, and she wanted to imagine that he had never existed. But she said, "Okay."

"I'm staying at Caesars. There's a beautiful restaurant here. I could send a car. At seven?"

She wanted to say that she would get there herself. But even these words would not come out of her mouth.

"Yes," she said finally.

Jimbo wanted to get married.

"I always wanted to get married, Honorata. We got started badly. Your uncle . . . your uncle cheated us both. But I'd like to start over. Please."

When he spoke, she was afraid. Her lungs swelled as if they would burst from her chest, and yet she felt as if she couldn't get enough air. She struggled to speak.

"I don't want to marry you."

The room swayed around her, and everything looked blurry. It was a physical effort to say this. To resist. Her heart beat frantically.

"I understand. I'm older than you. I'm not very good looking. But I'm a kind man. I want a family. We could have a family."

Honorata closed her eyes because she did not want to look at him.

"I don't want a family."

"But you said —"

"I didn't write those letters. I didn't say anything. I don't want a family. I want to go home. I want to see my mother."

It was easier now. Now that she had started. She didn't have to do what he wanted. She didn't have to please him.

"You should go home and see your mother. Then come back. There are so many opportunities in the United States. It would be easier for you to stay if we were married. You could bring your mother here."

"I want to go home."

"Of course you can go home. I can make the arrangements tonight. But after, please, Honorata, please give me another chance."

He looked stricken. Honorata didn't know how he could be saying these things. They frightened her. She wanted to forget the months in Jimbo's home, the sound of him opening the door to her room, the squeak of the bedframe as he climbed in. She remembered his hands, slippery on her back in the bath. She heard his steady snoring, asleep beside her. The gap between the shutter and the sill would slowly lighten, from deep gray to silver to white, and he would get up, or take her one more time and then get up. How could he imagine this meant something to her? How had she endured it?

"I love you, Honorata."

She looked straight at him, but in her mind she was thinking of the woman in the casino, of June, in her pink jacket and high ivory heels.

"I never want to see you again."

He stared at the ornate candlestick on the table, and she slowly removed the ring from her finger. Her voice trembled.

"If you contact me, I'll . . ." She didn't know what she would do. "I'll call the El Capitan."

She said this, and the floor did not crack open, the ceiling did not fall, he did not stand and strike her. He looked at his plate, and he fingered the leather folder that held the bill, and it was possible that his eyes were wet. Honorata didn't know, she couldn't look, she could hardly breathe. She had said what she wanted to say, and she got up fast, leaving the ring beside the plate, afraid to hand it to him. Then she walked as quickly as she could across the great glittering room; she wouldn't be able to say it again, she had never said something like that before in her life. Would he rise up, would she take it back, would the planet stop spinning? She, Honorata, had dared to resist.

19

Coral had been teaching for four years, so she both was and was not surprised at the letter. It arrived in July, and explained that the district would be adding portables to her school, and that she would now be teaching music in portable number five. The unit was undergoing renovation, but all expectations were that it would be ready for occupation a week before school started.

She called the district and tried to get someone to tell her a little more. She was pleased to hear it would be large — larger than the music room that had doubled as a stage in the cafeteria — but sorry to hear that it had been built "thirty, well, at least thirty" years ago. She asked about air-conditioning, and from the careful way the woman answered, she gathered that the unit had a swamp cooler, which "works really well in our desert environment."

Whatever.

Still, she was unnerved when she saw the unit. There were six portables, and number five was set down right where the kids played hopscotch, four-square, and cat and mouse. The top of the hopscotch frame — a rectangle with the word *Home* — angled out from the bottom of the unit, giving one the slight sense that the portable, like Dorothy's house, had fallen from the sky. It was a dirty beige color, with dents in the aluminum sides, and a rickety-looking set of stairs leading to a pressboard door that was also painted beige. The whole unlikely heap appeared as if it had been dumped in a vat of dun paint; there wasn't a pipe or a hinge or a fitting that was not the same drab color.

That night, Coral met her friend Paul and some of his buddies for a drink at the Elephant Bar. The place was loud, and Coral tried to avoid the glass eyes of the gazelle head mounted on the wall near her. Paul's college friend Koji was in from Tokyo — he was going to be doing some work in Vegas — and the guys were in high spirits. Coral told them about the beige portable, and though she meant the story to be funny, her voice shook, and her eyes started to water.

"Okay, that's one drink too many for me."

"They'll do anything to kids here," Paul said. "My nephew just got told that he'll be in double sessions until at least December. He has to get up and go to school from six to noon, but his sister is at the elementary school from nine to three. So my sister has a week to work something out with her boss."

"Can you paint the portable?" Koji asked.

"Great idea!"

"I don't know," said Coral. "I've never seen one painted."

"I could design something for you. I'm here till Wednesday. You could paint it this weekend, before school starts."

"Koji's a designer. He does work at all the casinos," Paul explained.

"I'm pretty sure I couldn't get permission to paint it by this weekend. It's okay. The building really doesn't matter. It was just upsetting to see it. I mean, who chooses beige paint for little kids?"

Paul wouldn't drop it.

"Let's do it anyway. What's the worst that could happen?"

"I get fired?"

"Come on. For making it beautiful? I think the worst thing that could happen is that we have to paint it back."

"Listen, I don't even know who to ask."

It went on like that for a while, with Coral's protests getting weaker and weaker, and the guys getting more and more excited about doing it.

And that's how P5 came to be the sunflower portable. The whole thing was covered in huge yellow blossoms that draped over the sides from the top, and down the rickety stairs, and across the door. It made one smile just to see it.

Three months later, she got a call from Koji.

"I don't know if you remember me?"

"Remember you? Are you kidding? The sunflowers are incredible. I'd love for you to see it."

"Oh, I'd like that. I'm going to be in Vegas in two weeks. That's why I was calling."

"Are you in Tokyo now?"

"Yes."

"What time is it there?"

"About noon, Thursday."

"It's Wednesday night here."

"I know. Is it a bad time? Are you eating?"

"Oh no, it's fine."

"Well, I'm going to be in Vegas, and I have tickets to this show. It's a preview of *Mystère.* Have you heard of it?"

"Of course. I loved Cirque du Soleil last year. In the tent? It was amazing."

"Yeah, that's it. This is a Cirque show, but it will be permanent. Treasure Island built a theater for it."

"I read about that."

"So, umm, *Mystère* opens Christmas day, but there's a private showing for special guests on the twenty-third. I have two tickets. I was wondering if you'd like to come."

Coral felt flustered. She couldn't remember very much about Koji, other than how wonderful his design for the portable had been, and she certainly hadn't been thinking about him as a date.

He filled the silence. "It sounds like maybe the answer's no. Sorry."

"No."

"Well, it was nice talking to you."

"No. The answer's not no. I just — I'm sorry, that was stupid of me. I'd love to go. It sounds wonderful."

"Really? Well, great. I get into town the twenty-second. I'll call you, and we can figure out the details?"

"That sounds good."

"Thank you, Coral. It was nice talking to you."

And just like that, he was off the phone. She hadn't asked him why he was coming to Vegas, or more important, told him how the kids had reacted that first morning of school. One mother started to cry. Some children had jumped in the air, yelling "flowers!" The principal didn't even get angry. She told Coral that the district wouldn't maintain it, that Coral should have gotten permission to change school property, but she didn't say anything about changing it back, she didn't ask Coral to tell her who had painted it. Coral was taken aback. She'd been steeling herself for some sort of formal discipline, wondering whether the union would back her or not.

But the sunflowers were terrific. The kids were proud of P5. Coral watched them crossing the blacktop from the main building in their mandated rows and saw them grin as they approached the sunflower portable. Students were always suggesting ways to paint the rest of the school. Some fourth-grade girls had started a petition to have every portable painted as a different kind of flower, and Coral overheard children talking about the various ways they would paint the school or their classroom or their own homes. The portable became so popular that the kindergarten teachers started walking their kids out there for music class even though Coral had always gone to their classrooms instead.

■ ■ ■ ■

At the end of December, Koji picked her up in his hotel limo, and they rode to the Strip a little bit awkwardly. Coral couldn't quite remember what he looked like, and she had hesitated before choosing her highest heels. She wasn't particularly tall, but would she tower over him? Would he care? The Strip was wildly crowded, and there were so many people jammed onto the sidewalk to watch the pirate show at Treasure Island that the driver dropped them off a block away, and Coral tottered on her heels as she and Koji wove between the cars and the tourists to get to the casino.

It turned out that Koji's company had something to do with the huge drums that anchored *Mystère*'s musical score. He explained to her that the largest one had to be built on the stage and that there wasn't a door big enough to remove it. The casino surprised Coral. Treasure Island really was all about pirates, and it looked more like Disneyland than Vegas, but it was fun. Everything about Vegas was fun right now. The whole city rocked with the energy of the casinos, bigger and better and wilder every year. A lot of money was being made, and people were popping between LA and Vegas like it was a morning commute; anything seemed possible.

Mystère had its own lobby, filled with locals for this performance. Coral saw Althea's boss Ed near the bar with a woman who looked like she couldn't be twenty-one. Some Cirque performers, wearing skin-tight suits in green and orange and black, catapulted off the stairs leading to the balcony seats, and there was a little scurry of movement when Kevin Costner walked in. Koji excused himself and came back with a glass of white wine for her. She had barely started it when the doors opened, and people rushed to see the theater.

Inside, the room was filled with giant, abstract shapes in dark blues and greens. Coral craned her neck, looking to see what was above and behind. Koji pointed out the largest drum, the *ō-daiko,* high above their heads. He said it weighed a thousand pounds. All around her, she could hear the chatter of other people pointing out one inventive detail after another. They had excellent seats, and Koji smiled at her pleasure.

"Americans are so brash. They have fun. I love it."

"Well, I don't know if Vegas is very typical

of America."

"I think it is. I think it feels quintessentially American."

"When I lived in California, my friends didn't like Vegas. Most of them said they'd never even come here — 'cept maybe to see me."

"I bet they'd like to see this."

"Yeah. I mean, people visit from all over the world."

Koji grinned. "Yes. We do."

There was a reception after the show, and Koji had been invited. Coral was uncomfortable there. She hadn't realized Koji would know so many people, and she felt conspicuous; not Coral out on a date with the friend of a friend, but a young black woman on the arm of a Japanese businessman. It made her self-conscious. She excused herself to find a restroom, and coming back, she saw Marshall Dibb.

She knew who he was, of course. He was running the El Capitan now, with his mother. She tried to ignore the presence of the Dibbs in Las Vegas; told herself she had no reason to know anything about June or Marshall. From time to time, a story ran in the paper. The El Capitan was a classic, and the Dibbs kept it up even though the big casinos were corporations now, and everyone said the small resorts were on their way out.

Odell Dibb had been dead a long time.

Still, technically, this was her brother.

Marshall was fair and tall, and Coral was slight and dark. He looked like his father. Which meant that she probably looked like her mother, and even now, this thought hurt. But Coral had seen Marshall on the local news, she had studied him once when they were in the same restaurant. And as before, she saw herself in the way he moved, in something about how he was jointed, in the shape of his ears, in the way his hair lifted off his forehead. It wasn't a resemblance a stranger would remark on, but it was unmistakable if one knew.

Marshall Dibb looked her way and smiled. He must have noticed her staring. She smiled back awkwardly and turned abruptly, looking for Koji. He was nearby, watching her.

"You're not having fun?"

"Of course I am. It was an amazing show. The music, the drums, they were incredible."

"But now, here, you're not having fun."

"I'm ready to go home."

"I'll call the car."

"Thank you."

■ ■ ■ ■

In bed that night, Coral pulled a pillow over her head and tried not to think about Marshall Dibb.

How could he be her brother?

She felt no connection to him. He didn't know she existed. And here they were, in the same small town if you were a local, and she might be running into him for the rest of her life.

Seeing Marshall made her feel like she didn't have a home. Las Vegas was his town. He was practically royalty. Son of a casino family. Still, it was her town too. She'd grown up here. Where else would be home?

And that old feeling, that deep pressing emptiness, rushed back. The sense that she didn't have a place, that she didn't belong, that she had somehow been cut adrift when she was four days old, and also that, somewhere, someone wanted something from her.

"I'm a Jackson. I'm a Jackson as much as Ada and Althea and Ray Junior. Augusta Jackson is my mother." It was ridiculous to say these things aloud, and yet doing so made her feel better.

Would she ever tell Marshall Dibb her story?

Would she ever sit down with him and say, "I think you're my brother"?

And what would be his reply? Would he see the proof in *her* walk, in her ears, in the rise of her hair?

Could he know that she might exist? Could someone have told him?

That was the thing. She didn't care if Marshall Dibb ever knew who she was. She didn't want him for a brother. She didn't want to live in Las Vegas as the bastard black child of a casino pioneer. She had thought through this scenario before, and while Althea and Ray Junior and Ada now knew everything that she and Augusta did, nobody else knew. Augusta had kept her secret for her, and if she could have a life in Las Vegas — a life separate from the mystery of her birth; a life that was hers and had nothing to do with the Dibbs; with all the people that would find her birth fascinating, a story worth telling, even a story about Vegas — if she had any chance to live free of that, it was possible because Augusta had kept this secret so well. Augusta and Odell.

But what if Marshall did know she existed? Or knew she might?

What if Marshall was the one person in the world who might know who she was?

Over the years, Coral had come close to

270

contacting Marshall. She knew odd bits of information about him: the telephone number at his office, that he had bought a home the year after she bought hers, that he wasn't married, that he played in a recreational baseball league. She didn't want to know these things about him — didn't want to think of Marshall Dibb at all — but each time she had considered reaching out to him, each time she had prepared herself for what he might say, she had learned a little more. And every time, she had changed her mind. There was more to lose than there was to win. Why would Del Dibb have told Marshall about her, if he had worked so hard to keep her a secret all these years?

Still, the desire to know something about the woman who had given birth to her never quite went away, and remembering Marshall Dibb's casual smile in her direction made her scrunch the pillow down on her head and kick her feet, and finally stand up and find a movie and slip it into the VHS. There was the whir of the tape being pulled into the machine, and the clicking sound of it dropping into place, and then the film started: *North by Northwest.* It would be as good as anything else right now.

20

Going home was not as Honorata had imagined it would be. It took two days to get to Manila, and when she arrived, the airport smelled of gumamela, which made her think of Jimbo's house instead of the bubble paste that she and the other children had once made from its flowers. She panicked in the airport — tired and dehydrated, of course — but more and more, she found she couldn't settle down, she couldn't rest still, she was stricken with moments of coursing emotion, when she felt she had to bolt, or scream, or twist the neck away from the head of an animal. These moments were terrifying in their suddenness and in their violence, but nothing she tried made them easier. Honorata found an empty room down a long hallway, and there she put her head between her knees.

From Manila, she took a jeepney to Mayoyao. When it stopped to pick up passengers in San Jose City, she got out and threw up in the bushes. She shuddered there until the driver honked, and then she wiped her mouth with some leaves and stumbled back onto the jeepney. It smelled of sweat and *lumpia* and cassava and garlic. Some children at the back argued about who was sitting by the window, and a group of young girls experimented with lipstick in purple and magenta and black.

Everything leapt at her: the colors, the smells, the sounds. After San Jose City, the brightly painted bus began to climb into the mountains, and the fields were so green, the sky so blue, the air so soft; it was even more beautiful than she remembered. And yet already Honorata felt strange. She was wearing pants, and the other women were wearing skirts. She wanted to lean out the window and look down the valleys — see the road hanging off the side of the mountain, and the river far below — but she could hardly keep her eyes focused on the seat in front of her. She felt sick. She didn't want to throw up again, and every lurch and jostle of the jeepney threatened the possibility.

She had not told her mother she was coming, because she didn't want her uncle to know. She hoped that he would not be in the village; that he would be in Manila. It hurt to think of him in the city, what he did, the women he found, the letters he had someone write for them. But she could not do anything about her uncle. She had traveled without stopping for days, and she wanted *Nanay.*

The jeepney let her off about a mile from her village. Honorata started to feel better as she walked the familiar route, even if her suitcase felt heavy. Coming around a bend, she saw her uncle standing with two other men. She stared at him, but to her surprise, he did not acknowledge her. He turned and left the path, and she did not see him again while she was in Buninan.

She had come to take her mother back with her. This is what she had decided. This is why she had come so far, so abruptly, without telling anyone she was coming, without stopping to rest, without stopping to think about what had happened in the middle of one night, in a casino, in Las Vegas, in America, in a place impossible to describe or quite to remember now that she was back home, in a world entirely green and quiet and fresh. If her mother was with her, Honorata would know what to do.

But her mother was not ready to leave her home, not ready to cross an ocean when she had never been more than fifty feet off its shore, and even that was only once, when she had traveled very far, perhaps a hundred miles, to the sea. In Honorata's lifetime, her mother had never been to Manila. She did not want to go with her to the United States.

Still, what her mother knew, she knew well.

She knew instantly that Honorata was pregnant, which is how Honorata knew that it was true.

She knew quickly that Honorata would not return to Buninan.

She understood that the baby was not Kidlat Begtang's, and that it belonged to a different world.

She could not know what her brother had done — she might never believe this — but she knew somehow that Honorata should not see her uncle.

And in knowing that, everything was settled.

Because one could not live there and not be fully of the family. She could not live near her mother and avoid her uncle. There wasn't any way to separate family like this.

Perhaps in her mother's mind, the choice that Honorata had made so many years before — to leave Buninan with the boy from the village across the fields — was the only choice that mattered. Everything else came of it, and her mother, who had never lived anywhere but Buninan, accepted that life was to be played forward. She taught her daughter this.

But Honorata's mother didn't know everything. Honorata had not left the village, the place where her father's bones were kept, because she had been rebellious or unhappy. She had never dreamed of going away as a girl, and she hadn't wanted any other life than the one she had known. She had run away to Manila because one day she had gone into a field with Kidlat — one day she had made a sudden and unexpected and defining choice: so human, so universal, so absolute in its impact — and after that, there had been no way back to the life she had lived or intended to live. The life with which she would have been happy.

Of course, another girl would not have had to leave. These things happened, even in Buninan. They were an ordinary fact of life: perhaps Honorata was one of the few girls unaware of this. But other girls had not fallen in love with this boy. Kidlat had an uncle who had lived in America. He had a cousin who had been to Jamaica, and a friend who worked in Taiwan. Kidlat was not willing to play his part in the village script: the one that would have allowed Honorata that afternoon in the field. Kidlat would not marry Honorata and take her home to his village. If Honorata wanted, she could come to Manila with him. They could have a new life there. That was the option he offered.

So she, the precious only daughter, the one who had never wanted to leave, she, Honorata, thick with regret, with longing, in a kind of shock but also wild with desire, with love, with the feel of Kidlat's touch as vivid in her mind as it had been on her skin — insatiable skin — Honorata had followed Kidlat to Manila. And everything that came after, all of it — the tiny apartments; the city friends; the nights wondering where Kidlat was, and if he would come home bruised or even, once, burned; the movie; the bakery; her uncle; the flight to Chicago; Jimbo; the El Capitan; the coins clinking in the plastic bucket; the lights whirling and horns sounding when all the wheels spun to the same Megabucks logo (lucky Honorata — Honosuerte); the young men, drunk, running toward her in their polo shirts; the baby (not Kidlat's) now inside her — all of it, came from that instant. It was that instant after she'd thought Kidlat had stopped loving her, after he had gone to Manila when they were seventeen and come back wanting nothing to do with her, after she had mourned losing him, and then bumped into him, and neither had expected to see the other, and their attraction was so strong, their bodies drawing nearer — as if they were each on one of those moving walkways she had not yet known existed — angling toward each other, magnets propelling to their own fates, their shoulders actually bumping when they finally met, so out of control of their forward movement to each other that they did not quite recognize when they had reached the same spot. They had bumped and then turned and walked forward, shoulder not quite grazing shoulder, elbows not quite touching, and casual words spoken: "I haven't seen you." "Will you be at the festival?" And before them, the field, so green, so silent, and nothing else said and nothing else thought, but knowing nonetheless where they were going and what they would do, even if the actual words would have startled her and stopped her and sent her to a different fate entirely.

After a few weeks, Honorata left the village. She had sobbed, wanting her nanay to come with her, and her nanay had held her tightly. It was true, she agreed, Honorata must go to America, but no, she would not go with her. She would not walk onto a plane, fly across an ocean, speak a language she did not know. It was not possible for her in the same way that living where she could see her uncle was not possible for Honorata. Somehow the world had dropped between them — Honorata and Nanay — and how it had happened did not matter. Life could not be reversed.

In the days after Honorata accepted that this was true, at least for now, everything about her time in the village felt precious. She sat underneath the wooden floor of her mother's home, her back against one of the four thick trunks that held the house well above the ground, and remembered the games she had played there. At night, the rain fell softly on the grass roof. She walked about touching things, smelling them, rubbing against her cheek the dented pot her mother used for cooking and tasting the leaves of the bush with purple flowers. She did not know when she would return to Buninan or who she would then be. As she left her village, as she walked along the road to catch the jeepney, sipping the *salabat* her mother had said would ease the sickness, she imprinted every sensation: the shape of branches against the sky, the smell of rice growing, and the sounds: of birds, of children playing *luksong-baka,* of a cloud rat startled from its branch. In Chicago, she had heard the whistle and chug of busses, the honk of car horns. In Las Vegas, there had been clanking and bells, the crashing of coins into trays.

From Buninan, Honorata went first to a hotel in Manila. Not a grand hotel in Makati or Ortigas, but still her room was big and there was no garbage piled next to the building. At night, the shops closed, and the streets were quiet. She stayed there another week, looking for Kidlat, trying to find out where he had gone, if anyone was in touch with him. Finally, she found Rosauro, who told her that Kidlat had gone to Mindanao, that he was headed to Davao City, or perhaps he had changed his mind and found a way to Palawan.

Rosauro had been with Kidlat when he had found out what happened to Honorata. Kidlat had shouted and said he would hurt her uncle, but they both knew that he would not hurt him. Kidlat and Rosauro already knew what her uncle did in the city; they had known for a long time, but Kidlat hadn't thought there was any reason for Honorata to know. Nobody had imagined that her uncle could do what he did. Did Honorata need anything? Rosauro asked. Kidlat was his *kuya*. He would do anything for Honorata.

She left Manila the next day.

She had not given up on bringing her mother to the States, and she thought that her nanay would come eventually, after the baby was born, after she accepted what her brother had done to her daughter. But Honorata had given up on finding Kidlat. Too much had happened; it had been a mistake to want to find him. Perhaps she had thought that Kidlat would persuade her to stay in Pilipinas, perhaps she had thought he would have a way to shield her from her uncle, perhaps she had imagined the life they would live with all her money. But seeing Rosauro brought it back: the way it was, not the way she pretended. There was the movie, what had happened, that she had done it for Kidlat, and that he had then left. There was her uncle, there were the months with Jimbo, and, strangely, there was the woman who had helped her in Las Vegas. All of this made not just Buninan, but even Manila — not just her village, but even Kidlat — wrong for her.

The Honorata who had lived in Manila did not exist anymore. Sitting on the edge of the bed, in that clean hotel room larger than any apartment she could have imagined a year ago, Honorata shook with this idea. For an instant, her teeth clenched, her muscles contracted, she wanted to strike something, she wanted to hit someone, she would not be able to bear it; the anger was a cold-hot rush of necessity. Then she inhaled, once, twice, she put the thought carefully aside, she unfolded her fingers and closed her eyes. She sat perfectly still for a long time.

If that Honorata did not exist, the one sitting on this bed did.

Nanay was right. The only way to live life was forward.

When she was fully calm, when she could take in air without hearing it, she repacked her suitcase, bumped it down the stairs of the hotel, and walked along the crowded street until she found a taxi. "To the airport," she said, and as she rode, with the car lurching and the smell of exhaust making her sick, she thought about the possibilities. She thought about what she had learned of the United States, about the snow in Chicago, the lights on the Strip, the grocery stores with their long aisles of boxes and cans. She thought of the television shows she and Kidlat had watched in the bar where he worked: *Charlie's Angels* and *The Brady Bunch* and *L.A. Law.* She remembered the way America looked in those shows, the blue skies and the ocean and the houses so new and big. She pictured the women — their long feathered hair as they sped away in a car; or the mother with the short bob, smiling as everyone in her family did what she wanted.

When she got to the airport, she didn't hesitate. She didn't hesitate because she wasn't the Honorata who had left Buninan for Manila a decade ago. She wasn't the Honorata her uncle had put on a plane a year ago. She wasn't even the Honorata who had sat in this airport, head in her hands, just weeks ago. She was on her own, and there was no one to protect her, and she did not need protection. She had won a jackpot, and she was pregnant. Hono*suerte.* She had a passport, and she would buy a ticket to Los Angeles. *Bahala na.* Come what may. She would live in the city of angels.

She took a room in a hotel near the Los Angeles airport, and a taxi driver showed her the nearest hospital. At first, the man at the hospital was reluctant to help her. She couldn't register for a birth without a doctor, and how long would she be staying in LA? Did she have a permanent address? So she went to a Catholic church, and there the woman in the office helped her find a doctor, and also asked where she was living and if she could afford an apartment. With her help, Honorata rented a furnished apartment in Inglewood, not too far from the hospital. She told the woman at the church that she was planning to buy a house, before the baby was born, if she could. The woman gave her a puzzled look but did not ask any questions; instead, she gave her the name of a congregant who was also a Realtor.

"We don't have a large Filipino community here," she said. "You might be more comfortable in Eagle Rock. Or West Covina. The Realtor will know."

Honorata thought about these words. The enormity of what she had done, leaving Pilipinas after she had found a way back, felt like a wave sweeping her out to sea. She could not think about this now. She couldn't think about whether she would buy a house in Eagle Rock or Inglewood, couldn't imagine driving the maze of roads she had seen from the window of the plane, all those neighborhoods, all those people, all those communities — some with Pinoy and some without — and did she want to live with them? Would there be tamarind and pandan and lemongrass for cooking? Would her child speak Pilipino? Would she always be shunned, a mother without a husband?

It overwhelmed her, and the plan that she had worked out carefully — that she had written down and repeated to herself over and over as she flew all those hours — no longer seemed so clear. What was she doing in LA? She didn't know anyone here. She didn't know anything about the city. She couldn't buy a house and set down her life, her child's life, without knowing anything. It was too big. It was too much. Why had she thought she could do it? Where did she belong?

Honorata spent the months before her baby was born in the furnished apartment, ricocheting between days she felt strong and days she felt weak. There was almost never a day in the middle, a day of balance. She was super Honorata or she was disgusting Honorata, and the seesaw nature of her own temperament exhausted her. She began leaving the apartment only to attend morning Mass, or to talk quietly to the priest in the dark confessional stall on Saturday afternoons, or to buy food and the things she would need to bring a baby home. She didn't call the Realtor. She tried to avoid the woman from the church office, though the woman looked for Honorata sometimes and stopped to ask how she was feeling, if she needed anything. One day she brought a box of new baby supplies to Honorata's apartment, and Honorata blinked back the tears as she showed her the diapers, the sterilized bottles, the baby wipes, and the blanket with a matching cap that a parishioner knitted for all the new babies.

"Do you have someone to go with you, into labor?" the woman from the office asked.

"Yes," Honorata said.

The woman seemed to know she was lying, but she didn't say anything. The next Saturday, after her confession, a priest came out from the sacristy, wearing street clothes, and waited until she was done praying, until she had awkwardly shifted her belly and pulled herself up from the kneeler. Then he reached over to help her stand fully upright. He asked if she had a minute to talk, if they could walk outside, and when Honorata went with him, he invited her to join a young adult group that met on Tuesday evenings. "Some people have children, and others are single," he said, "but they will be people your age. You might enjoy it."

Honorata did not commit to going, but she noticed that the priest was also about her age, that he had very large ears and that he walked gracefully, as if he might suddenly turn and spin. He wasn't particularly earnest, which she appreciated.

Her contractions started in the morning.

They continued all day, and when she called the doctor's office, they asked her to time them, and when she said they were coming every three minutes, they told her to go to the hospital, not to delay, and did she have a bag ready?

She had a bag.

Honorata had had little to do but prepare for this day for months, so she had a bag for herself and another for her baby, and on the top of that bag were the blanket and the cap the parishioner had knitted. She called the number of the taxi company she always used, but when she said she was having a baby and needed to go to the hospital, the dispatcher hung up. Frantic, she found the phone book someone had left under the brown leatherette couch in the main room. The front cover was ripped off, and Honorata was not sure how old it was, but there was an ad for a taxi company on the back cover. Shaking, she dialed it carefully.

When the dispatcher answered, she gave her address slowly, said she was ready right away, but not why she was going to the hospital. Then she stood outside on the sidewalk, and waited, and the taxi came in just minutes. The driver, from some African country — she couldn't quite understand what he said to her: something about the baby, something about his wife — dropped her off at the emergency entrance, and she walked in by herself, doubling over when a contraction came, and carrying the two bags, one in each hand, like ballast.

The birth was easy.

Nanay had told her it would be easy — that her births were easy, and her mother's too. When she said this, a look had passed across her face, and Honorata knew she was thinking that Honorata's baby might be different, might not be like any other baby they had birthed. Her mother had this thought and decided not to say it, but Honorata had seen it, and her mother had seen her see it, and they said nothing of this to each other.

So Honorata was not counting on an easy birth, and yet it was.

Malaya was born just after midnight. When the nurse, a Pilipina, handed her the baby, already wrapped tightly in a pink blanket, with a pink bow fastened to a lock of hair that looked quite black, with her eyes squeezed narrow — from the antibiotic, the nurse said — and her face wide and red as a beet, Honorata experienced something she would later think of as the only true religious moment of her life. It was awkward to hold her, lying there almost flat in a bed, and the baby's body wrapped too tight to fit naturally against her own, and yet the instant that she had the weight of her in her arms, the moment she looked into those ointment-smeared navy eyes, Honorata felt her own body begin to grow, as if the edges of her were expanding and then loosening, wavering, shimmering, dissipating; as if she were not held inside her body at all but existed everywhere and enormous and without shape. She was at once formless and formed: holding her baby carefully so there was no chance she would fall, though her physical body — her arms and shoulders and back — were weak and tired.

And that was the moment in which Honorata let go of the fear that had gripped her in the furnished apartment, with its stained tan carpet and its cream-colored walls and the plastic flower in an orange pot in the corner. That was the moment in which she knew she could do it, that she was free, that she had a daughter and a purpose and the strength to do whatever it would take. She was not a foreigner, an outcast, a sinner, a whore; she was a mother, and, incredibly, she had her own money, and nothing that came after this would be as hard as what had already been. This was the revelation.

They kept her in the hospital for two nights, bringing Malaya to her every three hours to nurse and also when she would not stop crying. Honorata could not get her to stop crying either, but it didn't matter, it didn't frighten her. In the village, there had been babies that cried all the time and babies that did not, and at a certain point, they all became children just like any other.

From the hospital, she sent a telegram to the church for her mother so that she would know she had a granddaughter, and then, in a moment of inspiration, she sent her a second telegram. She had decided to move to Las Vegas. She would buy a house there, and there would be a room for Nanay. Her mother could not live eight thousand miles away from her granddaughter, and as soon as possible, Honorata would be home to fetch her for a visit. Nanay would have to learn to fly.

21

A woman had moved into the house at the top of the cul-de-sac, but Coral had been unable to say hello. She often heard her neighbor drive in, because she braked and then revved again as she managed the slight incline to her garage, but the woman kept her door shut and picked up her mail quickly, without looking to see who else might be on the street. Finally Coral left a plant and a note at her new neighbor's door. The gift was gone the next morning, but nobody stopped to acknowledge it.

It was another week before Coral realized the woman had a child.

On Saturday, Coral saw her pushing an elaborate stroller toward the park. She watched her go by, and when she noticed her returning, she stepped out the front door and said hello.

"Hello," the woman replied. She didn't look directly at Coral.

"My name's Coral. Welcome to the neighborhood."

"Thank you."

She looked down, uneasy. Coral thought she must be shy.

"May I see your baby?"

The woman looked up and flashed a small smile.

"Her name's Malaya."

"What a lovely name." Coral walked to the stroller, and looked at the little girl. She was asleep, her cheek flushed, and one curl, moist with sweat, was pasted to her small pink ear.

"Oh, she's beautiful."

At this, her new neighbor smiled fully, and her face, which had seemed still and severe, was suddenly open and pleased. She reached out to move the brightly woven blanket off her daughter's shoulder, and as she did so, her fingers lightly caressed the infant's soft skin.

"Did you make her blanket? It's so intricate."

"My mother made it. In Pilipinas. Where I'm from, we make this cloth."

"It's wonderful."

The woman didn't speak, but she also didn't move away. She stood there, gazing at her baby, and Coral shifted awkwardly. It was sweet, the way this mother looked at her baby, but intimate too, as if Coral should not be standing right next to her. She started to step away from the stroller, and the woman spoke.

"My name's Honorata. I move here from the Philippines."

"Well, welcome, Honorata. I hope you like it."

"Have you lived here long?"

"On this street? Nearly three years. But I grew up not far from here. I'm a native."

Coral was used to people commenting on this fact, but, of course, Honorata was too new to know that native Las Vegans were rare.

"So you choose this neighborhood because it's a good one?"

"Well, I like it. And it's close to the school where I work. I'm a teacher. I teach music."

"At a Catholic school?" Honorata asked.

"No. At a public school. Just a few blocks that way."

"I'm going to send Malaya to Catholic school."

The baby stirred then, and made a little noise, like the bleat of a calf. Honorata stroked the child's cheek, and made a shushing noise with her lips slightly parted. Coral turned to go back inside.

"It was nice to meet you. Let me know if I can do anything. Just knock."

Honorata looked at Coral.

"Do you like that house there?"

"That one? With the dead grass?"

"Yes. Do you like it?"

Coral wasn't sure where this was going.

"Umm. Well, I wish they still had the water on. Nobody's lived there for about a year."

"Oh. So not good house?"

"I don't know. The house's fine. I'm not sure what happened to the owner."

"You don't want to buy this house?"

"That house? No."

"I might buy it. The Realtor told me that rental homes are good investment. Lots of people to rent homes here."

"Oh. Probably. That's cool."

"So, okay with you?"

Coral paused.

"I don't want to buy that house. It's nice of you to ask me."

"Okay. I find out about the owner."

"I think if you call the county, they'll tell you who owns it. Or you can ask your Realtor."

"Thank you. Very nice of you to tell me."

Honorata smiled at her.

"You're a teacher?"

"Yes."

"You look young."

"Actually, I'm thirty-two."

The baby was fussing now, and her neighbor moved the stroller back and forth, trying to get her to settle. Still, she didn't move on.

"That's very good. Be a teacher. Have a house."

Coral laughed.

"My mama agrees with you. It was nice meeting you, Honorata. Take care."

"Bye, Coral."

At this, the baby let out a cry, and her mother bent quickly toward her.

Coral didn't see much of her neighbor after that. On weekends, she sometimes saw Honorata pushing the stroller toward the park, and when the evenings cooled off, she could hear her singing to the baby, in a language Coral couldn't make out, in the backyard. In the spring, an older woman came to visit, and when Coral stopped to talk with Honorata, she learned that her mother had come to live with her. Coral had never seen anyone who might be the baby's father on the street, but she didn't pay close attention. It was possible that there was a father; that he visited Malaya at times.

One day Coral's niece Keisha came over to play, and when she saw Honorata and Malaya on the street, she rushed out to say hello. The child was learning to walk now, pitching one foot forward at a time and swinging like a pendulum from her mother's hand. She was a beautiful baby, fairer than her mother, but with her mother's bright, plump lips and dark-fringed eyes.

Coral watched from inside the house as Keisha crouched down and began to talk to the little girl. Malaya laughed at something Keisha did, and Coral saw Honorata smile and then show Keisha how to take the baby's hand, how to steady her as she threw one eager foot in front of the other. After a little, Keisha came running in.

"She says I can go over and play with Malaya one day!"

"Really? That's great."

"I told her I wanted to babysit, but she said that I would have to get older first."

"Yeah. Playing with her is a good way to start. She's learning to walk?"

"She's so funny. I tried to let go of her hand, but she just sat down on her bottom."

Althea came by later to pick up Keisha and

stayed to eat dinner. Malcolm was at basketball practice, and then the team was going to the coach's house to eat pasta so the players would be ready for the middle school tournament the next day.

"I can't stand the coach. He loves Malcolm, of course, and I appreciate that. But he says these things that make my skin crawl."

"He asked Malcolm if he was planning on a basketball scholarship," Keisha piped up. "That's why Mom's mad."

Althea raised an eyebrow at her sister.

"Did your mom tell him Malcolm is planning to be a doctor?"

"Malcolm told him."

"And he clapped him on the back and said he really liked to see a kid dream big." Althea sounded like she might spit.

Coral looked at Keisha. "I wouldn't want to be Malcolm's coach and step on your mom's toes."

Keisha laughed.

"Don't say those things to her, Coral. You just wait till you have a son."

"Auntie Coral's going to have girls, Mom. Did I tell you I get to play with the baby down the street?"

"What baby?"

"My neighbor at the end of the street."

Coral rinsed off the cutting board and handed it to Althea. "She has a little girl. Learning to walk. Keisha ran out and met her today."

"That's great, Keisha."

"I asked her if I could babysit."

"You're too young to babysit."

"That's what she said. But she said I could play with her."

Althea turned to Coral. "Keisha's planning on you having a daughter."

"Well, that might be a bit complicated."

"Are you still dating that guy? From Japan?"

"Sort of. He's only here a week or so a month."

"Well, do you know what he's doing those other three weeks?"

"You mean, do I think he has a wife and kids in Japan?" Rising on her tiptoes, Coral pulled down the cow pitcher that Keisha liked to use as a glass for milk. "No, I don't. But he might date someone there. He said he wasn't dating anyone in particular. I haven't told him I wouldn't go on other dates."

"And do you?"

Coral shook her head. "Now you sound like Mama. No, I'm not dating anyone else. I like Koji."

"Okay. Just be careful. This is Vegas. A lot of guys come here once a month."

"I don't think it's like that."

"And a lot of time can go by."

"Now you really sound like Mama."

Althea laughed and wrapped her arm around Coral's shoulders. Keisha was there, so they didn't talk about it anymore. Coral knew why her sister was concerned. You didn't grow up in Vegas without knowing the possibilities. Still, Koji was important to her.

The day after Keisha had gone out to play with Malaya, there was a knock at the door.

It was Honorata.

"Hi. Do you want to come in?"

"I was wondering if you could help me?"

"Sure. Is something wrong? Is your daughter okay?"

"Oh yes. Thank you. She's with my mother."

Honorata didn't seem to want to come in, so Coral stepped outside and sat on one of the chairs at the front door. Honorata took the other. She was nervous.

"Would you like a cup of coffee? I have some ready."

"No. I just have a question. I want to change my daughter's name. And I want to get a trust. I thought you could help."

"Me?"

"Yes."

"I think you have to go to a lawyer."

"Yes. You grew up here. Do you know a lawyer?"

"Umm. Well, sure. A friend of mine's a lawyer. He grew up here too. He probably does this sort of thing."

"What's his name?"

"He might be expensive. He works for a pretty big firm."

"That's good."

Coral assumed that she meant the big firm.

"His name's Darryl Marietti. And he works at Lionel Sawyer. I can contact him and tell him you'll be calling."

"Thank you."

"Sure. I'll do it today." After a bit, Coral asked, "What are you naming your daughter?"

"Naming her? Oh. No, I keep her name. I'm changing her last name to Begtang. Mine's Navarro."

It didn't seem right to pry, but Coral wondered if her neighbor would say why she was changing her daughter's name. She didn't.

"Keisha was thrilled to play with Malaya

yesterday. She's getting so big."

Honorata smiled. "Yes. She's almost walking. Eleven months."

"That sounds early."

"The doctor says she's very bright."

"Well, that's great. It's so nice that your mother's here too."

"Yes, now she's here, I'm going to get a job. At the church over there. In the office. Four mornings a week."

"That'll be convenient."

"Do you know I own three houses? On this street? I bought that one too." Honorata pointed to the house next to her own.

"Wow. I noticed the sign was only up one day. Will your mother live in one?"

"My mother?" Honorata looked confused. "No. She live with me." Then she thought for a moment. "Your mother? Does she want to rent house?"

"Mama? Uh, no. She has her own house."

"Okay. Very convenient. To have your mother on the same street."

Coral laughed. Ada would love this conversation.

"Yes. Very convenient. Listen, I'll call Darryl. Let me know if it works out."

Honorata never said anything about the name change, but Darryl mentioned it once.

"That woman you sent me? Your neighbor?"

"She's a character, right?"

"She's loaded."

"Really?"

"Yes."

"Was she married? I've seen her mother. I don't think she has any money."

"She didn't tell me where the money came from. Said she was never married. Just wanted to change her kid's name. Freaked out when I told her we had to publish it in the paper. We had to put it in the *LA Times* too, because the baby was born there."

"So, bad-dad story."

"I guess. Or maybe she's a sex worker."

Coral choked. "She really doesn't strike me as a sex worker."

"Well, she got that money somewhere. And that kid. You never know, Coral. It's not as if there's a sex-worker type. She's very good-looking."

"Honorata?"

"Drop-dead. Did you even look at her?"

"Yeah, I mean, I guess she's pretty. She's so nervous when I talk with her, I didn't really notice."

"I'm a man. We notice."

"*Ohhh*-kay. Well, so did she do it? Change her daughter's name?"

302

"Yeah. She was pretty upset about the advertisement, but I showed her how someone would have to be looking pretty closely, and she made a big deal about it not being anywhere but here and LA. After that, it was just a verified petition in family court."

"Did it go through?"

"Well, no dad showed up. The judge could have refused it, but that's rare. Hers was fine. Kid is Malaya Begtang."

Coral raised her glass.

"Daughter of a sex worker."

"Or a drug smuggler."

"Card cheat?"

"Romance novelist?"

Coral laughed out loud. Whenever she saw Honorata after that, hurrying in and out of the neighborhood, wearing her lace veil on Sunday mornings, she smiled.

22

Virginia asked Honorata what she thought of the priest's sermon.

This was something of a ritual. Molly said they were like Monday morning quarterbacks, calling the shots after the game had already been played. This made no sense to Honorata, but Virginia tried to explain it.

"A lot of games are played on Sunday, and then everyone whose team loses tries to figure out what the coach should have done to win. It's called Monday morning quarterbacking."

This was not helpful to Honorata.

"It means that after the fact, people try to call the game differently."

Honorata didn't particularly care if she understood Molly's reference or not, but she wanted to seem interested. Molly had been working there only a few months.

"Is the quarterback the one who guards the goal?"

"What?"

"I think that's a very hard position. Because if he keeps the ball from going in, the game just goes on. And if he misses, everyone is upset. I wouldn't like to be the quarterback."

"I think that's a goalie. Like soccer."

"Oh."

Honorata looked down. She didn't know why she had started talking about soccer. It was on her mind lately because there was a player in the news named Wohlmann, and the name made her jump. He wasn't even American, though. It had nothing to do with James Wohlmann. Still.

"Anyway, what did you think of what he said? About joy?"

At Mass, the priest had said that Catholics should be joyful. He said that joy was the natural expression of faith, and that the parishioner who followed all the rules but didn't feel joy was missing the point of a faithful life.

What Honorata thought was that the priest didn't know that much about life. He'd never lived in another country, he'd never been with a woman. He didn't have children, he didn't even pay his own bills. She didn't think she would say this to Virginia.

"I thought . . . I thought he wrote it very carefully."

Virginia laughed. "Carefully!"

"What did you think?"

Virginia might think anything. She was very surprising. She'd worked in the office for years, and she was devout, but she could be irreverent. Honorata didn't quite know what to think of her.

"I think he's got his head up his ass. Telling people to be joyful. Like that's something on tap."

Honorata wasn't sure what to say. It was very unusual, someone who worked in a church office and said "head up his ass."

"Doesn't it make sense, though?" she said. "That God would want us to be joyful?"

"Oh, what's God got to do with it? We're talking the Catholic church. Sex is joyful, but only if you're married and ready to have eight more babies. If you're one of God's chosen ones, which means you're also a man, then you can't have sex at all. Where's the joy in that?"

Honorata didn't answer. She didn't want to tell Virginia that when the priest was talking, she'd been thinking about how little he could know about her life. He looked at her and saw a little Filipina lady, something like her nanay, which was fine with Honorata —

306

which was the way she preferred that he see her — but still, how could somebody who couldn't tell the difference between Honorata and her nanay tell her how to feel?

"It's very American," she said at last.

"It's American? That's interesting. What do you mean?" Virginia leaned forward and waited for Honorata's reply.

"I mean, telling someone what to feel. A feeling is . . . A feeling isn't . . . I don't think you can tell someone what to feel."

"Exactly! Feelings aren't on tap. Only a priest could come up with something like that."

Honorata didn't know what "on tap" meant, but she did know that Virginia was big on what priests didn't know. She said it had something to do with her parents naming her Virginia, for the Virgin. Also, she believed the problems in the church came from ignoring women.

Molly asked why Virginia worked at the church if she thought it was such a mess. Honorata knew what Virginia would say. She'd heard it before. Virginia said that she was a true believer, and that she was quite sure God was happy to have her in the church, encouraging it from the inside.

Honorata thought about the other things the priest did not know about her.

He didn't know about her village. He didn't know what it was like to grow up as if one were part of the earth, the way that she and the other children were part of the green leaves and the rain and the sky. He didn't know about the ladder she climbed into her home, or the way that home was dark and close and smelled of the rice stored under its thatched roof. What could the priest know about what it had meant for such a child, one who ran naked in rain or sun, and made the other children laugh by bobbing her head sideways like a *tamsi*, to move to Manila, with more people than even a teacher could count, with its tin-sided shanties, and human waste running down mud roads?

More than this, how could the priest know what Honorata felt about what had happened to her: about the men who had made the video, about the one who had violated her, about the way her uncle had watched that tape? What could he know about the months in Chicago and the fat American man in her bed every night? How she still felt about all of this, how the feelings came to her at night, how they made her want to scream, how she would never be sure of herself again, of who she was, of what she might do. Could the priest imagine that the little girl who had lived in that village — who was *herself* — seemed almost other-worldly to her? Even with a daughter of her own to help her remember, a sturdy American child, Honorata could not quite summon up what it was like to have once been that little girl in a green world.

Still, with everything the priest could not know, she didn't like the way Virginia talked about him. He was a kind man, the priest. He had been kind to her, and he was kind to the people who came to the door, looking for help, and to the people in the parish, so many of whom were old and had no one to look out for them. That was one thing about America. A lot of old people were left all alone.

Americans went bonkers if a child was left alone, but if you worked at the church, then you knew that all sorts of old people — just as helpless as a child, some of them — were alone. And nobody seemed to care too much about that. But the priest did. And actually, Virginia did too. She was as kind as the priest.

Last week, Honorata and Nanay had attended a program at Malaya's preschool. It was the first program of the year. And since it was Malaya's first year of preschool, Honorata had not known what to expect.

She dressed her daughter in a gold satin dress with a white lace neck, which Malaya kept pulling at; before the night was out, the lace was torn, and Malaya was saying "That feels better, that feels way better!" to anyone who looked at her. Nanay said she could fix the lace.

The room where Malaya had preschool was filled with so many toys and so many bits of colored paper hanging from the ceiling and plastered to the walls and piled on the teacher's desk that it had made Honorata feel dizzy. She wouldn't be able to think calmly in such a room. When they arrived, Malaya wanted to play with her friends on the jungle gym. Honorata made her stay and greet the teacher, but Miss Julie said, "Oh, let her play. That's what all the kids are doing." So Malaya had run outside, and Honorata had seen her sliding and trying to hang from a bar and turning a somersault in the dirt with her underwear right in the air.

In her remarks — that's what they were called in the program, "Miss Julie, Remarks" — the teacher stressed the importance of being independent. She said that at Sunny Days Preschool, four-year-olds hung up their own backpacks, four-year-olds took themselves to the restroom, four-years-olds solved sharing problems on their own. These seemed like very unusual remarks to Honorata. What else would a four-year-old do?

Miss Julie also said that she encouraged children to think their own thoughts and to stick up for their own ideas. While she was saying this, one of Malaya's classmates, a boy, was yelling "Bang! Pow! Shazam!" Honorata looked around to see if his mother was coming to get him, but everybody sat smiling on the very small chairs. Nanay was one of the ones sitting and smiling. She couldn't understand a word. Honorata thought about asking what Miss Julie would do if the child's idea was not a good one, but she decided against it. She didn't feel comfortable speaking.

After the teacher's remarks, the parents were free to wander around the room. A man wearing a blue T-shirt said hello.

"My name's Mark. Father of Adam. You're Malaya's mom?"

Honorata was not sure how he knew this. She nodded.

"I'm a single dad. I feel sort of awkward at these things. You?"

Honorata wondered if he was insulting her. How did he know she was a single mom?

A ring. She didn't have a ring. She wondered if it would be lying to wear one, for Malaya's sake. She gave the man a discouraging look and turned away.

Later, he tapped her on the shoulder.

She didn't want to talk to him.

"Hey, listen, I'm sorry. That came out wrong earlier. Miss Julie's my sister, so that's how I know you're Malaya's mom. She told me Malaya didn't have a dad, so I was just trying to be friendly. I didn't mean to scare you. I'm really sorry."

He did look like Miss Julie.

"I'm sorry that Malaya doesn't have a dad. I know that's bad." Her voice didn't come out strong, as she intended.

"What? No. That's not what I meant. Hey, no big deal. Like I said, I'm a single dad."

He hadn't seemed mean, more like a puppy, but Honorata had walked away, and when she could persuade Malaya to leave the sandbox, she and Nanay had gone home.

Virginia was still talking about joy, and Molly had apparently stuck up for the priest.

"Molly," Virginia said, "the problem is not with the idea, it's with the command. Of course, we should feel joy. Of course, we are meant to enjoy this world."

Was that true? Were we meant to enjoy this world?

Did Honorata feel joy?

When it was the morning of Malaya's birthday, when Honorata had impulsively pulled over at the pet shop, a dirty little place, not at all reassuring; when she had gone in and seen the gray kitten, fluffy and blue-eyed, and known that it might not be healthy, that getting a pet from one of these stores was not a good idea, that in any case Malaya couldn't be relied on to care for a pet yet, that a cat would shed hair and snag its claws on the silk fabric of the dining room banquette; when she had thought all these things and brought the kitten home anyway; when Malaya had stood there, shocked to absolute stillness, with tears pouring down her cheeks, so surprised and so happy, and yes, so utterly joyful; hadn't Honorata felt joy then? Hadn't she laughed and sat down on the floor, and set the kitten near her daughter's feet, and watched while Malaya bent her knees and squatted in her Swiss dot dress and gently, oh so gently, stroked the kitten with one small finger?

Surely that was joy.

And was it not joy when she walked the three short blocks from her home to the church office, and let herself in with the key, and poured the honey over the *pandesal* she had baked that morning, and brewed the coffee, and opened the blinds, so that when Virginia and Molly and the priest walked in, they would know the day was starting right?

Wasn't it joy when she spent the afternoon in her garden, wiping the bugs off the rose petals with her fingers and wrapping the sweet pea vines on the trellis? Wasn't it joy when she and Malaya stopped at the Blockbuster to choose a movie, and then walked to the Dairy Queen for an ice cream dipped in red candy, and then sat in a heap on the couch with Nanay while Malaya shrieked in delight as an enormous dog shook mud all over his owner's bed or stood on his hind legs to eat the Thanksgiving turkey? Malaya used her whole body to watch a movie — jumping to her feet to bounce up and down when something funny was about to happen, or throwing her arms out wide to sing "roll over baked oven" whenever the music started up again.

That was joy.

Honorata wanted to say something about joy to Virginia and Molly. She wanted them to know that she felt joy, that her daughter did, that joy was possible even if there was also a great deal of pain, but she couldn't find the right words. She wasn't quick enough, and Virginia always spoke so fast.

What Honorata said was: "Malaya has a kitten, and even when he scratches us, we love him."

Virginia looked at her quizzically.

Molly said she loved cats, and that she'd had her cat YoYo since he was three weeks old. She'd fed him with a bottle, and he still crawled in her lap every time she sat in the one particular chair that she'd fed him in.

Just then, the priest walked in.

"So, Virginia," he said. "What was wrong with my sermon?"

"We were talking about cats," said Virginia.

The priest laughed. "I bet."

Honorata didn't know how they had ended up talking about cats. She had started it, but it wasn't what she meant. It would have taken her a long time to explain what she meant, and it wasn't really that sort of conversation, this Monday morning quarterbacking. It was more like a ritual, like a way to start the week, and it didn't matter too much what anyone said. It had taken her quite awhile to figure this out.

It was confusing, being in America.

It wouldn't have occurred to her to think

about whether she felt joy or not.

What occurred to her was whether or not she was doing the right thing each day. Whether she was using the money in the best way, whether she was raising Malaya to be a good person, whether her nanay was happy, whether she was a fair landlord to her tenants, whether her work at the church was correct.

She liked Americans for thinking about things like joy, even if she thought that someone should have made that little boy stop yelling when the teacher was talking. And the man, that Mark. Maybe he was just being friendly, and there wasn't any reason to feel afraid of him, and maybe he hadn't meant that he knew she was not a nice woman. Maybe he didn't think things like that at all.

But Honorata did. She regretted the mistakes she had made, how foolish she had been. It didn't seem fair that she had won a jackpot and that she had a daughter, and that her nanay was here with her. She didn't deserve these things. She tried to be as good as she could, to make up for everything she had done wrong before, but she knew that it wasn't really like that. People didn't get what they deserved, you couldn't hold off bad luck by being good, you couldn't say

you earned your good luck. You just got
what you got, and did the best you could,
and tried not to be afraid of what might
happen next. At least, that's how Honorata
did it.

23

She found out at her annual appointment.

"Coral, are you aware that you're pregnant?"

She was not.

She was thirty-six years old, and she had always used birth control. No wonder the school nurse's perfume had seemed so pungent.

Pregnant?

Her heart fluttered dangerously.

What would Koji say?

Their relationship was, well, unconventional. He wasn't even in town most of the time. Augusta had stopped asking Coral what their plans were. The answer was that they didn't make plans.

Two years ago, she and Koji had traveled to Japan. Coral had assumed she would meet his family; that he was bringing her home for that reason. But he didn't introduce her. They'd had a wonderful time. Koji took her to his favorite places — temples and ball fields and gardens and the sea — and each morning, he carefully assembled a tray and fed her *natto* and pickled vegetables before she dressed. But she never met his father, his mother, his younger brother. It wasn't difficult to decode what that meant.

After the trip, Coral had decided she needed to move on from Koji. Althea had been right, way back when. A lot of time could go by; a lot already had. For several months, she spent the weeks when Koji was not in Vegas living as if they had separated. She allowed herself to go on dates and told her closest friends that she was looking for someone with whom she could have a family. But each time Koji arrived in town, she accepted him right back. He was always so pleased to see her, he had one suitcase filled with food he would cook for her, he wanted to hear about everything that had happened in his absence again, even though they had often talked about it on the phone. Also, he had a present to celebrate Malcolm's MVP award at the high school championships; he had found a kimono for Keisha that she might like; had the little girl in the fourth-grade class come back to school or not?

After awhile, Coral accepted that she didn't want to meet anyone else, that she didn't want another life, that she loved Koji even if it wasn't the life she had imagined. She wasn't ready to let him go. Still, she knew she should tell Koji how she had felt in Japan. How she had waited to meet his family, how she had started to realize she might not, how she had not known what to do, how she had lain awake, heart pounding, wondering whether everything she thought was true between them was not true. What if he had a secret life? What if he didn't care about her in the same way she cared about him?

For months, she promised herself that she would talk with him on his next trip to Vegas, but each time, she found a reason not to do it. Finally, on a day when puffy white clouds foiled an impossibly blue sky, and the sweet smell of star jasmine hung in the air like a kiss, she asked him.

"Koji?"

He laid his head on her shoulder.

"I wanted to meet your family. We never talked about this."

He was silent. His head was still on her shoulder, but the weight shifted subtly. Coral felt tears start in her eyes. She concentrated on staying calm, on not thinking ahead of this minute. Koji shifted and sat up, but he didn't look at her. Instead, he looked at the pool, at the vines snaking up the stucco wall behind it.

"My family's very traditional."

Coral said nothing.

"I don't care what they think, Coral. It's never mattered to me."

Coral kept her eyes averted.

"I wanted you to meet them."

What did he mean?

"You'd really like my brother. His wife would love you."

Coral concentrated on being perfectly still.

"I didn't want them to hurt you."

She tried not to think about what he was going to say.

"My parents wouldn't understand, Coral. They've never left Japan. They don't like how their country's changing."

She knew what was coming.

"My father lost his brother in the war. He hates America."

Breathe in, breathe out.

"They don't believe in mixing races."

There it was.

And Coral had wept. The pain had burst out of her in great gulping sobs, and Koji had said, "I'm sorry, I'm sorry, I'm sorry," and held her and wept too. And when it was over, when they sat huddled on the bench under the glorious sky on the beautiful day, they had not talked more about it.

Coral couldn't bring herself to talk about this. It wasn't Koji's fault. It wasn't anything he could fix. But the pain was so fierce and so hot and so unbearably personal, it reached so far inside, to so many other experiences, to so many memories, to classmates calling her "halfie" and "zebra," to saleswomen standing just outside the dressing room door when she needed a new pair of jeans, to certain things that had been said to her late at night in those nightclubs where she and Tonya had sung, to a thousand other moments, uncountable memories, whispers and intimations and slights so subtle they couldn't register as slights, and yet they built up, they piled one on top of the other until the weight smothered one, until the thought of just one more assumption, one more stupid comment, one more sidelong glance, made her feel as if she would never stand again.

Not long after that morning, Koji asked Coral to marry him.

And Coral said no.

She remembered how very stricken he had looked. His face on that day was seared in her mind. But she couldn't marry someone who might just feel terribly guilty.

Gradually things got easier. It had been a

year and a half, and Koji still came to Vegas as often as he could; if anything, the relationship deepened. They settled into a partnership, one that was almost the same as a marriage.

Now Coral didn't know what Koji would say when she told him she was pregnant. He had mentioned children when he proposed. For the last year, Coral had told herself, over and over, that she was probably already too old.

Apparently not too old.

Coral told Ada first.

She felt closer to Althea, but it was easier to talk with Ada about some things. Her sister was an hour away in Pahrump, living with some guy who grew marijuana for a living. Nobody said that, of course. Russ was a "farmer." Grew vegetables for some of the restaurants on the Strip. They said stuff like that. But really he grew marijuana, and Coral pretended not to know, and Ada pretended that a multi-ton marijuana operation was some offshoot of the way she'd lived when she was young: when she had followed around a couple of bands and lived in a house where nobody cared what color anyone was, or who slept with whom; where they all raised one another's kids, and laughed about which ones might be blood related after all. In Ada's case, it didn't matter. Her two kids both looked exactly like her, and whoever their dad was (dads were?), he must have hardly had any genes, because Serenity was Ada's double, and Alabaster — Alabaster, for a black man — was Ada if she'd been a boy.

Ada came to town to bring Augusta flowers. She had filled the back of her car with them, and she called Coral to bring over more vases. It was a crazy Ada idea, but they had ended up laughing harder than they had in years. Coral came right over and got things organized. She separated the flowers by stem length, nipped off the ends of each one, and then filled every pot and glass and bucket in the house. There were bowls of flowers all the same color, and vases filled with daisies and roses and asters. She had tall, spikey arrangements, and flat, floating ones, and little sprays of wildflowers to set by the beds. She was showing Augusta her work, wondering where Ada was, thinking that she'd spent an entire Saturday afternoon finishing one of Ada's projects, when Ada finally poked her head in the door.

"There you are," said Coral. "Well, it's done. They look beautiful. They do. Extravagant — and beautiful."

"Done?"

Ada stepped through the door, her arms full of more blooms. And they both laughed. Because here was Coral, with the problem all resolved, and there was Ada, with no problem at all.

They ended up giving the rest to the neighbors.

And later, after Augusta had fixed some dinner, and they had sat and talked about Ada's kids — after Augusta had said she'd turn in early, she was an old lady now, and Ada had said, "Old lady my ass" and Augusta had reminded her kindly not to swear — then the sisters found the cognac left over from Easter, and they sat in the back, in the hot comfort of a summer night, and that's when Coral told Ada she was pregnant.

"I probably shouldn't be drinking this."

"Why, you pregnant?"

Like everything with Ada, it didn't go as Coral might have predicted.

"Girl, you got pregnant at thirty-six — we'd all about given up — and now you're going to have a baby. It's fantastic news. Wonderful. Why haven't you told Mama? Why aren't we dancing?"

"I'm afraid to tell Koji."

"Of course you are. I mean, what are you

325

guys doing? You're together, you're not. What's your deal?"

"Wow, Ada. Easy on the judgment. When did *you* ever have a normal relationship? With Russ, the drug dealer?"

"Hey, let's not go there. Come on. We're having a nice time. You're drinking, and you shouldn't be, so let's not waste it. This isn't about me. What I did. What my relationships are. I just don't understand your relationship with Koji. I mean, we all treat him like he's part of the family, but he's here, what, one week a month, and you don't go there, and he doesn't move here, and what are you doing? I mean, what's it been? Four years?"

Coral thought about Koji's family; about why she didn't go to Japan. Ada would understand this, but she didn't want to tell her. She didn't want to tell anyone. She didn't want Ada or Althea or her mother to know what Koji's family thought.

"It's complicated."

"It's always complicated, Coral. Give that up. Give up that thing you do."

"What thing?"

"That Coral thing. That everything-has-to-be-right, my-life-isn't-messy thing. Speaking of judgment."

"I don't judge you."

"You've judged me my whole life. And maybe I deserve it. But I'm just telling you, let it go. Whatever's bothering you, whatever's holding you back, let it go. Life's messy. Big fuck."

Coral looked down at her hands. Ada continued.

"I don't know what's going on in your head right now, but this baby's a beautiful thing. I know you want her. And I want her. And Mama wants her." Ada stood up. "What we should be doing right now is celebrating!"

So they did.

Her sister hadn't even stopped speaking, and the euphoria washed over Coral like a wave.

She was pregnant. She was going to have a baby. She, Coral, would have her own baby. She whooped. And Ada flew out of the chair, and wrapped her arms around her, and they both cried. Ada started it — she started the crying — and she said, "Coral, Coral, Coral, I am so happy for you."

Augusta heard them and got up to see what was going on, so they all sat there, late into the night, talking about Coral's baby, and what sort of baby Coral had been, and how Ada used to crawl into the crib and make her sister laugh by barking and neighing and mooing in her face.

On Monday, Coral called her doctor for a prenatal appointment and picked up a bottle of maternity vitamins at the GNC on Flamingo. Her mind was full of thoughts of the baby, of whether it would be a boy or girl, of what the nursery might look like, of whether it would be fussy or calm. The baby would be born near Christmas, and with maternity and sick leave, she could probably stay home three months.

She talked with Koji every night, as always, but somehow she kept the secret. He would be home in two weeks, and she needed to tell him in person. She needed to see his eyes, his face. If she didn't, she might never be sure of what he really thought. She tried not to think of what he would do, of how they might live, of the changes they would make. She was sure of Koji, but she was afraid too, and this fear was deep inside, and she had to be with him in person when he heard the news.

She started to bleed two days before he arrived.

It was a hot gush, unmistakable, in the middle of lunch duty. She made an excuse and ran out the door, leaving behind everything, even her purse. She raced to the emergency room at Sunrise, but it was too late. The baby was gone.

"Miscarriages at eleven weeks are not uncommon. I'm sorry, Ms. Jackson, I'm really sorry. You should talk to your own doctor about when to start trying again. She knows your body best."

And Coral had cried.

She had sat in the open exam room, nothing but a flimsy cotton curtain, not quite shut, between her and the child with the seizure, the old man with the chest pain, the woman who had been vomiting for days, and she cried. Her cries were great gasping shudders, mortifying cries, which she desperately wanted to stop, but she could not stop them. She sat and cried in this horrifying way, and everyone there could hear her. After a bit, a nurse said she was sorry and asked if there was someone she could call. And Coral said no, and got up, and then remembered that she didn't have any money, she didn't have her purse, so the nurse walked her to a quiet hall and gave her a quarter for the pay phone.

Two days later, Koji flew in. He always stayed with her, but she asked him to take a hotel room. She said she was sick, that she would see him in a couple of days; there was no sense in him getting it too.

"What do you mean, Coral? If you're sick, I want to help you."

"No, Koji. I don't want you here. I just want to sleep."

She knew she'd hurt his feelings, and that he had no idea what was happening, but she was wildly angry at him, afraid of what she might say if he were right in front of her.

She couldn't think what to do with herself, so she called her sister.

"Ada, it's Coral."

"Yeah, how ya feeling? Any fever?"

"No. I'm fine. I mean, my body's back to normal. The doctor said it would take longer, but —"

"Did you tell Koji?"

"No."

"Is he there?"

"No. I told him to get a hotel. I don't want to see him."

"You have to tell Koji."

"I know."

Coral hung up, but she didn't call Koji. She got into bed and tried to sleep. The next night, he rang the doorbell, and when he came in, when he took her in his arms, when she started to cry, when *he* started to cry without even knowing what had happened, she told him the story.

And then she said, "I think we should break up. I love you, Koji. I always will. But I don't want to do this. This isn't the life I want."

Koji looked at her, shocked.

"It's just not what I want. I thought it was okay. But it's not. It's not okay."

"What *do* you want?"

"I don't know. But it isn't this."

"You're mad at me because I was in Tokyo?"

"Yes."

"You didn't call me. You didn't give me a chance."

"What difference would it make?"

"I would've come."

Coral almost started to cry but steeled herself. "And that wouldn't have made any difference."

Koji didn't answer her then. He looked down at his hands, for a long while. Coral said nothing. She was thinking that she might never see him again, and that she had never loved anyone more than she loved him, and still, that she could not do it. She could not have a lover one week of the month; she couldn't keep living this way. She would not.

Finally, he spoke.

"I don't know what you want. But I do know what I want. I want you. I'll leave Japan. If you'll marry me, I'll marry you. We can live right in this house. I can get a job here in a week. And we can have another baby. That's what I want. That's what I've always wanted. Please. Say yes."

24

"Everyone plays soccer! Ashley, Brittany, Divya. They all get to play, *Ina.*"

"Why do you want to play this game? It's a boy's game."

"It's not for boys! It's for girls."

"You'll get very dirty. And kicked. People will kick you."

"I like to be dirty."

This was true, to Honorata's chagrin.

"I don't like you to be dirty, Malaya. And I don't like soccer. You could take another dance class. You could try ballet again."

"No! No, no, no! I hate ballet!"

"Don't yell. You didn't hate it last year. You loved your pink leotard."

"No, I didn't. I don't want to take ballet. I don't want to take tap. I don't want to take any dance class."

"You can't just quit your dance classes because your friends are playing soccer."

"Why not?"

Honorata didn't know why not. She knew she wanted Malaya to stop arguing. She was only in second grade, but already she fought so hard against her mother. It was these American schools. But Nanay was no help. When Honorata asked her what she thought she should do about Malaya, Nanay said, "Well, she's an American. She should do American things."

What did that mean?

Why didn't Malaya like the dance classes Honorata paid for? She had taken ballet and tap, and each year, there were at least four beautiful costumes for the spring show. Last year, Honorata had bought the largest and most expensive photo of Malaya in the package deal. It showed her daughter, right hip jutted out, hair pulled tight across her scalp, a red flower over her ear, and a little red-and-black costume with a short swirl of skirt and a rhinestone belt. Malaya's lips were red and her cheeks pink and her lashes so full they looked as if they were fake; the teacher had let all the mothers use her theater makeup to get the children ready. What little girl would not love that costume? That photo?

Honorata had the photo framed at Swisher's Frame Shop, with a little gold plaque that said "Malaya Age 6," and it hung over the dresser in her bedroom. When Honorata looked at it each morning, she felt pleased with her daughter, and with herself, for giving that daughter a childhood with dance recitals and lessons and all the things a little girl living in the mountains in the Philippines could not even imagine.

But soccer? Why did Malaya want to do something like this? The specter of Malaya's father, the one who was a secret, flickered in Honorata's mind. She didn't want Malaya to be anything like this man. At times she asked herself, *Who is this little girl?* When Malaya wanted to play a boy's game; when she jumped in the puddles in her brand-new shoes and got mud straight up the back of her pressed white blouse right before she was to go to school; when she sat rigid and screaming in the shopping cart at two years old, furious because Honorata would not buy her a tray of Jell-O chocolate pudding cups (how did she even know what they were?); when the school office called and said Honorata would have to come in, that Malaya had called another child a word the woman could not repeat on the phone; when these things happened, Honorata wondered where Malaya got these qualities. Why did she do these things?

And this is why it was so good that her

mother lived with them, and it was right that Honorata send her daughter to Catholic schools, even if it meant she would have to ride a school bus, and why it was so important that she watch what Malaya did, and the choices her daughter might make without knowing what it was inside her that made her choose them.

Even when Honorata had betrayed her family and run away to Manila with Kidlat, an act far more horrible than anything she could imagine Malaya ever doing, even then, Honorata had not been like Malaya. She had been in love with Kidlat — madly in love. But Malaya? Malaya was willful when there was no particular reason to be so. Malaya was not submissive as Honorata had been, Malaya did not want to please Honorata the way that Honorata had wanted to please Nanay and Tatay. Malaya had a wildness that came to her from somewhere else — that came to her from the man. That was Honorata's fault. But she would do what she could, she would protect her as much as she could, and maybe Malaya would change; maybe she would grow up. This did happen. Some wild children became serious adults.

And perhaps it was these fears, these unknown possibilities, that tipped Honorata over some days. Perhaps this was why she would occasionally wake up, after a year — or even longer — of perfectly normal mornings, and the light would shine in acidly, and the sound of a cup rattling on the tile would grate, and she would feel it about to happen, an instant before it did, and then it would be there, full on top of her, and unbearable, and no way to lift herself back up. There was nothing to do but wait, and take one leaden step after another, until one day, just as inexplicably, the light would shine clear again, and she would hear the three-toned trill of a bird out her window. Honorata would stand up, startled at how easy it was, at how gravity had somehow shifted, and how she did not have to press against nothingness, but instead almost lifted, almost elevated, with each step she took.

On those dark days, everything would stretch out impossibly. She would pick up her toothbrush, and the puddle of whitish gel at the bottom of the cup would accuse her: you can't even keep this clean. She would step out the door, her fingers gripped a little too tightly on Malaya's, and her daughter would protest: "Ina, stop touching me!" She would make herself a cup of strong, sweet coffee and allow herself to sit in the thickly padded wrought iron chairs she had bought for the patio, and she would not be able to push the chair into any position at which the sun did not shine too brightly, or in which she was not looking at something left undone, or from which the pool did not beckon like a siren: come in, come here, give up, give in, sink, forget, sink. So she would not sit down but would go to her desk and finally call about the outside sprinkler that still did not have the correct water pressure, even though she had paid a garden service twice. And when she talked to the receptionist, her voice would quiver, and then she would bark angrily at the young man who was not sure which house she meant, and then she would hang up the phone and feel mortified at what they must be thinking, what they must be saying, about the crazy Pilipina with all the houses on Cabrillo Court.

And day after day, it would go on like this. After awhile, her mother would start making Malaya *suman* for breakfast, and she would hear Malaya say, "Lola, I don't want *tuyo* in my lunch," and she would hear the murmur of her mother's voice, *"Ang pagkain na ito ay mabuti."* Then Malaya would call, "Mommy, get out of bed!" But Honorata would not. She would lie there, tight like a stick, and she would hear the door open and close, and then awhile later, hear her mother return, and Honorata would not answer when her mother called to her. Only when the house was completely quiet — when she had counted dully to a thousand and then two hundred more — would she get up and dress and follow the to-do list she had made for herself the night before, exactly.

And then one day she would get out of bed when Malaya called to her, and she would thank her mother for helping, and she would make a peanut butter and jelly sandwich for Malaya's lunch, with an apple and two pieces of candy. And when they walked out the door to the bus, her fingers would rest lightly in her daughter's hand, and Malaya would tell her about the boy at school who could do a backflip, and about the teacher who had been to Rome and seen the Vatican, and about how she might grow up and sing onstage like Madonna. "Isn't Madonna a pretty name? And her dresses are beautiful, Ina."

And that night after dinner, when Malaya would wrap one of Nanay's scarves around her middle like a sari and totter into the kitchen in Honorata's heels, singing, *"Nothing like a good spanky"* — and Nanay, her English suddenly much better than it had ever been in the supermarket, would ask, "What? What is she saying?" — that night, Honorata would laugh. She would laugh until the tears leaked down her cheeks, and Malaya, delighted that she could make her mother laugh, would sing louder and louder, *"I just wanna hanky panky!"* And Nanay would look more and more dismayed, and Honorata would think that probably she should not be laughing, and that this might be one of Malaya's bad choices, but she would not be able to help herself. The laugh would boil up from somewhere far below reason, and it would bellow out of her, unstoppable and cleansing and bringing with it a joy she had so recently believed she would never feel again.

And what was this? How was it that she could not predict these feelings? Or direct them? And what did it matter, if right this minute she could feel this elation, she could look at her perfect, improbable, irrepressible child, and know suddenly that if she had not been so irrepressible, she would not have existed at all? It was all part and parcel of one thing: the fear and the horror inextricable from the beauty and the joy, at least for her, at least for this family. And really, if she had been given the choice — the whole choice, the good and the bad, the pain and the glory — she would have taken it. She would have said yes. Who knows, maybe she *had* been given that choice; maybe there was a reality in which she had chosen this life, somehow, someway, in that realm in which the truth was grander than anything one could know with the mind, but which did not, for Honorata, have anything to do with religion or a church or the way in which people spoke of these things.

■ ■ ■ ■

Engracia:
The One Whose
Heart Was Broken

■ ■ ■ ■

May 8, 2010
In the Midnight Cafe

There was a bill on the floor of the almost empty Midnight Cafe. Arturo could see it through the bars of his cashier cage, and since it was slow, he watched it flutter in the slight breeze from the air-conditioning, and wondered who would find it. His guess was that whoever picked it up would immediately put it into a slot machine, probably Megabucks, since there was one nearby. To a gambler, found money was lucky money.

It was one of the maids. She looked tired, coming off the night shift. She had stopped to get a fifty-cent cup of coffee, and the old man watched as she lifted her eyes from the Styrofoam cup, spotted the fluttering bill, and then leaned over to pick it up. It was more than a dollar; he could see it in the way she straightened. But she didn't play the money.

She tucked it into a pocket of her pale-blue dress.

She leaned against a pony wall that separated casino cardholders from the regular line when the cafe was busy, which wasn't often anymore, and finished her coffee. Then she shifted her purse, large and cracked, with an oddly bright buckle at the center, and dug around in it for her ID and an envelope. She approached the cashier cage.

"Cash check?"

"Small bills? ¿En billetes pequeños?"

"Sí."

"Una noche difícil, ¿eh?"

She looked startled that he had spoken about something other than her check. She must have worked alone all night. The hotel was even slower than the casino.

Her eyes caught his, but she did not speak.

She was young. She hadn't looked young, stooping for that bill, but she was. Arturo wished he could say something to her. He was an old man now, and he knew what it was like to work in a hotel, to work all night, to move from room to room with a heavy cart — and here was a room trashed by someone on a Vegas binge and there was a guest, weaving down the hall, drunk and unpredictable. And all night long, she would have worked silently; she would have observed and been mute.

Perhaps she had felt nervous, perhaps she had felt irritated, perhaps she had simply moved through it all, leaden, as she looked right now.

Why did his eyes water as he stamped her check and opened the till to count her cash? Getting old had made him foolish. She was lucky to have a job, and there was nothing wrong with working as a maid.

"Gracias," she said, taking the small stack of twenties.

"De nada, Engracia. Gástalo sabiamente."

Spend it wisely. Why did he say things like this?

"Voy a comprar un patín para mi hijo."

A skateboard. For her son. She was old enough to have a child with a skateboard.

"He'll be happy."

"Sí. Eso espero."

She had a wide face and when she smiled, her eyes narrowed into deep-set black ribbons. Arturo smiled back, pleased to think that she had a son, that she could buy him a gift, that the boy would be happy.

He had worked at the El Capitan for forty-three years. Had known Odell Dibb, and worked for June when she doubled the size of the place, and then for their son, Marshall. Now the Dibbs had all left, and the El Capitan should have been gone too. Marshall had sold to a Chinese investor who immediately announced that the casino would be torn down. But the economy fell apart, and everything in Vegas just stopped: overnight it seemed. There was a huge empty lot down the street where the Stardust had been imploded, but the El Capitan hadn't closed and hadn't disappeared; it just sat, and nobody, not even the rich people, had the money to get rid of it. Most of his carnales had gotten out while they could, but Arturo figured he'd just ride the ship down. There weren't any jobs anywhere, and who would want an old Mexican guy with bad lungs?

Of course, they all had bad lungs after a lifetime inside casinos. The word now was that it was best not to go to a doctor, not to do anything; the doctors wanted to operate, wanted to confirm cancer. But of course it was cancer. All that smoke, all those nights. Surgery just stirred things up, made you die quicker. Marge said that she'd had black spots on her lungs for nine years, and she would not let a doctor touch them. Just leave those spots sit, and if you were lucky, your own tissue would encase them — that was Marge's idea. She was a tough old broad, and she'd been right about a lot of things. She could be right about the lungs too.

Arturo didn't know. He didn't like doctors

much, and he didn't know anything about his lungs. The world was for young people, like this maid, anyway.

25

Engracia struggled to unhook the head of the vacuum cleaner from its notch on the canister. Cleaning Ms. Navarro's house was different from cleaning a hotel room, and she got tired of doing everything a different way in each house. It was strange how trivial things could bother her, when, in fact, she cared nothing at all about what she was doing, or how her day went, or whether something got done. Even now, if the plastic bit of this vacuum snapped off, she would feel bad to have done it.

Sweating, struggling to wrench the pieces apart without making a sound that might draw Ms. Navarro near, she cracked her elbow against the washing machine.

"Mierda."

Ms. Navarro appeared in the door.

"Do you need help?"

"No. I'm fine. I — I fix it."

Ms. Navarro had followed her around the

first two times she had come. She wasn't used to having a maid, and had given Engracia the job only because one of the priests had asked her to do it. This made Engracia nervous. She wondered what she sounded like to Honorata. An idiot, probably. Her English was fine but not when she was rattled. Diego had chattered away in English, and she had understood perfectly. She hadn't even told him to speak in Spanish, as most of the other mothers did, because it pleased her that he could speak so well.

Diego.

"I'm making something for Malaya. She'll be home in a while. Can I fix you a plate?"

"No. Thank you. I'm not hungry."

Ms. Navarro's daughter had purple and green stripes in her hair and a tattoo that looked like a serpent winding up her neck from somewhere inside her shirt. Engracia rarely saw her but found her a bit alarming. She could not imagine letting one's child look like that.

"I make the beds now."

"Don't worry about my mother's room. She's staying with a friend who had surgery this week."

Engracia nodded and started up the stairs with two sets of sheets, thinking that she could be done with Malaya's room before she got home. Sometimes the girl would skip school, and when she did, she would stay in bed until well past noon. Her room got the morning sun, and Engracia was amazed that she could stay asleep, swaddled in blankets, with the sun beating in and the second floor so warm that Engracia would feel slightly nauseous as she scrubbed out the shower.

Someday she would return to the El Capitan to work. They had told her she could have her job back any time she wanted, at least if the El Capitan was still open. Engracia was thinking about it. She didn't like working in homes, and while she appreciated that the padre had gotten her these jobs — that he understood she needed something to do every day — eventually she would go back to the El Capitan. It was just hard going back, as if her life were still the same.

Malaya's room had a deep-orange wall and a poster of Manny Pacquiao on it. Diego had been wild for boxing too; it was something he shared with his dad. Juan was in Las Vegas twenty years ago when Chavez fought Taylor — it was the first time he had crossed the border — and he and Diego had spent hours watching old fights on YouTube

and hashing out why Chavez was the great-
est Mexican fighter of all time.

This is how it was for Engracia, day after
day, alone with these memories, these
thoughts. She supposed it would be like this
until she died — until finally she died —
because she agreed with the padre: she did
not have the choice about how long she
lived.

Engracia snapped Malaya's sheet expertly
under the mattress. She tugged the com-
forter up straight, and placed the girl's collection of pillows and teddy bears back on
the bed. The room was a sort of archeology
of girlhood: a row of puppets on one bookshelf, a doll-sized American Girl dresser and
bed in the corner, a pile of CDs with titles
scribbled in blue and green marker: *Aimee's
Mix, Road Trip 1987, Don't Listen to This
Sober.* There were photos of little girls on
soccer teams and at Fern Adair dance recitals; there was a dried-up corsage, a Home-
coming Court banner, a collection of flip-
flops, tangled necklaces hanging from a
metal stand, and a leopard-print padded bra
on top of the bureau.

Engracia flicked a feather duster across
these surfaces. She thought about Diego's
room, for the short time they had lived in
Las Vegas together. It was a closet, really,

but there was a small window and room for his bed. Apart from that, there had been almost nothing in it: just an old jacket of Juan's spread on a stool and a small pile of books from the school book fair.

When Juan was detained, Engracia knew she would have to leave Pomona. She told Diego that it would be better if they were far away; that her papers might also be inspected, that they would have to lay low for a while. Her friend Pilar had suggested Las Vegas. It was cheaper than California, especially now, because the economy was so bad. And there were still jobs in the casinos, if you knew someone, and Pilar did: Engracia could work as a maid in one of the old hotels. Engracia didn't want to move because Diego was happy with his friends, and this was the only world he'd ever known.

But she couldn't reach Juan. The only reason she knew he was still in jail, just sitting there, was because Ramón had told her. Ramón knew things, knew people everywhere. Engracia had asked him when Juan would be back, but Ramón had not replied. He had shaken his head, said times were tough, and that Juan had been caught already twice before. Engracia did not tell Diego that Juan was still in jail, that he was waiting to be deported, or that she was running out of money and could not afford their apartment.

That night, Engracia tossed and turned, and then finally threw up in the toilet. This was why Pilar had talked about Las Vegas. She had known that Engracia would be on her own, would need someplace easier than Pomona — cheaper, with steadier work. Engracia resisted, but only for a few days. This was not the hardest thing she had done. It was easy to do hard things for her son.

She had crossed the border when she was sixteen, with a friend of a friend of Juan's. Engracia had found out she was pregnant, and she had known she didn't have much time. If she was ever going to leave, going to follow Juan, she would have to do it now, before the baby was born. And so she had. She had done this enormous thing on her own, without telling her mama or her papa, without kissing her little brothers good-bye. She'd given birth in a hospital filled with women like herself, and the nurse had not concealed the anger she felt at what Engracia was doing, and Engracia had had to force herself not to care about the nurse, not to need her, as her body twisted and gripped. In her mind, she thought that this pain could not be right, could not be normal, but of course it was normal, and she gave birth to a perfect Diego, who waited to cry until the doctor rubbed his feet, and then stopped crying the moment that Engracia took him in her arms.

Afterward, Engracia asked for a piece of paper and a pen. She wanted to write it all down, everything that had happened, so that she could send it to her mother. This is how tired she was: she knew her mother didn't have a phone, but somehow forgot that she didn't know how to read. Engracia could not send the letter. If she sent a letter, someone would have to read it to Mama. Her brothers were still too young yet, so it would be someone from the village. It would embarrass her mother to hear someone read aloud Engracia's words: about what it had been like to give birth to Diego.

Juan had not been there. He was working, moving farther and farther north, but he had made it back in time to take her and their son out of the hospital, to bring them, carefully and solemnly, to the little apartment in Pomona. She had been so proud of Juan, who had gotten them a place to live, just one big room, but all theirs. They had not shared it with another family. And this is where they had lived for nine years. She and Juan and Diego. By the time that Engracia left, the apartment was unrecognizable from the room they had first taken. Juan had painted the walls yellow, and Engracia had made everything herself: the curtains and the bedding and the flowered cover on the couch where Diego had slept with his thumb in his mouth, and the sound of his suck, suck, suck like an ocean lapping.

They had been happy. She had known Juan since before her *quinceañera* — they had met at the parade for Nuestra Señora de Guadalupe — and as soon as she turned fifteen, he had made the long walk from Jerez to her village to find her. Juan was older, and he had already been to the United States, already worked a few seasons in a raisin plant. He was full of ideas for what they could do, for how they would live, for the lives their children would have. In the meantime, they could send money back to her family.

And this was what they had done.

Engracia was proud to help her parents, proud that her brothers could go to school, proud that her papa, who had hated working in the States, could stay and grow peppers on the land on which he had always lived. These were not hardships: she and Juan enjoyed the life they had made. They liked being in a city — in an American city.

They liked taking Diego to the park, and watching people on the streets, and buying ice cream on Fridays when they got paid. Diego was a funny little boy, and he made them laugh. They would play on the floor with him for hours. Juan used to invent silly songs, and Engracia was not too shy to dance in the park, or to run wildly down the beach with her arms above her head on the days when they took the bus to the ocean.

There were all those good years to shore her up, and if she had been capable of crossing a border and having a child and making a home when she was sixteen, then she could certainly find a way for her and Diego to live until Juan got out of jail. This was not even hard, it was just life. She still had the rent in the box they kept hidden. Engracia had ignored the landlord pounding on the door, ripped the sheet of paper from the door without reading it. She would have to go quickly, and she was sorry that there would be no time to let Diego get used to it. She picked him up at school on Friday, after getting his records from the office, and told him they would be moving to Las Vegas on Sunday. Even though Diego was already nine, he cried, and begged to stay a little longer. But because he would be afraid if he knew how little money they had, she did not explain why she refused.

Her son was subdued on the ride up I-15. They stopped at McDonald's, and she bought him everything he liked: the double cheeseburger with bacon and a Dr Pepper and a hot fudge sundae. They sang *"Hay un hoyo en el fondo de la mar"* for miles, and she made sure Diego beat her each time. For a while, it was fun, but as they got farther from Pomona, after they crossed the Cajon Pass and drifted down and past Victorville, even Engracia felt daunted. She pointed out the giant thermometer in Baker, which didn't seem to be working, and Diego looked out the window, at the desert stretched brown and barren and relentless as far as the eye could see. Cars were strung along the freeway like seeds on the backside of a fern, and the sun beat down even though it was January. They finally saw what they thought was Las Vegas in the distance, but it was merely a collection of overeager casinos at the state line, with a huge roller coaster in the parking lot, and just after that, a low concrete building, ringed with barbed wire, in the middle of nowhere.

The drive was sad, and the move was harder.

Diego was not happy in their new home,

and he did not like his new school. Pilar's friend had gotten Engracia a job at a casino called the El Capitan, and she had told her about the apartments near Maryland Parkway, where everyone spoke Spanish and she would not need a deposit. But the neighborhood was rough, much rougher than where they had lived in Pomona. All night long, Engracia heard loud talk and fighting, sudden shouts, and the undulating whine of police sirens. She did not let Diego outside after dark, and she worried about the kids he walked home from school with, even while she was grateful that another mother had invited Diego to have breakfast at her house when he woke up alone, hours after Engracia had left for work.

Engracia did not think the school was so bad. She had gone to a meeting for Hispanic parents, where a man in a suit and tie talked with them about college. His Spanish was very good, and he told them there was a lot of money for Hispanic children who wanted to go to college. They could go to the best schools in the United States. And then a woman, a *mexicana,* spoke. She explained that the children who got this money had to go to school every day, had to take AP classes when they got to high school, had to join the debate team or the math club, and stay after school when they could be home taking care of younger children. Engracia heard one father say that he did not want his child to leave home, and he did not understand a college that preferred math club to a child who helped his family, but Engracia did not feel this way. This is what she wanted for Diego. This is why she had left her family, so that Diego could live differently.

It had been Juan who had first felt this way about America, who had given her these ideas about their children. But when he finally called, the day he arrived back in Jerez, he said that maybe they should all go back to Mexico. Life was so much easier there; one didn't need very much money to live in the village. Engracia was shocked. They had never considered returning to Zacatecas.

After the meeting, she wandered the school, looking at the walls filled with children's art: watercolor paintings and origami sculptures and brightly colored maps that showed small children in different cities around the world. Peering in the windows of a classroom, Engracia saw a row of computers and three bookshelves stacked with books — even though the school had its own library where the meeting had just been held — and plastic cups filled with markers and paintbrushes and rulers.

Engracia had gone to school. It was a long walk, very hot, to the next village, and the school had been just two rooms: one for the younger children and the other for the older ones. There was a little building in the back, with three pit toilets, and in between there was a dusty field where the children played at recess. The teacher, Senorita Consuela, was from Mexico City. She had been to the national museum filled with stone figures too heavy for fifty men to lift and also to the house painted blue where the artists had lived. Engracia had liked school.

Weeks went by, and still Diego did not thrive. He gained weight. He pretended to be sick in the mornings. He would call her at work and beg not to go to school, saying his stomach hurt, he had a fever, he could not get out of bed. And she would make him go to school, not listen to his pleas, and wonder at how long that would last. How long would he relent and do as she asked, and when would he figure out that there was nothing she could do if he did not go?

One night at dinner, Diego was animated. A scientist had visited the fourth grade. He had dipped a rose in nitrogen and made it freeze. He had showed slides of Death Valley and told about the Indians who had lived there, and the giant boulders that rolled mysteriously, leaving tracks in the dry earth, even though no one ever saw them move and they were too big for any living thing to push.

"Can we go see them, Mama?"

"The boulders?"

"Yes. They're sailing stones. And where the Indians lived. And the castle."

"Maybe, *papí*. Maybe in the summer, if you get good grades."

"Could Papa come?"

"I don't know."

She regretted telling him that they might go to Death Valley. She was afraid of this place. She didn't want to go there without Juan. "Do you still like to skateboard? Maybe we can get a skateboard for summer."

Diego's face dimmed.

"*Sí,* Mama," he said slowly.

At this thought, Engracia dropped Ms. Navarro's laundry basket to the floor.

The clothes at the top rolled onto the floor, and she heard Ms. Navarro walk to the bottom of the stairs to see if something had happened. Engracia did not call down to her. A tight band stretched across the bottom of her rib cage, and squeezed. She doubled over, trying to breathe. Padre Burns had said that it was good to remember, that she had to let her feelings out, but she couldn't bear to remember; it took her breath away. But then, what difference did it make if she could breathe? And as soon as that thought came, her body relaxed, the cinch around her middle eased, and air filled her lungs.

She picked up the clothes that had fallen, and the basket, and started down the stairs carefully. Ms. Navarro wasn't standing there anymore — Engracia could hear her in the kitchen — so when the bell rang, she set the basket carefully on the bottom step and hurried to open the door.

The man was large, and older. His face was quite red, as if it were always that color, and at first, he seemed nervous.

"I'm looking for Honorata Navarro. Is she here?"

Engracia hesitated. Perhaps she shouldn't have opened the door. She struggled to find the right words.

"Just a minute."

She started to close the door to look for Ms. Navarro, but he put his foot in the jamb and then said calmly, "I'd like to speak with her if I could."

Engracia looked from his foot to the door to the empty hallway behind her. "Ms. Navarro!" she called.

As soon as she spoke, the man entered the doorway. He didn't move farther into the house, but stood on the entryway floor, waiting.

Engracia's heart beat faster. Why had she answered the door?

"She's not here," Engracia tried. "I'm sorry, she's not home right now."

"I'll wait."

"No. You can't stay here. You have to leave."

Her voice was weak, but at least she was finding the words she wanted.

Just then, Ms. Navarro rounded the corner. Engracia was looking at her, past the man, and the shock on her face, it actually went white, made it clear that she should not have opened the door.

"I'm sorry. I try to tell him to leave . . ."

"Rita," said the man.

"Honorata," said the trembling Ms. Navarro.

26

Life perfects us, if we let it.

I have reached a moment in which I might be almost pure. I don't wish for things. I think I finally see life: how nature is, what it means to live and die, how there is nothing at all, nothing, except in what one might do for someone else.

I've reached this place at a time when I am something like an old dog. My fur is pocked with bald spots, my skin spotted with twisty disturbing growths, my teeth smell of rot; there is always a whiff of urine or feces about me. In short, I live to do something for others, and the people around me are busy steeling themselves, summoning the courage, to do for me. Marshall tries so hard to be loving, and I know the effort it costs him, now that I am slow and dribbly and unreliable and more or less mute. It's ironic, of course. A divine sort of joke. Almost, but not quite, I even see the reason why it should be so.

"I thought you ought to know my heart's on fire."

"Singing again? You sound happy."

"The flame it just leaps higher."

"Oh, June, you're wet. You know where the bathroom is. Why'd you do that?"

"I've got my love to keep me warm."

"You have to try to keep up. It's not nice."

Helen is a lovely person, very competent. Del would have hired her in an instant. She's not as much fun as Jessy, though. Jessy will put on a record and dance with me, or bring me a bit of the dessert she made the night before. When we walk, she doesn't seem to care that I am slow, and she brings along a little vase, with water, and collects a nosegay as we go. I can't tell you how this pleases me. (Actually, I really *can't* tell you. Isn't that funny?) I sing and sing as we walk along, I can't stop myself; it makes me so happy when she finds a flower, especially if I have spotted it first and am hoping she will see it.

"Today's physical therapy. Matt will be here in ten minutes, and now you have to change your clothes. Come on."

"I can't give you anything but love, baby."

"All right. I'll just bring your clothes in here. And then you change, okay? You have to hurry, June."

"Scheme awhile, dream awhile."

I'm not trying to frustrate Helen, though she thinks I am. If I wanted to make her mad, I couldn't. I can't seem to make things work the way I intend. Words are the worst, and eating is hard, but even getting dressed. I'm thinking about putting my pants on. Fifteen minutes ago, I was thinking about getting up and going to the bathroom. There's nothing wrong with my legs. I'm slow, but I can get up, I can move. It's just that if I try to do one thing, something else happens. And then when I feel something about that, a different feeling comes out.

It's caused a lot of misunderstandings.

Marshall comes to dinner when he is in town, and begs me to eat. He cuts my food smaller, and talks about how tasty it is, how it came from this restaurant or that chef, what the ingredients are, and I sit and look at him with a silly grin on my face, but my hand doesn't go to the fork, my mouth doesn't open. When he tries to feed me, I tighten my lips and shake my chin, and the food falls on to my lap.

"Mom," he says. "Please try. Just eat one bite."

And I remember saying the same words to him when he was too small to talk, and I wonder if he was thinking something other than what I thought he was. Probably he just wanted to play, probably peas tasted bitter to him, but now I see everything differently. I see all the moments of my life differently now that I am actually trying to open my mouth, trying to neatly take the food my son offers, trying not to make him feel mocked by my mysterious grin. And purse go my lips, and shake goes my chin, and twinkle go my eyes, as if I have annoyed him for fun.

"That's good," says Helen. "Thank you for getting dressed. And you wrapped up your wet clothes. I'll take them."

That's how it works. If my mind is distracted, if I'm thinking about Marshall, then I am also putting on clean pants and neatly wrapping up the dirty ones. Only I didn't know I was doing it. I'm more surprised than Helen to see that I'm ready for Matt.

"Howdy, Mrs. Dibb. How are you today?"

Matt always says howdy, but he doesn't look like a cowboy. More like a dancer. I smile at him, and apparently I really do, because he smiles back.

"Ready to work hard?"

"Nine little miles from ten-ten-Tennessee."

"Okay, sounds like a yes."

It is a yes! I feel good today. Matt asks me to stay standing, so my knees buckle and he catches me under the elbow so that I don't fall. I want to laugh about this with him, but of course I can't, so I try to get my mind to rest. My trick is that I think about nothing, that I pretend there is nothing around me, there is nothing for me to do, and then, sometimes, my body will be a little less of a rebel.

"Matt," I say. "Nice day."

"It *is* a nice day. That's really good, June. Thank you."

My eyes water, I am so pleased with myself.

He keeps me firmly by my elbow, and without telling me what to do, he walks me slowly down the hall and toward the back door. I like to have my exercises outside, even if it's hot. I've always loved the sun. Just before we walk outside, my legs lock. I push back against him, as if I don't want to go.

"She's in a mood today, Matt. I think she wants to stay inside."

Matt doesn't listen to Helen. He hums a little tune, something I don't recognize, but I try to get it. What is he humming? And just like that, we are out the door and in the sun. I love Matt.

■ ■ ■ ■

"That's probably enough for today. Are you tired?"

I'm not tired. I want to keep going. I don't want to go in the house. I don't want to watch television. I don't want to take a rest. But Matt is already leading me back to the door. I, of course, am walking along as fast as I have all year.

"So here I am, very glad to be unhappy."

When I sing, the words I want come out. Sometimes, anyway. I don't know how it works. I can sing the lyrics to songs I don't even remember knowing. I never know what I will sing until I hear my own voice. But a lot of times, the lyrics make sense. Isn't that crazy? Believe me, it makes me a lot crazier than anyone else. One thing I can't control, though, is how I sing them, so right now I sound as cheery as a little bird. But I don't want to go inside.

Matt grins. *"Do you still believe the rumor that romance is simply grand,"* he sings. Matt sings in a trio at the Venetian. He'd like to be a musician full-time, but it hasn't worked out yet. Isn't that amazing? That I would get a physical therapist who sings? It's not, really. It's how the world works. If we could just see it.

"Since you took it right on the chin, you have lost that bright toothpaste grin," I sing back. I know I'm smiling now.

"I did it my . . . way!" Matt belts out.

And I laugh.

Which is exactly what I wanted to do, and sometimes happens, especially with Matt. He leads me inside, so our session is done, but I am happy. I look at the ground and think as little as I can, so that I feel this.

"You tired her out." Helen comes over and touches her palm to my cheek. She does things like that when someone else is around.

"Maybe. She's pretty tough. Right, June?"

I shimmy with my shoulders and wink. I can just imagine what that looks like, now that I'm eighty-two.

"There's the spirit!"

"Okay, Miss June. I think you're ready for a little rest now."

I wish I could give Matt a hug, but my head flops forward and shakes a bit, I don't know why, and he puts his hand on my chin and says he will see me on Thursday. And then, like he does every time he leaves, he sings:

"S'wonderful, s'marvelous, that I should care for you."

And my head flops further forward. I can't even see him leave, which is for the best, because I am crying.

Marshall will be fifty-four on his next birthday. That's how old Del was when he died. He thinks of it, I'm sure. Partly, he's just a bit of a hypochondriac. Goes to Scripps for daylong medical testing and all that fuss. Marshall knows more about his hormone levels and genetic profile than I know about my own hair.

Not that anyone wouldn't wonder.

His dad drops dead without a hint, and his mom ends up a raving idiot. Singing Christmas carols at a Jewish wedding and asking the cute young man at the table on the other side of the restaurant for a dance. He thinks these things mean something — that they express deep down desires I no longer have the ability to repress — but if they mean something, I sure as hell don't know what. They feel as random to me as they do to anyone else. I try to laugh. I mean, I *would* laugh if I could do what I intend. I think I must have had something to learn about humility, and now I am learning it.

Of course, Marshall's hoping to avoid ending up like Del or me. I hope he doesn't end up like this too. But the game's rigged:

there's no way to win this one. It's possible to play in an entirely different way if you really see that. That's what I wish I could say. That's what I wish I knew how to share. This is a game you can't win, so don't play to win. Play to play. Play to keep everyone else in play. That's the long game here. That's what I want to tell him.

Marshall moved to Santa Monica after he sold the El Capitan. He and Janie bought a condo years ago, and the kids spent all their vacations there, so it made sense to make a permanent move. When he visits, he asks me if I'm ready to come to California. He says there are some nice assisted living programs, or I could live in the old condo, with caregivers, just as I live now. He seems to think that I'll go downhill if he moves me out of this house — this house and all its memories.

I don't know.

I don't feel like the house is me at all. I wouldn't mind going to California and seeing the kids once in a while. But I don't have a way to tell Marshall what I want, and I don't try. I don't empty my mind or start singing or make any effort to communicate what I think at all. This way, Marshall will choose what he wants. He'll leave me here if he doesn't really want me that close, or he'll take me there, and I'll live in the condo or in assisted living, and it will be what he wants.

But I do like seeing him. I love the kids.

I know that it's not fun for them to see me. I don't think there's much in the experience for them. So I don't want to want it. But I do.

I have hours, days, months to think about things.

I think just fine.

I think about my childhood. I think about my *bubbe,* and how she talked to me in Yiddish, and how I must have understood when I was small, even though I didn't later. I think about the cabin at Kittatinny Lake that we shared with our neighbors two weeks every summer, and how it felt to have my back hot with the sun and then how cold the water was. I think about my neighbor's dog Pal, who would come to the lake with us and then go with me as I rambled farther than anyone else in the woods. Momma would say that it wasn't safe, but Poppa would say, "She's okay. She has the dog."

There were ponds all over that country, and Pal and I would find one, and then I would throw sticks, and he would chase them, over and over. I can almost feel those summer mornings, the smell of the water and the trees, the quack of northern shovelers in the reeds, the heft of a good solid stick in my hand. There was one pond Pal didn't want to go in. He went in once or twice, then whined and barked and wagged his back end trying to get me to follow him away. "Come on, Pal!" I said, "Fetch!" And I hurled the stick as hard as I could, and Pal wiggled and waited and plunged in and jumped back out without fetching, and just as he barked again, loud, there was a huge sucking sound, and the water spun, and Pal barked madly while I watched, frozen, as a whirlpool formed right in the center of the pond. And like that, with one huge roar, all the water disappeared down into it.

They were old mines, those ponds, and if Pal had been in the water, he would have gone down that whirlpool with it. I ran all the way back to the cabin, yelling about what I had seen, and after I had finally gotten out my story, so that everyone could understand me, Momma started to cry. She kept saying, "Thank goodness you didn't go in! For once, June, you thought before you acted." She said it over and over, kissing me and crying, and Lew, who was my neighbor and in fourth grade with me, hugged Pal and said he was a hero, and looked at me and said, "Why did you take him? He's our dog. He could have been killed." And even now, more than seven decades later, I hear Lew saying this, and I hear the cracked fear in my mother's voice, and I remember how it felt to see that water begin to turn and to hear the sound it made, and the way the pond disappeared.

I think about other things too.

I think about how my son called himself "Hammerin' Marshall" after he hit a home run to win the opening game in Jaycee Park when he was thirteen years old. I swear he actually grew taller thinking about that hit, and a few years later, I remember the suddenly deep sound of his voice when he asked his dad whether he was also worried about Hammerin' Hank Aaron, whether Del thought maybe something was going to happen to Hank that winter, when he was one long ball shy of Babe Ruth's home run record. I couldn't even look at Del when he answered Marshall, couldn't bear all the memories our son's enthusiasm brought up. There were so many people who didn't want a black man to surpass Babe Ruth — he got death threats — and so many people who did. Hank Aaron had grown up in Mobile, and, of course, every time that fact was mentioned on the nightly news, I thought of Eddie.

I think about the first years running El Capitan. I think about Del. I think about Cora. I think about my mother and my father. How someone once vivid, vibrant, present in this world, can suddenly and absolutely be absent from it. Sometimes I think the joke is about to be revealed, that Del or my father will suddenly come around the corner, and how we will laugh and cheer and feel as if we will explode with joy in discovering that of course the impossible *was* impossible: that the people we loved have not disappeared completely and forever, lasting only in my memory, which is nearer and nearer to not lasting at all.

What if we could just see each other now and then? A quick hug, one dinner, a sunny day? What about that? It would be enough, wouldn't it? If we all got to shimmer in, here and there, and feel the cold rush of sea wave against bare ankle, the whisper-soft skin of our grandmothers, hear the low rumble of my poppa reading a bedtime story, or an eight-year-old Marshall singing "Zip-a-Dee-Doo-Dah" under a tree? It doesn't seem too much to ask of a universe so vast, that the absolute be a little less absolute, a little more bearable, a little more as it really feels: that the people I love are still present, are still real, are still near me.

■ ■ ■ ■

"It's time for dinner. I've cooked a piece of salmon." I'd forgotten Helen.

We'll have dinner, and then she'll go home. Jessy will be here tomorrow. There's no one with me at night. Everyone worries about this except me. I might fall, I might do something I don't mean to do, it isn't perfectly safe. But I hope Marshall doesn't hire someone to be with me at night. I'll miss that little bit of privacy, even if I mostly sleep through it.

"It's only a paper moon, sailing over a cardboard sea . . ."

"Take a bite now, while it's warm."

"But it wouldn't be make believe if you believed in me."

I pick up my fork and tap it on the table to the rhythm of the song. I am feeling good, and I mean to eat, but this is what the fork does.

27

Engracia should not have opened the door.

Ms. Navarro and the man stared at each other for a long moment. Then he said, "How could you? How could you keep my daughter from me?" and his voice squeaked, as if he were a child, a tiny, high voice in a huge man's body. Ms. Navarro did not answer. She turned quickly, but before she could move, the man rushed forward and grabbed her; he held Ms. Navarro between his arms and refused to move.

"Call the police!" she said to Engracia.

Engracia stepped toward them, and the man wrapped his arm tighter around Honorata, lifting her tiny body a few inches off the ground. "Stop!" he barked. "Nobody is calling the police."

Engracia saw his great arm wrapped around Ms. Navarro's thin neck. It seemed that he could snap it as easily as she snapped a sheet onto a bed. She froze, unsure what to do, and then he gestured, using Ms. Navarro's body as a sort of pointer, and Engracia stumbled into the study next to the entrance, the only room downstairs with a door.

Behind her, the man half carried, half dragged Ms. Navarro into the study. Her face was curiously slack. She neither struggled nor screamed.

"I have a gun," he said. "I don't want to use it. I don't even want to get it out. But I will."

And he moved his jacket aside, so that Engracia could see it, resting there against his soft, heaving belly.

"I want to talk. I want to talk with Rita. And you'll have to stay here and listen."

Engracia nodded her head, her eyes glued to Ms. Navarro's face, which remained oddly calm, removed.

Then he turned back to Honorata. "I'm going to let you go. Don't scream. Don't run. We're going to talk."

Sweat poured down the man's neck and into his shirt collar. He was panting, looking around, trying to figure out what to do.

He released Ms. Navarro, and she stumbled to the nearest chair, sunk into it, looking like a child more than the intimidating woman she had seemed an hour earlier.

"My name's Jimbo," the man said to Engracia.

"Engracia."

"What? What's your name?"

"Engracia."

"Sit down there. Just be quiet. I don't want to hurt you. I'm not going to hurt anyone."

Engracia tried to take a breath, but her lungs were constricted; she could not seem to inhale. Which was strange, because she didn't care if she lived or died, and she had already had the thought that perhaps this strange man — this sweating fat man, too old to be breaking into someone's house, with his gun, and his belly, and the hair limp on his head — was the answer she had prayed for.

Still, the body resists destruction. She knew that.

Her heart pounded, and she tried again to breathe, but her chest did not fill. The room looked to her as if someone had blown red smoke into it.

"I don't know what you're talking about," Ms. Navarro said. "You're going to go to jail."

The man stared at her but said nothing. Engracia expected him to erupt, she expected to see fury in his eyes, but instead, she saw pain. He looked as if he might cry.

"You won't get away with this. I know you've been looking for me. I've been here all along, all these years. And you never found me? You can't even find someone easy to find."

The man looked confused. Ms. Navarro kept speaking.

"Why are you here now? Why did you come now? All these years. I thought you had stopped looking."

"I never looked for you."

And again, Engracia saw that he was not angry, that the violence with which he had grabbed Ms. Navarro, ushered them into this room, was somehow not there. The terror of those few seconds was still present, though. Even her skin was alive with it.

"You never looked?"

"I never looked."

"Why are you here now?"

And at this, the man let out something between a wail and a cry. And he threw his hands to his head, and his whole body shuddered. When he lifted his arms to his face, Engracia saw the gun again, a black handle, the glint of metal. The gun gleamed there, waiting. He spoke.

"How could you?"

"I don't know what you're talking about."

"Malaya. *Malaya.*"

The name came out the second time like a wail. Engracia could see that the man was losing control.

Ms. Navarro did not react to her daughter's name. But she spoke anyway.

"What are you talking about? What Malaya?"

Engracia watched silently, trying to understand the game these two were playing, remembering what the man had said already, that Ms. Navarro had kept his daughter from him.

The man grabbed Ms. Navarro's arm. His fat white fingers dug into her skin, and she called out, but he did not release her. He held her arm, and looked at her, staring into her eyes, and Ms. Navarro shook all over and turned her eyes away first.

Malaya was his child.

Engracia could see it.

She could see it in their eyes, in the way they interacted, in what was not said. Slowly, she reached into the deep side pocket of her pants, where her cell phone was. She'd had the phone for only a few months; she could still remember the salesman explaining how to call 911, that all she had to do was open the phone and hold down the 9 button, that a chip in the phone would bring help to her.

The salesman had showed her this feature, and Engracia had cried, tears dripping down her face, at how wrong he was, at how little he knew of what phones could or could not do in an emergency.

But this was different.

This was Las Vegas, and her cell phone would work. If she could find a way to press the 9 and hold it, someone would come.

Her fingers fumbled, searching, searching.

"What are you doing?"

His voice was loud and panicky. Sweat ran in rivulets down his face.

Engracia said nothing. No English words would come. She opened her mouth, and nothing, no sound at all, came out.

"Call the police, Engracia."

"Shut up!" Jimbo turned back to Engracia. "Don't call anyone. That better not be a phone in your pocket. No one is calling anyone."

Engracia placed her hands on her lap, still unable to think of a single word in English. Taco came to mind. Taco Bell, Taco Time. Nothing else.

"I never looked for you. I respected your wishes. I thought you were in Manila, or back home. I never looked for you. I never even came back to Vegas. I never tried another woman. I never tried again."

Ms. Navarro would not look at him. She stared stonily at the floor, ignoring his fingers still buried in her arm, her body trembling, trembling. Finally, he released her arm and stepped away.

What was she thinking? Why was this man here?

"You knew I wanted a family. A wife. A child. How could you hide her from me?"

Now Ms. Navarro's voice cracked out of her.

"I didn't hide her. She's not yours."

At this, he reared back, looking as if he might slap her. But he stopped, turning his head and gritting his teeth so that his jaw jutted out from the fat fold near his neck.

Engracia put her hand back in the deep pocket of her pants.

"Don't lie. Please don't lie."

"Don't lie? Why shouldn't I lie? Who are you to tell me anything? You barge in my house. You show me a gun. You throw me in this room. If I got up now, you would shoot me. You would shoot me! This is respect? This is respecting me?"

Her voice rose hysterically. She stood up, enraged. And the man did not move; he did not make her sit back down. He stood against the wall, several feet from her, and now his shoulders slumped.

Engracia slid the phone from her pocket, and slipped it quietly behind her in the chair.

"Rita."

"My name is Honorata."

"Honorata. How could you hate me this much? How could you have done this to me?"

"I do hate you. I hate you! I have always hated you. What do you mean, how could I hate you? I hate you, I hate you, I hate you!"

Ms. Navarro was screaming, her hands scrunched into fists, her small body leaping closer at him, like a mongoose at a cobra.

Engracia silently opened the lid of her phone and slid her fingers slowly across the face of the phone. She had to be sure of the button.

The man looked at Ms. Navarro, and tears welled in his eyes.

Engracia stopped what she was doing, just for a second, engrossed by what she was witnessing.

"All I wanted was a family."

"Well, you can't buy one. You can't buy a person."

"I didn't buy you."

"You thought you could buy me. You thought your money, your man, your white, these bought me. You took me from everything."

He looked at her, still crying, and reached out his hand, as if to touch her arm.

"Don't touch me!" she screamed. "Don't touch me! Don't be in my house. Get away from me! Get away from here!"

"No!" he said. "No. She's my daughter. She's my daughter too. I will not leave."

"How do you know of her?"

"How do I know that Malaya is my daughter? That you hid her from me? That it's you who had no respect for me?"

"This isn't true."

"Of course it's true."

Ms. Navarro glared at him.

"It was Malaya who found *me*."

Engracia heard the shuddery sound of Ms. Navarro breathing. Otherwise silence.

"I got an email from a teenage girl who said she'd found me on the Internet, and she was pretty sure I was her father."

Ms. Navarro sat motionless, only the unnatural stillness of her face, her body, belying the shock she felt.

"She sent me a photo."

"Malaya sent you a picture of herself?"

"A photo of you."

Ms. Navarro's jaw tightened. Engracia could feel her rage. So could the man.

"You write to me. You ask me to marry you. You live in my home." He was angry now. His voice was like a knife, and Engracia's body lurched; the desire to run was so great.

"And then you win money. And I beg you to stay. But you go. And I let you. I never look for you. I leave you alone."

The man stopped and looked down. His back shook. It was three times wider than Ms. Navarro.

"And all . . . this . . . time." He drew the words out slowly. "All this time, you have our daughter."

"She's not yours."

"She's mine."

"Malaya's a young girl. She gets big stories in her head. She even has tattoos. She's not easy. She thinks you're her father, I don't know how she found out about you, but you're not her father. If she had asked me, I would have told her."

Engracia thought Ms. Navarro was probably lying, but the man was apoplectic.

"Stop lying!"

"I'm not lying. You haven't even seen her. You see a photo. She looks half white. You think you're her dad. You're not the only white man in the world, you know."

"Stop lying. Please, Rita, stop lying."

"I'm not lying."

Engracia was amazed at her defiance. She had started to calm down. She could think more clearly. The man was angry, but he was not paying any attention to her. Engracia waited to push the button on her phone, thinking she might be able to leave the room; that she might get a chance to tell the operator what was happening. If the police barged in right now, anything could happen. The gun was right there. Engracia had already noticed Ms. Navarro looking at it. Ms. Navarro wanted the gun.

"Do you think I flew out here, barged into your home . . . with a *gun* . . . because a seventeen-year-old girl thinks I'm her father?"

Honorata did not reply.

"We got tests. Malaya and I. We did the tests. She's my daughter, and you've always known this."

The air came out of the room. Engracia pushed the button.

In one motion, Ms. Navarro turned, screamed, and lunged at Jimbo's gun. He was a big man, but quick, and he dodged her easily. He clamped his hand on the gun but did not take it out of his waistband. Ms. Navarro slipped, banging her shin on the table and cracking her side into the chair,

as she struggled not to fall. Engracia slid off
the chair and made a run for the door.

"Stop!"

She kept going.

"I'll shoot."

"Run, Engracia, run!"

She couldn't see him, didn't know if he
had the gun out. She had her phone; she
could hear something on the other end of
the line. English. She couldn't think of any
word in English. *Taco.* Did he have the gun
out? Was she going to die? "Gun. Man," she
said, and closed the phone. She wanted to
die, but she didn't want to be shot. She
stopped and turned. He did not have the
gun out.

"Why didn't you run? I told you to run!"
Ms. Navarro's face was red with anger.

Engracia looked at the big man. He
seemed stunned, just as she felt.

"Did you call someone?" he demanded.
"Is that your phone?"

Engracia did not answer. Honorata
shrieked, "You're going to die! You're going
to jail! We're all going to die! What about
Malaya then?"

The man turned pale, and Engracia wondered if he was well. Perhaps he would faint.
He would collapse right there. He looked
right at Engracia, right into her eyes, and

with his big, fat, fleshy hand, he motioned for her to return to the study. She couldn't think. Her mind was flooded with what was happening, with how she might have been shot, with how she might have made it out the door — would he have shot Ms. Navarro? — with how she still might be shot, with how she wouldn't have to live. Her heart was pounding, she couldn't think. He motioned again with his head, and Engracia walked back into the study.

As she did, a memory so vivid came over her that for a moment she forgot there was a man, there was Ms. Navarro, there was a gun. She was in a field with her mother, standing between two neat rows of beans. She had let go of her mother's skirt, and walked along picking bugs off the leaves and smashing them between her chubby fingers exactly as she had been taught. She was much slower than Mama, in the row just next to her, so when her mother reached the end, she doubled back and walked toward the child, picking off bugs as she went. Each time they met, her mother made the sign of the cross on her forehead and said *"Que Dios te bendiga."* Engracia heard her mother blessing her, as clearly as if she were in the room then. And so she knew she would die, because her mother had come to say this blessing again.

She looked around. The man still didn't have the gun out, but he told Honorata to sit down — that they were all going to sit down. Nobody seemed to know what to do, but Honorata sat, and the man did, and finally Engracia. The three of them looked at one another.

28

He said he had never looked for her. He thought she was in Manila or home in her village. Was that possible? That he'd never looked?

For years, Honorata had trembled anytime she was on the Strip. She had avoided the El Capitan and Caesars Palace. If the newspaper ran a story with a picture of either hotel, if there was mention of the woman who had helped her — June Dibb — she squinted her eyes and tried to make out everyone in the photo; every shadowy person in the background. Was Jimbo there? She didn't think there was any way the Dibbs could know she was in Las Vegas. The worst part of coming here, of leaving the sad apartment in Los Angeles, had been the risk that somehow Jimbo would find out.

So why had she done it? Why, in that first rush of courage that swept in with Malaya's birth, had she chosen the one place where

Jimbo might also be? She was never going to play Megabucks again. She wasn't interested in gambling. But all alone in that hospital, sending a message to her mother about her daughter's birth, it had seemed to her that Las Vegas was the only place where something good had happened. Even before she had won the money, everyone in Vegas had been kind, everyone in the El Capitan had looked at her as if she were a person. She understood that they cared about her because Jimbo gambled a lot of money, but she felt it had been more than this. They had looked at her, and they had been able to guess who she was — what was happening to her — but they had not disdained her. They were kind.

That's why she decided to move to Las Vegas.

She had never seen any of those people again. She had never once seen anyone she met in those strange days at the El Capitan. Jimbo had not found her — she had changed Malaya's name, just in case — even though she had always believed he would.

He said he had never come back to Vegas.

He had never been here.

That was why she had never seen him.

And now he was sitting in her house — bigger and older and redder — with a gun jammed in his waistband and a fold of fat flopping over it, smearing sweat on the metal, and she was afraid and she was repulsed, and it didn't seem possible that he was Malaya's father. Though of course he was.

An image of Malaya — slim and taut and golden — wearing nothing but a T-shirt and boy shorts formed in her mind. Those boy shorts had astonished Honorata. They'd bought them together, and Honorata had been relieved when Malaya had not even asked to buy the tiny, lacy bits of underwear displayed on the main tables. Instead, she wanted cotton underwear that looked quite modest to her mother, so they had bought them in several colors. But the next Saturday, Malaya had wandered downstairs from her room wearing nothing but those underwear and that cropped shirt, and the boy shorts had been anything but modest.

Malaya was a freshman that year, and Honorata wondered how she had known what those shorts would do for her slim little figure. She saw too, for the first time, the body Malaya would have, how pretty she would be, how that little bit of Jimbo would fill out the curves of her slight bone structure. It was simultaneously pleasing and terrifying. She loved her daughter. She loved her beauty. She was not ready to think of Malaya in this way.

Also, seeing Malaya in those boy shorts had brought back her own adolescence. The wild desire she had felt for Kidlat even before she hit puberty, long before she had the words for what she was feeling. How old had they been? Maybe eleven. Two lean, narrow bodies, hardly different from each other, though one was a girl and one was a boy, and even then, being around Kidlat had set her skin to tingling, her heart to skipping.

They had gotten older, and their bodies had become different, and everyone knew that Kidlat and Honorata were in love, in adolescent love. Holding Kidlat's hand would make her feel slightly lightheaded, and they would spend the times when they were alone together — which were not that easy to get, because everyone in each of their villages watched them — they would spend that precious time talking and laughing and gasping whenever a hand touched a thigh, or bare toes twisted together. And when they could, they would kiss — such innocent kisses, really — but they would nearly knock Honorata to the ground.

And this is how it had been until Honorata was seventeen, older than Malaya when she came down in the boy shorts, and then Kidlat had gone to Manila with his father, and when he came back four months later, he was not interested in Honorata. He said hello to her coolly and made no effort to talk with her directly, much less be alone with her. It was crushing. She wanted to die. She couldn't understand it, and finally, one day when they met accidentally, she blurted out, "Kidlat, what happened? Why don't you want me anymore?" And Kidlat looked embarrassed, just for a moment, and then he said that he was not a boy; that in Manila he had been with a woman, really been with her, and he wasn't interested in Honorata anymore. He was trying to find a way to move to Manila.

It was unimaginable, what Kidlat had said. He had been with a woman? Her Kidlat?

How could he have done this? It was horrible. It was a sin. It was disgusting to imagine. It could not be imagined. For weeks, she grieved, and she did not eat, and she avoided seeing Kidlat, and her nanay kept asking, "Honorata, what happened? Is it that boy? That Kidlat? Forget that boy."

She had not forgotten him.

When she saw him again, he was preparing for the Imbayah Festival, lying on his back and leg wrestling with a friend. There was a group of boys watching, and everyone was laughing. When Kidlat won three in a row, he jumped up, and the boys yelled, *"Imbayah! Imbayah!"* while he grinned and slapped his friend on the back, the other boy smiling even though he had lost. Kidlat spied her watching, and, giddy as he was with winning, he came over to her. Then he waved away the younger boys, and after a few moments, she and Kidlat walked down the road and toward the green fields alone.

Honorata shook away this memory.

How could she be thinking of Malaya's pubescent body, of her own first delirious forbidden ineffable experience of a man, there in the field with Kidlat, after months of not talking, not touching, months of imagining him with someone else, her heart so broken and then so full? Even now, it was a memory that could engulf her. And Malaya? Malaya in the boy shorts? That had been only the beginning. The boy shorts seemed innocent now, compared with the rainbow hair, the black clothes, the tattoos: all these ways that her daughter did not look exactly desirable — at least not to Honorata — but did look dangerous, the opposite of innocent.

Malaya's father knew none of this. He was not part of her life.

She would not let him see Malaya.

No matter how much Jimbo frightened her, no matter what he did, she would protect her daughter. She would die here in this room, she would die, but she would not let him see Malaya. She would not let this man, this man who had haunted her thoughts, this man whose badness must be why Malaya had the peculiar hair, the serpent tattoo; she would not let this man see her daughter.

She felt sorry for the maid. Why did she have to be here today? Why was the world like this, that today, of all days, the maid should be here when Jimbo finally found her?

29

Coral had not gone in to school. She'd caught something when they were in Japan and wanted to shake it before Koji and the boys got home on Friday. The time change would be hard for them, and they hadn't done the homework they'd brought along. Gus was already worried about whether his coach would ever let him play again. There wasn't anything to be done about it. Koji's brother was very ill, and they couldn't wait for summer to see him.

Coral and Koji hadn't been prepared for how hard Isa would take this news. Coral thought the fact that their uncle lived so far away would buffer the boys a bit; that Koji's brother being ill would not upset them too much. But Isa, the namesake, was upset. He said he didn't want to be the only Isamu Seiko in the family, which was a funny way to put it, and Coral had been careful not to smile. It moved her that her youngest child would feel so deeply for Koji's brother. They were good kids, these labrapuggles of hers, avid for baseball and video games, at ease talking hip-hop with their cousin Trey or politely raising their hands to ask a question in Japanese at the *gakuen* on Saturdays. Would they remember her mama? Augusta had loved them so much. Coral wanted them to remember her; she could barely stand that Augusta had not seen Gus puffing out his cheeks to blow on his trumpet or Isa playing with Althea's new puppy.

At five o'clock in the morning, Coral had turned off her alarm, called into the automatic message that notified the district to find a sub for her, and fallen into a thick, anxious sleep. By nine, her room was flooded with light and warm, even though they had replaced the air conditioner last month — one of many repairs — and while she knew she needed the sleep and would feel better for it, she did not feel better right then. She forced herself awake, and then wrenched free of the hot, wrinkled sheets. With her head clogged and heavy, she sucked in a deep gulp of air. A hot shower would help, but she didn't have the energy to take it. She'd make some coffee, lie on the couch, try to rest.

Coral turned off her phone, so that she

wouldn't start reading her email, and tossed it in a basket on the shelf. It took half an hour to make coffee and a piece of toast, distracted as she was by everything lying uncared for in the kitchen. They had left for Japan quickly, and when she got back, she had spent every minute at the school, trying to get things ready for last night's music program.

Her body ached, and she moved slowly. On an ordinary morning, Coral would make oatmeal for breakfast, pack three lunches, and start something for dinner, all before seven. She and Koji alternated kitchen duty: on his weeks, he packed the boys' lunches carefully the night before and picked up fresh food from the market for dinner.

Even thinking about a normal routine made her tired. She walked over to lie down on the couch and then drifted in and out of sleep all morning, her raspy cough jerking her awake now and then. Coral finally got up to take a shower around one, and felt better after. She rubbed her body with a silky lotion, something that usually took too much time, and slipped on her favorite cotton pants, a soft old T-shirt, and flip-flops. She looked around the living room. There was Trey's guitar, and Coral thought of him, on the night before they left for

Japan, showing Gus how to play a funk riff on an acoustic.

Gus and Isa loved having their cousin back in Las Vegas. It pleased Coral too. Her boys had so few links to her childhood, now that both Malcolm and Keisha had moved out of town, now that Alabaster and Serenity were not coming to visit Augusta. Of course, the Las Vegas her children lived in was almost nothing like the Las Vegas in which she had grown up. She and her siblings had lived in the middle of a desert — chasing lizards and making playhouses out of old sofas that washed in with the floods — but Gus and Isa lived in a metropolis. They did not walk onto barren earth and see a million mysterious stars above, they did not turn away from a glowing Strip to see a night as black as pitch. The sky her sons knew was never black: the glow of today's Strip could not be made to disappear with the mere turn of a shoulder.

Trey had lived with Coral and Koji nine years ago, when he was fifteen. It had been a difficult year. Her boys were one and two then, and she and Koji were juggling full-time jobs and diapers and two kids setting records for serial viruses — all without sleep, of course. Then there was Trey: a teenager with a big loop of silver chains, heavy jeans draped around his knees, furious at having been shipped off to his aunt's.

Ray Junior had called late one night, his voice thin and strained, and asked Coral if she would take Trey, right away, before it was too late. A boy had been murdered, shot dead by another student as he walked out of Trey's high school. Coral never learned whether Trey had any particular connection to the boy who was killed. It didn't matter. She and her brother both knew how fast it could all move, how families put it together afterward: who their son knew and what he was doing and how he had ended up at the wrong place at the wrong time. Then you had all the time in the world to figure it out, to see how useless it had been, how trivial — the small details that had cost your son his life.

Ray Junior had seen the signs. He called Coral, and then packed his son into the car and drove ten hours straight to Vegas. Coral would never forget the morning they arrived, and how, just for a moment, she'd panicked, wondering if she could do it. Koji had seen this on her face; he'd given her a wink, and then reached up to give his nephew — already a head taller than he was — a lopsided hug.

Now they could laugh about that year, and

look what it meant to her boys to have Trey. He took them to UNLV games at the Thomas & Mack, and showed up at their school events, tall and good-looking and hip. On Saturdays, he drove them to Japanese school and did the end-of-day jobs usually assigned to Coral: washing off the chalkboards and sweeping the floors and taking down the Las Vegas Gakuen poster that temporarily concealed the Clark High School sign in the gymnasium. When Isa introduced Trey to his Japanese teacher, he said he was his brother.

Coral smiled, thinking of this, and then looked around for her phone. What time was it? She'd spent the whole day on the couch. She walked to the study, looking for her phone, and was surprised to see a wash of red light reflected in the hall mirror. What was that? She looked out the window, to the street. A police car in the cul-de-sac. That was unusual. Coral turned away, not interested enough to look further. As she did, she saw the black and white of a second car, then, was that a van? A SWAT van? On Cabrillo Court? She peered out the living room window and was startled to count three black-and-whites, and what was indisputably an unmarked SWAT van. What was going on?

Coral opened the front door, moving slowly, waiting to hear if someone called for her to stop. She stood in the shadow of the entry, where it would not be easy to see her, but where she had a wider view of the street. Two of the cars had officers in them, and two more officers were standing at the mouth of the cul-de-sac, looking at a laptop. She couldn't see anyone in the van and stayed very still, looking.

Across the way, Mr. Eberle opened his door and stepped outside. The police officer in the car in front rolled down his window and motioned for him to return to his house. Her neighbor looked confused, and then stepped back in and shut his door. Coral didn't see him go to the front window, though she imagined he was there, crouched down or standing in a shadow, watching just as she was.

The street was oddly still. No motor started, no dog barked, no child rode a bike. There was an air of waiting, and Coral waited too. She couldn't tell which house might be the problem. A few minutes went by, and then a maroon car pulled slowly up next to the officers on the street. One of them nodded toward the driver of the car and looked back at his laptop. The car sat, silent, but nobody got out. After awhile, one of the cops approached it. Coral saw the window roll down, and the officer lean in slightly, then gesture up the street toward Honorata Navarro's house before walking back to her companion with the laptop.

The maroon car did not move.

What could be happening at Honorata's house? Was it something to do with Malaya? Honorata and her daughter were going through a difficult year, and although the boys still asked if Malaya could babysit, she was rarely available anymore — and sometimes Coral was relieved. She loved Malaya, but she was not an easy teenager, at least not now. Coral felt sorry for Honorata; she tried so hard. She owned four houses on the street: her own and three she rented out. And she was a good landlord; her renters almost never left, the yards were neat, the cars were kept in the garages. It was probably because of Honorata that Cabrillo Court looked mostly untouched by the housing crash. A block in either direction, and every street had houses standing empty, with yards turned to flash dry tinder, and bits of trash lodged in the brown branches of dead euonymus shrubs and spikey pyracantha.

Coral shifted position in the entry and peered up the cul-de-sac to her neighbor's house. It looked as silent and still as the rest of the street. A curved concrete bench stood in Honorata's front yard — an oddly welcoming detail for a woman who didn't make friends easily — and the only movement on the street was a mockingbird resting on the back of the bench, his tail upright, and his body weaving a bit as he looked to and fro.

Coral looked back at the police officers.

There was a third person now, perhaps the driver of the maroon car, and Coral studied him, thinking it might be her friend Tom. Tom Darling wouldn't be here unless something big was happening. He might come out if there was a negotiation. Was that what this was? The man turned, and it was Tom. Coral had met him in a Leadership Las Vegas class nearly a decade ago. They were paired for the shift in a patrol car, and Tom had needled the officer driving them. "Hey look at that lowrider. Think his plates are right?" And the officer had thought Tom was serious, but Coral knew that Tom was being ironic, messing with the patrol officer to see how he thought. Or maybe he was trying to make a connection with her, a black woman riding in a white cop's car. She hadn't really known, even then, why Tom had needled their driver or what he really thought. Who was he making fun of? Maybe himself.

Still, Coral liked Tom. What was he doing here?

Coral almost went back inside. She wanted to get her phone. Maybe there was something on the news. But she was looking at Tom, thinking about whether she might go tell him she was there, when she saw the flash of the school bus pulling away in the distance. She looked at her watch. Three thirty. Malaya would be coming home.

30

Ms. Navarro had stopped talking.

The man had told her about the paternity test, and at first, she kept protesting. She yelled out, "You don't know Malaya! She gets these cockeyed ideas. She's very wild. She's tricked you, gotten some blood. You don't know how wild she is."

And the man stood there. Listening. Not saying anything. Not moving.

It was obvious that Ms. Navarro was wrong. This man, this huge man with a gun and a ring larger than her wristwatch, was Malaya's father. And Ms. Navarro did not want him to know. Had somehow hidden the child from him.

Now here Engracia was, with memories of her own child filling every cell in her body, in this ridiculous moment, with a man who might kill her, who might kill Ms. Navarro, who might kill himself. Who really, after all, had some reason for what he was doing.

Because who would not hate the person who had stolen your child from you?

She thought of Juan, and of how Diego had missed him, and, for some reason, of a time when Juan was galloping around the little apartment with Diego on his shoulders, and somehow galloped too high and banged Diego's head on a low section of the ceiling. Diego started to cry, and Engracia was annoyed. Then she saw Juan's face, crumpled and aghast. Diego saw it too, and the boy stopped crying to lean over and kiss Juan's cheek, saying, "Papa, it's okay. It didn't hurt. Papa, it's okay."

"Rita," the man was saying, "My lawyer phoned you as soon as Malaya and I did the tests. He sent you a letter. It was certified mail. I know you got it."

"I threw it away."

"You threw away a certified letter? Without opening it?"

"It was from Chicago."

"Did you listen to his messages?"

"No," she shook her head. "But you *did* look for me. You said you didn't."

"Malaya gave me your address. I didn't look for you."

Honorata stared at him defiantly, but all he said was, "You hated me this much?"

"Yes."

413

His voice was very soft. "I didn't hate you. I missed you."

Ms. Navarro looked at him, and Engracia could see the tremor in her back and her shoulders.

"I never meant for you to feel like that about what happened," he went on. "I thought you wanted to come. I thought you chose me."

The pain that crossed Ms. Navarro's face was unguarded and intense. Engracia understood that she could not speak.

"I'm not what you think I am. But I know why you feel that way. I've had years to think about it. To think about what I did. To think about how you felt."

Engracia looked from one face to the other. What had happened between these two? She thought of Malaya — that odd girl with the striped hair and the tattoo. This man might be surprised by Malaya.

"It didn't matter what you wanted. It was what you did."

"I know. I know that, Rita."

"Honorata."

"*Honorata.* I know what I did. I've spent seventeen years thinking about it. About your uncle. About how angry I was. About how I didn't care what that meant for you."

"She's not your daughter."

414

"She is."

"No. No!"

Engracia watched Ms. Navarro fold over then, her face in her hands, and she saw the tears leak out from her fingers, and she saw the way the man watched those tears, watched Ms. Navarro. And the room was very quiet.

The telephone rang.

Engracia jumped.

"Don't answer it."

They had all been sitting, frozen in place, for a while. Ten minutes? Half an hour? It was impossible to tell. Engracia's mind wandered. She felt her mother near, though she knew her mother was in the village — she would be making tortillas, and talking with one of the other women while she waited for her sons to come home — and yet Engracia could feel her presence, as she had longed to feel her presence when Diego was hurt, as she had tried to feel it night after night in the months since. But her mother was here, somehow, now.

The phone stopped ringing. And then started again.

They all ignored it.

Engracia shifted her position, and the man said, "You have to stay here. We stay here until we figure this out."

Engracia settled back into her seat. Ms. Navarro did not move, the man did not move. It was not clear what would break the stillness.

"Honorata, I'm not here to hurt you. I tried every way I could to reach you."

"That's why you bring *a gun*? To my *home*?"

The screech in her voice startled all of them. A vein in Engracia's temple throbbed. She looked at the man.

"I shouldn't have brought the gun."

"Get rid of it! Get it out of here! I'm not talking to a man with a gun."

"Will you talk with me if I put it in my car?"

Ms. Navarro stopped speaking again.

The phone rang.

"Honorata, I don't want this gun. I shouldn't have brought it. I wasn't going to bring it in. But I — I don't know, I couldn't reach you. I've been sitting in that car, outside your door, all morning. I got — I got crazy. Sitting there. Thinking."

Ms. Navarro would not look at him. She had moved inside herself; Engracia could not guess what she was thinking or feeling anymore. Had anyone heard her say "Gun. Man"? Was there anyone who had an idea something was happening here?

Engracia was not afraid — or not completely afraid. Her body still shook; she feared the rip of the bullet. She feared how death would happen. She waited for Honorata to grab the gun. She waited for the struggle, the sound. How much would it hurt? Dios had put her here. He had put her here for a reason. So she would pay attention. She would be ready. She would be grateful for these last moments, how it felt to see and smell and hear, how her skin tingled, how she could sense her mother — but not Diego. Her son was too young, she had decided, too young to let her feel him.

Just a few months ago, Diego had asked her about a gun.

"Mama, have you ever held a gun?"

"No, Diego. Why are you asking me this?"

"Mateo says his brother has a gun, and he got to hold it."

"Diego, you must not go near that gun. Mateo shouldn't be touching a gun."

"I didn't touch it. I didn't even see it."

"Guns are very dangerous. Where does Mateo live? Who's this brother?"

"Forget it, Mama."

"I will not forget it. I'm very serious. You mustn't go near that gun. If Mateo has it, you go away. You leave. *Entiendes*?"

"*Sí*, Mama."

That conversation had kept her awake for weeks. Diego walked home from school with Mateo. She didn't know the boy's mother. How could she have moved her son into this neighborhood? To Vegas? Juan would have known they should not live on this street.

Juan.

She had called him from the hospital, because he was still in Mexico.

"It's Diego," she sobbed. "He's hurt."

"Where are you? I'm coming. I'm coming now."

She didn't know how Juan had done it, how he had crossed the border, how he had gotten to Vegas so fast. But the next morning he was there, in the lobby of the Children's Hospital, and when she went down to get him, to explain to the receptionist that he was Diego's father, that he could come with her to the special room for family, he had started to cry, and his tears came so fast they soaked the collar of his shirt, and he could not speak, and she could not speak, and they had stood in the middle of the room, with people everywhere, some silently engrossed in their phones and others rushing by, wearing pale blue scrubs. She and Juan had stood there, collapsed in each other's arms, and sobbed.

The phone rang again.

It rang and rang, and finally, Jimbo answered.

"Hello?"

His face was alert. Then surprised. He looked out the window and moved closer to the wall, peering up the street.

Engracia looked too. She saw the red glow against the stucco wall of the neighbor's house. There was a police car out there. Someone had heard her say *gun* and *man* after all.

Her heart quickened its already skittery beat.

She looked at Jimbo's face. Was he angry?

He looked startled more than anything. Startled, and strangely vulnerable.

"I . . . I don't know what to say. It's not what you think. That's not what's happening."

The man was listening to someone on the line. Ms. Navarro stirred, and he looked over at her abruptly.

"Help!" she called. "Help!"

The man cracked the phone into the receiver and whipped around toward Ms. Navarro.

"Stop it!"

Ms. Navarro stood up, enraged now. She scared Engracia. She might do anything.

Anything could happen now. Anyone might live or die in the next seconds and Engracia, who knew what would happen to her, was having trouble concentrating. She thought of Juan, sobbing at the hospital, and she remembered the doctor asking them about the organs, and then, the night after the burial, when Juan drank glass after glass of whiskey.

Diego had gotten hurt in Engracia's care.

Juan had drank all that whiskey.

"Ms. Navarro."

Her voice came out small, and at first, Ms. Navarro did not look at her.

"Please sit with me?"

Ms. Navarro looked confused, and even Jimbo seemed unclear about what Engracia had asked. He started to say something, but stopped. Engracia motioned to the seat beside her, and Ms. Navarro stood a moment there, looking from Jimbo to Engracia, looking at the spot where the gun was hidden beneath his shirt, looking at the phone behind him. Then, awkwardly, as if she had not quite committed herself to the act, she stumbled toward Engracia and sat where the younger woman had indicated.

Engracia took her hand. Her bones were small, smaller than Engracia's, smaller even than Diego's, and Engracia could feel the beat, beat, beat of Honorata's heart through her skin.

Taking Ms. Navarro's hand helped Engracia.

At almost the same moment, she and Honorata looked up at Jimbo.

He looked back at them, and for a moment, Engracia saw it in his eyes: he was wondering what the hell he was doing. How had he gotten here, in this room, with a gun, and two women cowering beneath him?

"I'm sorry, Honorata."

She did not reply.

Engracia could still see the red glow of the police cruiser against the stucco of the house next door, and she noticed that the man stayed near the wall, out of reach of the window.

"Where's Malaya?" Jimbo asked. "I'd like to see her."

He did not say it, but Engracia thought that even Ms. Navarro must be thinking it: he wanted to see her before he died.

Silence.

Ms. Navarro was silent, and Engracia was silent, and the man did not ask again. Instead, he leaned against the wall and lowered himself slowly to the floor.

"Why didn't you read my letter, Honorata? Why didn't you give me a chance?"

He sounded sad, and resigned. Engracia wondered if he would kill himself there in front of her, and, for a moment, she closed her eyes, not wanting to see.

Ms. Navarro made a startled noise. Engracia opened her eyes, and Jimbo looked up.

"Is it Malaya?" he asked. "Is she here?"

Ms. Navarro glanced out the window, to the street. Engracia wondered if she could see the police car; if she knew what the red glow meant.

"Is she outside?"

The man stood up, peering toward the window. "I just want to see her once. Please."

Ms. Navarro said nothing. She pulled her hand away from Engracia's, sat up straighter on the couch, perched, alert and waiting and without speaking.

"I could have seen her, you know. She wanted to meet. I came here today to tell you I knew; to tell you we would be meeting. I didn't want to go behind your back."

Honorata stared at him then, her face a mask.

"I don't know why I have this gun. I don't know why I came in this way. I got so worked up. Waiting. I was so mad."

His voice trailed off, the enormity of the

error he had made — of the consequences it would bring — becoming clearer.

"Did you call the police?"

"Yes," said Engracia.

"You were right. Of course. You should've called the police."

The man sounded sad more than anything else, and his fingers reached inside his jacket. He touched the handle of the gun, reassuring himself it was there, or wondering if it was, or deciding, perhaps, what he should do now.

The phone rang again.

31

Coral grabbed her phone and her keys, and raced out the door. She heard someone yell, "Hey, lady. Stop!" But she did not stop. She ran straight for Tom Darling, her eye on the school bus, and the girl who was just now getting off it.

"Tom, it's me, Coral."

"Coral?"

"This is my street. I live here."

"Well, this isn't a good time. If you just go back inside, everything will be fine."

"No, Tom. The girl over there. She lives in that house. She's coming home from school."

"Shit."

Tom radioed to a patrolman at the end of the street.

"That girl. Hang on to her. She can't come up this street."

Coral saw the police officer look around, spot Malaya, and head toward her. She saw the girl see the officers, then the patrol cars, then look behind her toward the spot where the school bus had just idled. She would be afraid.

"I know her, Tom. Can I go to her?"

Tom looked around. Saw the girl's startled stance, saw Coral's concerned face.

"Yes. But don't say anything."

"I don't know anything."

"Get her off the street. Your house is too close. Ask the officer where to take her."

Coral turned and walked toward Malaya, who was talking to one of the policemen and had her backpack half off her shoulder, as if she were about to drop it and flee.

"Rick," Tom said into his radio, "my friend Coral is coming at you. She lives on this street. Knows the girl. Take them somewhere together. Keep her close by. And get the girl's cell phone. Make sure you have her phone."

Coral could hear Tom's voice on the officer's radio as she approached, and when Malaya looked at her, Coral tried for a reassuring smile. The girl simply stared, her eyes darting to her house, to Coral, to the officer. The backpack slid farther down her arm. Coral knew she wanted to run, was calculating which way to go, if she could get away. They wouldn't shoot a girl — they wouldn't — but Coral wished Malaya looked less wild. She had pulled her hair all to one side to reveal the shaved scalp above her ear and the tongue of the tattooed snake that twisted toward her neck.

Malaya had been such a beautiful little girl. Honorata used to dress her in elaborate dresses on Sundays, with a bow tied in her silky brown hair, and during the week, Malaya would walk to the school bus in a plaid skirt and a crisp white blouse. Even then, she was a funny child, knocking on Coral's door and selling Girl Scout cookies while carrying a small stuffed deer whose name was Horns. "Horns likes the short-bread cookies the best. That's the one Horns eats." Trey had adored her. Called her Malaysia, which had made Malaya angry the first time he said it. "Don't call me that . . . *Fatboy*," she had said at eight years old, her feet wide apart.

Fatboy! Trey had laughed and laughed. "Okay, Malaya, I won't call you that. But I meant it as a compliment. Malaysia is a very beautiful country." As if Trey knew anything about Malaysia. Or even where to find it on a map. He was always quick, though.

"Well, it's not my name," Malaya had said, much more amenably.

"Oh, I know that. I won't get it wrong

again." But the next time Trey had seen her, he called out, "Hey, Malaysia! How are you today?" And he had given her his big Trey grin — he towered over her, fifteen and already six foot three — and Coral had been sure Malaya would be angry, or worse, cry. But instead, she laughed and said, "Hi, Fatboy!"

And that was that: the little girl and the almost man were friends that year. Trey introduced her to his high school friends as if she were a peer, and Malaya brought him drawings she had made at school, or things she found in the patch of undeveloped desert behind their cul-de-sac. Even now, on the rare occasion that Trey came by and Malaya happened to be out, they greeted each other fondly. He still called her Malaysia, and she called him Trey; she allowed him to gently tease her about the black clothes, the laced-up boots, the zany hair, and the gold chain hanging from her belt loop.

"Malaysia, you're scaring little kids. Why do you wear that stuff?"

"You scared of me, Trey?"

"Of course I'm scared of you. You're covered in black and chains, and you got that freaky tattoo. How'd you get your mother to say yes to that? You're too young."

"Well, I got friends. They think I look twenty-one, not just eighteen."

"Yeah, well, take it from me, baby girl. Those might not be the friends you need."

"Come on. You gonna get all over me too? I got a mom for that."

"Nah, I'm not saying nothing. You always beautiful to me, Malaysia."

In the house, Trey would ask Coral what was going on, why Malaya looked so wild, but Coral didn't have an answer. Malaya almost never came by this year, and Coral worried about her. She walked with her head down and a hunch in her shoulders that had not been there before.

"You think she's gonna be okay?"

"Oh, I hope so Trey. High school can be tough, right?"

"Yeah. Her mom should get her away from those friends."

Coral smiled at this.

"I love that kid," he added. "She makes me laugh."

"I know you do."

Coral nodded to the police officer and set her hand on Malaya's arm.

"Come with me. I'm not sure what's going on here, but these guys are good. We just have to lay low a bit and let them take

428

care of this."

"Why are they here? Where's my mom?" The girl was panicking. Who wouldn't be?

"I don't know. But I know that man. He's a good guy. It's going to be okay."

"Is this about my dad?"

"Your dad?"

"My dad. I have a dad. He said he was going to visit me. Is this about him? I want to see him."

"I don't know. I didn't have time to ask about anything. I don't know if it's about your dad."

Of course it was about her dad. If anything would bring a SWAT team onto a neighborhood street, it was a domestic issue. They wouldn't take a problem with a dad lightly.

Malaya had never said anything about a dad.

All those years ago, when Honorata had asked for help changing Malaya's name, and Darryl had thought she was a sex worker, Coral had just assumed Malaya's father could have been anyone. But obviously that wasn't true. Malaya knew who her dad was.

Where had Honorata gotten the money for those houses? Who was Malaya's father?

One of the patrolmen led Coral and Malaya to the far end of the cul-de-sac, where another officer was setting up a shade canopy, like the ones Althea used to put up for Keisha's soccer games. They were getting ready for a long stretch; no one would be hurrying this.

"Honey, you hungry? I can ask someone to get us food."

"No."

The girl didn't say anything else, and Coral stood there, wondering how bad this might get.

The officer pulled out two lawn chairs and motioned for Coral and Malaya to sit down. Malaya was nervous, popping up and down on the balls of her feet, and Coral placed her arm around the girl to encourage her to be still. She didn't want the officer to think Malaya was on something — her appearance was incriminating enough. And it wouldn't help Malaya to get worked up before she even knew what was happening. They sat down in the chairs; the girl let Coral take her hand, but turned and stared off toward where the bus had been.

An image of Malaya a year or so earlier, standing in Coral's kitchen with a plate of *biko* that her grandmother had made, came to mind. Coral was talking with Malaya when Isa came running in the door, shouting, "Mom! Something bad happened!"

Coral's heart beat faster. Her youngest

son held something in his hand, his eyes teary.

"What is it?"

"A toad. Do you think it's Ichiro?"

Gus had found a toad in the parking lot at school and brought him home in his shirt. He'd lived in the backyard for months, and Koji could do a pretty good imitation of his low *bwrrracking* call, but nobody had seen or heard him for a while. Now Isa held out the slightly rotting body of a toad that had been run over by a car.

"Isa, put that down. It's not clean."

Isa set it on the kitchen table and ran to put his arms around Coral. Gus walked in, dropping his backpack next to the toad.

"Mom, I told him to leave it in his glove."

"It's okay, Gus."

"Do you think it's Ichiro?"

"No. I don't."

"How do you know?" Isa choked out.

"Well, Ichiro's bigger."

"Are you sure?"

"Yes."

"And he'd be even bigger if he were smashed like that, right, Mom?"

"Gus."

"Can we bury him?"

Malaya said she would help, and Gus found a Mickey Mouse T-shirt that was too small for either boy. Her sons wrapped the toad carefully in it before digging a hole near the plum tree and burying him.

"Can we sing a song?"

"How about 'Froggy Went A-Courtin'?'"

Coral gave Gus the warning eye, but Isa said, "That's a good song." And so the four of them sang it. When they finished, Isa said, "Bye, Ichiro's friend. We liked you." And Malaya took the little boy's hand and told him that he had done a really nice thing for the toad. Gus said he had helped too — he had done most of the digging — and then they all went inside to try the sweet rice cakes that Malaya had brought over.

Was that the day they had the conversation about physics? Malaya had surprised Coral, talking to the boys about her high school class.

Gus had started it.

"My teacher said that because of quantum physics, being happy isn't just good for the person who's happy, it's good for everyone else. For the whole universe."

"Because of quantum physics?" Coral was pleased to think this had caught Gus's attention.

"Yeah. Everything affects everything else."

"So being sad makes everyone else sad?" Isa asked.

"I don't know. Maybe."

"We talked about that in my physics class." Malaya flipped her long hair to one side. "It has to do with the forces that connect elementary particles, like electrons."

Gus looked at Malaya, pleased that the older girl knew what he was talking about.

"Yeah, it's physics. That's what my teacher said too."

"I don't know what physics are," said Isa.

"It's a science. It's the study of atoms and things."

"Oh."

"Somebody in my class asked if one sad person made everyone else sadder" — Gus jumped up and sat on the kitchen counter as he spoke — "and we had a whole conversation about how something good might make the whole universe better, and something bad, like war or murder, would make the whole universe worse."

"I feel sorry for the sad people," said Isa.

"That's just what I thought," said Malaya. "Like it's not bad enough that they're already sad, but somehow they make everything worse too?"

Gus frowned. "I don't think that's what my teacher said. She just said the thing about happiness."

Now Malaya wound her hair on top of her

head, and stuck in a pencil to hold it in place. "Well, I thought about it a lot — and I decided that it's really about love. And hate. I think that loving something makes the universe better, and hating something makes it worse. So if someone is sad because they love someone, then they are still making the universe better, because it's really about love."

Coral remembered the way Gus had scrunched up his face and shifted in his seat when the older girl said the word *love.* And she remembered the way her own eyes had filled, and how she'd wanted to say something — something that told Malaya what a lovely thought it was, something that made Gus more comfortable — but she was afraid to try to speak right away, so it was Isa who had replied:

"Then our toad helped everyone, because he made me feel sad, and I love him."

Malaya laughed and lifted Isa high in the air.

"That's right, Isa monster!"

And Isa had laughed and said, "Put me down," and they had all taken another piece of *biko.*

Now Malaya stood up from the rickety folding chair, nearly banging into the police officer behind her.

"I don't want to sit here."

"We have to stay here. They might not tell us anything for a while. But it seems really calm. That's a good sign."

Malaya looked at her, and Coral waited to see if she would say something, but the girl just sat back down.

They stayed there, quiet, until Tom came over.

"Hi. Malaya Begtang? Is that right?"

Malaya looked at Tom and nodded yes.

"Listen, I know this must be scary for you. Things are going fine, though. We just want to go real slow, make sure there's nothing happening. We don't have any indication that anything is, and I'm sorry to scare you like this."

Malaya's lip quivered. Instantly, Coral saw her as she had been at four, at seven. She looked tough, but of course she wasn't.

"This doesn't look routine, but it is routine in some situations. And we're always happy when we've overreacted. Okay?"

The girl nodded, but did not say anything.

"Just sit tight with Coral here. You couldn't be in better hands right now."

Malaya looked at Coral doubtfully, but Coral smiled, and the girl tried to smile in return. She was trembling now, and getting close to tears, so Coral waved Tom away and looked right into Malaya's eyes.

"It's going to be okay. I'm right here with you."

"Do you think my dad's there?"

"I don't know, honey. Why do you think he might be?"

"Because I found him. And because he said he would visit me. And I told him where I lived."

There was a pretty good chance that this was about her dad.

"I really don't know anything at all. I just saw the police cars, and I came out because I know Tom. And then I saw you."

"He didn't seem like a bad man. My dad, I mean."

"Well, we don't know anything. Let's just stay right here, with what we do know."

"I just wanted to meet my father."

"I understand that."

Coral's voice caught, and she batted back tears that rose in her eyes. Incredible. That she could still feel this pain, after all these years.

"I know how you feel."

Malaya looked directly at her; she'd caught the change in Coral's voice. She waited.

"I don't know who my mother is. I mean, I had a mother, she raised me, but she isn't my biological mother. And nobody knows who that was. You're only about the fifth person in the world to know this about me."

Malaya did not seem exactly surprised.

"Does it bother you? I mean, do you want to know her?"

"Yes. I've spent my whole life wanting to know who she was. But there isn't any way to find her. I've tried. Or I did try, for a long time."

"I'm sorry."

I'm sorry. It made Coral want to cry.

"Thank you."

Coral didn't speak for a while then, and Malaya held her hand, squeezing her fingers ever so gently, and Coral struggled with the lump rising in her throat. She was supposed to be the one helping Malaya.

"I found him on the Internet," the girl said.

"Yeah," Coral managed to reply. "That makes sense . . . How did you know where to look?"

"I didn't. I just looked up my mom, and there was a thing about how she changed my name when I was little. I used to be Malaya Navarro, but now my name is Begtang."

"I knew that."

"You did? Well, I thought my dad must be

named Begtang all the time, but the notice was for my father, to tell him my mom was changing my name. So that made me think she was trying to hide me."

"Hmmm. Okay. Then what?"

"Well, it was kind of an accident. I was looking in these old newspapers, and I couldn't find anything about my mom, so I was just looking for anything about someone from the Philippines. Which was sort of stupid. But there was an article about a woman who had won all this money. She won it at a casino, and she had only been in this country for like ten months. So it was a big story. And I just read it, because it was kind of interesting, even though it was too old. It was before I was born."

Coral was really interested now. This Malaya was surprising in so many ways.

"You found this on the Internet?"

"Well, it wasn't easy. Because the search engine in the paper isn't very good. So I went to the library on Flamingo, and the librarian helped me."

Coral thought of her own trips to that library, straining her eyes to see the faded microfiche records of Del Dibb's life.

"That was smart."

"Anyway, this article about the Filipina who won the money, I just read it for fun, because I wasn't finding anything. But there was a picture of her."

Coral knew what she was going to say.

"It was my mom."

Unbelievable. Incredible story.

"Her name was Rita Wohlmann. And she was married to this guy James. From Chicago. It was really easy after that. I just Googled him. He runs a big company, and I sent him an email."

"Wow. Wow! That's really an amazing story."

"Yeah. Like, did you know my mom won more than a million dollars?"

"No." She felt almost giddy listening to the girl. Malaya had done it. She'd found her dad. It made Coral want to jump up and cheer, even in the middle of this — what? — incident.

"And she was married. I mean, like, I've spent my whole life trying to explain to people why I don't have a dad. And there was this real asshole kid in fifth grade; he said I was a bastard. Which is stupid. Because half the kids I know are bastards. Just not the ones at my school."

Coral reached over and hugged Malaya awkwardly in her chair. She was so proud of her, and she was sorry about the fifth grader who had called her a name.

It was unbelievable that Malaya had actually found some record of her mom in the paper. With a different name. That's what it took. Some luck. At one point when Coral had been hunting for her mother, when she'd been doing research yet again, she had gone into some chat rooms and talked with other people looking for their parents. Usually straight-up adoptees, whose records were sealed. And the ones that found them — the mothers who found their babies or the children who found their parents — they almost always got lucky. There was one stray detail that turned out to be true, wasn't part of the standard story, and that detail led to everything else. My mother had eight siblings and was over six feet tall. My mother was an identical twin, and her brothers were identical twins too. Stuff like that.

And with genetic testing, all you had to know was that it was possible you had the right person. From there, if everybody agreed, you could actually be sure. She wondered if James Wohlmann really was Malaya's father. The girl was young. Honorata could have been married, but that didn't mean he was Malaya's father.

"What did your father say when you emailed him?"

"He asked me for a photo. Of my mom."

"And you sent it?"

"Yeah. And then he asked me if I was willing to do a test. To prove it. He sent me a kit, and then I sent it back to the company, with my blood and stuff."

"So, you're sure."

"Yeah. He's definitely my dad."

"Did he know about you?"

"No. He didn't even know my mom had a baby."

"You were a big surprise."

"Yeah. I guess so."

"Does he have a family? Kids?"

"No."

"You're the only one?"

"Yes."

Coral saw Tom walking toward them again, and he signaled her to meet him.

"Malaya, I see my friend Tom. I'm going to ask him if he knows anything. Okay?"

"Sure."

"I see a cooler over there. I think you can probably have a Coke if you want it."

"Okay."

Coral walked to the back of the canopy and then over to the next yard, where Malaya could not see her talking with Tom.

"Tom, what's going on?"

"We're not sure. We think there's a situation, and we've got a visual, but we haven't seen a gun. Nobody seems to be being held."

"Have you knocked on the door?"

"Not yet. That's the next step. We called, and a man answered once, but he hung up pretty quickly. We're just taking our time. No need kicking it up a notch too early."

"It's her father."

"Yeah? What's the story?"

"Malaya found her father online. He didn't know she existed. He had her confirm it with tests, and then he told her he was coming to see her."

"Okay. That's helpful. Know anything about the relationship? With the mom?"

"Not much. They were married. She's from the Philippines. He's from Chicago. They came out here, and she hit a jackpot. Malaya says she won a million dollars. So I'm guessing that was the end of the marriage. And he never knew she was pregnant."

Tom whistled.

"Yeah. That's a bombshell."

"Only in Vegas, right?"

Coral glanced over at Malaya, who was talking to a police officer who looked barely older than she was. "Any idea how long?"

"Not really. I mean, I'd like to talk to him on the phone first. Get a sense of the guy before I knock on the door. But if he won't answer, that's the next step."

"You haven't heard anything in there? Is something happening?"

"So 911 got a call. Couldn't make out much, except some woman who said 'gun' and 'man.' We sent a patrol over, and he got a visual just from the neighbor's yard. Two women. One man. No visible gun. No ropes. Looks like a tense conversation. It's not a lot to go on. But your information helps."

"The other woman is her grandmother. She lives with them."

"I don't think so. She's young. Looks Hispanic. Maybe the housekeeper?"

"Oh." Coral was surprised that Honorata had a housekeeper. "Well, I've seen someone get off the bus before. But the grandmother lives there too. You haven't seen her?"

"No. Damn. I have to ask the girl about her. Where the grandmother's room is. I don't want to scare her, though."

"Malaya?"

"Yes?" The young officer walked away, avoiding Tom's gaze.

Coral knew Malaya would be frightened by Tom's question, so she put her hand on the girl's thin back. Coral could feel her trembling even as she looked up at Tom defiantly.

"You have a grandmother? She lives with you?"

"Lola? Is Lola okay?" Malaya looked to Coral with fear.

"I'm sure she is. I was just confirming that she lives in your house."

"Yes. But she's not here right now. She's staying at her friend's house."

Coral and Tom looked at each other. She could see his relief.

"Do you expect her to come home today?"

"No."

"Okay, thank you. That's all I need right now."

"Is this about my dad?"

"Coral told me about your dad. That helps us. But I don't know. Listen, nothing's happened. We're being very cautious. It's really helpful if you just stay here."

Malaya looked at Tom, and Coral hoped she would not get angry. She had heard Malaya and Honorata shouting more than once. Tom reached out and took the girl's hand. "Thank you. You're doing great here. I really appreciate it." This calmed Malaya, and she shook her head and dropped to the grass in one fluid move.

"Whatever. My mom's going to be really mad if it's my dad. And she's crazy."

Tom looked down at Malaya a minute, as if he were about to say something. Then he thought better of it, nodded to Coral, and walked back toward the police officers in the cul-de-sac.

32

"Mi shebeirach avoteinu," June sang as sweetly as a child in a choir.

"Oh, Miss June, that's beautiful," said Jessy.

"M'kor hab'racha l'imoteinu."

Her voice was clear and strong today, as if she were a younger woman.

"I wonder if you could teach me your prayers? I could sing them with you."

June banged her hand sharply on her knee.

"Do you think Miriam has a songbook? Or that you could bring one home with you from services this week?"

Her leg jutted out straight.

"Arf!" she said.

Jessy laughed.

"I'll mention it to Miriam when she comes by later, so she can help you get it."

"Ruff!"

"Can you sing it again?"

June flopped her head toward her stomach.

"Oh, I'm sorry, June. Let me hum the tune for you."

She had a pretty good ear, Jessy. She had the tune right, all the way through, though of course she had heard only the first two lines. She hummed it over and over, and June pushed the puzzle pieces around on the jigsaw puzzle, and knocked the one border that was finished to the floor.

Jessy bent down to pick up the pieces while still humming, and June noticed the red glare of a police cruiser's light flashing in the street. She watched it in a sort of dazed way. It made her think of Christmas, and of the neon lights of the El Capitan's Christmas display, and then of the dripping red and white stripes of a candy cane already licked.

"Ooooohhhhhhh!" she called.

"It's just a police car, Miss June. The light's out at Eastern, and there's an officer directing traffic. It was like that when I drove in."

"Oh doctor, I'm in trouble," sang June.

"Well, goodness gracious me," sang Jessy.

Jessy beamed at June, and June wished she could tell her how beautiful she was — how gloriously beautiful — though she supposed that Jessy did not think she was pretty at all. What Jessy thought of herself was there in her clothes. Today she wore a long-sleeved black cotton T-shirt that bunched up awkwardly under the lightweight fabric of a flowered halter-style dress. She wore black spandex shorts under the dress, and her heavy red-splotched legs disappeared into inexpensive maroon ankle boots, with a sharply angled heel that made her wobble as she walked. These clothes touched June.

Sometimes Jessy took her on excursions, to the indoor garden at the Bellagio or the Barrick Museum on UNLV's campus. And on the way home, they would stop at a convenience store for Diet Cokes, and sometimes for Diet Cokes with chocolate donuts. Jessy would lead her in and carefully fill two giant Styrofoam cups with ice and soda, and June would look around and wish that she could make herself say hello to the little girl touching all the bags of Doritos or to the old man with the Sponge-Bob backpack and the plaid pants.

It was the sort of place Marshall would never believe his mother could be, where no one else she knew would ever take her, or imagine that she had been, and June loved these trips. Sometimes the stores reeked of smoke and were filled with signs forbidding things: no debit cards for purchases under five dollars, no checks cashed, no standing near the machines, no loitering, no change available. In these stores, there was almost always someone with hollowed-out eyes waiting to buy a pack of cigarettes, or jutting a hand into June's face and asking for a dollar. The Cokes cost twice as much in these places as they did in the cleaner stores, the ones with cheerful clerks and a display case of fresh donuts and a clear plastic box where you could leave change for the people at Opportunity Village.

One time June noticed a woman give a dollar to someone begging outside a store, and then she saw the panhandler walk in and buy his own jumbo soda — the day was so hot — for eighty-five cents. And the cheerful clerk, with a broken tooth and her hair pulled back over a broad bald patch, asked the man if he would like to leave his change for Opportunity Village. The panhandler looked at the clerk, and then at the photos of the middle-aged men who worked at the training center, and then at the change in his palm. He tipped the nickel and the dime into the plastic box. "Thank you!" said the clerk, to which the man replied, "Of course."

Seeing this made June shake her head

violently and caused her to bump Jessy, and there was a little fuss about the spill and her dress. June couldn't explain that her head shook because the man had given away the coins in order to help someone else, and because she never would have seen this if Jessy had not taken her into the Circle K — into the place that someone like June would never go.

On Friday evening, a van picked up her and Miriam and took them to services at Congregation Ner Tamid. June had known Miriam for almost fifty years, and while they had not really been friends, time had knit them together. Now they were both widows, they were both old Jews, they were both longtime residents of the same declining neighborhood, with wide, low-slung houses far too large for them and yards that stretched a hundred feet in every direction. When they made their way to the van on Friday nights, they passed through sunken living rooms and marble entryways and chandeliers weighted with crystal drops that coruscated light and memories as if they were the same thing.

It was Miriam who had asked June to donate to the campaign to build a synagogue in their neighborhood decades ago, and

Miriam who had persuaded her to make a much larger donation when the synagogue decided to move to the suburbs years later. June had given the first time because it was easy, and because she and Miriam saw each other at school gatherings, and because her father would have been pleased to know she did it. She gave the second time because, at a certain point, after she had mostly retired from the El Capitan, after Marshall was busy with his own family, after she had started to recognize the first symptoms of whatever was wrong with her now, she had taken to stopping by Ner Tamid from time to time.

Initially, she simply walked in the garden or by the wall that proclaimed itself to be the Moe B. Dalitz Religious School, and the staff got to know her and called out her name when she went by. Finally, she started to come to services on Friday nights.

It was a reform synagogue, and the call-and-response in English surprised her at first, but the prayers were the same as she had always known them. The Hebrew came back to her effortlessly, easier almost than English sometimes, and the standing before the ark, the mournful sound of the Sh'ma — not a mournful prayer at all — and the little children who padded up to stand around the bimah when the rabbi called them up each week; these all moved her. When she was a child, the rabbi did not invite the children this way. She had tried to be quiet in synagogue.

But the congregation built its new synagogue and moved miles away from where June lived. The old building was a Baptist church now. The rabbi's assistant sent a van for her and Miriam each Friday night, and it stopped at the Sunrise Villas, and then, with the seats usually full, made its way to the new Ner Tamid on Valle Verde Drive. June had been determined not to like the pristine building, in spite of having helped fund it, but it was impossible not to appreciate the warm cream of the Israeli marble, the flicker of green palo verde leaves through the glass on either side of the bimah, the drape of the heavy velvet cloths that surrounded the arc. Too, the seats were comfortable, the sound system excellent, and the same rabbi and the same cantor led the services each Friday night.

Of course, June was not the same as she had been.

Miriam had always been as petite and small as June, and she was too frail to help her friend make her unsteady, unpredictable way into the temple. Usually the bus driver helped June down, and then one of the members of the men's club took her arm, and danced with her, back and forth and tipping giddily away from wherever she intended to go, until she was seated with a heavy and unreadable siddur in her lap. She suspected that the usher handed her the prayer book in the hope that it would provide ballast. June hoped the same, though she had learned not to count on it.

Tonight she made it all the way to the Mi Shebeirach — the prayer for healing — without attracting any attention to herself. She longed to sing, though she could rarely get any sound to emerge for these prayers she had known her whole life. This evening was no different. June concentrated on thinking about something else: her breakfast that morning or the outfit Marshall had worn to an Easter egg hunt when he was four. Sometimes this allowed her to sing. She would hear her own voice, slight but on pitch, as if it were someone else's. Now the sanctuary's lights were dimmed. Small twinkling bulbs had been strung through the potted trees, and the rabbi read out the names of those in need of healing, while the cantor prepared to lead the Mi Shebeirach, and some people behind her stood and said the names of people who had not been on the rabbi's list.

"Michael Jackson!" June yelled.

The rabbi nodded her way.

"Salvador Dali!"

The rabbi nodded again and then turned slightly to look at the cantor. The woman at the piano began to play the first haunting notes.

"Mu'ammar Gaddhafi!"

June could not stop. She was standing now, and this bizarre list of names was flying out of her mouth, louder and louder. Miriam tugged on her elbow, and the usher from the men's club hurried toward her, and she wished he would hurry a little faster, the old bum, and at this thought, she erupted into laughter. At least June didn't call out any more names, but her hilarity was so absolute and so infectious that at first the rabbi gave a gentle smile, and then he nodded encouragingly to the usher — the man really was slow — and then suddenly, June heard the cantor give a snort, and someone to her left laughed, and then there was a titter and another laugh, and a whole row broke down, and then some member of the choir. Finally, the cantor was laughing and could not stop, and the rabbi, who had great control, gave in and started to laugh as well.

When it was over, when the usher had her firmly by the arm and near the door, when Miriam looked away whether because she could not bear to see June like this or because she might start to laugh again — there was no way to know — the rabbi said, "Well, there's nothing more healing than laughter," and the congregants clapped, and June did that damn shimmy thing with her shoulders — good grief, there was no humiliation too great — and the service went on. June sat next to the usher on a padded bench in the hallway, which is where she ended up from time to time and did not mind so much. She could hear everything.

June thought about asking Jessy to come with her to services next Friday night, so that she could hear the cantor sing the prayers all the way through. Then, too, maybe it would make her laugh if June pulled such a stunt again. It would be good to see Jessy laugh.

33

The phone rang six times, but Jimbo did not answer it.

Ms. Navarro sat back on the couch without saying what had alerted her; what she had been listening for. But she was thinking about something. Engracia could see that her attention had shifted. What was it?

She still held Honorata's hand in her own. She squeezed it lightly, but Ms. Navarro did not respond. She had not responded to Jimbo's questions either, or to what he had said about Malaya. About how he could have already seen her. About how he had come to tell Ms. Navarro that he was going to see Malaya. He hadn't wanted to go behind her back.

"If you'd just opened the letter. You would have known she found me."

"This isn't my fault."

"Isn't it?"

They sat silently again, the red glow of

the police cruiser on the wall outside, the sound of the phone, ringing, ringing, still in their ears.

Malaya. She would be coming home from school now. Engracia couldn't see a clock, and she didn't have a watch. But the light in the window. It would have to be about the right time. What would happen if Malaya walked in now?

These were, perhaps, the last moments any of them would be alive. They all knew it, and they were all afraid, and somehow the experience linked them: the woman who had lied to the man, the man who had a gun, the woman who did not know if she wanted to live or die.

Jimbo was still sitting on the floor, his back against the wall with the window. Honorata leaned into the couch, but Engracia could feel her alertness. It was one thing to wonder if she wanted to die, it was another to imagine a teenage girl walking through the door right now. Engracia could not bear it that Malaya might walk in. That something might happen to her.

"*Mi hijo* died," she blurted. "My son. Diego. He died."

Her voice came out cracked and accented. Engracia concentrated. She would have to say this in English. They would have to hear her.

"He was ten years old."

Ms. Navarro let go of her hand. Engracia did not move. Out the corner of her eye, she saw the man looking. She stared at the table in front of her. The wood was ornately carved, with a thick slab of greenish glass in the center. Through the glass, she saw her own foot in its dirty white sneaker. She could see her heel and then, under the glass, the rest of her foot, as if it had suddenly grown larger.

"I have only one child. He died."

Silence.

"When he was a little boy, he told me that when he grew up he would give his money to everyone on the street, to everyone who was hungry."

Ms. Navarro shifted slightly in the seat next to her. Engracia saw that the red glow of the police cruiser was also reflected in the greenish glass, just at the edge, a sliver of red.

"He said he didn't know why people walk by people who are hungry, who ask for food. 'Why do we do that, Mama?' I told him we do not have enough money to feed everyone. That my job was to feed him. And he told me that his job was going to be to feed them."

She inhaled deeply. Her heart thudded dully in her chest, and her stomach, fluttery and unsettled for the last hour, cramped. Still, it was not as hard as she thought to speak. Engracia had no one to tell about Diego now. The padre. Mary from work, who had come to see her. But she wanted to talk about her son. She wanted someone to know who he was. And she wanted these stupid, stupid people, who had their daughter, to stop it.

When Diego was small enough to swim in the bathtub, he had put his face in the water and said he could see Dios. When he was three, Juan took him to the Los Angeles County Fair, and they came home with two fish in plastic bags. Diego named them Hombre and Nacho. One time in first grade, he jumped out of line before he was supposed to leave the teacher and came running up to Engracia: "Mama, I can write in Spanish! Not just English. There are words in Spanish too!" Even then, he liked to crawl between her and Juan in bed, and sometimes, if he thought she was asleep, he put his thumb in his mouth and stroked her cheek with his small, gentle fingers.

Remembering the feel of his fingers on her skin nearly choked her. As always, she wanted to cry, she wanted to scream, she wanted somehow to force the universe back on the track it was meant to be on. But nothing, nothing that she did, nothing that her body could do physically, could express the horror of what was true, of what could not be changed. Even tears, the instant they fell, or screams, at the moment of sound, became nothing at all, worse than no movement, no sound, because they were so much less than what she actually felt and so much less than how utterly unbearable this fact was.

"He wanted to go to Death Valley. A scientist came to the school, and told him about the sailing stones. He wanted to see them."

She stopped. This was hard: what Diego had wanted and what she had done. Engracia listened for any sound in the room, her eyes not leaving the coffee table with her foot, distorted by the green glass, beneath it. Ms. Navarro and the man still said nothing. It was as if time had stopped. There was no gun. There was no argument. There was no girl about to walk in the door. There was just this moment, with Engracia hanging in space, concentrating, trying to tell them. She had to tell them now. Before Malaya came in.

"When the scientist came, Diego was

happy. He didn't like Las Vegas. He missed his papa. But he liked the scientist."

Engracia heard the man sit down flat against the floor.

"I wanted Diego to go to college. I told him to study hard. Maybe he could be a scientist."

There was no other sound. The phone did not ring.

"Diego was afraid here. Without his papa. One boy even had a gun."

Honorata made a sound.

"And I was afraid. I was afraid of the boys here. I was afraid of the men on the street."

Everything was coming out all wrong. She wasn't making sense.

"He wanted to go to Death Valley. But I was afraid to take him there. By myself."

Engracia closed her eyes. She could not tell this story. She could not talk about what she had done. She could tell them something else. Something about Diego.

"His name was Diego Alejandro Juan Diez-Montoya. He was born in *Abril,* in San Diego, the United States, on the eleventh. Every year, I decorated his cake with flowers."

Out the window, the stucco continued to glow red. Engracia looked up and saw a shadow move — a man on the wall, perhaps.

She heard Jimbo stir, as if he were getting up. Maybe the man on the wall would shoot him now, before she had told them, before they understood. She had to tell them.

"He wanted to go to Death Valley, and I was afraid to take him, so I bought him a skateboard.

"But he was disappointed. He still wanted to go to Death Valley.

"So I told him I would take him to Red Rock, to the trails there, and we would look at the paintings the Indians made a thousand years ago. And on a different day, we would go and see the sailing stones.

"I told him we would go on Saturday, when I came home from work.

"But first I had to sleep that day because I work all night. So I told Diego to watch the television and to wake me at noon. I told him do not take the skateboard outside. Because his friends are too crazy. And he does not know how to ride it yet."

Engracia shuddered. *Por favor Dios mío, ayúdame.* Help me.

"Diego woke me at noon. And we got in the car right away, so we would have lots of time to find the paintings on the rocks.

"And he was quiet. Tired. I say, Diego what's the matter? But he say he is fine, he is happy, he wants to see the rocks.

462

"I know something is not right, but I think it is these boys, his friends. Or maybe he watched the news on the television, and something happened. I wait, because he will tell me when he is ready."

Ms. Navarro shifted in her seat, and, very gently, she put her hand on Engracia's back. Engracia accepted this because she knew Ms. Navarro wanted to help, and she knew she was sorry about Diego, but also, she did not like it. Because even now, nothing anyone did ever helped. And also, Ms. Navarro hid her daughter from her papa.

"I turned on the wrong road, the one before the Red Rock, and we drive a long way, looking for another sign. And Diego is very quiet. He says, 'Mama I am sick. My head hurts.' And then he throws up. In the car."

" 'Diego,' I say. 'You should tell me you're sick. It's the car. It's too hot.' But Diego is not listening to me. His eyes don't look at me, they are not looking at anything, but there are tears. I see tears in his eyes."

Engracia saw that the man was no longer looking at her. He was holding his head in his hands, staring at the floor.

"I know he is sick, and I don't know where I am, so I try to call an ambulance. I stop the car, and I get out my phone, and the

463

call doesn't work. I say, 'Diego, Diego, wake up. What's the matter?' "

But Diego did not reply. He leaned his head on the window, with the mess from the getting sick still in his lap, and he did not answer, and he did not look at her.

"So I start the car, and I turn around, and I drive very fast. There is no one on that road. It's not going to Red Rock. And I keep dialing and dialing, and my phone does not work."

Diego threw up again. Engracia tried to hold him, tried to pull his head under her arm while driving with the left hand, and pushing on the buttons on the phone with her chin. She couldn't do it. She couldn't hold him and drive and phone. Diego was limp now, so she put his head in her lap, and she drove the fastest she had ever driven. Finally, there was the road she needed. She stopped. And the phone worked. And someone must have seen how desperate she looked, right through the window, because a car stopped and then another, and everyone tried to help.

Was it better to drive him to the hospital? To wait for the ambulance? In the end, she left her car on the side of the road, and a man in a Mercedes drove her and Diego very fast toward town, and when he saw the fire engine, sirens blaring, coming toward them, he pulled over. One paramedic worked on Diego and tried to rouse him, and another paramedic asked her questions. Before they put them both in the ambulance, the first paramedic said, "Where did he get this bruise? Here, behind his ear?"

And that was when Engracia knew that he must have fallen, that he must have taken the skateboard, that he must have gone outside when she was sleeping. And, of course, he would not have told her that he fell, because he would not have wanted her to know that he had disobeyed.

"He died in the hospital. Two days later. When they asked me if they could turn off the machine."

Engracia could not say more than this. She could not keep speaking, even if these idiotic people, who had their daughter, did not understand. She had tried. She and Diego had tried. If this is what Dios wanted, she had tried.

There were tears on Ms. Navarro's face now. She stretched her arm all the way around Engracia's back, and when she squeezed, Engracia could feel how her body had changed. Her breathing was ragged, but her body was no longer rigidly on alert.

Instead, it was soft, heavy, pressing into Engracia.

"I didn't know. I'm so sorry."

Engracia relaxed into Honorata's arms. She was a mother too. Engracia knew that the other woman had spent seventeen years afraid of just the thing that had happened to her.

A horrible sound erupted from the man.

He was crying. He was crying, and he was trying not to, and his face was hidden, and his big, fat body shook. Engracia thought that he cried like a child, without any ability to hold himself back. He snorted, and his nose ran, and he could not catch his breath, and his body twisted and shook. She was grateful for how deeply he suffered. He suffered for her, for Diego, and, somehow, this helped.

Just then, the doorbell rang.

At first, nobody moved. It rang again, and there was a loud knocking.

Engracia looked out the window and saw a man crouched on the wall and another across the street. They were wearing helmets and military gear, though surely they were the police. They were watching her in the window, and they were looking toward the front door — toward whoever was ringing the bell.

Jimbo looked up.

"I'm sorry," he said. "I'm sorry, Honorata."

And then he looked at Engracia. "I am so sorry."

Engracia saw in his eyes that he had given up, and she thought that he might shoot himself now, but that he would not shoot her and he would not shoot Ms. Navarro. They looked at each other, the man's face swollen with his tears, and red, like the glow of that light on the stucco.

"I'm sorry about your son."

Engracia looked at Ms. Navarro, who was watching them, her face stricken, no longer angry.

Engracia leaned over to the man. He had been sitting on the floor, and she was on the couch, so when she leaned over, and he put his arms around her, they met in a kind of crouch near the floor. He put both his arms around her, and as he bent his head near her face, she said, "The gun. Give me the gun." He didn't reply. She didn't know if he had heard; if he understood. Engracia wondered if there was a gun trained on the two of them now, someone out there waiting for some distance between her and the man, someone trying to understand what was going on in here.

"The gun."

She said it with urgency, because there wasn't much time. The person at the door was knocking loudly now, and he was yelling something, though she wasn't sure what.

Jimbo gripped her shoulders tightly. Engracia slowly moved her hand forward, toward his soft body, toward the gun stuck in his waistband. The man said nothing. And then she had the gun in her hand, and before she separated from the man's embrace, she dropped it in the deep pocket of her cotton pants.

"Open up! Police!"

Engracia and the man separated, and they looked at Honorata, who was looking out the door of the study, toward the hall.

Almost at once, they all stood. Engracia waited for the shot, the bullet that would come through the window.

"This is the police. Open the door!"

Honorata moved out of the room, toward the door. There was no shot, and so Engracia and the man followed. She didn't look at Jimbo, she didn't say anything; she could feel the gun against her leg, pulling the band of her slacks lower.

Honorata opened the door, and the policeman said, "Ma'am, is everyone all right in here? We've been calling you. We had a call earlier. What's going on?"

And Honorata said, "Everyone's fine. But I want this man to leave my home. I want him to go."

"Has he hurt you? Is there a gun?"

Jimbo and Engracia stood behind Honorata, the three of them all staring at the police officer. Except for his size, Jimbo looked the least frightening of all. An old man, older than he had been two hours before, with his eyes still swollen, and the sweat beaded in his hair and beneath his ear and along the collar of his shirt.

"I'm ready to go," he said.

"Well, ma'am, what's going on here?" the officer repeated. "Has this man been holding you? Has he hurt you?"

And there was a silence, while Honorata looked at the police officer, and Engracia looked at Honorata, and Jimbo looked down at the floor.

"No. He didn't hurt me. He didn't hold me. I just don't want him in my house anymore."

"Are you sure about what you're saying? We can hold him. We'd like to ask all of you some questions."

Honorata drew herself up — she was not much more than five feet tall — and she said firmly, "This is my home. I didn't call you. I want this man to leave, and he's ready to leave. I want you to leave too. I didn't call the police. I don't need you."

The police officer turned around and looked at another man standing a few feet behind him. That man shrugged his shoulders and raised an eyebrow.

"Someone called us, ma'am. There was a 911 call from this address."

Honorata did not answer.

"Ma'am, we understand these situations can be really complicated. But we want to be sure you're safe. We don't want something happening to you later. Do you understand?"

"I understand that this is my home, and I didn't call the police, and I haven't done anything wrong."

"Nobody thinks you've done anything wrong, ma'am. We just want to make sure you're safe."

"I'm safe. But my daughter. She should've come home by now. I heard the school bus. Do you know where she is?"

Engracia felt Jimbo go rigid. He looked up, out the door. The police officer saw him look.

"Sir, what are you doing here? How do you know this woman?"

"We're old friends," said Jimbo quietly. "I

470

was in Las Vegas, and I came to see her."

The man standing at the edge of the yard, behind the police officer, came forward then. He said, "Mrs. Navarro, is that right?"

Honorata nodded yes.

"I'm Tom Darling. I'm a lieutenant in the Metro Police Department. We got a 911 call from this house a couple of hours ago, and we've been watching you pretty close. We have your daughter just on the next block. She's fine. But we didn't want her to come home until we knew that everything was okay here."

Honorata nodded. "Thank you."

"So, before we let anyone go, we'd like to talk with each of you. Just for a minute. One by one."

Honorata turned and looked first at Engracia and then at Jimbo. Their eyes all caught, and their faces did not move. They stood silent and immobile, and an agreement was made.

"Okay. Would you like to come in?" Honorata asked.

34

When Coral and Tom talked a few days later about what had happened, he said that they had gotten lucky; the waiting had paid off. There was no doubt in his mind that there'd been a gun, that the man had been holding the two women; the whole thing could have ended in a very different way. But the gun got ditched somewhere. They patted him down; they searched the room where the three of them had been waiting. And what else could they do? The two women insisted there was no gun. Honorata Navarro wanted the police off her property.

Family fights were dangerous. Things could go any way at any time, and in ways a police officer couldn't predict. James Wohlmann didn't seem like too bad a guy — no record — but Honorata had taken a risk by letting him off, by not telling the police what happened. Not one of the three had been cooperative. Tom didn't know what had

472

gone down. But Coral was right. The man was Malaya's father, and he hadn't known she existed. It didn't look like her parents had been married, though. There was no record of a marriage.

Another strange thing that stood out: the housekeeper hadn't been working there very long. None of the three knew each other very well. And yet, the two others, they were protective of her. It was just a feeling, but he and the investigator had both picked it up: how Honorata and James had each been careful of the housekeeper.

By the time she and Tom spoke, Coral knew what had happened. She knew what Tom and his colleague had sensed, and why. Malaya had knocked on her door the next evening, and again a few days after that. So Coral knew what Honorata had told Malaya, and she knew why they were protective of the housekeeper. She also knew a little about why James Wohlmann had come to the door, though she didn't know if there had been a gun. Malaya had not said anything about a gun.

When it was all over that day — after the police cruiser had escorted Mr. Wohlmann out of the neighborhood, after the SWAT team and two of the patrols had left, after the young officer had started to take down the canopy and smiled at Malaya when she jumped up to help — Coral had walked with Malaya down the cul-de-sac. Before they got to the end, Honorata had come out running, and she and Malaya had embraced. They were both crying, and Coral thought about how difficult the last year had been for them, about Malaya asking to spend the night after babysitting so she wouldn't have to go home, about Honorata saying that American girls didn't listen to their mothers. It wasn't easy raising a teenager, and maybe it was harder for Honorata, who was mostly alone and who had grown up somewhere so different.

Coral said good-bye to Malaya and gave Honorata a hug, and then watched the two of them walk into their house. She had been going to offer Tom a drink, but when she turned to go back to her house, she saw the small form of the housekeeper, waiting at the bus stop on the road.

"Tom, I'll call you this week. Okay?"

"Sure. Thanks, Coral. You really helped us out. No days off for the weary, huh?"

"Yeah. Give me a school music program any day of the week."

"Yep. This is one peculiar town."

"See ya, Tom."

And Coral had grabbed her bag from the

kitchen counter where she'd left it hours earlier, eased her car out of the garage, and driven over to where Engracia stood, looking, from behind, like an old woman.

"Hello?"

"Yes?" The housekeeper looked startled.

"My name's Coral. I'm a friend of the Navarros. Malaya was just with me, while you were in the house?"

The woman looked about anxiously. The bus wasn't coming. There was no one around.

"Listen, I don't want to scare you. I just thought you might want a ride home."

"No. No, *gracias.* I take the bus."

"Please. You've got to be worn out. You don't have to talk. I'll just drive you wherever you want to go."

The woman hesitated.

"Look, it's after six o'clock. The busses don't run very often now. You could be out here a long time."

Engracia looked at Coral, pulled her thin sweater together at the front, and then said yes, she would be grateful for a ride.

But Coral hadn't taken her home. The woman, who said her name was Engracia, asked to be taken to the Catholic church, St. Anne's, on Maryland Parkway.

"It's close to my home. I can walk from there."

So Coral took her to Saint Anne's, and watched while she pulled open the heavy door and stepped inside the sanctuary. They'd said very little in the car. Coral had asked her if she could get her something to eat or drink, and Engracia had refused. Coral had explained that she was the choir teacher at a high school, had taught music at an elementary school before that, that she had known Malaya from the time she was a baby.

To this, the housekeeper said very little.

"Listen, what happened to you today. It might have been pretty traumatic. It might come back to you. And if so, you should talk to someone. The priest or something."

Coral felt foolish saying this: it was none of her business, and she didn't know why she'd said it. She just wanted to say something. It had to have been terrifying, and this woman seemed so forlorn.

Engracia looked at her strangely.

"Today?"

"Yes. I mean, I don't know what happened, but — well, it must have been frightening."

"Today didn't scare me. Today doesn't matter."

It was a strange reply. Sad. Coral didn't know what to say in return.

"Okay. Well, I'm sorry. I'm not prying. I wish you well."

"Thank you for the ride."

"You're welcome."

Coral still felt foolish, but she was glad she'd driven Engracia. The bus really might not have come for hours. And it was much too far to walk.

It wasn't until the next evening, after Malaya had told her some of what had happened, that she understood what Engracia's strange words had meant.

35

The man stood at the door a long time before ringing the bell.

He had walked up the steps quickly, with confidence. He had been about to push the bell, and then paused, his hand just inches from the button. He stood there, thinking, hesitating. And then he dropped his hand to his side and stared at the door.

Unless the person inside was watching for him, there was no way to know he had arrived. It took him a long time. More than five minutes. Maybe ten. His chest heaved slowly, in and out. Who knows what he was thinking. Whether he was afraid. The minutes, the years, he might have been reliving.

He rang the doorbell.

Jimbo was wearing a suit. A very nice navy suit, with a white shirt and a narrow mustard-colored tie. His shoes were expensive, of course, and recently polished. He looked good. Not old and red and fat, as he had looked that day.

"Honorata."

He handed her a bouquet of white roses and a box of croissants from Bouchon. He must be staying at the Venetian. She started to say his name, to say hello, but seeing him so soon after the way he had terrified her, even though she had invited him to come this time; suddenly Honorata didn't trust herself to speak. She took the flowers and motioned him to come inside.

Jimbo did not look at the study as he passed it. He followed the line of her arm, directing him to the table in the kitchen. It was a sunny nook, and outside the bay window, the wisteria was thick with its violet blooms and the door to the backyard was open, so that they could hear the bees buzzing, delirious in their lavender nirvana. An old woman, very tiny, sat with her eyes closed and her face to the sun near the far wall. Rita's mother. He set the pastry box on the table. Honorata opened a cupboard and found a vase.

"I'll just put these in water."

"Sure."

"I've made coffee."

"That'll be nice."

And he stood there, so large in her kitchen,

too large for the narrow wooden chairs, and he didn't seem to know what to do, whether to stand or to sit, what to say.

"Please sit."

He looked around, perhaps wondering where Malaya was. Honorata did not say she was upstairs, probably listening.

"Here are some plates. And napkins. I'll bring you coffee."

Jimbo nodded his head, but did not risk speaking. He pulled out a chair and settled himself into the seat gingerly. Honorata's kitchen made him feel like crying. There were embroidered curtains at the window over the sink and a red wooden frame where cups hung crookedly. A small ceramic tiger, made by a child, sat in the kitchen window, along with a dusty popsicle frame surrounding the faded photo of a small girl. There was a set of brightly decorated canisters for flour and sugar and tea; there was a teakettle on the stove. The yellow-and-blue mat near the sink was folded under at one corner; Honorata straightened it with her foot while she clipped the ends of the roses.

It was everything he had wanted, everything he had hoped for, everything he had finally put aside that night at Caesars when this very woman had told him she never wanted to see him again. A wave of bitterness passed over him, a taste like bile, but almost immediately, he felt remorse. It wasn't her fault. He knew this. He had known it a long time. But he had wanted a family. There had been so much loneliness. And when Malaya had found him, he had almost gotten them all killed. He wanted, suddenly, to be out of this kitchen, away from her. He pushed his chair back from the table.

"Do you want cream and sugar?"

He paused, about to stand.

"No."

And too, there was the way she had yelled, *I hate you! I hate you!* over and over. All these years later. She still hated him. Had anyone ever hated him before? Jimbo wasn't the sort of person people hated. Usually he was someone people did not notice. Old and fat and somehow unappealing; for as long as he could remember, he had sensed the way that he was slightly repellent to others. He didn't know why. He kept himself very clean. He wore good clothes. He spoke respectfully. But it had always been there, like a pheromone that repelled.

"Thank you for coming," Honorata said quietly. "I know you could have met Malaya without me. She would have gone with you."

Jimbo said nothing.

"But my mother's going with you tonight. You understand?"

"Of course. I'm glad she'll come."

"I was wondering what you're going to do. Where you're going to go with Malaya?"

Jimbo had given this a lot of thought. All he really wanted was a chance to see her, to listen to her talk, but he wanted her to enjoy it too.

"I thought maybe we would see Celine Dion tonight. Or *Jersey Boys*. Has she seen those?"

Honorata looked taken aback.

"You're taking her out?"

Jimbo was equally flustered.

"I'm not taking my *daughter* out. I just want to do something nice. I'm sixty-six years old. I don't know what Malaya likes."

Upstairs, Malaya was startled. Sixty-six? She didn't know anyone whose father was sixty-six. Courtney's dad was almost that old, but Courtney was part of his second set of kids. Courtney's mom had been friends with one of his older daughters when both girls were in grade school. That was pretty creepy if your mom had been your dad's daughter's friend. Courtney had to explain it three times to Dani, who just could not get it.

Well, whatever. Jimbo was definitely her dad. And after all this work, she was going to meet him. She looked herself over critically in the mirror and then started down the stairs.

"Hi."

They hadn't heard her coming.

Honorata was surprised to see her daughter looking so pretty. She'd brushed her hair long and straight, with a clip in the back, and she was wearing a buttoned shirt that covered most of that horrible tattoo. Her makeup was pretty too. A little mascara. Pink lipstick. Had she taken out her nose ring?

It had been a long time since Malaya had looked like this. Maybe as far back as that dance sophomore year, when she had worn the royal blue dress they found at the Fashion Show Mall. Malaya had actually whooped when Honorata agreed to buy it for her; she was so sure her mother would not let her have it. And then they had gone together to a salon to have Malaya's hair put up and her nails done in a bright contrasting pink, and she had been so pretty, so happy.

Had Honorata actually worried about that dance? Worried about the boy and the party bus and the group of friends all dressed up, posing for photos in the park? It was so innocent, compared with the friends Malaya had found the next summer, compared with the way she had started dressing after her job at the movie theater; after the boyfriend, Martin, who was so thin it had to be drugs, with his shaved head and his chains and those ridiculous boots. "Mom, you don't know anything about who's nice and who's not!" Malaya had yelled at her. "You don't have any idea what kids are like!" And Honorata had remembered how distressed her own mother had been when she kept disappearing with Kidlat, and so she had not put her foot down, but she should have. She should have stopped Malaya; at least she wouldn't have that tattoo.

Jimbo thought he had never seen a more lovely girl. She was taller than Honorata, and her face was a bit like his mother's. His eyes watered. He wanted to say hello, but he was trying very hard to stay composed. He stared at her and then looked down. He was helpless.

"Malaya. This is Mr. Wohlmann."

Everyone seemed uncomfortable, and still Jimbo could not bring himself to look up. This was terrible. He was the man. He was the father. But he didn't want to lose control. He didn't want to embarrass her.

"I'm glad you came."

Her voice was familiar, from the message she'd left on his phone. He had played it over and over, but he had not called her back. He had been afraid to chase her away, without ever getting to see her.

He took a deep breath and stood up.

"Hello, Malaya. It's an honor to meet you."

He was funny. An honor. And he looked like he was crying. Which was sort of embarrassing. But it was nice to think he cared that much. That he really wanted to meet her.

"Malaya likes movies. And she's very good at dancing."

Her mother was so awkward. Malaya was annoyed that she had said this.

"Not really. I mean, everybody likes the movies. And I just take dance lessons. It's not like I'm going to be a dancer or something."

Honorata was surprised. Malaya always said that she was going to be a dancer, whenever she told her daughter that this was not a job, not a career, not a practical plan for a smart girl.

"I'm sure you're a very good dancer."

This was the first thing he said to his own

daughter. And it came out oddly. He knew what Honorata thought of him: that he was some sort of sex monster. Which was about as far from the truth as something could be. But he was going to make it all worse. He didn't know what to say to this girl, to this very young girl in front of him. He felt sick.

"I like science too."

"Really? What do you like?"

"Chemistry. My chemistry teacher's pretty good, and everyone thinks she's too hard, but I like that it's hard. And I like being in the lab. I might study chemistry in college."

Honorata did not recognize this daughter. She had said she hated chemistry and that Honorata should not be surprised if she failed, because the teacher was a witch.

"I studied chemistry in college," Jimbo offered.

"You did?"

"Yes. I'm a chemical engineer. Or I was. I started my own company a long time ago."

Malaya didn't say anything.

"Do you want some pastries?" Honorata asked. "Mr. Wohlmann brought some."

Malaya shook her head. And they all stood there, uneasy.

"Do you want to take a walk?" the girl asked. "Just down the block?"

Jimbo looked at Honorata. He saw her

freeze, and he knew that even now she was afraid. He was about to say no, to tell his daughter he'd rather stay in, when Honorata spoke.

"Stay in the neighborhood, Malaya. Just walk around here."

Malaya nodded, and Jimbo said, "Yes. Yes, I would like to take a walk."

Honorata felt lightheaded as she watched the two of them walk toward the front door. Jimbo wasn't frightening now, the way he had always seemed in her mind or the way he had been just weeks before. If she were meeting him for the first time, she would notice how self-conscious he was, how his hands trembled, how his voice was too high for his size. She would notice that he kept his head lowered slightly, as if anticipating a blow.

How could he have once been terrifying? He was rich. He looked rich. And he was big. But he was the opposite of frightening. He looked like someone who would always have time to read at Sunday Mass, to help with the ushering, to replace the bulletins in the pews. When she lived with him — it was amazing that she could have that thought without fear — when she lived with him, he had talked and talked and talked. So many words that washed over her, that she could not remember, even then, even an hour after he stopped talking, and she thought now that he must have noticed she did not remember, that she did not pay attention, and this hadn't mattered, because — and how could this be the first time she had realized this? — because nobody ever listened to him. He was used to being ignored.

It didn't change what he had done. It didn't change the horror of what her uncle had done, of those months in Chicago, of all the memories that had played over and over again in her mind all these years, but it did somehow relieve her. The money she had won, the daughter she adored, her whole life: it was connected to this. To Jimbo's loneliness. To the way he seemed as if he thought he were about to be struck. This was an idea that surprised her. That Malaya had come not from violence but from sorrow.

Coral backed out of her garage slowly. There were people walking in the street, and she looked down at her phone, to see if she had any messages, while they walked by. She clicked through the list — Ada's riot of emoticons and a cat video from Isa — and then she backed her car onto the street.

It was Malaya walking. Malaya and an older man, quite large. They were straight ahead of her, and in her rearview mirror, she caught sight of Honorata standing near her mailbox, watching the two. Something about her pose alerted Coral, and she looked again. Was that Malaya's father?

His head was tipped down, listening to his daughter. He was a big man, but he walked lightly. Beside him, Malaya Begtang's face was lit up. She was talking, and her hands were moving, and while Coral watched her, she took a little skipping step, either to catch up with her father's stride or out of pleasure — Coral couldn't tell. She looked young, younger than she had seemed in a long time, and Coral thought of the little girl who would stop by to show Trey her artwork, or to ask if she could give the little boys some *suman* her grandmother had made. That little girl had been so beautiful, so full of light.

For a second, Coral imagined she saw that light shining off Malaya's rainbow hair, reflecting on her father's navy suit. She thought of her own boys, of the way they still curled into her lap or into Koji's, like animals claiming their owned territory. She thought of Trey, and of her husband standing on his tiptoes to rest an arm around his nephew's shoulders. She thought of her brother telling everyone at school that she was a 100 percent Jackson. She thought of her mother, holding her hand as they sang at Macedonia Baptist on Sundays. And here was Malaya, looking into the face of the father she had thought she might never know.

Malaya and her father reached the corner. As they turned to walk toward the park, the girl looked back, past Coral in her car, to her mother still standing near the mailbox. The girl looked, and she smiled, and she waved. Tiny in the rearview mirror, Honorata waved back.

36

Coral had lived in Las Vegas for nearly all of her forty-nine years, but she had never set foot in the El Capitan. It was ironic that she would be headed there now — nearly two years after it had been scheduled for demolition, more than three decades since her father had died, now that her brother no longer owned it.

But Engracia worked at the El Capitan — had apparently worked there before her son had died — and she had been so reluctant to meet with Coral, so reluctant to discuss that day or what she had done, Coral wasn't about to complicate things by not accepting the first place she suggested. Engracia would come to the Midnight Cafe at nine in the morning, just after her shift ended. Coral had intended to be there early, but Isa couldn't find his baseball mitt, and Gus had yelled that if he were late, he wouldn't get to play and why did Isa always lose his things, and so Coral had stopped to help Isa find his glove, and Koji had given her a quick kiss; she could catch up with them later.

She was on her way to the El Capitan to meet Engracia at the request of Honorata.

Her neighbor had knocked on the door a few weeks after the incident and asked if she had time for some tea. She had made a cake, if Coral wanted to come down. So Coral, who wondered why Honorata had not called first, raised her eyebrow to Koji, ruffled the top of Isa's hair, and told them she'd be back in an hour or so.

Honorata's house was very clean. There were several pieces of furniture made of black lacquered wood, and, as usual, there was not a speck of dust showing. There were embroidered pillows on each chair, and embroidered curtains in the kitchen; Honorata had made these. It was a cheerful room, very light, and Honorata's mother was there, playing something on an iPad.

"Hello, Mrs. Navarro. It's nice to see you."

Honorata's mother stopped playing her game long enough to stand up and give her neighbor a hug. "Hello, hello," she said. Coral had never heard her speak much more English than this, but Nanay had been sending Malaya down with plates of *lumpia* and *pancit* for years. Coral knew that Nanay appreciated how Malaya felt about them: had noticed the hours Keisha spent playing with her when she was a toddler, had observed Trey's gentle teasing when she was eight, knew how much Gus and Isa had loved their babysitter.

Honorata motioned for Coral to sit down, and then she brought out a cake, decorated with coconut and set on a clear glass cake stand.

"It's a beautiful cake."

Honorata's mother nodded approvingly.

"Good cook. My daughter good cook."

Coral thought of Augusta, who had lived in her own house to the very end. She had never been sick enough to leave it, though Coral had always thought that her mother would one day live with her, and that she would have the chance to care for Augusta in the way her mother had cared for her. But it wasn't to be. At seventy-six, which wasn't so old, her heart gave out. They'd always known it would be her heart.

Honorata sliced the cake, poured some tea, and placed three sections of tangerine on each plate before handing one to Coral and another to her mother.

"Is Malaya home?"

"She's asleep. I want to talk before she

comes down."

"Of course."

Coral had thought Honorata might want to explain about Malaya's father, but she didn't say anything about James Wohlmann. She must have known that Malaya had told Coral everything, but Honorata didn't give Coral any more information. This also made Coral think of Augusta, and how her own mother had never felt the need to explain herself. Still, Coral had just seen Malaya walking down the street with her father; she wondered how things were going.

"My housekeeper, Engracia . . ."

"Yes."

"I'm worried."

"Malaya told me about her son."

"Yes. But that's not why I'm worried."

"Oh."

Honorata did not continue right away, so Coral took another bite of cake. The grandmother patted her arm in an encouraging way. Finally, her neighbor continued.

"She's nice person, this housekeeper. Wise person. Even though she's very young."

Honorata wiped some crumbs off the counter, added some more cake to her mother's plate, picked up a napkin that had fallen to the floor.

"She might not be legal. Immigrant, I mean."

"Right. Well, I don't think what happened here will matter. The police don't turn that sort of stuff over to Immigration. And she didn't do anything."

"Yes. I see."

"Is she still working for you? Is she worried Immigration will find her?"

"No. She hasn't come back to work here."

Coral could have predicted that Honorata would not tell her why. Her neighbor didn't have ordinary conversations with people. Talking with her was like throwing a ball against a cracked wall: it bounced back, but not necessarily the way you predicted.

"She took the gun."

"What?"

"She took Jimbo's gun. She hid it in her pocket. The police didn't search her."

"Wow."

"That took a lot of courage. To take a gun when she's not legal. Right?"

"Well, courage is one word. It was definitely a risk."

"She just did it. She understood the problem. She understood how everything was going to go bad, how it was going to go bad for Malaya's father. She just fixed it. She fixed the problem, all by herself."

"I guess. I'm not sure. I mean, if Malaya's father had had a gun, they would have arrested him. I'm sure of that."

"Maybe he wouldn't have let them take him."

"Oh. Yeah. That would have been bad."

"It would have been bad for Malaya," Honorata said. "She would never recover from this. In her own house. After she found him. So mad at me."

"Yeah. I think you're right. I think that would have been terrible for Malaya."

"So. Engracia. This young woman. Who lost her child. She saved mine."

Coral's eyes watered. It was true, probably. If Engracia had gotten the gun away from Malaya's father. If it was because of her that the whole thing hadn't exploded.

"Does Malaya know this?"

"No. Malaya doesn't know her father had a gun."

"She told me about Engracia's son. How Engracia told you and her father about him."

"Yes, she knows that."

"So, what are you thinking?"

"I'm thinking that a very nice woman has a gun, and is not legal, and also, her son has died."

Yes. Coral agreed. The gun was dangerous

in anyone's hands, and certainly in Engracia's. She'd be deported in a minute if she were caught with it. And, too, she was awfully vulnerable right now. A gun could be dangerous in so many ways.

"Have you talked with her? Asked her about the gun?"

"No."

"Do you think you could do that?"

"No."

Coral waited.

"Engracia doesn't like me, I think. She doesn't like that I didn't tell Malaya's father about her."

"She said this?"

"No."

"Well, okay. But you're just going to call her and ask about the gun. See if she got rid of it. Where it is."

"Maybe the police are listening to my phone."

"I doubt it."

"Maybe her number doesn't work anymore."

"Her phone? Did you try it?"

"Yes. It's disconnected."

"Well, I don't know how we would find her. Do you know her last name?"

"Montoya."

"Okay. Engracia Montoya. Illegal immigrant. We're not finding her."

"I worry about it every night. I worry about her. I want to help her."

"Well. How did you hire her? Do you know someone that knows her?"

"Father Burns. From Saint Anne's church. He asked me to hire her. He knows her."

"Okay. Well. Call him."

This was getting a little frustrating. Why was Coral here?

"No. I can't call. She won't take my call, and Father Burns won't tell me about her."

"So?"

"You could call Father Burns. You could talk with Engracia."

"Me? That doesn't make any sense at all."

"It does. You're a teacher. People feel safe with teachers. I want to give her some money." Honorata pulled out an envelope thick with cash. "For saving my daughter. You can give this to her. And you can tell her about the gun; about how they will deport her."

Honorata pushed the envelope of cash across the table, and Coral was looking at it, thinking this felt weirdly wrong, like a drug deal or something.

"I don't know anything about deportation. Nothing."

"Your husband's an immigrant."

Coral couldn't think of anything to say. Koji had been an American citizen for years. And Honorata was an immigrant too. Her neighbor could be so odd. It was kind of her to want to give this money to Engracia, Coral appreciated that, but it wasn't anything Coral could do for her. The boys wanted to see a movie today. She had hoped to bag items for the Salvation Army to pick up. It was time to go.

"Please, Coral. I trust you. Just call her. Find a way to give her the money. Get the gun. Make sure she doesn't have the gun. I can't sleep at all. I think of her every night, and I need your help."

Coral wasn't sure what to say. She didn't want to get in the middle of this. But the truth was that she'd been thinking about Engracia too. She hadn't known about the gun, of course, but she remembered the housekeeper sitting in her car, wanting to go to the church, looking for a place that was safe. Malaya had said her son was ten years old. So was Isa.

Oh, what the hell. Augusta would have said yes.

"Okay. Honorata, I'll try. I'll see if I can find her, if she'll talk to me. I don't know when. But I'll work on it. I'll let you know."

She regretted it the second she said it.

499

But it was too late. Honorata's face was transformed. Coral rarely saw her neighbor look unguarded in this way. Her eyes were bright, and she was smiling, and she reached out to take Coral's hand.

Well, all right. This would be awkward, but she would do it.

Coral didn't do anything about the envelope of cash for several days. She told Koji what Honorata had asked, and he raised his eyebrows when he saw how much money it was, but he told Coral it wouldn't hurt to try. For sure, Engracia could use the money.

On Wednesday, she looked up the number for Saint Anne's and left a message with the receptionist asking the priest to call her.

"Hello?"

"Coral Jackson? This is Father Burns."

"Father, thanks for calling. I appreciate it. Listen, I'm looking for a woman. She did some housekeeping for my neighbor. Her name is Engracia Montoya?"

"Oh, Engracia. Yes. She isn't working as a housekeeper now. I'm sorry."

"Oh no, I don't want her to clean my house. I wanted to talk with her. I wondered if you had a phone number."

"Well, um . . ."

"I gave her a ride home one day. Some-

500

thing happened in the neighborhood, and I gave her a ride. And I've been worried about her. I know about her son. I know she lost her child."

"Yes. Engracia has had a difficult time."

He sounded like an old man, rather formal, like someone with money. Not quite the way she imagined a priest.

"I just want to make sure she's okay. And there's something else. Something I want to talk to her about. I have something to give her."

"Well, I can see. Perhaps I can call Engracia. She'll have to call you."

"Sure. Here's my phone number. If she wants, all three of us can talk. If that would make her feel better."

"Well, I'll see. She'll probably be here tonight, and I'll ask her. Okay?"

"Thank you, Father."

Of course, Engracia did not call. Coral had to call twice more, feeling a little more foolish each time, but she had this stupid envelope of cash, and there was still the question of the gun. Coral was not about to ask Father Burns if he knew about the gun. She did say that she knew someone who wanted to give Engracia a gift.

She almost missed the call when it came.

It was early on a Saturday morning, not even light. She didn't recognize the number, and she was just about to roll over and fall back to sleep when she thought of Engracia.

"Hello?"

"Hello," Engracia's voice was very quiet. "I'm Engracia Montoya."

"Engracia, thank you for calling. This is Coral. I drove you home, awhile ago, after the thing . . . the thing with the police."

"Si."

"How are you?"

She didn't reply.

"I mean, uh, I hope you're doing well. I called you because I was hoping we could meet. Ms. Navarro wants to give you a gift. She appreciates what you did that day. She's very grateful. And she'd like to give you something."

"I don't want anything."

"I understand. I do. But maybe we could just talk. Ms. Navarro is worried about something else. She wants to be sure you're okay."

"I'm okay."

"Do you think we could just meet? Just for ten minutes? I can meet you anywhere. At your house? At work?"

"I don't want anything."

"Engracia. You saved a whole family. You saved Ms. Navarro's daughter from a lot of pain. She's grateful. Please, just meet with me."

There was a long silence.

"Please. Don't hang up."

"I work at the El Capitan."

Coral's heart skipped. She would never be free of that place.

"I could meet you after my work. In the Midnight Cafe. I get off at nine."

"Today?"

"Yes."

"That's great. Thank you, Engracia. I'll be there."

She didn't say good-bye. Coral heard the phone click, checked for the number. It looked like a hotel. She had probably called from a room in the hotel.

So here she was now, racing to make it to the El Capitan before nine, and wondering what exactly she was going to say to Engracia Montoya. She had the money with her, but mostly there was the issue of the gun. Engracia might not reveal the truth about the gun, but maybe Coral could just tell her some of the risks of having it. How much more difficult Immigration would be if she were caught with that gun.

Thank God she was alive.

She figured Father Burns would have told her if something had happened, but he didn't give away much information. Each time she called, he just said that he would give Engracia the message again.

Coral took a shortcut to the back side of the casino, but a fence blocked the road a short ways from the hotel, so she pulled her car onto a patch of gravel and made her way around the fenced area on foot. Construction had stopped so fast on the Strip, when the money dried up a few years ago, that nobody had bothered to even move the trucks or the cranes or the lifts off the lots where the new casinos were to have been built. They just sat there, hulking, rusting beasts, and behind this array of them stood the faded façade of the El Capitan, with its arched entry and its old-fashioned neon and some of the letters missing in the sign: "C–me On In! Ge– Rich!"

The Midnight Cafe was just to the right of the main entry, in an older part of the casino. The whole place looked dilapidated, though the newer half had a tropical 1980s feel, whereas the older part was darker and lower, with wood paneling on the walls and a deep red fabric above it. The cafe sign was an old-fashioned marquee with a 1950s pin-up girl splayed across the letters M-i-d-n-i-g-h-t, and Coral gathered that the room had once been a nightclub. She took a booth on the side, facing the door, so that she would see Engracia when she entered. It was 8:55. Her shift had not yet ended.

Coral looked around to be sure Engracia wasn't there. Then she picked up the heavy leatherette binder that held the menu.

"What'll you have, honey?"

The waitress looked at least sixty, with bouffant hair and a big, smothering bustline and a Southern accent, though she might have lived in Vegas for decades.

"Coffee, please. I'll order when my friend arrives."

"No problem. Cream and sugar?"

"Just cream."

The cafe must have been remodeled shortly before the economic crash. Enormous black-and-white photos ringed the wall; they looked like they might be pictures taken at the El Capitan in its early years. She could see a line of showgirls, a group of men standing around a roulette table, and what might be Del Dibb posing with a little girl and smoking a big cigar.

Coral looked down at the menu. Her stomach did a small flip. She wished that Engracia worked somewhere else. This casino meant nothing to her, and yet in a way, maybe *she* meant something to *it*. She didn't like being in here. Didn't like that photo of Del Dibb.

The menu told the story of the cafe. It had started as a nightspot, the Midnight Room, and in the heyday of the El Capitan, it had been one of the premier clubs in town. Sammy Davis Junior had played there. And Jimmy Durante. Marlene Dietrich had stopped by to see Eddie Knox, and sung a duet with him. They'd kept it a nightclub even after they had expanded the casino, ran small local shows in it: revues of past hits, things like that. After June Dibb retired, her son Marshall had turned the nightclub into a cafe and decorated it with these enormous vintage photos from a starrier past.

Coral looked around for Engracia. It was 9:10. She probably had a time clock to punch.

"More coffee, honey?"

"Sure."

"Want a pastry? Tide you over?"

"No, thanks. She'll be here any minute."

But she wasn't there any minute.

Ten minutes passed, then twenty. It was 9:40. Obviously Engracia wasn't coming. Coral had upended her whole morning, was going to miss Gus's game, and then just sat here, drinking cup after cup of pretty good coffee.

"You sure you don't want something to eat, honey? It's on me. I won't charge you."

"Oh, thank you. No. I'm going to go. I was really hoping my friend was still coming."

"She doesn't have a phone?"

"No. But she works here. She's a maid. Do you know if there's anyone I could ask?"

"Well, you could try Arturo. Over at the cashier desk. This is payday, and a lot of the maids cash their checks when they get off."

"Okay. Thanks."

Coral paid her bill, left a large tip, and walked over to the cashier. Arturo was an old man, wearing a brocaded vest and a shirt with silver tips on the collar.

"Hi. I'm looking for someone who works here. A maid?"

"I might know her. I don't know."

"Her name's Engracia. Engracia Montoya. She got off at nine today?"

Arturo gave her a funny look.

"You know Engracia?"

"Yes. A little. She called me this morning, about five. She asked me to meet her at nine."

"Well, she's gone."

"Oh. Do you know where?"

"She cashed her check."

The man seemed to hesitate.

"I'd really like to see her. I have a gift."

The man looked carefully at Coral. Finally, he spoke.

"She wasn't wearing her uniform. Maybe she's not coming back."

Coral thought about this.

"Because she has to give back her uniform if she quits?"

"Yes. I work here a long time. And the maids cash their checks with me. But when they're not wearing their blue dresses, sometimes they're not coming back."

"Did you talk with her?"

Arturo was quiet. He looked down as if he was not sure whether to say something or not.

"Please," Coral said. "I want to help her."

"I don't know anything. She didn't tell me she was leaving. Maybe she comes back tomorrow."

"Okay. Did she say anything?"

"No. But Engracia and I . . . When I see Engracia, I say a prayer. We say it together. Because of her son."

Arturo's eyes were very sad, and Coral felt her own throat tighten. Poor Engracia.

"Thank you. Thanks for your help. My

name is Coral. If she comes back."

"If she comes back," he said.

Coral was about to leave the casino and hike back across the abandoned construction lot to her car when she realized she had left her sunglasses on the table at the cafe. She walked in, and immediately, the waitress called to her from across the room.

"Your sunglasses?"

"Yes. Did you find them?"

"I have them. On my way. Let me just drop this plate."

Coral turned and looked at the large black-and-white photo nearest to her. It was Del Dibb, of course, Del Dibb as large as life, standing with a big grin on his face, his hand resting on the shoulder of his wife, who was seated in a chair below him. June Dibb was a slight woman. Coral remembered the one time she'd seen her, when Augusta took her to Del's funeral: more than thirty years ago, the day she first learned who her father was. June had worn a hat and sunglasses, and Coral still remembered her motionless small foot in a high heel.

She looked at June now, mostly to look away from Del. She was very pretty, with curly, dark hair and a long, pale neck. She sat with one knee crossed over the other, and Coral recognized the slim foot in the high sandal that she had fixated on so many decades before. June had her hands in her lap. She was wearing a big diamond ring. But it was the oddest thing. Her hand was so familiar. It looked exactly like someone else's hand. Like a hand she knew.

And with a sudden, sickening jolt, Coral realized that June's hand looked exactly like her own. Long narrow fingers with wide shell-like nails and the wrist unnaturally thin, the bones on the top of the hand visible and the thumb with its disproportionately large first joint. With something like horror or exaltation or maybe just shock, Coral followed the line of that hand, of those fingers, of June's laughing, delighted face, right to where she was looking: to the third figure in the photo, a man, who looked back at June, and there was no mistaking the feeling in his eyes. The man was Eddie Knox, and here they were: her parents.

37

Engracia had stayed in Las Vegas because she could not leave Diego there alone. Juan had to go back to Mexico. It was dangerous for him in the States. He could end up in jail for much longer than a month. And her mother, her father, her brothers, they had not been able to come to the funeral. Juan had offered to bring them, but it was harder than one imagined it would be. They didn't have passports. They didn't even have identification cards. There was no way to get them there in time. Her mama could not come with a coyote.

So the padre had been there. And Juan. And Engracia. And Mary from the El Capitan, with a whole group of maids. And the man who cashed her check. One of the nurses from the hospital came too. And the mother who had given Diego breakfast each day, and Mateo, the boy with the gun. Pilar drove up from Pomona with Maria and

Javier and Oscar. When Pilar saw Engracia, she started to keen: "I'm sorry, I'm so sorry, I should never have told you to go."

And through all of that, Engracia had been numb.

She had said hello and accepted their hugs, and even answered as to whether she had eaten, or whether she was cold in the air conditioning, and as to how beautiful the flowers from the ICU team were. None of it was real.

It had been real in the hospital.

It had been real after she and Juan had said the doctors could stop the machine, after the nurse had explained that Engracia could stay with Diego, could get in the bed and hold her son, but that as soon as he died, as soon as his heart stopped beating, they would have to take him away fast. Because of the organs. Because Juan and Engracia had said they could take their son's organs.

It was Padre Burns who said that would be okay. Who said he thought it would help. He said that child-sized organs were so rare, they would probably keep another child alive. Juan had said no, he would not allow it, but Engracia had said yes. Somewhere there was another mother, so she had said yes.

"No, Engracia. No, not this!" Juan had cried.

"Si, mi amor. Si."

And so she was all by herself in a city she barely knew and hated deeply. Now that Diego was not with her, the street in front of her apartment did not frighten her. The sounds of the sirens, the shouts, people running at night — these felt right now. The world should be falling apart. There should be shouts and sirens and wails in the night. How else could the world be?

At first, she had not been able to imagine returning to the El Capitan. So the padre had found her some work in people's homes. And then there had been the strange day at Ms. Navarro's house, and after that, she had not gone back to those jobs. She wanted to be home with her mama, with Juan — who was fixing her uncle's abandoned house for them. He wanted her to return to Zacatecas, to her village. Juan no longer wanted to have his own business and make a lot of money in the States; he wanted to stay on the dry hot land, grow beans and eat tortillas, and play in a mariachi band as his father had done.

Yet Engracia could not leave Diego, the only American in the family. So she had returned to the El Capitan. She rarely spoke to anyone. She went to Mass every day, and sometimes she went twice. Most days, the padre came and offered her some tea, and they talked about the Mass, or the way it was taking so long to get cold this year, and sometimes, but not enough, they talked about Diego.

But now it was done.

She would have to leave.

She couldn't face the teacher. She didn't want to know anything about Ms. Navarro or her daughter or the man with the gun. She didn't care about a gift. She had called the woman named Coral because the priest had asked her to, and she had agreed to meet with her because she didn't know what else to say. But as soon as she had done it, she knew that she would leave. She would finish her shift, cash her check, and go to Padre Burns. Then she would say good-bye to her son, lie down on his grave and eat some of the dirt, and she would go home. To her mother. To Juan.

A few days later, she stood talking with the padre while a sedan idled nearby.

"I've paid them already," he explained. "They'll take you all the way."

"*Si.*"

to not have enough money, but he was glad he had done so.

He had said that Engracia belonged to this land as well. He wished that he could stay longer and help her to know this. But now he was going to meet his grandson, and he would hold Diego for her. He would make sure her son knew how much he was loved. He and Diego would have some fun.

38

Today I had a brain scan. An MRI.

It was Marshall's idea, of course. I have seen lots of doctors, and they suggest different diagnoses. Alzheimer's. Senility. A form of Parkinson's. I don't quite fit any of these. Aphasia. For sure, I have aphasia, though I am not sure Marshall or the doctors understand this as clearly as I do.

Anyway, there is a new clinic in town. A brain center. And Marshall has given them money in my name, and now I have to do more tests. With the brain doctors. Though I've been seeing doctors all along. I don't mind, if it makes Marshall feel better, though I don't think these tests are going to help. Maybe there is a medicine for me, but it seems more likely that I'll be one of the ones that help the doctors figure things out for the next generation. That's okay. That pleases me.

I had a good life. A long life. And we all

have to die.

I don't want to die, though. I wish I could have been like my Aunt Ruth, who died last year at ninety-nine and lived on her own, without help, until just before. But Ruth was extraordinary. Most of us aren't like Ruth. I'm not. It's a funny thing. To know there is nothing left but to die. To know that one has already gotten the good life, already missed all the things that might lead to an early death, and still, for life to seem so short. Still to want more. Even with an existence like mine. When I can't do anything I mean to do. When I spend my days with people who are paid to take care of me. Yet I still like it. Living, I mean.

I still hear the birds sing. I still notice the sunlight dappled on the table, the way the light moves when the leaves tremble. I still love music. I still have memories. I dream. In my dreams, I sometimes see them all. Del and my father and my mother. Marshall and a tiny, pink-swathed girl. Even if I am not dreaming, even when I am just remembering, it's all so vivid. My life comes back strongly. So many sounds: music and laughter and tears and Marshall's toddler voice: "This way, Mommy! Let's go this way." The feelings come back. All of them. Excitement and rage and contentment and fear. I'm not ready to give it up. I don't suppose I ever will be. And even now, it still seems like there must be something I could do, there must be some way to slow it down. But of course there's not. There never was.

Helen took me to the appointment. We had to be there early, before seven. And Helen couldn't figure out how to get into the place, though we could see it from a long way off. A bizarre, curving building, with a metal roof folded in on itself, and the walls appearing to tip, as if it were all about to slide, or implode, or collapse upon itself. No wonder Helen couldn't figure out how to get to it. It was disorienting to look at. Which is kind of funny, for a brain center. Like when some of the newer casinos piped in oxygen to get rid of the smell of cigarette smoke, they said, but really, because it made people feel good, and so it was just one more way to keep them inside the place. Maybe this crazy-looking building makes its patients feel a bit crazy, like they belong there more than they had thought they did. I laughed, and Helen said, "It's not funny. Marshall told me not to be late." Which, of course, was funny to me.

The technician took me into a little room with Helen, and explained that I would have to wear nothing but the robe, and that the most important thing was for me not to move during the testing. Was I claustrophobic? Had the doctor given me something to take? What time had I taken it? Helen explained that I had taken something to relax me at six — I didn't know that — and also that it was best for him not to tell me what to do. It would be better not to give me instructions. Maybe it had something to do with whatever Helen had given me at six, but this made me laugh too. It was true, of course. Giving me instructions was a disaster. But then, my mother would have said the same thing. I laughed and laughed. Helen looked a bit exasperated; she was still upset about not being able to find her way into the parking lot, and the technician started reading the notes on his clipboard. Maybe it was notes about me; he stopped telling me what to do.

His name was Ahmad, and he helped me lie down on a narrow table in a room that was glaringly white, and he placed my head on a pillow, and fit some earphones over my ears, and put something in my hand to hold. It was all very easy. My body didn't jerk or cramp. I just lay there and he silently positioned me, and pulled a sort of metal frame over my head. Then I heard a small motor, and the bed on which I was lying slid slowly backward until I was encased in a white tube.

"Mrs. Dibb, are you feeling all right?"

The voice came through the earphones, but I did not reply. I felt sort of woozy, like I was about to fall asleep.

"This first test will last about thirty seconds, and you'll hear some funny noises. Okay?"

It sounded like a lawnmower, swooshing toward me and back, not quite touching my toes.

"Good, Mrs. Dibb. Thank you. This next test is longer. It's the longest one. It will take nine minutes and thirty seconds."

He gave such oddly specific times. As if I had a watch or could see a clock. All I saw was white. A white metal frame twelve inches above my head, and, beyond that, a white metal tube, like being inside a fluorescent bulb.

The nine-minute test was a spring being sprung — *twang thump* — at regular intervals, and I imagined a circus tent lifting slowly into the air, each *twang thump* the sound of another tether breaking loose. *Twang thump,* and a red-striped corner lifts. *Twang thump,* I can see sky beneath the flapping section. *Twang thump,* the fabric dances in the wind. *Twang thump,* round and round the tent, until finally, nine minutes and twenty-seven seconds later, the tent lifts: a soaring, spinning candy cane sphere, bright against the blue sky. And just before Ahmad asks how I am doing, I see a little girl, dark-haired as I was, looking up and pointing at the sight.

The other tests are less relaxing. For four minutes, there is a high-pitched series of whirs and clicks that remind me of my grandson playing video games at the beach house, and then there are three or four more tests, all identified for me by their duration: this one three minutes and thirty seconds, that one forty-five seconds, the next one five minutes. I have lived long enough to hear the sound of magnets taking photos of my brain, and I am pleased about this, and I wish I could live longer, to see all of the other things we will discover.

Afterward, I am very tired. Helen takes me home, and I go to the sunroom, where I like to take a nap in the afternoons. I don't know how long I'm there, a few minutes, a few hours, but I wake to the sound of the doorbell ringing, and then of Helen telling someone — someone she doesn't recognize, I can tell — that I am not available, that I do not take callers without an appointment, that the woman can call my son, Marshall, if she wishes to see me.

"Please. My name's Coral. I just want to say hello. I think she'll want to see me."

"No. I've asked you to leave, and if I have to, I'll call the police."

"Of course. I understand. You're doing your job, and I know Ms. Dibb is not well, I know I'm asking a lot. It's just, I really want to see her. And I think she'll want to see me."

By this time, I have gotten up and headed for the door. Whatever Helen gave me this morning makes me loopy, but it also seems to help me do what I want. I crack sharply into a hutch. Well, at least it sort of helps me. I am headed to the door, if not in a very direct way.

"Oh! Oh! Oh!" I call.

"Miss June, it's okay. You're all right. There's nothing you need to worry about out here."

Helen is annoyed. At me, at whoever is at the door.

"Oh!" I call louder.

"Ma'am, you'll have to go. I'm busy."

I can't see what is happening, but I don't hear the door close. I can't hear what the woman who is there says.

"Let it snow, let it snow, let it snow," I sing, bizarrely.

"Everything's all right, Miss June. I'm coming."

"Rockin' robin. Tweet, tweet, tweet! Rockin' robin." I am coming full speed now. I've taken a route through the dining room, instead of straight to the front door, but the singing is helping me get there.

"Hopping and a-bopping and a-singing his song."

I come around the corner and catch sight of my visitor. She's a black woman, maybe fifty, wearing a well-cut suit and good shoes and holding a leather bag. I don't know her, which is disappointing, because I thought she said I would want to see her.

"There was no reason to get up," Helen says to me.

"Hello, Mrs. Dibb," says the woman in a strangely strained way.

"Tweet, tweet, tweet!" I sing.

The woman looks toward Helen, who isn't about to explain anything to her. Helen tells me to go back to the sunroom — I really don't like Helen very much — and then she tells the woman that I have had a very long morning and cannot be disturbed.

"I'm sorry to bother you. I'd like to come back. Maybe another day this week? I'd just like to talk with Mrs. Dibb for a little bit."

"I told you to contact Mrs. Dibb's son. If

he says it's okay, then that will be fine."

I flail my right arm wildly, and it knocks against the entryway table, which hurts, and which also causes a picture frame that is standing there to fall over. Helen comes over to steady me, and the woman looks at me intently. I think about Matt, I think about him singing "S'wonderful," and the way the sun helps me stretch when we do our therapy sessions outside. I concentrate on Matt as hard as I can, and sure enough, I say what I want to say.

"Please stay. Please stay now."

"Miss June, I don't think that's a good idea."

"Helen, go in the kitchen."

"I'll stay with you, Miss June."

"No!"

My voice is sharp, and the woman listens to the two of us quietly, without saying anything, and then she says, "What about if Mrs. Dibb and I just sit down, right over there? Mrs. Dibb?"

And she reaches out her hand, and I take it, and, miraculously, we just walk over to the two chairs arranged by the fireplace, and I sit down, without a jolt or a jerk or a pull in the wrong direction. The woman holds my hand lightly, but she does not let it go when I sit down. She looks at it; she looks at my hand as if it means something to her, so I look at it, and I look at hers, darker than mine, but similarly long and slender. We both have shell-shaped nails. I never liked my nails, but they look sort of nice on her.

Helen rustles over, impatience brimming.

"Tea," I say.

I'm feeling really proud of myself, which is a mistake, because it will almost certainly put an end to this little moment where my body seems to be listening to me. The woman sits down in the chair next to mine.

"My name's Coral Jackson. I teach choir at Foothill High School."

Oh darn. I hope she's not here to ask for money.

"But that lucky old sun got nothin' to do but roll around heaven all day." I'd rather sing than talk about money. If I wanted to do something with my money, I wouldn't be able to do it. Marshall handles all that, and I can't even tell him that I want a bite of dinner.

I've already stopped thinking about Coral Jackson, but she surprises me by picking up my song.

"Fuss with my woman, toil for my kids, sweat 'til I'm wrinkled and gray."

She has a beautiful voice. Beautiful. I

stomp my feet and shake my head a bit. And she keeps singing.

"While that lucky old sun has nothin' to do, but roll around heaven all day."

"Roll around heaven all day," I sing back.

She smiles.

"I'm sorry to come without calling. I was going to call your son, Marshall."

She knows Marshall.

"But . . . but I . . . I didn't do it."

Is this about Marshall? Is he okay? How does she know Marshall?

"I mean, I will call him. I'm happy to call him and tell him that I want to visit you. I just . . . I was nearby. I just stopped."

I wish she would sing again. I try. *"Would you like to swing on a star? Carry moonbeams home in a jar?"*

Something about my singing bothers her. I see her lip tremble, and her forehead crease. She looks down at her hands.

"My mother is Augusta Jackson."

It's a familiar name. But, of course, there could be a lot of Augusta Jacksons. Who was Augusta?

"She worked for your husband a long time ago."

Augusta Jackson! Of course. Ray's wife.

"No, no, no," I say, nodding my head and smiling.

"You remember her?"

She understands that I meant yes. This is Augusta's daughter. She's coming to say thank you. All those years that Del took care of that family. And Leo kept it up after, whatever it was that Del had arranged.

"My mother told me a story."

It's nice of her to come and see me, an old woman. I wonder if Augusta's still alive. She was about my age. A little older, maybe.

"She told me a story about your husband."

Are those tears? There are tears running down Coral Jackson's face. But she keeps talking, as if they aren't even there.

"It was 1960."

So Augusta's daughter is a teacher. She dresses nicely for a teacher. It's great to think that Del helped her somehow. He loved Ray so much. This must be Ray's youngest, the one that was the same age as Marshall.

The woman is looking down at her lap. She seems to be having trouble speaking. I want to pat her on the knee, tell her it was really so little. That money. She shouldn't feel a debt, because her father had been so important to Del. Del would have given Ray much more than that if he'd lived. And also, nobody had ever really known what happened when Ray died.

I don't like to think of those days. How naïve I was. How little I understood. I sing to stop thinking.

"Ol' man river. That old man river. He just keeps rolling. He just keeps rolling along."

She doesn't join me this time.

She keeps looking down, and I can hear the teakettle whistling, and I know Helen is making some tea for us.

"I get weary, and sick of trying. I'm tired of living, and feared of dying."

I hear Helen pick it up in the kitchen. She can sing too, though she almost never sings with me. *"And ol' man river, he just keeps rolling along."*

The woman looks up. She is clearly crying; she seems really upset. I feel bad for her, and I want so much to tell her that it is okay. That things will be okay. Whatever is wrong. Things will work out. I really believe that. If you just get lucky and stay alive, a lot of things work out.

"Augusta wasn't really my mother."

I wish I could nod my head, look like I'm listening to her. I am listening, but for some reason, I have decided to do a little bebop rhythm in my chair. My shoulders are shaking, and my head is bobbing, and I feel lucky just to be able to see her face out of the corner of my eye.

"Odell Dibb brought me to her as a baby. When I was just a few days old."

What?

"He didn't tell my mother . . . Augusta . . . where I came from. He just asked her to take care of me."

I have flung myself out of the chair, and I am banging my head against the fireplace. Helen comes running.

"What's going on here? Miss June, stop! What did you say to her?"

Coral Jackson is on her feet, and she is trying to capture me in her arms, she is trying to keep me from banging my head — pound, pound — on the wall. My head really hurts, and my stomach is sick, and I can't get my body to stop convulsing, but I am trying to look at her, I am trying to look at Coral Jackson. Coral! Of course. Coral!

Helen comes and pushes Coral out of the way.

"You need to leave. You need to leave this house right away!"

And I can hear Coral trying to catch her breath, crying, and saying, "I'm sorry. I'm so, so sorry. I just had to see you. I've been looking —"

And at that, I wrench myself away from Helen, and just by accident, I am facing Coral, I am looking at my daughter, at the

531

person I never once stopped dreaming about, at the person I did not think I would ever see, and I can't say anything I want to say, I can't control my expression, I can't tell her in any way how fervently I hunted for her, how I didn't know where to look, how Del died, how she wasn't in Alabama, how there was no one to ask. How I hoped. Until there was nothing left to hope for. Until I could not imagine any wild, serendipitous, impossible way that I could find her. How had she found me? And really, how could it be that I would never be able to tell her how much I had wanted to find her?

Tears stream down her face, and I can see that she is about to leave. That she doesn't know what else to do. That it is all too much. And I think of Eddie, her father, and how she looks more like me than like him. But her voice. It's beautiful. She has Eddie's voice.

"In this world of hope, in this world of fear."
Just like that, the song comes to me.
"I'll be your rock. And you'll be my cheer. Every moment with you is so dear."
Eddie's song.
She knows it.
I see it on her face. She knows the song. She knows why I am singing it. She knows

that I know.

And like that, my daughter steps forward and takes my wayward, truculent, unruly body into her arms.

So that we can dance.

ACKNOWLEDGMENTS

The correct answer to who made it possible to write *'Round Midnight* is everyone I ever loved, and everyone who ever loved me. My editor, wise soul, suggests I make the list a bit shorter.

So I'll start at the top of the marquee. My husband, Bill Yaffe, for his great stores of patience, kindness, and humor (I noticed). And my editor, Trish Todd, for her counsel, her insight, and her commitment. Without her, no dream comes true.

There are others. My spirited agent Stephanie Cabot. All the cool kids at Touchstone — *if this is our ride, then my hands are up and my eyes wide open* — especially Susan Moldow, Tara Parsons, David Falk, Shida Carr, Kelsey Manning, Meredith Vilarello, Kaitlin Olson, Leah Morse, Cherlynne Li, Loretta Denner, and Philip Bashe (plus a coolest-of-all button for Wendy Sheanin). Those brave first readers: Jamie

Jadid, Jodi McBride, Deb Newman, Vicki McBride, Randee Kelley, Tracy Conley, and Maya McBride. The College of Southern Nevada, for championing my journey. Dawn Stuart, whose Books In Common so enriched my author life. The Gernert Company, particularly Ellen Coughtrey. For meaningful favors: Grace McBride, Yolanda Hernandez, and Third Chan. And for delighting me: Leah Deborah and Noah Max.

To publish a novel is to find oneself suddenly immersed in a new world. To the readers who shared their deeply felt experiences. To the authors, who encouraged and allowed and celebrated, without hesitation. (In particular, Joanna Rakoff, Patry Francis, Margot Livesey.) And to the booksellers, those fairy godparents. Thank you. Two small words that do not begin to say all I feel.

ABOUT THE AUTHOR

Laura McBride is the author of *We Are Called to Rise* and *'Round Midnight*. A graduate of Yale and a Yaddo fellow, she teaches at the College of Southern Nevada and lives in Las Vegas with her family.

The employees of Thorndike Press hope you have enjoyed this Large Print book. All our Thorndike, Wheeler, and Kennebec Large Print titles are designed for easy reading, and all our books are made to last. Other Thorndike Press Large Print books are available at your library, through selected bookstores, or directly from us.

For information about titles, please call:
(800) 223-1244

or visit our website at:
gale.com/thorndike

To share your comments, please write:
Publisher
Thorndike Press
10 Water St., Suite 310
Waterville, ME 04901